D0436207

ALSO BY JAMES M. TABOR

Forever on the Mountain

Blind Descent

THE
DEEP
ZONE

THE DEEP ZONE

A NOVEL

JAMES M. TABOR

BALLANTINE BOOKS NEW YORK

The Deep Zone is a work of fiction. Names, characters, places, and incidents are the products of the author's imagination or are used fictitiously. Any resemblance to actual events, locales, or persons, living or dead, is entirely coincidental.

Published in the United States by Ballantine Books, an imprint of The Random House Publishing Group, a division of Random House, Inc., New York.

BALLANTINE and colophon are registered trademarks of Random House, Inc.

Library of Congress Cataloging-in-Publication Data
Tabor, James M.
The deep zone : a novel / James M. Tabor
p. cm.
ISBN 978-0-345-53061-5
eBook ISBN 978-0-345-53228-2
I. Title.
PS3620.A258D44 2012
813'.6—dc23
2011040477

Printed in the United States of America on acid-free paper

www.ballantinebooks.com

9 8 7 6 5 4 3 2 1

Book design by Liz Cosgrove

This book is dedicated to
Elizabeth Burke Tabor,
who makes everything possible.

There is as much biomass beneath the earth's surface as there is above it.
—Thomas Gold, PhD, Cornell University

They believed in a reality with many layers. The portal between life and where the dead go was important to them.
—William Saturno, PhD, Boston University

Only the Devil has no inner demons.
—ancient Cuicatec saying

PART ONE

CONTAGION

ONE

SOME NIGHTS, WHEN THE WINDS OF SPRING RISE UP OUT OF Virginia, they peel fog from the Potomac and drape it over the branches of dead trees trapped in the river's black mud banks. Streamers pull free and flow into the mews of Foggy Bottom and the cobblestoned alleys of Old Georgetown, float over the chockablock townhouses, and finally wrap pale, wet shrouds around war-fortune mansions.

A black Navigator pushed through this fog, driving west on O Street until it left behind the homes of the merely rich and entered a realm of oceanic wealth. The SUV turned onto a drive of gravel the size and color of corn kernels and walled on both sides by Madagascar barberry nine feet tall and bristling with three-inch thorns.

In the backseat, the passenger stared at the red spikes and thought about crucifixion.

The Navigator passed through a series of remote-controlled gates, the last of which was hung with warning signs:

DANGER
10,000 VOLTS
EXTREME HAZARD
STAY CLEAR

It stopped in front of a mansion of rust-colored brick and white marble. Flowers like red fists filled white boxes hung beneath windows of wavy, distorted glass. Boxwoods carved into strange shapes lined the circular receiving area in front.

The driver got out, a tall man blacker than his black suit, lips like overripe plums, skin smooth as polished onyx. He wore sunglasses, despite the hour. His accent was thickly African: "Sair. We hair."

The passenger stepped onto glistening cobblestones. A warm and moist night, fog coiling around his legs, air fragrant with boxwood and the coppery bouquet of those red flowers. The Navigator dissolved in mist. He climbed granite steps, their edges rounded off by a century and a half of wear, to a columned, curving porch that reminded him of the foredeck of an old sailing ship. He was reaching for the knocker, a massive brass cross hung upside down, when the door swung inward.

Standing before him was a tall woman wearing a blouse of lime-green silk and a white linen Dior skirt cut above the knee. She had shoulder-length red hair and green eyes and she was so beautiful that looking at her was like gazing at the sun: impossible to regard for more than seconds.

"Good evening. I am Erika. Thank you so much for coming." Lilting, musical voice, traces of Ukraine or Belarus. She extended a hand, cool, long-fingered. She smelled faintly of gardenias.

"My pleasure."

"Mr. Adelheid has been expecting you. Please."

He followed her down a long, dusky hallway floored with Italian marble, smooth and white as ancient ice. In pools of yellow light on the burgundy-painted walls hung what he took for reproductions, a van Gogh, a Renoir. Then he stopped.

"Excuse me. Is that a real Picasso?"

Erika glanced over her shoulder. "Of course. They are all originals."

She brought him to a pair of doors from an old century, some European castle or palace, pushed one open, touched his arm, and left.

A man came forward holding a heavy crystal tumbler. He wore tan gabardine slacks pressed to a knife-edged crease, a black double-breasted blazer, a French blue shirt open at the collar, and a pale rose ascot. The visitor had never actually met someone who wore an ascot and had to keep himself from staring. The deep, resonant voice on the recordings had led him to expect someone huge and powerful, but this man was as slim as Fred Astaire and moved with the same languid grace.

A man who never hurried, he thought. *Not once in his life.*

For all his elegance, there was nothing effeminate about the man. Quite the opposite; he moved through space like a perfectly balanced blade.

"Bernard Adelheid." *Ahdelheight.* Accent here, too. Faint, indistinct. Swiss? Dutch? "We are so glad you are here. You must be extremely busy."

"You know government. Too much work, too few people. Always."

"Always." A handshake, mild, dry, brief. "What do you drink?"

"What are you having there?"

"Fifty-year-old Laphroaig, neat." He held his crystal tumbler aloft. The room was high-ceilinged and dimly lit and the golden whiskey seemed to collect light from the tall white candles in brass wall sconces. There was a fireplace the two of them could have walked into. He could not see into the farthest corners of the room.

A hundred dollars a glass if it's a cent, he thought. "I'll have the same, then."

Mr. Adelheid poured him four fingers from a Baccarat decanter on a sideboard of medieval proportions. They clinked glasses and the host spoke in German:

"Mögest du alle Tage deines Lebens leben!"

They drank, and Mr. Adelheid said, "A very old toast. Eleventh or twelfth century. From the Teutonic Order, some say. Or perhaps der Bruderschaft St. Christoph. It goes, 'May you live all the days of your life.' "

"Good advice. Even if easier said than done."

"Not if one has the means."

He raised his own tumbler, swirled the liquor, inhaled its spirit, a scent like lightning-struck oak.

"Remarkable, isn't it?"

"Beyond words."

"As some things are."

"Including this house." He could feel the halls and countless dark rooms winding around him like the passages and chambers of a great cave, dark space with weight, pressing, a sense of threat. "Is this yours?"

"Is my name on the deed? No. It belongs to a family of my acquaintance."

"It looks very old."

"Built in 1854 by Uriah Sadler. A shipowner."

"What kinds of ships did he own?"

Mr. Adelheid smiled. "Fast ships with big holds and hard crews. He was a slave trader."

He thought of the black man who had let him out of the car. "Your own crew. Impressive."

"You mean Adou. Yes. A Ugandan. Mostly civilized."

He saw chopped limbs, brained babies, changed the subject. "The place is huge."

"And bigger than what you can see. Captain Sadler had unusual tastes even for a slaver. The cellar beneath is vast. Rooms with granite walls and drains. To contain the screams and flush the blood, I've been told."

"A horrible time." He could think of nothing else to say.

Mr. Adelheid sipped, watched him. "I hope you will stay to dine with me."

"I had planned on it."

"Wonderful. Please, come and sit."

They took places at a table set for four. Crystal and silver sparkled on white linen. He had never been good at small talk, but Mr. Adelheid was extraordinary, so after a while he felt as though he were in one of those foreign films where people speak endlessly across fabulous tables, every utterance freighted with wit and irony. They talked about Washington's execrable weather, the visitor's workload, AfPak, one subject flowing smoothly into the next. Mr. Adelheid made a story about hunting wild boar in Russia sound like an elegant fable.

A waiter appeared, removed his empty tumbler, replaced it with a full one.

"Shall we begin with some Strangford Lough oysters?" Mr. Adelheid smiled, then looked abashed. "I'm so sorry. You do like oysters, don't you?"

The few raw oysters he had ever eaten had made him think of toilet bowls. "Absolutely," he said.

The waiter set down silver plates with the slick, pink things in iridescent shells on crushed ice. Mr. Adelheid tipped one to his lips, slurped, savored. Steeling himself, the guest did the same. A taste like very dry champagne with a hint of salt wind. He smiled, agreeably startled.

"Incredible, no? I could eat them every day." Mr. Adelheid lifted another. "This morning they were in the Irish Sea."

They concentrated on the oysters. He had always known that certain people lived this way: palatial homes on estates that sprawled like counties, enormous yachts, exquisite women, the food and drink of royalty. Relishing ecstasies *every day* about which he could only fantasize.

He had never known how such lives were made. Now he might learn.

. . .

When he had finished eating the oysters, Mr. Adelheid pushed his plate aside, dabbed his lips.

"Let us speak now. You have a very important job at BARDA. The Biomedical Advanced Research and Development Authority, yes?"

"Yes."

"Created in 2006 by President George W. Bush to counter biowarfare threats and responsible for, among other initiatives, Project BioShield."

"Yes."

"Fascinating work, I imagine. Would you care to tell me about it?"

He paused while the waiter set down new plates. Velvety, chocolate-colored filets in a scarlet sauce. "Medallions of Black Forest venison with Madeira and black truffles," Mr. Adelheid said. Then wine, poured into crystal goblets from a bottle with a label like parchment. He had drunk wine, of course, even, on a few occasions, in very expensive restaurants. Now he understood that he had never tasted *great* wine.

How many other great things had evaded him in this life? He suddenly felt regret so intense it made his eyes glisten. Too quickly, he brought the wine glass to his mouth, spilling a few drops onto the immaculate tablecloth, embarrassing himself. His moist eyes, the soiled linen—he felt thick and stupid in the presence of this polished man.

"I do microbiology. MDRBs."

"Excuse me?"

"I'm sorry. Multiple-drug-resistant bacteria."

"Is it like in the movies? You know, exotic germs, that kind of thing?"

A little flare inside him. "Calling them germs is like calling diamonds rocks. They are miracles of evolution. And beautiful. Think of a spiral nebula on the head of a pin. Every color in the universe."

"You speak of them as friends."

"We get along well. I respect them. And admire their good qualities."

"Which are?"

"Astonishing evolutionary speed, for one."

"Do you work in space suits?"

"Sometimes. Those in BSL-4."

"What does that mean, exactly, 'BSL-4'?"

"Biosafety Level Four. The highest security level. Positive-pressure environments. Chemturion protective suits. Respirators. Disinfectant showers and ultraviolet germicidal lights. Double-door air locks. Unbreakable labware."

Mr. Adelheid nodded, touched his right ear with the tips of two fingers. The door swung open and Erika walked in. Even moving, she seemed to be in repose. Everything about her was . . . *perfect*. Her legs, body, face, eyes—not one dissonant curve or angle.

"Good evening, Erika. Would you care for a drink? Some champagne, perhaps?"

"No thank you, sir."

She sat, crossed her magnificent legs, and something caught in his chest.

"Erika, you have met our friend." No name offered, none asked for.

"Enchantée."

"Would you like to spend time with our friend?"

"I would love to." A voice like chimes, exultant, as if it were the greatest opportunity life had offered.

He almost dropped his fork, fumbled, felt like a fool.

"Would you find that agreeable?" Mr. Adelheid smiled at him.

He hesitated, thoroughly unsure how to respond.

"We could have Christina come in. Or Gisele."

"No, no." He reddened. "No. I mean, *yes,* of course, I would find that agreeable."

"And Erika, would you like to accommodate our friend's wishes?"

"Oh, yes." She placed her fingertips on the back of his hand, four small, cool circles on his hot skin. There was something about the way she moved, slowly, dreamily, as though underwater. "There is a villa in the Mediterranean, on an island all its own, with a waterfall in the bedroom. Floors of pink marble, walls of glass." She flicked her eyes at Mr. Adelheid.

He smiled. "No rules we do not make, the only laws those of nature."

His thoughts twirled, huge black eyes, white fog, shining oysters, golden whiskey, scarlet wine, a turquoise sea scattered with flakes of light. This woman's scent, heavier now, gardenia sweet. He closed his eyes, breathed.

I could use some air.

"Thank you, Erika." She rose and turned to their guest.

"I hope to see you again."

"And I . . . yes, me, too."

He watched her leave, moving through space as though without weight.

"To the victors go the spoils." Mr. Adelheid raised his glass again.

"God in heaven." He drank, eyes closed.

"Would you like to learn more?"

"That's why I came."

Mr. Adelheid nodded. "Fine. But let us enjoy this good food first. We should never rush our pleasures."

"Live our lives."

"Indeed." Mr. Adelheid did something in the air with his right hand, some ancient benediction, and picked up his knife. They ate in an island of light in the great shadowed room. With a silver knife he cut the venison and forked to his mouth pieces dripping with sauce. They ate and did not speak, the only sounds in the room those of their chewing and breathing and the insistent buzzing of one invisible fly.

TWO

THE LIGHT IN THE ROOM RIPPLED, CANDLE FLAMES DANCING with currents of air. He ate, drank wine, so overwashed with pleasures he forgot for long moments who and where he was.

After a time, with half of his venison uneaten, Mr. Adelheid laid down his silver, dabbed his lips. His fingers were slim and very long, tendrils with shining tips.

To leave food like that. His own plate had been clean for some minutes.

"Well. We would be very grateful for your help."

"Leave BARDA and come to work for you?" He did not know who Mr. Adelheid worked for. But surely it would be made clear. Or would it?

"No. Not leave BARDA."

"A mole, then." *Crude*. He regretted it immediately, blushed.

The fly, buzzing again. An expression passed across Mr. Adelheid's face, like clouds scudding over the moon. "An observer."

"What would you want me to observe?"

"Most antibiotics today are derived from one original source, is that not true?"

"Yes. Actinomycetales. Discovered in 1940 by Selman Waksman. He got the Nobel for that work."

"But germs are winning the battle. So I have heard."

"Hundreds of thousands of people die every year from bacterial infections we can no longer treat. In the U.S. alone. Other places, the numbers are . . . appalling."

"Hundreds of thousands of *reported* deaths. The true total is much higher, isn't it?"

"Of course. Did renal failure or hospital-acquired infection kill Mr. Jones? One checkmark in a different box on a report. An easy choice for dirty hospitals. Which most are."

"And your facility—BARDA—is trying to produce an entirely new family of antibiotics."

"Among other projects. But yes, that is one main thrust of the work."

Mr. Adelheid smoothed his ascot. How old was the man? The visitor could not say with any certainty. Forty or sixty. His skin was smooth, eyes bright, movements lithe. But there was something ancient about him, Sphinx-like, an inscrutable repose.

"Consider this. The new currency of power is *information,*" Mr. Adelheid said.

"Really?" The Laphroaig and the wine were making him bolder. "So given the choice between a ton of gold and a terabyte of information, you'd take the terabyte?"

"On the surface, an easy choice. A ton of gold today is worth $45 million. No paltry sum. But: what if you have golden *information*? Do you have any idea how much money has been made from Dr. Waksman's antibiotics?"

"Billions, I would guess."

"Trillions."

"Don't you have politicians who can help you?"

"Of course we have politicians. And others. But no one like you."

"So what do you need, exactly?"

"Exactly? At this very moment? Nothing. But there will come a time. Very soon, we think."

Keeping his eyes on the table, he said, "You want me to be a spy."

Mr. Adelheid made a sound as if clearing something unpleasant from his throat. "Spies make death. Our wish is not to take lives but to save them."

"For a profit."

"Of *course* for a profit." His tone suggested that any alternative would be irrational, like living without breathing. "What are millions of human lives worth?"

"Priceless."

Mr. Adelheid regarded him in silence for a moment. "You know of Reinhold Messner? The great mountaineer?"

"I know he climbed Mount Everest solo."

"And without oxygen. In Europe, a god. Messner said, 'From such places you do not return unchanged.' "

"I don't climb."

"Mountains are not the only realms from which we may not return unchanged."

Mr. Adelheid reached into his blazer, produced a slip of green paper the size of a playing card. He slid it to the middle of the table. A deposit ticket from Grand Cayman National Bank for *Fifty thousand and 00/100 dollars,* payable not to a name but to an eleven-digit alphanumeric sequence.

"An appreciation for the pleasure of your company this evening. You need only the PIN. Which I will give you."

"For doing what?"

"For joining me tonight."

"*Fifty thousand dollars* for a few hours?"

"Of course."

It was dizzying, but another question had to be asked. "How much for doing the . . . observing you mentioned?"

Mr. Adelheid named a figure that made his heart jump. For a moment the room blurred and sang like a plucked string. He put his hand on the table, a few inches away from the green slip. Thoughts skittered in his head.

So this is how it feels. He watched as his hand, possessed, slid toward the green paper.

"I urge you to think carefully." Mr. Adelheid's voice made a strange echo in the chamber. Or was it the whiskey and wine? "This threshold, like Messner's realm, is one you cannot recross. Be certain."

It came out, quick and harsh, as though he had been waiting most of his life to tell someone. "I have a doctorate from a good university. Nineteen years of government service. I make eighty-seven thousand, four hundred and seventy-six dollars a year. I have been passed over for promotion three times. I do not want to die having had only this life."

Mr. Adelheid regarded him thoughtfully. "And there was that unfortunate business with your wife. Forgive me: *former* wife."

So he knows. Of course. He would know everything. He bit off each word: "Yes. The 'unfortunate incident.' "

It had been nine years, but like a gangrenous wound, this one would never heal; in fact, like such a wound, it seemed to grow deeper and more foul as time passed. Even Mr. Adelheid's veiled reference made his rage flare. And not just rage. A hot and breathless shame for the losses—and for being one who'd lost the great things.

Mr. Adelheid said, "It was unfortunate. *She* strayed. And yet—"

"—and yet her lawyers took *everything*. The house, our savings, the antiques . . . our *dogs*."

"The Airedales, yes. And it goes on."

"Oh, yes. On and *on*. Do you know, after she left me, I had to move into a *condominium*"—he said the word as though it were an obscenity—"in one of those subdivisions with hundreds of them, all identical, lined up. It could be Bulgaria. Every morning I drive from there to BARDA, walk the same two hundred and nineteen steps to the laboratory, and at the end of each day I walk the other way. Week after month after year. That does something to a man." He paused for breath, aware that he had not spoken to anyone like this for longer than he could remember.

"I am so sorry." There was something like sympathy in Mr. Adelheid's voice.

The guest's fingertips lifted, extended, dropped down on the edge of the deposit slip. His chest felt like thin blown glass. A red spot, wine he had spilled, stained the linen beside his hand.

He put the ticket into his shirt pocket.

Mr. Adelheid lifted his wine glass for a toast. "Welcome."

"Thank you." They drank.

As his latest swallow surged through him, he felt empowered. "You know who I work for. Am I permitted to ask who you work for? My guess would be BioChem." The largest pharmaceutical, headquartered in Zurich, operating in every developed country and many undeveloped ones.

"No. Nor any other pharmaceutical concern. Are you familiar with the Dutch East India Company?"

"I know that it raped Asian countries for centuries."

"No. It was the world's first multinational corporation, and the first to issue stock. A government unto itself, with global reach."

"The Dutch East India Company became corrupt and collapsed."

"As do all empires."

"What I meant was, you can't be working for the Dutch East India Company."

"A descendant."

The waiter brought balloon snifters of cognac. Mr. Adelheid sniffed, drank, smiled with closed eyes, a bliss like lovemaking.

"I wasn't aware it spawned any."

"A little knowledge can be dangerous. Too much can be fatal. I can tell you that the object of our present discussion has no headquarters, no corporate papers, no employees. Only members and friends."

"Are you talking about some kind of international cabal? Freemasons, Templars, that kind of thing?"

A barked laugh. "God, no." Mr. Adelheid paused, considered. "Think of an enormous, invisible web. If you touch it even lightly the whole web shivers."

"Can you give me an example?"

"I could give you many. Cancer is to our era as infectious disease was to the last. One in three persons alive will contract cancer of some kind."

"Yes."

"There is a cancer vaccine, though."

"What?"

"Oh yes. Almost nine years now."

"Can't be. The government would not allow that."

Mr. Adelheid laughed and the candle flames shivered.

"The *government* has nothing to do with it. The government houses the lowest common denominators of our species."

"Why?" He already knew the answer, but the question asked itself. Mr. Adelheid frowned.

"Healthy people do not buy pharmaceuticals."

A fellow worker, killed by brain cancer, had taken a medicine called Orbitrex. Thirteen hundred dollars for six small blue pills. Every week. For months.

He knew that what his host was describing was wrong, but in this moment he could believe that it did not compare to the greater wrongs life had inflicted upon him. And there still existed in him a deep, silent place where all things rang one of two ways. Mr. Adelheid's words rang true. Really, he had always known, or at least suspected. But how could you keep going and not bury that deeper still? There was no other way.

"So we near the end of our evening together." Mr. Adelheid stood and came to him and they clasped hands again. This time, Mr. Adelheid locked eyes and held his hand and forearm in an astonishing grip, like a tourniquet tightening.

"*So* pleased. More than you can know. Before you depart, I would like to show you the house. A historic place, truly fascinating. More cognac?"

"*No*. But thank you."

"Very well." They walked into the hallway, as dimly lit as the huge room they had just left, and then toward the rear of the house. At the end of that hall they turned right, into another. The passages and chambers were draped in black crepe shadows. Mr. Adelheid held a cigar that trailed blue smoke. *When did he light that?* The visitor could not remember. Mr. Adelheid drew on the cigar and its tip flared red. They walked and walked, along halls and through rooms, passing many closed doors. At last through one whose hinges squealed and down a narrow, creaking stairway, poorly lit, into darkness from which rose odors of damp earth and stone and decay.

He followed the red coal of Mr. Adelheid's cigar as if it were a beacon, down one dirt-floored passageway after another, turning corner after corner, and for the first time began to feel afraid. The surface underfoot was rough, and he had to take care not to stumble. Every so often he stooped beneath massive beams.

Mr. Adelheid stopped by a door five feet high, thick, rough-hewn. He could not stop thinking of spiders and snakes. Cellars always did that to him, and *this* cellar . . . Mr. Adelheid pushed the heavy door open and ducked into the room. He followed. There were no electric lights. Candles burned in rusting sconces. Massive iron rings, affixed to walls and ceiling, scabbed with brown rust. The smell in the room was stomach-turning, heavy with filth and mold.

The stone floor sloped down toward a central drain. Mr. Adelheid walked to the drain, drew on his cigar. The tip flared red. There was the buzzing of the fly again, louder now, closer to him. For an instant he thought that he might have felt the brush of tiny wings on his lip, but he saw nothing in the gloom. He could not take his eyes off the drain.

"In rooms like this, Captain Sadler took his pleasure. An underground passage led to the Potomac. Still does. Bodies were carted down and consigned to the river, which carried them to the sea."

"Why did you bring me here?"

"You know why. This is a very serious thing, this new realm you now inhabit. *Caveat venditor.*"

Let the seller beware.

Mr. Adelheid glanced around the chamber one last time. "Remarkable place, isn't it? The kind from which you do not emerge unchanged. Nor ever forget."

Upstairs again, they walked to the front door, which began to open as they approached.

"One more thing you should know." Mr. Adelheid drew on his cigar, peered through blue smoke. "You will have company at BARDA."

"You mean other . . . observers?"

"Yes."

"Doing the same thing I am?"

Mr. Adelheid tilted his head, exhaled smoke. "Enough to know that they are there."

Observing, he thought. *Observing* me. *Is that what he means?*

He needed to know something. "How do you find . . . people like me?"

Mr. Adelheid drew a red line in the air with his glowing cigar tip. "You find us."

"But I never did anything. You reached out to me first."

"We have done this for a very long time, and we are exceedingly patient," Mr. Adelheid said. "Not unlike you scientists. A few unguarded words. An indiscreet letter. Financial transactions of a certain kind. These and other things."

The word came to him: "Signals."

"Indeed. And the strongest signals are those of distress."

Like a moth caught in a web, he thought.

"Adou will drive you back. You will hear from me. For now, go and live the days of your life." Mr. Adelheid disappeared into the mansion.

The guest stepped out onto the porch and almost bumped into Adou. The place had been ablaze with light when he arrived, but now the porch was as dark as the deck of a slaver on a black Atlantic night.

He could just discern Adou's outline, shadow against dark. Then a lighter clicked and Adou touched fire to the tip of his cigarette. He had taken off the sunglasses. One empty, ragged eye socket flared red in the yellow flame.

"Come." It did not sound like a request this time. Adou moved off, as sure-footed as a midnight cat. He came behind, stumbling into the darkness.

THREE

THE BULLET HIT FATHER WYMAN BEFORE HE HEARD THE AK-47 report. No surprise, that. Haji's AK rounds traveled a mile in two seconds, *way* ahead of their sound. You never heard the one with your name on it. So to Father Wyman's way of thinking, only fools and ground pounders ducked and flinched in firefights. When they were Oscar Mike, he stood tall in his up-armored Humvee turret, head on a swivel, hands on his fifty-cal's oak, cigar-shaped grips, thumbs on the butterfly trigger.

Father Wyman was not a priest. He was a heartland patriot less than three years out of high school, but he loved to read his Bible and to hold prayer meetings for the other troopers, so that was what the men in Viper Company at Combat Outpost (COP) Terok had taken to calling him. Wyman's was not a foxhole conversion. He'd inherited from his father and mother an unshakable belief in the Book's literal truth. It was not an ancient tome of mystic parable, but practical wisdom by which they lived their lives, day by day. They trusted it as farmers trusted their land and wealthy people their money. They read it more often than newspapers. They had no faith in soiled politicians and godless scientists. Anyone with eyes to see and a mortal soul knew that the Bible had survived centuries of sin and dark horror to bring them light. Why would God have saved it for them otherwise? When they touched their Bible, opened it, read from it, its power was as real as wind and fire.

Wyman was as big as he was devout, six-three and 210 pounds. His machine gun was bolted to a wheeled carriage that rolled around the circular track of his Humvee mount, so he could easily man the gun one-handed. He had seen the muzzle flash two hundred meters out. The haji fired—a good shot, considering the AK-47's notorious inaccuracy—and dropped down behind a washing machine–sized boulder, no doubt thinking himself safe.

Too bad for you, Mr. Haji. Viper Company was equipped with "Badass"—that was what they called the new boomerang anti-sniper detection system (BADS), which used passive acoustic detection and computer-signal processing to locate a shooter with pinpoint accuracy. Badass's developers, like those who created audible aircraft-crew cockpit warnings, knew that the male brain responded best to a female voice. So, while he was still running on adrenaline, in his earpiece Father Wyman heard a sultry young woman say, "Target bearing one-nine-one. Range two-zero-seven."

When he turned in that general direction, a bright red dot appeared on a particular boulder, two football fields distant, in the image in his monocular eyepiece. The red dot remained on that boulder no matter which way Father Wyman turned his head. A yellow dot representing his aim point, with computer-calculated elevation and windage adjustments, also appeared in the eyepiece. When the yellow dot merged with the red, a green dot appeared and the woman's voice breathed, "Target acquired," followed by a soft, continuous tone.

Father Wyman loved the fifty-cal because it was more light cannon than machine gun. It could reach out and touch at two hundred meters, no problem. Wyman depressed the trigger twice with his good thumb and the gun bucked. He felt the detonation of each round, the blasts milliseconds apart.

BAM-BAM-BAM-BAM-BAM-BAM. That one blew apart the boulder.

BAM-BAM-BAM-BAM-BAM-BAM. That one blew apart the sniper.

"Scratch one haj . . ." Wyman said, but then the adrenaline ran out. White-faced, with his shoulder squirting blood, Wyman dropped out of the turret and collapsed on the Humvee's floor.

DeAengelo "Angel" Washington was a Crip from South-Central, but he had been born again, was just as Bible-struck as Wyman, and the two had grown as close as brothers. Angel had been riding shotgun with his SAW—squad automatic weapon—up front. He jumped back, pulled Wyman's body armor off, stuck a tampon in the tubular wound, pushed three ampicillin caps into Wyman's mouth, and gave him water.

"That hurt, dog?" Angel was holding Wyman in his arms. Wyman was big, but Angel was built like Mike Tyson.

"Not too much." Smiling, voice soft, dreamy. "I get him?"

"You got the mother. Dog meat now."

Angel turned and screamed "*MEDEVAC!*" at the Humvee driver, Corporal Dorr, a quiet young soldier from Arkansas, who was staring back at them, wide-eyed and slack-jawed. *"CALL MEDEVAC, DOORKNOB, YOU DUMB CRACKER, 'FORE I SHOVE MY KA-BAR THROUGH YOUR EARHOLE!"*

Wyman and Washington were paratroopers of Viper Company, 503rd Parachute Infantry Regiment. COP Terok sat high on one side of a steep, twelve-hundred-meter mountain overlooking Afghanistan's Korengal Valley. The Korengal River flowed through the valley's green floor, throwing silver loops around yellow fields of wheat, disappearing into the blue distance. Early in the mornings, white clouds curled around the black mountain's flanks and hid the valley floor completely, and at such times Wyman and Washington agreed it was so lovely and peaceful that it could have been heaven. But this was perishable heaven, and by 0800 hours sun seared away those clouds, uncovering a valley of death laced with infiltration routes for veteran fighters from Pakistan.

Just after noon, orderlies rolled Wyman on a gurney into Terok's medical unit. He looked pale and spooky-eyed, but he was conscious and holding a black pocket Bible on his chest with his good hand.

"Hello, Sergeant," said Major Lenora Stilwell, MD. She was trim and pretty, with short brown hair and kind eyes and freckles from the Florida sun. Her Tampa practice was orthopedic surgery; her Terok practice was gunshot wounds and blast trauma. Not so different, she told the people back home—surgery was surgery. But that wasn't true. It was very different.

In a way, Wyman was lucky, getting to a real doctor so quickly—and he had, incongruously, the Taliban to thank. Because Terok did such a good job of sending hajis to meet their seventy-two virgins, the Taliban had targeted it for annihilation. Then, of course, the Army had decreed that Terok would never fall. Dien Bien Phu and Khe Sanh redux. More, bigger, fiercer Taliban attacks, worse atrocities. More troopers, arty, gunships, Bradleys, drones. Taliban and Terok, two scorpions in a jar, stinging each other slowly to death.

The one benefit of the Army's commitment was a combat support hospital (CSH). Most COPs had plywood cubicles with extra sandbags where medics stanched bleeding, doped up the bad cases, and waited for Chinooks. Terok had an actual little hospital with two surgical theaters, two ten-bed wards, twelve nurses, and three doctors. One was Lenora Stilwell.

"Hello, ma'am."

Good strong voice, Stilwell noted.

"Are you hit anyplace other than the shoulder?"

"Don't think so, ma'am." The kid was grinning now. Amazing.

Nurses scissored off his uniform, started IV ampicillin, removed the tampon, irrigated the wound.

"What's your name, Sergeant?"

"Daniel, ma'am. Wyman." That stopped her. Stilwell's son was named Danny.

"Do I hear a little Kansas there?"

"Yes, ma'am. Delacor, Kansas. You, ma'am?"

"Tampa." Stilwell probed, assessed. His jaw muscles clenched. "Ketamine twenty cc's IV," Stilwell instructed a nurse without looking. "Through and through. You are a lucky young man, Daniel."

"Ma'am?"

"Bullet missed bone. A couple centimeters lower and you're minus an arm. I'll clean you up, start you on antibiotics, get a drain in place."

"So then I can go back?"

"Back where?"

"With the squad. Angel and all."

"You'll be here awhile. Maybe Kabul."

"No way. Really, ma'am?" Kabul was the home of CENMEDFAC, the big military hospital. He looked more troubled by that possibility than by the wound.

"Way. We want you to have that arm for a long time. Hey, it's not so bad here, Daniel. We have some vivacious nurses."

"Ma'am?"

"Hot."

"*Oh.* Well." The grin returned. "Thass good. Thank you, ma'am."

He yawned, the ketamine working. Without his combat gear, Wyman's wide blue eyes and towhead buzz cut made him look more like the high-schooler he had so recently been than the expert killer he was now. That had been the hardest thing for Stilwell. Not the gore and carnage—those she saw in operating theaters every week. But the youth. Kids too young to drink whiskey in a bar damaged in every imaginable way and some that were simply unimaginable until seen. That was the hardest part.

Her Danny was fifteen and talking about enlisting already. In a few years, a doctor in some godforsaken corner of the world might be ministering to him. Her eyes felt hot. She put a hand on the exam table to steady herself.

"Are you okay, ma'am?" She had thought him asleep, but he had been watching, concerned, up on his good elbow now. *He* was worried about *her.* Stilwell patted his healthy shoulder, eased him down.

"I'm fine, Daniel. I was just thinking . . ."

"Ma'am?"

"Nothing. You go to sleep, Sergeant."

Wyman rubbed his eyes like a little kid and dropped right off.

The next morning Angel visited. Wyman's bed was one of ten in a long, rectangular room. Only two others were occupied: by a corporal who had dropped an eighty-pound mortar tube on his foot and a Humvee driver with back injuries from an IED.

The *quiet* struck Angel. Outside there were whapping helicopters and thrumming generators and outgoing arty thumping like the drums of God. *Never* quiet. Here, it felt weird. *Dead.* Angel stopped at the blue curtain drawn around Wyman's bed.

"*Wy.* You awake? How you doin', dog?"

"All good, Angie. Come on in here."

Angel thought Wyman looked normal, a little drowsy maybe. His shoulder was bandaged and he had needles in both arms.

"What they sayin', Wy?"

"No biggie. Hit muscle, missed bone."

"How long you be in here?"

"Doc said couple of days." Wyman was not going to mention Kabul. Bad juju.

"Ain't the same without you on the five-oh, Wy."

"Roger that. Anything happening?"

"Same ol' same ol'."

Wyman yawned. "I think they been giving me a little dope." Crooked frown. "Don't like th' stuff."

Angel chuckled. "Oh my. Back in the 'hood, dog . . . No, forget that. Look, Wy, I'm gonna go, let you sleep. You need anything?"

"All good, Angie. Thank you f' comin' over here." Eyelids drooping.

"You send for me, you be needin' something, hear?"

"I will. See you later."

"Roger that." Angel started to leave. Then he turned back and put a hand on Wyman's good shoulder. "You sure you don't need nothin'?"

"Needa get back on the fifty." Wyman tapped Angel's hand with his fist.

"All right. I'm gone."

"Hey, know what? The nurses in here are *vivacious,* man."

"They what?"

"Hot." Wyman laughed, a groggy chuckle. Angel, not sure what the joke was, laughed, too. If it made Wyman laugh, it was a good thing.

Lenora Stilwell returned that evening, expecting to find Wyman better. Instead, he was feverish, BP and pulse elevated, skin sallow.

"Ma'am, I think I'm coming down with flu or something." He said this without being asked.

"What are you feeling?"

"Hot. Sore throat. My body hurts."

"How about the shoulder?"

"Hurts, ma'am." Paratroopers' pain thresholds were off the charts. If this one was telling her it hurt, it *hurt*.

She removed the dressing and a yellow reek rose from his wound. Between tribiotic ointment and IV ampicillin, Wyman should have been infection-free, but Stilwell was seeing puffy, whitish flesh flecked with dark spots, bacterial colonies oozing pus like rancid butter.

Stilwell cleaned and irrigated Wyman's wound, applied more tribiotic, replaced the drain, and put on a fresh dressing.

"There's some infection, Daniel. I'm putting you on a different antibiotic, tigecycline. And something for the pain."

This time he did not argue. "Thank you, ma'am."

"All right. Rest, drink a lot. I'll come by later tonight."

She did not return then, nor most of the next day, nor even the next. The same action that kept the doctors and nurses up to their elbows in blood for almost four days kept Angel and his squadmates in the field as well. On the first day, Viper and Tango companies surprised insurgent units moving in daylight, a rare thing but, as it turned out, no accident. The firefight quickly became a complex encounter that unfolded according to a careful plan—the insurgents' plan.

They did not hit and run, as usual. In fact, they made contact and then engaged even more aggressively, taking a page from the old North Vietnamese Army tactic of "hold them by their belts." This clutch of death negated the Americans' artillery and most of their tactical air support. The initial action became a running battle that the insurgents seemed to have no interest in breaking off. Going to ground during the days, they were resupplied with fresh fighters and matériel each night and renewed their attacks on multiple fronts under cover of darkness. The KIAs and MIAs mounted. After the first day, medevac helicopters flooded Terok with an endless red stream of wounded troopers.

Angel wasn't a casualty, but once he was finally back at Terok, he fell asleep in his gear and didn't wake for ten hours. It was late afternoon, six days after Father Wyman's wounding, when he walked back into the ward—which, though still white, was no longer silent. The ward was filled with damaged troopers. Extra beds had been rolled in. Instead of the silence that had greeted him before, Angel now heard a sound that made him think of chanting by drugged monks, an endless chorus of moans and cries from soldiers in morphine-proof pain. The mobile unit's flimsy floor and walls seemed to vibrate with the sound.

There was also a funny smell he had not noticed last time, a sour tang like meat gone bad. He stopped in front of Wyman's drawn blue curtain.

"Wy. Hey, Wy. You up, dog?"

No answer.

"Wy?"

Angel eased the curtain aside and stepped in. Father Wyman was lying on his back. Blood soaked the sheet covering him and had gathered in dark red pools on the floor. Wyman's breathing sounded like steel wool being dragged over a washboard. Angel stepped forward and pulled the sheet back, smearing both hands with Wyman's blood. Silver dollar–sized patches of Wyman's skin were missing, exposing red, raw muscle. His left cheek looked like it had been chewed by animals, the white eyeball floating in blood. He smelled like a slaughterhouse.

"MEDIC! MEDIC! I need a medic here!" Angel kept screaming until a slim, white-coated doctor with short brown hair and a blue flock of following nurses pushed him out. Somebody whipped the curtain closed. Other soldiers—the few who could manage—were sitting up in their beds, staring, looking at each other: *What's going on, man?* Angel, terrified as he had never been in battle, backed out of the ward wide-eyed and open-mouthed, tears of fear and horror streaming down his face as he left a trail of wet, red bootprints going the wrong way.

FOUR

LEAP DAY IN NORTHERN FLORIDA, AND A TALL YOUNG WOMAN with short hair was opening the Deep Enough Dive Shop for business. She was thinking that the peculiar month's extra day was going to muck up the bookkeeping, but that was getting ahead of things. She wore khaki shorts, a red Hawaiian-print shirt with the tail out, and New Balance running shoes. She was tanned the shade of tea, her naturally blond hair sun-bleached almost pure white. She had square shoulders and runner's legs. Her forearms were corded with muscle and veins from climbing, her hands scarred and as rough as a laborer's. Her nose had a slight crook in it.

A squat man with a bodybuilder's physique walked in while she was arranging a new display of Liquivision dive computers behind the counter. He wore tight red swim trunks and a yellow tank top and his biceps and calves were like loaves of bread. The man's way of walking made his Teva sandals slap the floor like flyswatters smacking a tabletop. “I need a guide to dive the Boneyard.” The man’s voice was high and boyish for one so armor-plated. Tourist sunburn, last night’s margaritas on his breath. “I heard this shop had the best guides.”

“Are you cave certified?”

He showed a TDI C-card that affirmed that Thomas Brewster of White Plains, New York, was indeed full-cave certified. “Also deep diving, decompression, and trimix. You want to see those cards, too?”

“No. There’s no deco or trimix on the Boneyard dive.”

She was thinking that if were up to her, she might not take the guy—impatient, puffing out tequila fumes. But Mary Stilwell, sleeping one off herself, had given Hallie this job after the fiasco in D.C. Mary was her best friend, but not much of a businesswoman. An inch-high stack of unpaid bills sat on the card-table desk in the back office. No time to turn away customers.

“I’ve done the *Doria* twice. *Empress of Ireland,* too. Plus Nowhere Caverns and Bottom of Hell.” Brewster said this in a flat voice, but his face shone with pride.

“What did you think of the *Doria*?” Hallie had always wanted to do that dive herself.

“Tell you the truth, I was freaking terrified the whole time.” With that, she liked him a little better. “Two-knot current, ten-foot viz. Risk my life for some crockery? But now I get to say I did it.”

She smiled. “There is that.”

“So what’s this gonna cost me today?”

“It’s three hundred dollars for one guided dive, five-fifty for two. We’d do the Boneyard first, maybe Sink to Perdition in the afternoon.”

She waited, knowing that the guys over at Divers Down charged two hundred for the one-dive package.

He glanced around the shop. “Who’s the guide?”

“I’m the guide.”

“Can I see your C-card?”

"Sure." She reached under the counter. "I'm NAUI, TDI, and NOAA certified, bonded, licensed by the state of Florida."

"Hey. Just kidding. Can we go now?"

"Like, right now?"

"Yes."

The patience of tourists, she thought. The options: stay at the shop for four hours or until whenever Mary came in, sell some fins and masks to tourons who would call them "flippers" and "goggles," or guide Thomas Brewster and make three hundred, maybe five-fifty, for the shop. Bird in the hand.

"Let's go."

The shop was two miles north of Ginnie Springs Park on State Road 47. With Brewster following in his black Escalade, she drove the shop's red F-150, windows cranked down. It was very hot already, but she loved the moist air, sweet with gardenia and hibiscus and orange blossom and, when the wind was right, with the Gulf's saline tang. Welcome change from the diesel and sewer reek of D.C.

They parked in a dirt lot and carried their gear to a wooden dive platform by the water. Nearby, families who could not afford trips to the Gulf or the Atlantic were picnicking on fried chicken, potato salad, burgers, and Budweiser, drawn to the shade of the park's big live oaks and the cool springs' turquoise water.

Assembling her rig, Hallie looked over Brewster's gear. Double-steel 100-cubic-foot tanks, Halcyon buoyancy compensator with Hogarthian rig, dual Atomic regulators, redundant NiTek dive computers, fifteen-hundred-dollar Halcyon cave lights, OMS fins with steel-spring heel straps. *Maybe I was wrong about the guy,* she thought. It was a new thing with her, judging quickly and harshly, and, she understood, a direct result of the mess in Washington. It had soured her as surely as a cup of vinegar spilled into a bottle of good wine. Easier to get it in than to take it out, was the problem. Hanging around with Mary, who had been an Apache pilot in Iraq and was scarred in body and soul, was not the best cure.

She explained the dive plan: one-third of their air going in, one-third coming out, one-third in reserve.

"Sure, sure," Brewster said. "SOP."

"There is no SOP in cave diving, Mr. Brewster. And especially not in the Boneyard."

He nodded, stared back, after a while looked away. "Right."

"I lead going in, you lead coming out. The line is clearly visible all the way to the Boneyard Chamber. Viz should be good but not great, thirty feet or so. We've had rain."

"Any obstacles?"

"One restriction. Tight, but no doffing gear required."

"I'm gonna shoot some video." He held up a Nikonos digital video recorder with integrated lights that, she knew, retailed for about five thousand dollars.

"Gas allowing, not a problem."

"So what actually happened in there?"

They had been donning gear as they talked and were almost ready to enter.

"Two good divers drowned in 1998."

"How'd it happen?"

"Nobody knows."

"Why are the bodies still there?"

"Recovering would have been too dangerous. Plus both had wills stating that if they died in a cave, they didn't want people risking their lives to bring them out. And, so I heard, the state thought it would help prevent repeats."

"Law of unintended consequences kicked in, though, am I right?"

"What do you mean?"

"The place is famous now. Like the *Doria*. Everybody wants to dive here, go see the skeletons."

He had that much right. They ran through predive routines, made giant-stride entries, hovered at ten feet to perform bubble checks and S-drills. She vented gas from her own Halcyon and settled to thirty feet, the water sweetly cool after the heat above. The cave mouth was a dark hole in a pale underwater wall. Inside, beyond the entrance, she shone her light on the white guideline on the cave floor. Brewster pointed at his eyes, gave the circled thumb and forefinger: *Okay*.

Hallie tied off line from her main reel to the permanent guideline. She pointed in the direction of their intended travel, watched him acknowledge by repeating the gesture, then took them down toward the Boneyard, spooling out line as she went.

The first quarter mile was like the intestinal tract of a giant worm, ten feet in diameter, bending and twisting, striated limestone walls flaring green and white and black in their dive lights. The bottom was tan silt, fine as flour; the particles would remain suspended in the water for an hour if disturbed. The only sounds were the hissing and burbling of their regulators.

Hallie loved being down here. She had been in her first cave at six, just a touristic operation, nothing special, Luray Caverns in Virginia. But that day something went *click* deep inside, and she had loved going into caves ever since. Sometimes she thought of herself as a troglodyte, one of those creatures, perfectly adapted to the cave environment, that died if brought out into the light. She wouldn't die and she loved light, but in caves a certain ancient calm took her over. Very different on the surface, where type A genetics drove her like wind behind a sail.

They each had two lights on their yellow helmets and bigger primary lights affixed to the backs of their right hands with surgical tube straps. Every twenty feet, Hallie looked back between her thighs at Brewster. He was moving well but breathing hard, blowing out a steady stream of bubbles.

Four hundred yards in and forty-five feet deep, they came to the restriction. The ceiling dropped and the walls closed in, leaving an opening the size of a refrigerator door. It was called the Jaws of Death, something Hallie had neglected to mention to Brewster. She slipped through and hovered, waiting. His head and shoulders made it, but his big chest and double tanks did not. Instead of relaxing and emptying his lungs, Brewster started throwing his hips and legs around and yanking on rocks with his hands—bad mistake. Before he silted them out, she grabbed both his wrists, gave them a hard jerk, made eye contact, held up an index finger: *Stop*.

He did.

She signaled again, pushing down slowly with both hands: *Relax*.

He nodded, backed off, tried again, and worked his way through. They reached the Boneyard Chamber in ten minutes. The main cave passage continued to the left, and the short feeder passage to the chamber dropped steeply fifteen feet down to their right. Hallie went in first. The chamber was shaped like a bell, thirty feet in diameter at the bottom, no bigger in diameter at the top than an oil barrel.

Brewster came in and settled down toward the skeletons, whose bones flashed white in his bright dive lights. They were on their backs, where the weight of their tanks had pulled them. As their flesh had decayed, their mask straps had loosened and the masks had fallen away. The eye sockets gaped, black holes in the white faces.

Brewster videotaped ten feet from the skeletons for thirty seconds. He sank lower until he hung a foot above them, the sharp light making the skulls shine like silver. Then he jerked and spun, dropping his Nikonos. Inside the mask his eyes looked wide and wild.

Hallie had seen it before. The skeletons had spoken: *We died in here. You can, too.* He had begun to imagine their deaths, the panicked breathing, thickening silt, the flailing search for the exit in zero visibility. Thrashing and gasping, tangling bodies, panic feeding panic, air coming harder as tanks emptied, frantic last gasps, thoughts flickering out, and then . . . nothing.

She knew that Brewster's deep, reptilian urge for self-preservation would be screaming, *Out!* He charged, tried to shove her out of the way. Hallie grabbed his harness and spun him around and smacked him hard on the side of the head, just beneath his helmet, with the steel handle of her primary light. Not many things could cut through panic, but good old-fashioned pain was one. She gave him a shake, held up one finger: *Stop!* For a moment she wasn't sure, but then he got control of himself. She looked at his pressure gauge: *1,300 pounds*. They had started with 3,000. *He should have signaled for the turnaround long ago.*

We're going back, she signaled with a twirling forefinger. *Now.*

He nodded.

She went first, frog-kicking and pulling herself along with handholds to get more speed. She had dropped her primary reel in the Boneyard. No time to be rewinding line now. Brewster was breathing so hard it looked like his regulator was free-flowing. At the Jaws of Death she slipped through. Brewster got stuck again, flailing and scrabbling. Hallie hung back, knowing that panicked divers not infrequently took their buddies with them. Two minutes passed before he finally muscled through.

And then, suddenly, his bubbles stopped. He grabbed his secondary regulator. No bubbles. She could not believe he had breathed both tanks dry that fast, but here they were. She gave him her primary regulator on its seven-foot hose. His eyes were bulging as though someone were pumping air into his skull.

Breathing from her own secondary, which she carried on a shock-cord necklace, she started out again, careful not to pull the regulator away from him. Fifty yards from the cave mouth, it began to feel as though she were sucking air through thick cotton. She took several long, deep breaths, locked the last down in her chest. Brewster spit his reg out and tried to grab her. He breathed in water, convulsed, went limp. She grabbed his harness and began swimming backward, towing him on her chest.

Hallie was a national-class free diver who could remain motionless at forty feet for almost five minutes. But hauling Brewster, who weighed more than two hundred pounds, and whose double-steel tanks weighed another hundred, she was burning through oxygen.

No choice. She swam on toward the circle of light. It was small and too far away and she knew they were not going to make it. Hypoxia hit, burning in her chest, her peripheral vision contracting, thoughts slowing. She felt sluggish and numb. Very soon her blood CO_2 level would trip an autonomic breathing reflex, and that would drown her.

Nothing to do about that.

Swim.

She kept kicking hard, pulling on rocks with her free hand, her vision darkening to points of light like the last two shimmering stars in a black sky. Beyond thought, beyond feeling, her body kept working, hauling, pulling. Then she was falling away from the dimming stars, away, and then she was gone.

She did not remember bringing herself and Brewster through the cave entrance. When she came to, she was swimming toward the platform, Brewster in tow.

"Need help here!"

People ran down from the picnic area, hauled Brewster onto the platform.

Gasping, she puked into the water. "Put him on his left side!" Hallie said. She dumped her own gear in five seconds, climbed onto the platform. Brewster's face was gray, lips and fingernails blue. She cleared his airway, rolled him onto his back, performed fifteen chest compressions, started CPR. Sour fluid came out of him. She breathed, pumped, breathed, pumped. She heard someone calling 911.

"I thank he's a goner." A woman in the crowd, nearly hysterical.

This was country; EMTs would take time. Hallie began to feel light-headed, her arms burning. She kept at it, breaths and compressions, over and over and over. It could have been ten minutes or an hour, she wasn't sure. Was that a siren? She couldn't be sure about that, either. Foul liquid kept leaking out of Brewster's throat and nose, but she ignored it. A child in the crowd was screaming. A man bent over her, red-faced, fearful.

"Lady, I don't think he's gonna—"

Just then Brewster bucked, convulsed, spewed vomit. She rolled him over onto one side as two EMTs in blue jumpsuits shoved through the crowd.

"What happened?" The EMTs, sweating like laborers from their run in the heat, were breaking out oxygen and defib kits.

Hallie and Brewster knew exactly what had happened. But she said, "Equipment failure. His regs silted up."

Hallie leaned close, as if to give Brewster a light kiss, and whispered into his ear. "You were lucky."

Vomit-smeared, eyes stretched wide, he grabbed her hand. Squeezed, pulled her back down. Whispered, *"Thank you."*

"No worries."

She patted his shoulder and left.

FIVE

MARY WAS THERE, RED-EYED, GREEN-FACED, CLUTCHING A mug of black coffee in one hand and a Marlboro in the other when Hallie came in. The paramedics had taken Brewster to their local hospital, worried that he might have aspirated vomit and possibly collapsed a lung as well. Hallie had sat with two state troopers, giving information they needed for their report. It was almost two by the time she made it back to the shop.

"I got a call. What the hell happened?"

Mary's voice was deeper and rougher than cigarettes could make it. Insurgents in Iraq had done that, bringing her Apache down with a Stinger and filling her lungs with fire.

Hallie told her.

"Jesus Christ. How *are* you?"

"Trashed. Can I take the afternoon?"

"For sure. Those guys want a word with you, though."

Mary nodded toward the back of the shop, and Hallie saw the red, wrinkled mat of scar tissue on the left side of her friend's face, a sight she would never get used to. Then she let her eyes travel farther.

She hadn't noticed the two men by the racks of masks and fins. Gray business suits, white shirts, and ties with wide, diagonal stripes. One tie was red and gold, the other blue and green. Both had little American flag pins in the right lapels of their suit jackets, short, razor-cut hair, and cheeks shaved so close they gleamed.

"I don't think they're looking to dive." Mary blew smoke toward the men.

Hallie approached them. "Can I help you?"

"I'm Agent Fortier," said the one with the red-and-gold tie. "This is my partner, Agent Whittle. We're with the Department of Homeland Security."

They showed ID folders with gold badges and photos.

Hallie flushed, folded her arms across her chest, pissed off just by the sight of them. "Let me guess. You're worried we're diving with terrorists, sowing mines in harbors or some such bullshit. Am I right?"

Fortier's mouth dropped open. Apparently people usually showed more respect. While Whittle coughed and examined a wet suit's price tag, Fortier maintained a neutral expression. "Can we speak privately, Dr. Leland?"

That surprised *her*. Hallie wasn't called "doctor" around here, where people just knew her as a dive instructor and guide.

"Nope," she said. "Let's do this tomorrow. Rough day at the office, gentlemen." She started to walk away, already tasting an ice-cold Corona, then stopped. "In fact, let's not do this at all. You want to see me, I have a lawyer you can talk to first." It wasn't true, but she thought it might get them off her back.

"Dr. Leland," Fortier's eyes flicked from side to side. His voice dropped to a whisper. *"This is a matter of national security."*

That did it. She whirled, eyes flashing. "I know exactly what it's a matter of. What, BARDA didn't screw up my life enough already?"

The agents exchanged glances. Then Fortier said, "You're right. We *are* here because of someone from BARDA."

"Uh-huh. So you can just—"

"We have a message from Dr. Barnard."

That stopped her. "Don Barnard?"

"Yes."

Dr. Donald Barnard had been her boss at the CDC. The only one who had stood with her when her world came crashing down.

"Is Don all right? Why didn't he just call? Or come down himself? What is—?"

"Dr. Barnard's presence was required in Washington. He is . . . very busy."

Fortier looked truly worried—whether about Barnard or something else, Hallie couldn't tell.

"So you came all this way to give me a message?"

"Fifteen minutes, Dr. Leland. Please. But not here."

"I'm the blue Tundra outside. Follow me to my house."

"Nice place."

The first time Agent Whittle had spoken and his voice wavered. The oppressive, soggy, boiling heat. He had the fishy, white-lipped look people got before they fainted. Hallie saw it, but she was not feeling charitable. *If he can't take the heat, screw him.*

"Thanks," she said. The rented house wasn't really nice. Some shutters were missing, the faded blue paint was alligatoring, and the small screened porch listed. But inside it was neat and clean, with white-painted floors and walls, and smelled of fresh oranges. There was, however, no air-conditioning.

"*Warm* down here," Whittle said. He was a sizable man who appeared to be in good shape, but his voice sounded weak and thin. They were sitting in chairs at her chrome-and-Formica kitchen table, original equipment with the house.

"You get used to it. No worse than D.C. in August."

"It's February, though. How hot is it, exactly?"

"About ninety in here. Ninety-eight outside. So, not too bad. High humidity today, though."

"Lord God." Whittle loosened his blue-and-green tie, unbuttoned his collar. Mopped sweat from his face with a damp handkerchief. "I'm from North Dakota. It doesn't get like this."

Hallie was afraid he might actually keel off the chair. If there was one thing she did not need this day, it was a heat-stroked Fed flopping around on her kitchen floor.

"Hold on." She took a fluted pitcher from the refrigerator and poured three tall glasses of cold, homemade lemonade. Condensation filmed the glasses in a second. She added sprigs of mint from her backyard herb garden and brought the glasses to the table. Hallie sipped hers, studying the agents. Whittle gulped half of his lemonade, then held the glass against his forehead.

"*Thank* you." There was serious gratitude in his voice.

"About Don?"

"Yes. Just a second." Fortier put his briefcase on the table and begin working through its three combination locks.

Agent Whittle took another long drink of lemonade, then looked at Hallie in an odd way. "Could I ask you a question, Dr. Leland? It'll take Agent Fortier a minute here."

"Shoot."

"Well, I was wondering what happened to your friend back there."

"You mean Mary? The shop owner?"

"Yes."

"She was an Apache pilot in Iraq. Patrolling her sector one day when she monitored a combat patrol screaming for air support. Insurgents had them surrounded. Command denied their request. The fighters were known to have Stingers and the brass probably figured soldiers were easier to replace than choppers. Mary went in anyway. She saved the team, but the bad guys brought her down with a Stinger. Her copilot was killed. Mary survived the crash but . . . well, you saw. She should have gotten the Medal of Honor."

"What medal *did* she get?"

"None. 'Lieutenant Stilwell is dishonorably discharged for willful disobeyance of orders from a superior officer and wanton disregard for the safety of her copilot, her actions resulting in destruction of Army assets and the death of said copilot,' is how the court-martial finding read, if I recall right."

Agent Whittle blinked, looked out the window. "I'm sorry to hear that. You get a feeling sometimes. I lost a son in Iraq."

The words stung. At least Mary was alive. "*I'm* sorry, Agent Whittle. I have a soft spot in my heart for soldiers. My father was career Army." She reached forward and touched his arm, realizing that her eyes had teared up.

"Thank you." He continued to look out the window. Hallie hadn't added all her history with Mary, how they had been best friends at Georgetown University and she had gone on to graduate school at Hopkins while Mary abandoned plans for medical school and joined the Army instead. Mary had been chasing her Big Sister the Doctor's achievements all her life, and going to med school would have been just another step in her shadow. But flying an Apache—*that* would be something. Mary graduated from flight school at Fort Rucker second in her class and asked for the hottest region of operation, which at the time was around Fallujah in Iraq.

Agent Fortier set on the table what looked like an oversized BlackBerry, unfolded two side panels, pressed a button. One soft tone, then a cone of rose-colored light blossomed, and Don Barnard was there on her table. His head and chest, anyway.

The hologram spoke: "Hello, Hallie! Can you see me okay?"

It took her a moment to respond. "I . . . can see you fine, Don." The image was unbelievably real. Every hair of his big white mustache was clearly visible, his bushy eyebrows and sharp blue eyes and his weekend sailor's sunburn.

"I can see you, too. Amazing, isn't it?"

"This is *you* I'm talking to? Not some CG thing?"

"It's me. I just couldn't get away right now."

She smiled at the sight of him for another moment, then decided it was time to drive the conversation forward.

"What's going on, Don?"

His smile faded. "We have a problem, Hallie, and time is of the essence. I—*we*—need your help."

She actually laughed. "*My* help? Come on, they ran me out of there on a rail."

"You know how I felt about that. It was a rotten deal."

"I know that you were the only one in my corner."

"And I would be there again. Look, Hallie, can you come up here?"

"You mean, like *now*?"

"Yes."

"In a day or two, I guess. I work for a friend, Don. She'll need some—"

"Can't wait, Hallie. We need you now. Someone will speak to Mary."

"How did you know— Never mind. But you won't tell me why?"

"*Can't*. Even these things can be hacked. I'm sure the agents have mentioned national security."

"Was I supposed to take that seriously?"

"Indeed."

"This has nothing to do with the other business?"

"No. Nothing. My word on that."

"Okay." Hallie believed him, but wanted to be clear. "Those bastards can piss in their hats for all I care."

"I think we agree on that."

"I'll come. What happens now?"

"Agents Fortier and Whittle will take it from here. Thank you, Hallie. We'll speak soon."

His image dissolved.

"Do you have any idea what's going on?" she asked Whittle, who was drinking the last of his lemonade and looking better.

Her hospitality had softened their official crust. He smiled and shook his head. "For this mission we're just high-end errand boys, Dr. Leland."

"Do I have time to pack?"

"They'll have things for you on the other end."

"Jesus. Well, then I'm ready when you are, gentlemen."

They walked out. She locked the door and followed the agents to their black Expedition with tinted windows, where Whittle held a rear door for her. They had left the engine running to keep the air-conditioning on. She got in and it was like sitting down in a meat locker. When he saw that she was settled, he said, "Thank you, Dr. Leland," before gently closing the door.

This, she had to admit, was more like it.

SIX

"HALLIE!"

Donald Barnard, MD, PhD, had started at tight end for the University of Virginia in 1968 and '69. He was now twenty pounds heavier and decades older, but still solid. He hauled around his desk like a bear rolling out of its den, big hand extended, looking happy and relieved and exhausted all at once. Hallie brushed his proffered hand aside and gave him a long, hard hug, then held him at arm's length. She frowned.

"You look tired, Don." It was just after seven in the evening. She knew he started his workdays at six-thirty A.M.

"That makes two of us." He stepped back. "You remember Lew Casey? Lew was Delta Lab supervisor when you were here."

It was only then that she noticed the two men who had been standing off to one side in Barnard's large office while he and Hallie said hello. Dr. Lewis Casey was a short man in his fifties with milky skin, a blizzard of freckles, and hair like curls of rusty wire.

"I remember him very well. It's good to see you again, Doctor."

"And I remember *you,* Dr. Leland." Casey stepped forward, shook her hand. "I always admired your work. Tried to steal you for Delta, in fact."

She looked at Barnard. "You never told me that."

"Lew was not the only one, I can assure you." Barnard appeared, very briefly, sheepish.

"Thank you, Dr. Casey. I'm honored to hear you say that." Despite herself, Hallie was pleased.

"Lew does fine. And I'll call you Hallie, if that's all right with you?"

"Of course."

Barnard turned to the third man, who, Hallie could tell with a second's glance, was no scientist. Too neat, too polished, too perfect. Could have stepped out of a Brooks Brothers catalog. He was slim and tan, wearing a tailored, three-piece suit of fine brown wool and what looked to be handmade English shoes. His razor-cut brown hair lay tight against his scalp and he sported a meticulously trimmed mustache. *An otter,* Hallie thought. *Sleek and shiny and uncatchable.* CIA was written all over him. His handshake was firm, and when he locked eyes with hers something inside her shuddered. The man had done some things.

"David Lathrop. With Central Intelligence."

"Hallie Leland. With Deep Enough Dive Shop."

He got it, laughed. "Don has told us both a great deal about you. His admiration is unbounded."

She felt herself blushing. "Thank you."

They settled into red leather chairs at a coffee table across the big office from Barnard's desk. She hadn't been sure how it would feel, coming back to BARDA, but here in Don's office, at least, it was good. Barnard's time in government entitled him to several rooms with tall windows on the top floor of a building that was, by design, four utterly unremarkable stories above ground and tucked back in a declining industrial park in Prince George's County. The office walls could have been those of any senior bureaucrat in Washington, covered with framed citations, pictures of Barnard with his wife, Lucianne, and their two sons, plus photos of Barnard with senators and generals and presidents.

"Florida's obviously agreeing with you." Barnard looked pleased.

"Sunnier there. Smells better, too."

"You deserved a respite, Hallie."

"It's good for a while. But I'm already starting to feel . . ."

"Bored?"

"Unchallenged."

"That doesn't surprise me." Barnard fiddled with the big meerschaum pipe he had not smoked for fifteen years. "Well, you're surely wondering why you're here."

"You could say that. It's been a short, strange trip." Fortier and Whittle had put her on a Bell Jet Ranger helicopter, which had taken her to a government Citation jet at a restricted airfield, which had flown her to Andrews, where another helicopter had brought her here. It was well after dark now.

"The request originated at the highest level."

"You mean from the OD?" Office of the Director, CDC, of which BARDA was a part. Despite her fatigue, Hallie was sitting up straight, legs crossed, elbows on the chair arms, fingers tented.

"No. The White House."

"Yeah, right. Don, I came too far for jokes."

Lathrop broke in: "He's not joking, Dr. Leland. I can assure you. Shortly before you arrived we were on a videoconference with President O'Neil." He smiled. "It wasn't long, but it *was* the president."

Barnard nodded. "I've been briefing the president, Vice President Washinsky, Secretary of Homeland Security Mason, and Secretary of Health and Human Services Rathor every day."

She saw no humor in his eyes, just fatigue, concern, and—something she had never seen before in her former boss—a hint of fear.

"Okay. What's going on?"

Lathrop's voice was smooth and modulated, like an FM radio announcer's, but as he spoke this time it grew tight.

"Almost two weeks ago, one of our soldiers in Afghanistan was wounded at a combat outpost called Terok. Not seriously, but he was admitted to his base's medical unit. That's when it started."

"What started?"

"Watch this. Don?"

Barnard punched buttons on a remote. A large flat-screen monitor on a near wall glowed to life. Hallie watched as the image on the screen showed a room with lime-green walls. It contained a stainless steel table, sinks, scales, trays of evil-looking instruments, and a wall of cold-storage lockers.

A figure walked into the picture wearing a blue Chemturion Biosafety Level 4 suit. Inflated to maintain positive pressure, it looked like the space suits in Buck Rogers movies, right down to the clear, bucket-shaped hood and futuristic backpack containing the battery-powered personal life support system. The attendant opened a locker door and rolled out a stainless steel rack. She unzipped the orange cadaver bag and pushed it open, exposing the body inside.

Hallie came half out of her chair, gaping. "Jesus Christ! Did terrorists do that?"

"Iatrogenic. It happened in Terok's medical unit." Lathrop shook his head as he said this, as though having difficulty believing it, despite the grisly evidence before them at that moment.

"How?"

"Just watch for a bit."

The camera moved. Hallie saw close-ups, plate-sized patches of skin missing, exposed red tissue and even, in a few places, white bone. She had seen skinless cadavers in graduate school at Hopkins, but, treated with formaldehyde and phenol, they'd looked more like pink wax. This body was like fresh meat.

The screen faded to black. Barnard turned to Hallie. "That is . . . *was* Army Specialist DeAengelo Washington. A fine young soldier, from what I was told."

"Was he captured? Tortured?"

"No. He wasn't the one wounded. That young man is in another locker in the same morgue. It was ACE."

"*Acinetobacter*? Can't be. ACE doesn't do that."

"What do you know about ACE, Dr. Leland?" Lathrop asked.

"Thirty-one known species, thirty benign. One, *Acinetobacter baumannii,* is drug-resistant, but not often fatal in healthy adults. Transmissible by inhalation, ingestion, or through damaged skin. Lungs are the primary infection site, but it can also initiate in the urinary tract, stomach, or bowel."

She paused a moment, not sure how much they wanted to hear. When no one said anything, she continued: "ACE loves hospitals. It can live for months on a stethoscope or examining table. But the biggest infection vectors are catheters. Of all bacteria, ACE has one of the highest transmutation indexes."

"That's exactly right," Don Barnard affirmed. "All ACE species, including *baumannii,* have an extraordinary ability to exchange genes with each other through carrier viruses called bacteriophages. It's almost like the way ants communicate with pheromones. Information, including immunity to an antibiotic, can spread through an entire population with astonishing speed. A matter of hours, in some cases. Back in 2005, geneticists at Stanford broke the code of a new ACE strain and found the greatest number of genetic upgrades ever discovered in a single organism."

Hallie sat forward. "I remember that. But ACE only endangers people with compromised immune systems—HIV sufferers, the elderly, burn victims, chemotherapy patients."

"*And* people with severe tissue trauma." Lathrop sounded angry.

She understood. "Like wounded soldiers."

"Correct."

"Okay. But after ACE outbreaks in New York hospitals killed some older people in 2002, they dusted off a 1950s antibiotic called colistin. It worked. On some of the people some of the time, anyway."

"All true, Hallie." Barnard frowned, rubbed the pipe bowl with his thumb as if trying to remove something foul.

"So what happened over there? They didn't have any colistin?"

"They got some. It just slowed ACE down. And colistin is in very short supply. Nobody has produced it in any quantity for at least forty years."

"But surely ACE didn't cause what we saw on that video?"

"It did. We have conclusive test results."

"How?"

"It is a new ACE." Lew Casey spoke for the first time, sitting forward in the chair, elbows on knees, looking up at them from beneath wiry red brows.

That stopped her. "So this is biowar, finally?"

"Possible, but the intelligence people don't think so. More likely, antigenic shift."

"How did it do that to him?"

"This new ACE apparently grows in the bloodstream, then attacks organs and skin from inside out."

"Bacteria usually burrow deeper, where it's easier to propagate."

"This ACE does just the opposite. It wants *out*. And it gets out fast."

"Like being skinned alive, slowly." Hallie tried to imagine what it would be like, but then gave up. "No drug on earth could blunt that agony."

"No." Barnard looked grim. "None."

"It's *horrible*," she said. "But at least it's contained."

Barnard coughed, looked at the others.

"There are more cases?"

"His squadmate, a kid from Kansas, was the first—the zero man. Since then, two nurses and another patient in the medical unit."

"Who's in charge at that place?"

Barnard took a deep breath, let it out, rearranged his bulk in the chair. "An Army doctor. National Guard, actually. It's a field hospital with Level II trauma capability and that little morgue you saw, but they stabilize serious cases for transport to CENMEDFAC, in Kabul."

"He's still in there?"

"She. By herself, unfortunately. The Taliban launched a regionwide offensive. May or may not be a correlation. But there have been heavy casualties, so Terok's other two doctors were called to other COPs."

"She's dealing with wounded *and* ACE. Tough assignment."

"Yes."

"Well, at least that COP is quarantined. Terok, was it?"

Again Barnard hesitated, stared down at his pipe's empty bowl.

"My God, Don. People got out? *How many?*"

"Two went back to a forward operating base called Salerno, fifty miles east. But the big worry is CENMEDFAC."

"The mother of all Army hospitals over there."

"Right. Four patients were transferred there. All had contact with the cases at Terok."

"CENMEDFAC sends the worst cases stateside."

"Right."

"So it could be coming here."

"It *is* here, Dr. Leland." Lathrop, sitting forward. "Some of them arrived two days ago."

For a moment, nobody spoke. Hallie was stunned, the ramifications spinning out in her mind. As they sat in silence, Barnard's secretary, Carol, came in. It was well after working hours, but she would never leave until he did. She was a trim widow with a rust-red beehive hairdo and a different-colored polyester pant suit for every day of the month.

"Here you are. I thought you people might want a snack." She placed a tray with roast beef and turkey sandwiches and a big pot of coffee on the table.

"*Thank* you," Hallie said. "I needed this. Nothing since breakfast."

Carol put a hand on her shoulder. "It's good to see you again, Hallie. I've missed you."

Hallie smiled, patted her hand. "I've missed you, too, Carrie. You *and* Don."

After a moment, Carol left them. The men poured cups of coffee but took nothing to eat. Hallie gobbled half a sandwich, poured coffee, dumped in cream and sugar. Not her usual way, but she needed energy.

"So where do things stand now?" She got the words out through a mouthful of roast beef.

"Colistin is buying us some time." Barnard did not look relieved saying that.

"But it's like water building up behind a dam. Colistin is the dam," Lew Casey put in. "Those four cases from Terok remained at CENMEDFAC for three days. During that time they came in contact with dozens of patients and staff."

"Where did the cases go here in the U.S.?"

The two scientists looked at Lathrop.

"Reed got one, Bethesda another, and two went to the burn center in Georgia."

Hallie stopped chewing. "Those places are full of people with compromised immune systems. ACE will burn through them like fire in a hay barn."

"And it will keep going," Barnard continued. "There's constant interchange between military facilities like those."

"This is horrific. You've got thousands of sick and wounded soldiers in facilities all over the country. They might have survived combat injuries only to be killed in our own hospitals." Feeling her eyes fill, Hallie set her cup down. "Sorry, gentlemen."

"Don't worry. A little emotion is good for the blood," said Barnard, and the others nodded. "But it gets even worse. If this ACE can really attack healthy subjects as well . . ."

"The entire armed forces could be decimated. Not just the sick and wounded."

"You see now why your presence is so important."

"You need the drug we had been working on. Superdrug for a superbug."

"Yes. You were close. Another few months and I believe you'd have had a whole new family of antibiotics."

"Weeks, maybe." Hallie recalled the research very well.

"That's why Don wouldn't let me spirit you away, actually." Lew Casey sounded rueful.

"But I never finished. For obvious reasons. So Al must not have done it, either."

Barnard shook his head. "Dr. Cahner—Al—is a very good microbiologist. I know the two of you got on well. And did fine work together."

The two of them *had* worked well as a team, but it had been more complicated than that. More than twenty years older than Hallie, Al had reminded her, at first meeting, of those men she saw scrutinizing labels in supermarket aisles and reading books over the daily specials in chain restaurants. For their first months in the lab together, he spoke of nothing but work and always lunched by himself. He was never rude, just solitary.

But month after month they worked, pressed together in the microbiology laboratory, always conscious that they were in the company of Level 4 pathogens that had killed hundreds of millions of people throughout history. She came to respect Cahner's grace under pressure and the precision of his lab techniques. She sensed, too, that he recognized her own dedication to good science and, even more, admired her ability to handle demons like *Yersinia pestis* with steady hands.

After eight months they started eating lunch together in the canteen. His meal never varied: a Red Delicious apple, a carton of V-8 juice, tuna salad on whole wheat with lettuce and tomato. He wasn't much for idle chat, but she learned that he'd happily talk about microbiology. One day she mentioned that the CDC had just sent a team of pathogen hunters to some caves in Gabon.

Munching a bit of sandwich, he said casually, "Those African caves are nasty. I was in Bandubyo myself."

She almost dropped her coffee. *"Bandubyo?"*

He looked sheepish, meeting her astonished gaze. "Well, yes. It was back in—let me think—'03 or maybe '04."

"My God. Ebola-B was discovered in that cave. The worst of the Ebola family. What were you doing there?"

"I was part of a WHO team of virologists and microbiologists. Some people had contracted hemorrhagic fever after eating *Passiflora edulis* grown near the cave."

"Passion fruit."

"Right. We determined that fruit bats from the cave contaminated the crops. Passion fruit and cassava both, in fact."

"Bandubyo," she repeated, shaking her head. "That is supposed to be one hell of a cave."

"There was a lot of vertical. And to penetrate the dark zone we had to do some diving. Inside, the cave was clean. But from the twilight zone with its bat chamber on out—red-hot with what turned out to be that new species of Ebola virus."

"I hadn't realized you did that kind of fieldwork."

"Oh, when the need arises. I don't get out often enough to keep my skills *really* sharp. But I can still hold my own if I have to."

This was a side of Al Cahner she had not known about and would not have suspected. But he was trim and looked reasonably fit, so it was not completely outlandish to imagine him exploring wild caves. And she could not help but admire him for it. Penetrating viral caves was as bad as fieldwork got, partly because it was so dangerous and required a host of technical skills like rock climbing and vertical rope work and scuba diving. The really bad part, though, was that such caves sometimes housed pathogens of unearthly virulence.

"I gather you've done some cave work yourself," he said.

I wonder what else he knows about me? Hallie thought, but didn't press the subject. BARDA was not a large facility. People talked.

"Yes. For fun and work both. A lot of cave diving, too."

"It takes a special kind of person to do that for *fun*. It is dangerous business."

"There's no margin for error, that's for sure."

They talked a bit more about caves and viruses, then went back to their food. But the conversation had changed Hallie's perception of her lab partner. *There's more there than meets the eye,* she thought. And then: *All he needs is a little TLC.*

Their bond grew, and as the months passed they talked about themselves, laughed at odd fellow workers, bitched about the bureaucracy, damned do-nothing politicians—took the small risks that inched them closer together. Of all the things they talked about, Hallie was most surprised to find that Al Cahner was a walking encyclopedia of baseball statistics. He was especially fond of the 1950s—"baseball's golden age," he called it. He could recite ERAs and slugging percentages and double-play combos as if he were reading them off a page. He also delighted in the *sounds* of baseball. Not the smack of a fastball in a catcher's mitt or the ring of a cleanly hit home run. The sounds he found most beautiful were players' names, which he loved to recite, almost like a kind of poetry:

"Granny Hamner. Enos Slaughter. Ryne Duren." *Pause.* "Paolo Discomenides. Hart Workman. Joe Bolt." *Pause.* "Gino Cimoli. Rabbit Hopper. Artie Dedeaux."

Hallie had never been a baseball fan. One of her brothers had played cornerback for Duke; the other had been a flanker for the University of Colorado on a nationally ranked team. Both had been high school standouts, so she had been watching football games since she was ten. Nevertheless, she enjoyed listening to her lab partner's name-poems, and enjoyed, as well, seeing him smile.

On her last afternoon, when stone-faced security guards escorted her back to retrieve her personal effects, Cahner appeared stunned. The blood drained from his face so rapidly she feared he might pass out. But then, glaring at the guards, he asked what in God's name was happening. They just stood and stared. He turned to her.

"I'm leaving" was all she could say, and she knew it was only the first of many such encounters to come.

After several unsuccessful tries to learn more from her, he again fired sharp questions at the guards, who only shrugged. One said, "Hey, we don't know anything. We're just doing our jobs here, you know?"

Cahner started to berate the two men, but Hallie said, "It's not them, Al," and he let it go. So all he could do was stand and gape during the ten minutes it took for her to collect the pictures of her family, epidemiology reference books, laptop, back issues of *Science*. By the time she finished, she saw that he had composed himself somewhat.

As they shook hands for the last time, he held on and said, "This is horrible, Hallie. I don't know what to say. But if you ever need anything that I can provide, you must call."

She nodded and, still holding his hand, leaned forward and kissed him on the cheek, which made his eyes fill with tears.

Barnard pulled her back from those recollections. He said, "There has been no breakthrough."

She understood. "Or else you wouldn't have me here."

"Right."

With the coffee and sandwiches, she was feeling better, but sensed she was missing something still. "Why haven't I heard anything about this in the media?"

"Damage control at the highest levels. President O'Neil has

called in quite a few chits. But it won't stay contained for long." Lathrop sounded pained.

"How many military hospitals are there?" Hallie wanted to run the numbers.

"More than two thousand in the U.S. More overseas."

"How many patients in those?"

"As of six P.M. yesterday, 217,452."

"And not just from this war, but from others, right? Plus all those dependents hospitalized to give birth, get hernias fixed, whatever."

"That's right."

Hallie felt sick. "So it's not only active-duty soldiers. Families packed into bases, circulating through movie theaters, clinics, gyms, kindergartens. My God, the list is endless. You could not create better pandemic conditions if you tried. What's the transmission factor?"

"Unknown," said Barnard. "The other ACE is similar to smallpox."

Lew Casey continued: "Smallpox carriers take about seven days to become contagious. After that, in an urban environment, they infect an average of twelve people every twenty-four hours. Those carriers infect others. Exponential growth. A million or more in two weeks."

Lathrop rubbed his face. "Military bases, with higher population densities than cities, would be much worse. Ships at sea, submarines—the *Pentagon,* for God's sake."

Then Barnard spoke, in a tone Hallie had never heard him use before:

"'Potentially the worst threat since Pearl Harbor.' Those are not my words, but President O'Neil's."

SEVEN

HALLIE POURED HERSELF MORE COFFEE. SHE TURNED TO LA-throp.

"Is anything else being done?"

"Yes, of course. Everything possible with the information still on close hold, anyway. But it's all reactive."

"How long do you think we have, Don?"

"With colistin and aggressive containment, ten to fourteen days. No more."

"That's not enough time."

"No."

"So the only real hope is . . ."

"That highly classified work you had been doing here at BARDA."

Classified. BARDA.

She had been so focused on the burgeoning catastrophe that she had all but forgotten what had happened thirteen months earlier. Now those two words took her back to the small and windowless room—its smells of cigarette smoke and body odor, its contents a metal conference table, six chairs, and two men. The table and chairs were gray, the men were black and white.

"Please close the door and have a seat."

The black man's voice was cool, neutral. Neither rose or offered to shake hands.

"My name is David Rhodes. I'm the ARILO—agency research integrity liaison officer with the CDC's Office of General Counsel—for your case." He spoke slowly, carefully, sculpting each word, the cadence of a preacher at a funeral.

"My *case*?" Hallie had been peremptorily summoned from her lab and was not happy. "And who is *he*?"

"Agent Rivers is with HHS. Office of Internal Security."

Rhodes was smooth and utterly composed. A lawyer's lawyer. His cologne smelled like sun-warmed roses. The other one wore a cheap suit and his tie had a stain just below the knot. A double-dipping ex-cop or maybe ex-Bureau. *His* cologne smelled like industrial disinfectant. Rivers's face was a collection of wrinkles and pinches from a lifetime of frowning. Rhodes's was smooth as dark ice. He had a thick neck and that quiet, precise voice. A manila folder lay in front of him, perfectly squared to the angles of the table. Looking at it, and at his huge hands, she saw that he wore a Penn State ring. *Linebacker,* she thought.

"You need to know that I am in the middle of extremely critical—"

"We *know* whachure workin' on." Rivers cut her off, bored, looking at the ceiling.

"And we are aware of its importance." Rhodes kept his eyes on hers. "That's one reason we're here. There has been a security breach. Traced to you."

First came denial: she laughed. "A security breach? Is this some kind of prank? Did Don Barnard put you up to this? The lab people?"

"No joke, Doc." Rivers hacked out a smoker's phlegmy rattle. He did not cover his mouth, and microdroplets of saliva sprayed the table.

Buy time. "Show me some ID, gentlemen."

They had valid credentials. Rivers's included a gold badge with blue numbers. When he put his black leather ID folder away, she noted that he made sure to flash the Glock 9mm in its brown Bianchi shoulder holster.

"What kind of complaint?"

"It appears that you have been providing secure research information to an outside party for unauthorized remuneration."

She translated the bureaucratese in her mind. "You're talking about selling government secrets?"

"That's right."

"First, that is a lie." Hallie tried not to sound like it, but she was furious and afraid. "Second, if there is to be an investigation, you are required first to inform me and my immediate superior, allow me to retain counsel, and present your allegations before a panel headed by the associate director of science and including at least one CDC employee of my choosing."

"You've read your personnel manual." Rhodes seemed impressed.

Rivers did not. "What the *personnel manual* don't include is that with national security, that *personnel process* goes in the dumpster."

National security. Twenty-first-century McCarthyism.

"How long has this inquiry been going on?"

"I'm not at liberty to divulge that." Rhodes tapped the manila folder with his index finger. A fly buzzed around Rivers, who seemed not to notice. "But we're confident that a court would find probable cause to believe a security breach occurred and that you were responsible."

"This is insane!" Hallie jumped out of her chair. "I'm getting the hell out of here and calling my lawyer, gentlemen."

Rhodes's voice, soft but urgent, stopped her. "*Dr. Leland.* I seriously advise you to wait. Hear us out. Then you can always retain counsel . . . and so forth."

That was reasonable. Still furious, she sat back down. "So tell me."

"Emails have been intercepted. From your home computer to and from an external source, containing secure BARDA information. Deposits have also been tracked to an account in your name at Grand Cayman National Bank. They correspond to payments and dates in the emails."

"This is unbelievable. I don't have a Cayman account, Mr. Rhodes. Never have."

Rivers suddenly sat up straight, put his elbows on the table. "We don't even have to talk to you, Doc. We could refer this to the United States attorney. Like *that*." He snapped his fingers and in the small room it sounded like a slap. "For criminal charges."

It was like trying to fight her way through a whiteout in the mountains, no points of reference, cliffs and crevasses all around. Stop. Make them wait. "Rhodes and Rivers. What a coincidence."

No one smiled.

"What's in that folder?" she asked. "The charges?"

Rhodes pushed a single sheet of BARDA stationery across to Hallie. It had today's date. She read it, looked up in disbelief.

"This is a letter of resignation."

"Better for the gubment." Rivers poked a finger at her. "Better for *you*."

"Jesus Christ. Look, I need to think about this. To talk to a lawyer, at least. You can understand that. Isn't that my right?"

"Absolutely." Rhodes looked at her calmly. "But you should understand that we can make this offer here, now. On the table for this meeting. If you walk, it goes away."

"It was me, I'd take it." Now Rivers tried to sound collegial, supportive. She found him less nauseating the other way, but ignored him regardless.

"All it needs is your signature, Dr. Leland." Rhodes waited, watching her.

She was furious and terrified and confused. Her face felt hot. It was hard to get a good breath in the small room, its air thick with the men's smells.

"Who was I supposed to be selling data to?"

Rhodes glanced at Rivers. "I'm not at liberty to divulge that."

Nothing like this had ever happened to her before. She had no frame of reference, no experience to fall back on that might help her know how to react. But she did know that Washington was always all about leverage, and suddenly something occurred to her.

"What's CDC afraid of? Why are you doing this in secret?"

For the first time she saw a glimmer of uncertainty in Rhodes's eyes. He twisted the Penn State ring, looked at Rivers, who shrugged, more concerned with the little wart on his left palm that he was picking with the fingernails of his other hand. Rhodes took a while, appearing to consider his words very carefully.

"You know how important secrecy is to BARDA's mission. Therefore to CDC's. A very public security-breach trial could do irreparable harm. There are people in the government who would like for BARDA to go away. Every dollar spent here is a dollar not spent on guns and tanks. If you get my drift." With his two index fingers, he drew a pentagon in the air.

Leverage. Now she had some. Now they were afraid.

"I could walk out of here right now, gentlemen. Make just three calls. My lawyer, my senator, and the *Washington Post*." *Like there really is a "my lawyer,"* she thought. But they would not know that. Or . . . maybe they would.

"That's true, Dr. Leland." Rhodes's hands were folded on the tabletop again. "But you may know how much Washington lawyers cost. And as I said, if you walk out of here, we have no choice. It goes to the U.S. attorney immediately. There will be preliminary hearings, discovery, perhaps press conferences. Possible criminal charges, as Agent Rivers said. Think carefully. A government scientist selling top secret biological research—"

"Alleged," she snapped so sharply that Rivers looked up from his wart.

Rhodes nodded, smiled, happy to stipulate the parsing that, she herself knew, would make not a whit of difference. "Yes, alleged to be selling top secret research. Even if you are cleared, your career will be over. Why would anyone hire you when there are thousands of untainted microbiologists out there?"

"I'm telling you, Doc, you're better off taking what we're offering." Rivers's smile showed yellow smoker's teeth and a serious lack of flossing. She almost screamed at him to shut up. But she knew that Rhodes was right.

She could not afford a pricey lawyer. Her mother had some money, but Hallie would never ask for it. Even if she got a lawyer, the story would be in the *Post* and on the news programs for days. National news. International, probably. The media liked few things better than espionage stories. Genocide, maybe, and senators getting caught with bimbos or, even better, seducing pages of the same sex, but not much else. The stories would include her side, of course, but their *allegations* would have the real weight. She could see the headlines:

LEAKS FROM SECRET BIORESEARCH LAB
WOMAN SCIENTIST IMPLICATED

"You ever read about D.C. Jail?" Rivers seemed to know her thoughts, spoke while examining the wart on his palm. "I been there, Doc, dropping perps off. Terrible things happen. Especially to people like you."

"You can really do this?" She ignored Rivers, addressed Rhodes. There were not many things she feared, but Hallie was honest enough to admit that being locked in the District of Columbia Jail was one. The stories that came out of that place—broom-handle rapes, mutilations, medieval things.

"Yes. We can."

She could fight but, as Rhodes said, even if she won, she lost. Or she could sign. Go quietly. Live to fight another day.

Hallie had never been the kind of person who agonized over decisions. Weigh risks and benefits, figure the calculus, make the call. Another day always came. She looked up. Rhodes was holding out a pen. Rivers leaned back, smirking, fat hands folded on his paunch.

A part of Hallie wanted to curse them. Instead, she reached into the pocket of her lab coat and took out the Mont Blanc Meisterstück Solitaire her father had given her when she'd received her doctorate at Hopkins.

"I have my own."

Without hurrying, she uncapped the pen, signed her name, ignored Rivers, and looked Rhodes in the eye.

"You're doing a bad thing here, Mr. Rhodes. Sooner or later, we all pay for the bad things we do."

The fly buzzed around Rivers's head, and he still seemed oblivious to it. Rhodes kept his eyes locked on hers, saying nothing, but he rubbed his Penn State ring as if it were an amulet and she saw a flicker in his dark eyes, sudden and bright and quickly gone, that told her he knew it to be true.

EIGHT

NOW, IN BARNARD'S OFFICE, IT WAS NOT LOST ON HER THAT she could simply say, *Sorry, gentlemen, BARDA screwed me royally,* and walk right out.

But really, she didn't even come close to that. Instead, she sat thinking of the thousands of young soldiers. And not only young ones. Old ones, too, from older wars, hanging on in VA hospitals all over the country, living out their lives with whatever remnants of bodies and minds their wounds and wars had left them. And soldiers' families. It went on and on.

"You said Al is still working on the project."

"That's right."

"How much biomatter does he have left?"

Barnard looked embarrassed. "None, I'm afraid."

"It's all gone? Every last *milligram*?"

The basis of their research had been an extremophile from the

Archaea domain. She had retrieved the biosamples while on an expedition exploring a monstrous cave in Mexico called Cueva de Luz. She had brought almost 100 grams of viable organism out of the cave with her. Half of that had expired before they learned how to keep it alive. When she had left over a year ago, more than 20 grams had remained. In microbiological terms, that was a ton.

"I'm afraid so. Al's worked himself near to death, Hallie. I worry about him sometimes. And he took your departure hard. But at some point, science goes from craft to art. Al's a fine craftsman, but he's not an artist."

"Can we synthesize replicant?"

Lew Casey broke in: "We've tried for months. Can't get the mitochondrial dissemination right. It could be more months—or never."

"While thousands of hospitals become . . ." She searched for the right word.

"Death camps."

Hallie took a deep breath, sat back, rubbed her eyes. She hadn't slept now for almost eighteen hours, and the cave rescue had been exhausting. She needed fresh clothes, a hot meal, a shower, sleep. But others were in much, much worse shape. Sleep could wait.

"We have to go back to Cueva de Luz." She stared at Barnard. "There's nothing else."

"You cannot imagine how much I was hoping to hear you say that."

She'd said it, but not without dread. Cueva de Luz was a true supercave, thousands of feet deep and many miles long, located in the high, remote forest of southern Mexico and filled with bizarre and exotic dangers. *Journey to the Center of the Earth* but worse, and for real.

"It's not going to be as easy as it was last time." Barnard's voice was grim.

She gaped. "*Easy?* Don, it was a nightmare. I didn't think any of us were getting out. Two didn't, as you know."

"I know that expedition was hellish. But there are other complications now."

"Such as?"

Lathrop looked at his gold wafer of a watch. "Dr. Leland, we can fill you in later. Just now, however—"

She ignored Lathrop, addressed Barnard: "We'll need a team. That will take a week at least."

Lathrop smiled for the first time since she'd walked into the office. "Already done!"

"What? Where? When do we meet them?"

"Right now. You're the last to arrive. The others are waiting downstairs."

It was past nine P.M. when the four of them took a secure elevator to the lowest level that BARDA acknowledged publicly and then dropped on down to Sublevel 1, the first of four classified levels that it did not acknowledge. The elevator stopped. Barnard entered an alphanumeric code on a keypad, the elevator door opened, and they walked forward into a biosecure chamber with gray walls and blue germicidal UV lights. The door slid closed behind them and there was a soft hiss as the chamber's airtight seals engaged. Clicks and whirs, integrated sensors and analyzers scanning them for pathogens, explosives, biological material. Presently a group of lights on the air lock's far wall glowed green and the inner door slid open.

The limited access was essential, for reasons well known to Hallie. In January 1989, chimpanzees infected with Ebola Zaire virus had gotten loose inside a research facility in a Maryland suburb of Washington, D.C. They, in turn, had infected hundreds of other chimps. Before long, the entire complex became one vast Ebola-Z growth medium. Hot animals were running amok, others going crazy in their cages, still others breaking out.

Hallie did not routinely work with chimps, but she knew that they were eight times stronger than a human and could eat a man's face in ten seconds. If any of those animals had escaped, a pandemic of hemorrhagic fever with a 90 percent mortality rate and no known cure would have burned through Washington's civilian population in two weeks. It would have obliterated the constitutional line of succession like a wet sponge wiping chalk marks off a blackboard. There would not have been an executive, legislative, or judicial branch of government, nor any military command to speak of. Washington, D.C., would have been a cauldron of death.

In the end, only the work of some very brave people and more sheer luck than humanity had any right to expect had averted disaster. But the Monkey Business, as it was known forever after, had had lasting effects. To ensure that nothing like that *ever* happened again, the CDC had imposed fail-safe security precautions. Now a hot pathogen break might kill many BARDA people, but the bug would find no further hosts. Those BARDA lives would be the price of containment.

They stepped into a long corridor flooded with more watery UV germicidal light, cream-colored walls, tan floor. Though mostly administrative work was done here, some research was ongoing and the air carried odors of alcohol and formaldehyde and disinfectant. People in white lab coats and business suits moved in both directions, some pushing carts, others speaking into Bluetooth-style microphones attached to earpieces. It could have been a hallway in any government building, except that it was almost ten P.M. and everyone was in a hurry.

"How on earth were you able to get me back in here?" Hallie was a little surprised by how good it felt to be back in a place where important science was being done—*dangerous* important science, at that.

"Friends in high places."

"But . . . even after what happened?"

"I couldn't stop that at the time." Barnard's voice tightened with anger every time the subject came up. "But now that we have a *situation,* they were more willing to listen to reason."

"You put your career on the line for me, in other words. Again."

"And I never had a better use for it, Hallie."

"Hear, hear." Lew Casey reached up to pat her shoulder reassuringly.

They passed through an unmarked door that opened onto a sparsely furnished anteroom with another inner door, guarded by a U.S. Army Special Forces sergeant wearing a crisp uniform and a green beret. He carried a sidearm and had a Heckler & Koch MP7 submachine gun slung across his chest.

Barnard said his own name out loud, pronouncing the syllables carefully, and a green LED light came to life on a panel on the sergeant's desk.

"Good evening, ma'am, sirs." The sergeant nodded to each in turn. "Please go right in."

They walked through the inner door into a rectangular conference room. White ceiling, beige carpet, big flat-screen monitors on sky-blue walls. On a long mahogany table sat pitchers of water, juice, coffee, and plates filled with sandwiches and cookies. Five men sat at the table, and among those was her old research partner, Albert Cahner.

"Hallie!" He jumped out of his chair and came around the table to give her a hug, which she returned, laughing.

"Al! I'm so glad to see you again!" She thumped him on the back.

"It's wonderful to see *you,* Hallie."

They stood there grinning. He was as she remembered, though perhaps with a little more gray in the comb-over now, the circles under his eyes darker. Otherwise, he was the same old Al, wearing a wrinkled blue shirt with a flyaway collar and a skinny tie that had gone out of fashion ten years earlier. He gave her shoulder a final pat and went back to his place at the table.

She took an empty chair and poured herself more coffee. Don Barnard leaned against a wall. Lathrop addressed them.

"I know that you all have traveled hard and must be tired. So let me make a few things clear right away. My name is David Lathrop.

Officially I work for Central Intelligence, but for now I report to the secretary of Homeland Security, Hunter Mason. Directly. He reports to the president. Directly. They both know we're here."

Lathrop introduced Barnard and Casey, then turned back to those seated at the table.

"We thank each of you for responding to our requests, which must have seemed strange, to say the least. We are grateful beyond measure for your presence here."

While Lathrop spoke, Hallie eyed the three men at the table she did not know. She pegged them in her own mind as Blond Man, Dark Man, and Big Man.

"More introductions are in order." Lathrop gestured toward Blond Man. "Dr. Haight"—he pronounced it *height*—"is a medical doctor from Tennessee. Emergency medicine specialty. An accomplished technical climber, caver, and diver."

Hallie had thought he looked familiar, and now realized why. "You're *Ron* Haight!" she blurted. "You were on the cover of *National Geographic* last year. They called you 'the caver saver.' "

"Well, yeah, I was." Haight looked down at the table, grinning and shaking his head.

"Dr. Haight is justly famous for his rescue work," Lathrop said.

"Please call me Ron." Haight looked uncomfortable with all the attention, which Hallie found positively endearing.

"You were all muddy, with a helmet and dive mask on. It took me a minute to recognize you," she said.

"Hard to believe they'd put an ugly mug like this'un on the cover of such a fine magazine, I know." Haight's accent was Tennessee thick, his words flowing softly and slowly.

But Hallie thought he had a right nice mug. Haight's hair was almost as light as hers, worn in a ponytail. He was one of those rare blonds who have dark eyebrows; his were perched high on his forehead and far apart, like quotation marks at the ends of a sentence, making him look perpetually, pleasantly surprised. Beneath those eyebrows were angular features in a lean, open face. He was not tall but had the build of a serious climber, a compact bundle of muscle with about 5 percent body fat. He looked to be in his late twenties.

"It's an honor to meet you, Dr. Haight," said Hallie. "Sorry, I mean Ron. You saved a couple of friends of mine once."

Haight nodded, formal, graceful, as if he were bowing to a princess, the deathless courtesy of southern men.

Lathrop turned to Dark Man. "Dr. Rafael Arguello is a paleoanthropologist from the University of New Mexico and a member of the Cuicatec Native American population in Oaxaca, Mexico. He speaks several languages but, most importantly, Cuicatec."

Arguello was perhaps thirty years older than Haight. He had high cheekbones, olive skin, black eyes, and neatly barbered, shining black hair. His unshaven cheeks looked like someone had smudged charcoal over them. He wore a rumpled business suit and a white shirt with no tie, a professor whisked all the way from New Mexico on the strange wings of power.

"Dr. Arguello has done groundbreaking research on Native American shamanic practices. He underwent shamanic preparation and initiation himself. He also served as a cultural liaison officer with Mexico's military. And as a paleoanthropologist, he has explored many very serious caves."

"I should say how pleased I am to meet you, everyone." Arguello's accent was unlike any Hallie had heard. Neither Spanish nor English, but something more like the Comanche dialogue she'd heard when she had gone to New Mexico with Stephen Redhorse.

Finally, Lathrop nodded at Big Man. "Dr. Wil Bowman is in our government's service, on loan to us. He has the requisite skills—diving, climbing, caving. Plus, ah, appropriate security experience."

Bowman sat directly across the table from Hallie, wearing jeans, running shoes, and an old red rugby shirt. He looked to her like a six-four, 220-pound slab of muscle. His face was a collection of juts and angles: outsized cheekbones, thrusting chin, and prominent nose with a zigzag from more than one break. He had a straw-colored crew cut and a scar divided one of his eyebrows into two short dashes. Bright, hard, unblinking eyes the blue of glacial ice. He had the body of a professional athlete and the face of a warrior. Not beautiful, certainly, but a face that would have held her glance if she had seen him in a restaurant or on the street. His age was less apparent than the others', but she guessed about forty.

It was her turn. Lathrop said, "Dr. Hallie Leland, BS in microbiology from Georgetown University, PhD in microbiology, Johns Hopkins University. Extremophiles are her area of research. She is an accomplished climber and master technical diver. Her research has taken her into many caves."

"Is there anything you don't do?" Bowman looked at her, his eyebrows raised.

"Dishes and laundry."

She watched him, saw a flicker of something like amusement.

At the same time, Haight laughed out loud. Cahner chuckled, and Arguello said nothing. Whatever had been in Bowman's eyes was as quickly gone. *Not a man to have mad at you,* she thought.

NINE

BEFORE LATHROP COULD SPEAK AGAIN, A CELLPHONE BUZZED in his pocket. He retrieved it, turned away. "Yes, sir. Yes, sir. I understand. Yes, sir. Immediately, sir." He closed the phone, turned back to them. "Sorry. My boss."

Lathrop hooked thumbs in his vest pockets and took a breath. "Dr. Cahner was introduced earlier, and Dr. Leland knows him. Let's move on. All of you know *some* of why you're here, but none of you know all." Lathrop related the background that Hallie had already heard from Barnard. At the end, he repeated the president's comment about Pearl Harbor.

"Long story short, we need to *kill* this germ before it kills our military. Whatever your political persuasions, visualize the United States of America without armed forces. Fresh meat for the animals of the world. Al Qaeda would be in every city in a month, with the Taliban right on their heels. And those are just the obvious ones."

And not just us, Hallie thought. *A new kind of domino theory. Take down America and the others go, plunk-plunk-plunk. A world where men behead a woman for flashing an ankle.*

"Now about you. The five of you were distilled from a database of hundreds of thousands. Parameters included security clearance potential, fitness and health, unique skill sets, and a couple of other things. Think of yourselves as the only keys for a very complex lock."

He paused, looked at Barnard. "That's enough from me. Don?"

Barnard pushed off the wall he had been leaning against. "Let's back up a bit. The media has talked about 'supergerms' in the past, but that's wrong. They were bugs with acquired resistance, but bugs we knew. ACE, however, really *is* a supergerm. An entirely new species.

"Something called antigenic shift is probably responsible. Antigenic *drift* accounts for most evolutionary changes, but it works over eons. Antigenic *shift* can happen in weeks or days. Or even seconds, at the microscopic level. Viruses and bacteria have a special gift for it. Antigenic shifts caused the influenza pandemics of 1918, 1957, and 1968.

"We all knew this was coming. We just didn't know when. To kill a superbacterium, you need a superantibiotic. My section in BARDA had been pursuing one in Dr. Cahner's lab. He can tell you himself. Al?"

Cahner squirmed, ran a hand over thinning hair. "I, ah, well . . . maybe we should let Hallie—I mean Dr. Leland—explain. It was her work originally, and I, ah, just . . ." Cahner looked with desperation at Hallie, who knew how much he hated being in any spotlight, no matter how small.

She glanced at Barnard "Don?"

"Go ahead, Hallie."

She swigged strong coffee, then began: "Two years ago I accompanied an expedition to a remote cave called Cueva de Luz, in southern Mexico. It's a supercave, one of the deepest on earth. Maybe *the* deepest. No one knows for sure. The team included two hydrogeologists, a paleontologist, and me. Five thousand feet deep and four miles into this cave, I found a unique extremophile."

"Cueva de Luz means 'Cave of Light,' " Haight said. "Why is it called that? There's no light in any caves I've ever seen."

"I don't know." Hallie shrugged. "Maybe Dr. Arguello knows."

Arguello did not respond immediately. He seemed slightly uncomfortable with all eyes on him. He opened his mouth to speak, then held up his hands, shrugging. "It is not certain." *He knows more than he's telling us,* Hallie thought.

"Dr. Leland—" Lathrop said, to get things back on track. But Arguello was not finished. He had a question: "Wait. I do not understand that term, 'extremophile.' "

Hallie explained: "They survive where nothing should: geothermal vents twenty-five thousand feet deep in the ocean, arctic wastes, hyperacidic pools. And in caves. Some persist in absolute darkness for millennia.

"The extremophile I found looked like blue cottage cheese. We called it moonmilk. It was bioluminescent, like some arthropods. Tests revealed genomes we had never seen. Back in the lab one day, I accidentally dropped some onto a tray of petri dishes where we were growing DRTB—drug-resistant tuberculosis—colonies. Level Four biosafety suits are not conducive to fine motor tasks.

"We thought, What the hell, let's see what happens. The cultures looked like dried splotches of red-and-green vomit. After six hours, little white spots appeared. Three more days and the dishes were white. The DRTB was killed.

"You could spend ten careers and never see something like that. I damn near fainted, let me tell you. So this stuff was right on the outer edge of our science. Definitely from the Archaea domain, but like nothing we'd seen before. We tried it on other DRs. Killed every one."

"So why are we not giving this . . . this moonmilk to those soldiers right now?" Arguello sounded genuinely puzzled.

"Because," said Wil Bowman, "you can't give an organism in its raw biological state to humans. That would be like feeding people the mold from which penicillin is made." He spoke very softly, but with undertones that could be humor or could be threat. It was a voice that caught ears and held them. "Plus, they ran out of biomatter before learning how to replicate it."

Now, how would he know that? Hallie looked at him more closely. This time, when he returned her curious gaze directly, she actually felt a little twinge in her gut.

"Why don't y'all just send the troops down there and get some more?" said Haight, looking from Barnard to Lathrop to Casey, not sure who should answer.

For the first time, sleek Lathrop looked uneasy. He cleared his throat. "It's quite complicated, actually. But here's the situation. *Narcotraficantes* now control eastern Oaxaca, which includes Cueva de Luz. They are well organized, well armed, and savage beyond belief."

Arguello gripped the table, his face darkening with anger. "*And* they perpetrate the most horrible atrocities against Cuicatecs, *my own people*."

This Hallie had not known. Before, the region had been idyllic, high mountain forest dotted with white villages overlooking steep-sided, green river valleys. The Cuicatecs she'd met had been reserved but not hostile, always ready to gamble with homemade dice and share their ferocious sugarcane moonshine called *aguardiente*.

"There is more." Lathrop rubbed his forehead, stared at his fingernails. He half-turned to look at Barnard, who nodded. When he turned around again, his suit jacket moved aside just enough for Hallie to glimpse the butt of a semiautomatic pistol in a brown leather shoulder holster. That surprised her, but only a little. She knew the joke about the CIA being an employment agency for Skull and Bones, so a Yalie with a gun was not out of the realm of possibility.

"Mexico's army has gone after the *narcos*. It is war down there, unconstrained by niceties like Geneva conventions. The Cuicatecs, feeling invaded, are killing *narcos* and Mexican troops both. A total nightmare."

"More reason to send in troops, don't y'all think?" said Haight.

"Illegal-alien issues have strained our relations with Mexico to the breaking point. The demonstrations, riots, both here and there—you've all heard. Just now, we could not possibly insert military assets into their sovereign territory. Especially with their own military concentrated in the area."

"So how 'bout SEALs and Deltas and such? Those black ops guys."

"SEALs and Deltas are the best warfighters in history, but supercaves are one of the few environments they're not trained for." As Bowman said this, Hallie thought, *Well, then, bet he was a Delta*. She had never known any, but he fit pretty well her vision of one. Except for the "doctor" part. *What exactly is he a doctor of?*

"Then how in hell're y'all gonna get us in there?"

"Stealth insertion." Bowman bit off his words in short bursts. "Tomorrow night. No moon. Our good luck. Already planned. Assets staged. Ready to deploy."

With all of that laid out, it felt like those moments after a brutal fifteen-round fight when all anyone can do is wait for the decision. Nobody spoke. Haight had untied the ponytail and was running fingers through his blond hair. Al Cahner was looking at his hands. Arguello was tapping an index finger on the table. Bowman sat perfectly still, watching them all. Hallie noted that he was missing the tip of his left little finger.

Haight cleared his throat, spoke: "So let me make sure I understand. Y'all are lookin' at a catastrophe of biblical proportions. You pulled together a group of total strangers helter-skelter. Nobody but presumably Dr. Bowman has, ah, *security* experience. But y'all would have us sneak into the middle of a vicious drug war, penetrate one of the deepest caves on earth, retrieve stuff that probably won't survive the trip out, and then sneak back through the war zone, hopin' all the while that pissed-off, murderin' natives don't shoot us with poison arrows or blowguns or whatever. I don't work for the government, nor, apparently, do Drs. Leland or Arguello. Since y'all haven't said anything about payment, this obviously will all be from our patriotic fervor and the goodness of our hearts. Is that about the size of it?"

There had been an expectant pressure in the room, tension generated by crisis and challenge, Lathrop and Barnard working it, shaping it up to a climax. This, clearly, was not the one they had hoped for. The phone in Lathrop's jacket pocket vibrated over and over. He seemed not to notice. Barnard's head and eyes and shoulders drooped, like the top stories of a building keeling over slowly, reluctantly, resisting the downward pull to the very last. Barnard was not the kind of man who spent a lot of time looking at the floor. Hallie did not like what was happening here.

She glanced around the table. No one met her eyes except Bowman—who, she got the feeling, had been watching her first. Al Cahner was chewing a cookie, slowly, thoughtfully, as though it might be his last. Arguello was still tapping one finger on the table, rhythmically, as though to a song only he could hear. Bowman sat perfectly still, eyes locked with Hallie's. Having grown up with two brothers and a soldier father, Hallie had become very good at staring matches. The urge to look away was deeply instinctual, like the urge to gasp in air after a long bout of breath holding, but Hallie would not quit first. Seconds passed. Finally, Bowman pointed an index finger at her, mouthed the words *You win,* and looked away.

For his part, Lathrop appeared to know quite well what happened in Washington to those who carried bad news to high places. The phone vibrated again. He ignored it.

"I'm afraid that is about the size of it, Dr. Haight."

"Sounds like a pretty desperate thing." Haight looked from Lathrop to Barnard.

"We would be lying if we suggested otherwise." Barnard, returning his gaze directly.

Something had been building in Hallie, and she could contain it no longer. Bowman had distracted her, but now she stood up so quickly her chair tipped over backward and hit the floor with a bang. The door opened and the security officer stood there, surveying. Lathrop waved him back out.

"God *damn* it." Beneath the deep tan, Hallie's face was reddening. "How often do you get the chance to save thousands—maybe *millions*—of people from horrible deaths? We have just been offered the opportunity of a lifetime, gentlemen."

"We have to be clear, Dr. Leland," said Lathrop, "so there is absolutely no misunderstanding. People could die on this mission. It is, as Dr. Haight observed, a desperate thing."

In her head, Hallie heard her father's voice: *Every day, every single thing you do writes a page in the book of your life. You can write them, but you can never change them.*

"We could die driving to work and what good does that do anybody? But we're not going to die. We are going into that cave to get the moonmilk."

Ron Haight shook his head, laughed out loud. "Hell, this is the best deal I been offered for an ol' coon's age. Savin' people is what I do for a livin'. Hallie's right. I'm in like Flynn, y'all."

Arguello's index finger landed on the table and stopped. He arranged his face, swallowed, spoke formally. "When my time comes, I do not want to look back on this day and feel shame. I am going."

Al Cahner reached for another chocolate cookie. "I always intended to go." His voice was calm, confident. "It was never in question." The steel there surprised Hallie. It was not something she had heard during their time working together.

They all looked at Lathrop. He stared back, expressionless for a few seconds. Then he raised his coffee cup in salute.

"Lady and gentlemen, we have a team."

Hallie cut her gaze from Lathrop to Bowman. He winked, the movement nearly imperceptible, accompanied by the tiniest crinkling at the corners of his mouth. The wink and crinkles could have meant anything, but in Hallie's mind they caused these words to form: *Thank you.*

For his part, Lathrop looked like a man whose death sentence had just been commuted.

There followed a few long moments of silence as the full significance of their decisions sank in. Then Bowman turned to Hallie.

"You've been there. What can you tell us about the cave?"

She looked to Barnard, who nodded, and then she got up and walked to a whiteboard at the front of the room.

"Dr. Haight's probably the most experienced, but we've all been in big caves. Here's the thing, though. Cueva de Luz isn't a cave. It's a *supercave*."

She drew a line that plunged from the board's top left corner toward the bottom right corner with a lot of small, jagged steps in between. It looked like the graph of a badly failing business's cash flow.

"Cueva de Luz's profile. About five thousand vertical feet deep. A bit more than four miles from entrance to the cave's known terminus."

"*Known* terminus. So there is more unexplored terrain beyond that point?" Arguello asked.

"It keeps going and going. No one knows how far. We could tell that because wind was ripping up from somewhere deep beyond the place we stopped. Right after the mouth, this cave gets vertical quickly, so we'll pass through the twilight zone fast. Before you know it, the dark zone just ambushes you. And because of its size and depth, this cave has a special zone not identified in other caves. It's called the deep zone."

"Is that name because the terrain down there is different?" Arguello wanted to know.

"You're much deeper, so the watercourses are bigger, but it has more to do with the psychological impact," Hallie said. "You know that every human body has a unique response to altitude in the mountains, right? Depth and darkness don't affect the body that way, but they do the brain. Scientists have studied the phenomenon. Some believe it's neurochemistry. Down there, the brain knows it's a mile or whatever from the surface and doesn't like how that feels. Self-preservation is the oldest, strongest instinct. The brain will do weird things to keep its body alive, like drive a person to fatal panic. When that happens we call it the Rapture."

"Like the rapture of the deep, in diving?" Arguello asked.

"No. Most divers experience that—nitrogen narcosis is the real name—as euphoria. Some have taken off their masks and tried to talk to fish, others believe they can breathe water. It's like a five-martini buzz. The Rapture in a cave is like, well, like the worst anxiety attack you can imagine, multiplied tenfold. Just the opposite of euphoric: *horrific.*"

"It sounds perfectly delightful," Arguello said. Hallie stared—it was the first time he had tried to say something funny. Defusing fear, she knew, but that was fine—whatever worked.

"To continue about the cave," she said. "I'm assuming we all know the standard expeditionary caving drill: vertical work, diving, breakdown, squeezes, gas pockets. Right?"

She got the nods she wanted.

"Good. So let's talk about the major obstacles in Cueva de Luz. First one's a big wall."

"What is 'big'?" Bowman, professionally curious.

"About five hundred feet, lip to pit." Haight whistled, and even Bowman looked impressed. Cahner and Arguello exchanged worried glances.

"That's the Washington Monument," Cahner said.

"Right. Lots more drops of fifty to seventy-five feet each. At least one long flooded tunnel and maybe more, depending on recent rainfall. After that, the usual big-cave nightmares: squeezes, lakes, breakdown, rotten rock, some pockets of carbon dioxide and hydrogen sulfide, and probably a few others I'm forgetting."

"What provisions for our rescue if something happens?" Arguello asked.

"There are no rescues from deep in a cave like Cueva de Luz." Bowman, announcing grim news as if it were a weather report. "For one thing, there's no communication. For another, if you get hurt far down in a cave like that, evacuation is not a possibility. Vertical walls, flooded tunnels and sumps . . ." He shrugged. "We will be on our own. From start to finish." Though he was giving them facts that would unsettle most normal people, she found his words, or maybe the way they came across, reassuring, and it appeared the others' reactions were similar. *The power of a natural-born leader,* she thought.

Her eyes kept flicking back toward Bowman. Something about the man was pulling her. It wasn't purely his looks. He struck her as one of the toughest, most intimidating men she'd ever seen up close. Well, all right, it might have a *little* to do with the way he looked. But there was something else, intangible and ineffable, a pull like two magnets just close enough to generate attraction. And his eyes, his intense, hypervigilant, unwavering eyes, which seemed to be looking out from some great depth.

Which was when she realized the others were all looking at *her* looking at Bowman. She cleared her throat, continued: "The main thing to understand about Cueva de Luz is that we *don't* really understand it. We know more about the *moon* than about supercaves like this one."

"Hey, y'all did have some problems down there. Care to enlighten us?" said Haight, leaning back in his chair, hands folded over his belt buckle.

"It's true," Hallie said. "We did have some trouble."

"Like two ol' boys never came back."

She swallowed. "Yes." *Who else among these guys would know what happened?* Bowman, almost certainly. Al did. And Barnard. And Lathrop would. So it would be news only to Arguello.

"What was it, then? Where they spelunker types or what, Hallie?"

Serious cavers derided casual enthusiasts, called them spelunkers. *Cavers rescue spelunkers,* went the saying.

"They were good expeditionary cavers."

"So what happened to 'em, then?"

"We don't know."

"Y'all *don't know*?"

"We never found them. They were exploring a side passage and never came back. We searched for two full days and nights. No trace."

Ten minutes later she finished telling her colleagues everything she knew, which really wasn't much. No one spoke for a moment. Then Arguello did.

"Now I will tell you some more things about Cueva de Luz. Cuicatecs have inhabited that region for a thousand years. The cave is sacred to them. The place from which all life flowed in the Great Beginning. For them, the cave is a living thing. They call its spirit Chi Con Gui-Jao. It is a place of *great* power."

"What kind of power?" Cahner asked.

Arguello thought for a moment before responding. "Many kinds. Chi Con Gui-Jao guards the entrance to the underworld. He can take a spirit to La Terra de los Muertos, Land of the Dead. Or send it back to Tierra de la Luz, Land of the Light."

Cahner started to speak again, but Lathrop went first. "If I may. There will be time for this later, but now we need to focus. Are there any questions?"

Haight's hand went up. "I have one. I've been into some very big caves in my life, and to descend the vertical drops y'all described will take thousands of feet of rope that'll weigh hundreds of pounds. Too much for a small team to carry. How will we get down and up?"

"That's my department," said Bowman. "We won't be needing rope."

"Y'all aren't suggestin' we BASE-jump the drops, are you? We still have to get back out."

Arguello grimaced. "I do not know how to do that and have no desire to learn." Arms folded across his chest, he shook his head slowly back and forth.

"It would take too long to explain now. But we won't need rope." Bowman looked at each of them in turn. "Trust me on this one."

Hallie watched their reactions. The others seemed willing to do that. And so, somewhat to her surprise, was she.

"One last thing," Lathrop said. "We will have a small special operations team staged near Brownsville. Two-hour response time. But they are only for extraction from the surface, not rescue from the cave."

"Whoa, there." Haight held up both hands, like a cop stopping traffic. "I got a few more questions about little things like equipment, food, communications. An expedition like this would normally take months to organize."

Lathrop was ready. "We don't have time for 'normal.' You saw the pictures of ACE victims. We have, at the very most, ten to twelve days."

"And those things are taken care of." Bowman again.

"Righto, then. Any idea how long we'll be underground?"

"We have planned for seven days," Bowman said. "Two days to reach the bottom of the cave, one day there to collect material and rest, and three to come back out again. Plus one extra."

Lathrop looked around. "Thank you for your patience. Any more questions?"

"Just one more." Haight, hand up. "Really. Then I'll stop. Earlier y'all said, if I remember aright, we were picked 'cause we could get security clearances and we all had serious cavin' skills and such."

"Correct."

"Y'all also said, 'and a coupla other things.' " *He doesn't miss much,* Hallie thought. She remembered the phrasing now, but only after Haight had brought it up. Haight looked from Lathrop to Barnard and back to Lathrop. "I was just wonderin' about those 'coupla other things.' "

Lathrop and Barnard exchanged glances. Barnard nodded slightly.

Lathrop said, "Well, as a matter of fact, there were some other criteria."

They waited. He looked at the floor, then back at them.

"You are all unmarried, live alone, and have no children."

No one spoke. But Hallie thought: *In other words, expendables.*

PART TWO

CAVE OF LIGHT

TEN

THEY SPENT THE NIGHT IN GUEST ROOMS AT ANDREWS AIR Force Base. The next morning, after showers and breakfast, they were jetted to a military airfield at Reynosa, Texas. There they were outfitted with the caving equipment they would need: scuba rebreathers, mil-spec meals ready to eat (MREs), redundant lights, exposure suits—the best of everything that advanced research could create and government money could buy.

At eight P.M., when it was full dark, a jet-engined, stealth version of the Osprey vertical takeoff and landing aircraft spirited them two hours south. In the moonless night—a gift of pure luck, as Bowman had noted—they off-loaded in a clearing a mile from Cueva de Luz's mouth.

Bowman herded them back to the tree line and the stealth craft lifted off, its jets making not much more noise than idling bus engines. Without lights of any kind, in ten seconds it disappeared into the black sky and they were alone in southern Mexico's high mountain wilderness. The nearest village, a Cuicatec settlement, was twenty miles away.

They were all carrying heavy North Face backpacks. Bowman was the only one with weapons: a SIG Sauer semiautomatic pistol in a thigh holster, a huge dive knife worn in a scabbard strapped to the inside of his left calf, and, slung over one shoulder, a weird, futuristic-looking rifle with a carbine-length barrel, a circular magazine like the ones used on Thompson submachine guns, a lightweight tubular stock, and a pistol grip like an M-16's. Hallie had asked him if was a rifle or a shotgun during their ride in the stealth Osprey.

"Neither," Bowman had told her. "It fires ten-millimeter FAFO projectiles."

"What's FAFO?"

"Fire and forget. You put the laser spot on something, fire, and the projectile will find that target. The projectiles are explosive OSOKs—sorry, one-shot, one-kill designs. Like little grenades." He looked at her for a moment. "You like guns?"

"My dad was an Army officer. I grew up on a farm. I'm a hell of a wing shot. I'd love to try that thing."

She saw that he tried, but failed, to suppress a grin. "Maybe one day you'll get the chance."

Now, in the forest at the tree line, Bowman shifted his massive pack and whispered to the others.

"Okay, listen up. I've walked through this terrain in SatIm holograms and I've got GPS waypoints to the cave in a HUD on my NVDs. I'll lead. The rest of you follow in the order we briefed. Most important thing is noise discipline. Around here, the Mexican army patrols during the day, but *narcos* own the night. God knows what the Indians do. I do not want to hear one clink, rattle, or cough. It could mean our lives. Let's go."

A trail climbed out of the clearing's northwestern corner. Bowman led, Arguello came next, and then Hallie, Cahner, and Haight. After a quarter mile, the trail simply ended and then, even with the night-vision goggles, it was slow going. They were at about four thousand feet in mountain cloud forest. Warm temperatures, high humidity, and prodigious annual rainfall combined to produce 150-foot-tall oak and pine trees towering like giant temple columns over a forest floor overgrown with monstrous lime-colored ferns, tangled vines, and, most remarkably of all, a particularly vicious nettle shrub, *Cnidoscolus angustidens,* which natives called *mala mujer*—evil woman. The plant had beautiful leaves, like spiky, shining green hearts strewn with white spots. But they were covered with poisonous hairs and needle-sharp thorns that inflicted wounds worse than those of the Portuguese man-of-war. Stings could induce paralysis and, in extreme cases, even death. Had they all not been wearing one-piece, ballistic nylon caving suits, it would have been virtually impossible to make it through here.

Hallie expected Bowman to set a blistering pace, but he did not. Their progress was almost leisurely. Even though she was carrying close to forty pounds, she could have conversed easily with the others. No so Rafael Arguello, whom she could hear puffing and panting. She could understand his difficulty. As good as they were, the NVDs couldn't distinguish between slippery exposed roots and, say, a hunting fer-de-lance, so every step demanded caution. It was also hard not to blunder head-on into the *mala mujers*. And the most daunting challenges lay ahead. Once they entered Cueva de Luz, Hallie would become their guide. *Point woman*. Bowman would still command, but she would be in front.

She was concerned about the supercave, of course, but she had taken its measure before. The *people* worried her more. If Lathrop was right, with the exception of Arguello, they had all spent enough time down deep to be expert with the techniques. So it wasn't their experience that concerned Hallie. Depth and darkness could prey on a person's mind; she had seen brave and brawny men reduced to trembling wrecks after several days far down. She had—

She walked right into Arguello, who had stopped suddenly to avoid running into Bowman. Someone spoke, words unintelligible, the voice like wind-blown tree branches scratching on a wall.

Peering around Arguello and Bowman, in the NVDs' green glow she could see the luminous form of a man blocking their way. A small dog stood beside him, eyes glowing red as fire. The man was of average height, his face etched with wrinkles, wearing a shirt and pants that hung loose on his bony frame. His sandals looked to have been made from old automobile tires. On his right side he carried a machete in a leather sheath hung with frayed rope around his waist. He had a battered leather satchel draped over his left shoulder.

The old man spoke again.

Bowman looked at Arguello. Hallie noted that the big man had turned ever so slightly, so that his right shoulder and hip were away from the old man. His right hand hung easily, casually, by the SIG Sauer.

Arguello hesitated a moment. "Sorry. A very old dialect. He asked if we are here to kill *narcotraficantes*."

"Tell him we are not."

Arguello did, and the old man spoke more.

"He says that is a pity. Now he asks if we are here to kill the *federales*. The government soldiers."

"Tell him we're not doing that, either."

Arguello did, and the old man responded, his eyes straying to Hallie.

"He said that, too, is a pity. He also says that the high woman is very beautiful. The tall woman, he means. Even with the funny glasses."

Hallie wondered how he could see her at all.

"Ask him if there are *narcos* or *federales* close by."

"He says they are everywhere now. He calls them . . . ah, it is obscene. Something to do with the excretory function. But very bad."

"The *narcos* or the *federales*?"

"Both, I believe."

"Ask him how he travels on a moonless night with no light through a forest of *mala mujer.*"

The old man listened, chuckled, answered. Arguello translated: "He says that when you know *the way,* there is no darkness. And that he made friends with *mala mujer* long ago."

"Friends? Ask him . . . never mind."

The old man spoke at length then and Arguello translated again: "He says that he is sorry we are not here to kill the *federales*. They are stupid and careless, drunk constantly, and they shot his wife during a firefight. Also the *narcos,* drunk and worse, crazy on drugs. They took his two daughters and burned his home. Now he lives in the forest and kills those who get drunk and wander away from their camps."

"What's going on?" Cahner whispered from back in the line. "Why did we stop?"

The old man spoke again and Arguello murmured to Bowman: "He says Chi Con Gui-Jao is expecting us."

And Hallie wondered, *How would he know we are going to the cave?*

"Ask him why he approached us. Why he wasn't afraid." Bowman watched the old man, not Arguello.

After an exchange, Arguello answered, "He is a *curandero*. Shaman. He says that you give off good light. Not like the *narcos* and *federales*. Their light is like foul water."

The old man kept talking, apparently explaining something to Arguello.

"He says that he would accompany us but cannot until his business of putting out the, ah, 'filthy lights,' he calls them, is finished."

The old man spoke to Arguello once more.

"He says that the cave is another world," Arguello relayed. "One that—how to explain this—contains what we call heaven and hell. Many enter the cave and never return. Those who do return are different."

"Different how?" Bowman asked.

Arguello questioned the old man in his language and once again translated for Bowman. "There is no way to know," he said.

Hallie felt goose bumps rise on her arms. The old man was speaking the truth. On her other trip into the cave, she had experienced exactly what the *curandero* described. One of the hydrogeologists, a hard-core smoker, had a cold when they entered Cueva de Luz. It intensified with frightening speed, becoming pneumonia in both lungs before they reached the cave's terminus. If he had not disappeared, it was entirely possible that he would not have made it out of the cave in any case. Another of the men had flirted with her—just lightly, nothing offensive—during their trip down to Mexico. The deeper they went, the more powerful his lust became, the more insistent his advances, until toward the end she slept with her sheath knife in one hand inside her mummy bag. That man, too, had disappeared.

Bowman turned back, addressing the team: "We'll move out now." He swung toward the trail, and then froze.

The old man and the dog were gone. They had made no sound.

"Did you see where he went?" Bowman, tense, looking all around. "Anyone?" No one answered. "Let's get on. The sooner we get into the cave, the safer we'll be," he said.

I wouldn't count on that, Hallie thought.

ELEVEN

"YOU OUGHTA BE WEARIN' A HOT SUIT, DOC." THE SPEAKER was a young black sergeant.

Lenora Stilwell glanced up from her clipboard. The sergeant's name was Dillon. *Marshell* Dillon.

"Can't get anything done in those body condoms." Stilwell winked, prompting a pained grin in return. "Can't hear, can't talk, can't touch. Heck, you can barely walk in one of those. As for going to the bathroom . . ." She shook her head. "What kind of doctor would that be?"

It was early evening. Terok's field hospital was now fully quarantined and isolated from the rest of the combat outpost. From the rest of the world, for that matter. The NBC—Nuclear, Biological, and Chemical—guys showed up the day after the presence of ACE was confirmed. They sealed the unit, installing one biosecure air lock for ingress and egress, and distributed Biosafety Level 4 suits.

The "hot suit" Dillon had referred to was the sky-blue Chemturion Model 3530, made of a twenty-millimeter impervious plastic called Cloropel. It weighed ten pounds. The personal life support system backpack (PLSS) added another ten pounds to the total weight. A BSL-4 felt, when zipped and clipped, like a diver's heavy dry suit, but even stiffer. Every movement required extra effort, and the plastic popped and crinkled continuously. Then, too, they were so hot that it was possible to sweat out two pounds during an eight-hour shift, even with the little ventilator fan blowing.

Air from the PLSS backpack or an external supply kept the suits inflated to positive pressure, so that no pathogens could infiltrate even if a suit was breached. The integrated, bucket-shaped hood was made of thicker plastic that was clear enough when new but never remained so for long. It scratched and marred easily, so that seeing through one more than a few weeks old was like looking through a windshield spiderwebbed with cracks. After the antifog chemical wore off, which it usually did within a month, the plastic fogged up, making it even harder to see. The suits' sleeves ended in heavy, double-layer hazmat gloves that allowed only slightly more manual dexterity than winter mittens. Since the suit, when inflated, effectively doubled the wearer's volume and added a foot of height, it required constant mental recalibration to keep from blundering into equipment, other people, and containers holding pathogens so deadly that a thousandth of an ounce could depopulate the planet. Stilwell thought it was like driving an eighteen-wheeler after a lifetime of Hondas.

BSL-4 Chemturions were designed to protect laboratorians against nightmares from the invisible world, monsters like Ebola Zaire, superpox, pneumonic plague, and many others, including ACE, and they did that job well enough. But they were not designed to help an overtasked doctor in a combat zone do her work, and Stilwell had refused to wear one from the start. Since no one outranked her at Terok, no one could order her to wear one of the clumsy suits, and *that* suited her just fine.

"You don't wanna catch this stuff, Doc. It's amazing you don't got it already." Dillon was twenty-three, slim, his head shaved. He wore a wedding band and, Stilwell knew, had two young children back home in Atlanta, Georgia. He'd enlisted at eighteen, loved the Army, planned to make a career of it.

"Hey, you know about us doctors. We build up immunity. I've been exposed to so many bugs over the years, I'm probably immune to everything."

"I'm sayin' prayers for you, Doc." Dillon gasped, his face collapsing into a clutch of pain as Stilwell lifted the dressing from one of the red, suppurating patches on his torso. The infection had not progressed as far as those that had killed Wyman and Washington and the others. IV colistin was slowing it down. That was the good news. But it was gaining on the colistin, despite steadily increasing dosages.

"Sorry," she said. "Hey, tell me something, Sergeant. Did you ever hear of a TV show called *Gunsmoke*?"

"Only about a hundred million times, ma'am." Dillon's voice contained pain again, but of a different kind.

"So you know about Marshal Dillon? The character James Arness played?"

"Oh, do I ever, ma'am. Forget bein' a boy named Sue. The 'hood I come from, you named for a cop, that's two strikes right there."

"If you don't mind my asking, why would your mother do that?"

"She didn't, ma'am. It was my aunt."

"Oh? And how was it that she did the naming?" Stilwell was still probing, examining. *Keep him talking*.

"My mother booked soon as she could get out of the hospital, ma'am. I never seen her. My aunt and uncle raised me."

"I see. Well, why did she do it, then?"

"They never had a TV when she was growin' up. She didn't know anything about that show. Just liked the sound of the name."

"I guess it could have been worse."

"How so, ma'am?"

"She could have named you Festus."

He gave her a blank look. *Too young,* she realized. "Another character on that show."

"Oh yeah." Dillon nodded, his face screwed up in distaste. "That *woulda* been worse. Sounds like a disease. 'You got a case of acute Festus.'" He smiled briefly, but then his expression changed. "Ma'am, what's that stuff doing now?"

She never lied to her patients. "It's growing. But more slowly now that we're getting the antibiotic into you."

"So that drug's helpin' some, then?"

"It appears so, yes."

"I'm glad, 'cause it fu— um, it messed up my stomach big-time. Can't even keep water down."

"The other IV will keep you hydrated. We can feed you that way too, if we have to."

"Doc . . . you talked to my wife yet?"

"Not yet, Sergeant. Battalion has clamped down. No outgoing comm. I haven't talked to my own family for five days."

"They don't want to freak people out, right? I can understand that. But, Doc, if you do talk to her?"

"Yes?"

Dillon had been in more firefights than she could count and seen more horrors than she could imagine. He was one of their best, career Army, a cold-eyed, efficient killer but a sensitive leader of men. Rare combination, that. Now his eyes filled with tears.

"Doc . . . look. No bull now. I don't think I'm gonna make it. I know 'bout Wyman and Angel and the others. You're good at hidin' it, but . . . not that good. So, please don't tell her how bad I am, hear? She got enough on her plate, dealin' with the kids an' all. Who knows? Maybe I'll have one of them miraculous recoveries."

She looked down. There were no lesions between the elbow and wrist. She gave his arm a long, firm squeeze.

"Marshell Dillon, you listen. There's no way I think you're going to die. I don't want to hear you say that again. Roger that?" She delivered that stern-voiced, like an order, but her eyes were kind.

He smiled up at her, his own eyes still glistening. "Roger that, ma'am."

Stilwell finished examining the eight cases in Ward B and headed for the four in Ward A. In the hallway between the two wards, a nurse in a Chemturion approached. Stilwell laid a hand on her plastic-covered arm.

"Pam."

"Yes, ma'am?"

"What day is it?"

"What day? Tuesday, ma'am. Evening."

"Thank you. I sort of lost track."

"Um . . . ma'am? Permission to speak?"

Stilwell patted the nurse's arm, smiled. "You always have that with me, Pam."

"Yes. Thank you, ma'am. So, we're worrying about you."

"About me?"

"Yes, ma'am. It's not only going around without a suit. You're not taking care of yourself. Ma'am." Through the hazy plastic hood, Stilwell saw genuine concern in the young nurse's eyes. "You're not eating enough or sleeping. We're worrying."

"If you didn't have that suit on I'd give you a hug. I appreciate your concern, Pam. Really. But back in the day, when I was an intern, they called me 'Superdoc.' I could do more work than any two of the male doctors."

Pam looked skeptical, but a bit less worried. "Is it true you used to run marathons, ma'am?"

"That is true. I never broke three hours, but I never ran a race I didn't finish, either. Born with the stamina of a mule." Her expression turned serious. "Look, I'll be careful. I know that if I go down, I'm no use to you or these sick kids. But if you do see me screwing up, say so. Understood?"

"Yes, ma'am. Understood."

Stilwell patted her shoulder and sent the nurse on her way. *Now, where was I going? And what was I doing?*

"Uh, Major, ma'am, excuse me, there's a call." Stilwell turned to see another nurse, a young specialist from Baltimore, Michael Demrock, very thin, corn-silk hair. Not the brightest one she'd ever had, but certainly one of the best-hearted.

"Thanks. I'll catch it later. I'm going to—"

"It's a colonel, ma'am. Full bird."

"What does he want? Is he a fobbit?" Stilwell could feel her impatience heating up. She had never much cared for the fobbits, officers so called because they were denizens of the FOBs, forward operating bases, which were not really forward at all but were a world away to the rear. She disliked them for their tailored uniforms and Baskin-Robbins shops and McDonald's and Starbucks and bars, all of which FOBs offered. When the fobbits came, it was always about some missing piece of paperwork or with an admonition about her outrageous MPPs—her minutes-per-patient ratio.

"He kind of sounds like one, yes ma'am."

"What's his name?"

"Ah, Rubbish, ma'am."

"Rubbish? His name is Colonel *Rubbish*?"

"No, wait. That's not it. Ribbesh. Or something like that. It's kind of hard to hear in these suits."

"Did he say what he wanted?"

"Yes, ma'am."

She waited. After a while she realized that Demrock was waiting, too. *Patience, Major. He's just deferring to your rank.* "And what was it, Specialist?"

"You, ma'am. He said he wanted to talk to you."

Round and round we go, she thought. "Of course. You told me that already. Thank you."

"You're welcome, Major."

In her closet-sized office, she dropped into the wooden chair behind her desk and picked up the phone. "Major Stilwell."

"Colonel Ribbesh here, Major. They had to go a way to find you, apparently. I apprised them almost ten minutes ago of my need to speak with you."

A fobbit for sure. And he wants an apology for keeping him waiting. They were easy to spot when you could see them. Their uniforms were too clean, they had too much fat on them, and their skin was always too white. They were almost as easy to identify just from their voices. They never swore, didn't drop *g*'s, sounded prissy, used words like 'apprised.' Lenora Stilwell detested them.

"How can I help you, Colonel?"

A beat, then another. *He's surprised. Waiting for it.* She let him wait, glanced at her watch. She was overdue in Ward A. Those four soldiers would be waiting for her. Medicine was about drugs and scalpels and X-rays for sure, but healing was about heart; she had understood that long ago.

Finally he cleared his throat. "I'm battalion NBC liaison. I will be coming up to Terok. An inspection visit, orders from regiment. I wanted to apprise you of my ETA."

Regiment. That meant from the one-star, an alcoholic martinet named Gremble. "Your ETA. I see. What is it, sir?"

"Day after tomorrow, zero eight thirty hours."

Day after tomorrow. Fine. Great. From where she sat now, with a hundred things needing to be done in the next hour, that felt like a century away.

"Very well, Colonel. Thanks for letting me know."

When the fobbit spoke again, his voice was different. "Major, can you apprise me of the conditions up there at Terok?"

"The conditions, sir?" *What the hell did he mean? The weather? The four-star accommodations?*

He coughed again. "Yes." Pause. "I gather this pathogen is quite deadly."

He's scared. She could hear it in his voice. *Just tell him the truth.*

"It's the worst thing I've ever seen, Colonel. You've heard of Ebola Zaire?"

"Of course."

"Worse than that. More contagious, shorter incubation period, higher mortality rate."

"My God."

"Are you sure you need to make this trip, Colonel? We've got things under control here."

"Orders, Major." Ribbesh sounded like a miserable child who was being punished. She wondered what he had done to get on the one-star's bad side. "So . . . would you recommend full Biosafety Level Four protection?"

She laughed before she could stop herself, but cut it off quickly. No need to insult the man. "Not if you remain outside the hospital confines, sir. If you want to come in, then definitely."

Too late. He sounded very insulted. "All right, then. Thank you, *Major.* I will see you soon." He emphasized her rank just enough to let her know that he was pissed.

"I'll be here, sir."

"I'm sure you will." The line went dead.

She replaced the receiver and scrubbed her hands over her face, trying to push away the fatigue, the heaviness in her eyes and muscles and brain. In the drawer of her desk she found half a Butterfinger bar in its crumpled yellow wrapper. It might have been left over from the day before, or from some other, more distant time. She wasn't sure. She gobbled it anyway and washed it down with a cup of the mud that passed for coffee here.

"Time to go, Major." She pushed herself up and headed for Ward A.

. . .

They were no longer sending battle wounded into her hospital, of course, nor was Terok releasing any except under the strictest BSL-4 protocols. They *had* sent out infected soldiers before they understood what was going on, but there was no point in dwelling on that. Done deal. The four cases in A were the last to come in before ACE was identified. Two spec 4s, Ligety and Mayweather; Corporal Dancerre; and Sergeant Bighawk. All admitted initially with wounds—gunshots, fortunately, rather than blast damage—and all subsequently infected with ACE. She always began with the most serious first, and that was Sergeant Dane Bighawk, a twenty-four-year-old full-blooded Sioux from Nebraska. He had taken two AK rounds, one in the big right quadriceps muscle, the other in the right lower abdomen midway between his navel and his hip joint. Both were clean through-and-throughs. The thigh wound was nothing serious, but the abdominal wound was—or could have been. Passing through Bighawk's body, the bullet had nicked his colon, cutting a dime-sized opening. That hole should have leaked fecal matter, which would have virtually ensured the onset of peritonitis.

But Bighawk had been lucky—if you could call taking two AK rounds lucky. The squadmate who had tended his wounds had stuffed in two tampons, just as DeAengelo Washington had done for Father Wyman. No one knew which soldier first had the idea of using a tampon that way, but one thing was sure—they worked beautifully, being the perfect size and shape for bullet-wound battle dressings, and now every combat soldier carried some. The tampon in Bighawk's abdomen had stopped serious bleeding from that wound site and had also occluded the breach in his colon. Stilwell had explained that, and Bighawk had thought about it for a second. "So it kept the stuffing in the sausage."

She'd laughed. "An unscientific but perfectly accurate description, Sergeant."

That was the good news. The bad was that twenty-four hours after being wheeled in, Bighawk began to show the first signs of

ACE infection: spiking temperature, dropping blood pressure, searing sore throat, generalized pain. Lesions appeared about six hours after that, and now, a day later, the raw, red patches were spreading. Colistin was slowing ACE's burn through the young soldier, but not stopping it.

Stilwell walked quietly to his bedside. Bighawk was sleeping, thank goodness, the IV ketamine still working. She watched, listened to, and timed his respiration, took his pulse—still strong and regular—and felt his forehead. The fever was up. She'd use a digital thermometer, of course, but she remembered exactly how warm his forehead had felt four hours earlier, and it was definitely hotter now.

Bighawk's eyes opened, drooped, opened again. "Mom?" He blinked, looked at her from far away in a ketamine haze, yawned, then grimaced because that motion stretched one of the lesions on his left cheek. Relaxing again, he smiled up at Stilwell, reached for her hand. "Mom? What're you doin'?" He dozed off.

I need you awake, Stilwell thought. She put her hand on his muscular shoulder, squeezed softly, and his eyes opened again. This time he recognized her. "Hey, Doc. How're you doin'? I was just havin' a dream."

"About your mom, right?"

His eyebrows went up. "How'd you know that?"

"We doctors have secret powers, Sergeant. We can read minds."

He chuckled. "You're kiddin', I know, Doc. Must've been talkin' in my sleep. But we Sioux know medicine people *do* have special powers. Some of the stuff I saw as a kid on the rez . . . Unbelievable."

He closed his eyes, coughed, and Stilwell heard the pneumonic rattle in his chest. *What I wouldn't give,* she thought, *for some* real *special power.*

"So how'm I doin', Doc?"

Bighawk kept a brave face, but she could see the fear in his eyes.

"You're doing, Sergeant. That antibiotic I told you about is retarding the bacteria's spread."

"But you got no cure for it, right?"

"Not now we don't. But every lab and scientist at the government's disposal is working around the clock. They'll find one. Trust me."

"I do trust you, ma'am. Not much else, but you for sure."

Bighawk's words were like a lance through Stilwell's chest. She was the only thing standing between this good young man and a slow, agonizing death, and despite her reassurance, Stilwell was not at all certain that the government could find a cure for ACE. She wasn't at all certain of anything just now.

Two hours later, groggy with fatigue but needing to do one more thing, she went to her cubbyhole office, closed the door, and booted up her laptop. She wanted to write an email before catching an hour's sleep. She had written one to her husband and son during her last break. She wrote in time-saving email pidgin:

> Hey ther hows it going Vry cool here and little rain. sorry not been in bttr tuch bt crazy bsy jst now Wld love 2 hear frm u talked to momdad? Shoot me an eml catch me up
>
> SIS

It wasn't much but she had learned, through long experience, what would slip through the censors' nets. No mention of combat, no specific locations, nothing about casualties or material shortages or morale problems. Just Chatty Cathy stuff. But at least it was something, and maybe her sister would answer this time. It had been a long time since Mary had answered one of her emails, but Stilwell was not the kind to quit trying. She hit the Save button and put this email into her Outbox folder with the others she'd been writing, but could not send, since the ACE horror had begun.

TWELVE

ON THE MORNING OF THE DAY HALLIE AND HER TEAM BOARDED their flight from Andrews to Reynosa, Don Barnard poured coffee in Lew Casey's office. Barnard took his coffee black and strong, and still he grimaced when he took a sip.

"Toxic sludge," he said.

Casey, wearing wrinkled chinos, battered loafers, and a plaid shirt with no tie, raised his own cup in a toast. "Navy coffee. Keeps the brain sharp." Barnard knew about Casey's affinity for "Navy coffee." He had gone to Annapolis, done his five years on active, and realized he loved microbiology more than nuclear engineering. Resigned from the Navy, got his PhD, tried private enterprise long enough to dislike it intensely, and came to CDC, where he had been now for more than twenty years. He and Barnard had worked together for most of that time. Toward each other they behaved more like brothers than like supervisor and subordinate. "The hours you've got us working, we need it."

"I know, and I'm sorry." Barnard took out his cold pipe, fiddled, put it back in his vest pocket. "We're stretched thin. And it's going to get worse before it gets better. But we are probably the best hope for stopping this thing."

Casey waved the apology away. "It's not often I get the chance to beat up on you a little."

"How are *you* holding up, Evvie?" Barnard turned his attention to Evelyn Flemmer, the other person in Casey's cramped office.

"I'm one of those people who hate to sleep, sir. I can't stand wasting all those hours unconscious. So thank you for asking, but I'm doing fine."

Flemmer had called him "sir" during their first meeting, and he had waved the honorific aside with a laugh. She had blushed, giving him the impression, which time had done nothing to diminish, that she was unusually shy. "I'm sorry. It's a hard habit to break. My parents were big on proper manners, sir," she had said, flinching as she helplessly pronounced that last "sir." Barnard, raised in Virginia himself, knew that some southern parents still brought their children up the old way, which included respect for elders and for courtesy, as well—all in all, not such a bad thing. An upbringing like that could make the use of "sir" and "ma'am" virtually reflexive.

"I understand," he had told her and then, curious, had asked, "Were you raised in the South, by any chance?"

"Well, sort of, sir. Southern Oklahoma."

"Close enough." Barnard had smiled, and that was how they had left it.

Evvie Flemmer was one of Casey's best research scientists. Perhaps even the best who had worked for him, he had told Barnard. She was short and a bit stout and her wardrobe, as far as Barnard had been able to tell, was exclusively J. C. Penney. Today she wore a brown dress whose hem hung below her knees. Her legs dropped without a single curve into the practical black flats she wore every day. She used no makeup and kept her brown hair in a short blunt cut, easy to wash, easy to dry. She rarely smiled and Barnard had never heard her laugh, but neither was she openly angry or cynical. Just very, very serious, was how he eventually came to think of her.

Barnard knew that Flemmer was thirty-eight years old, single, and lived alone. She was brown-eyed and pale-skinned, not from Irish heredity, like Casey, but from spending virtually every waking hour in BARDA's laboratories. In all his time in government, Barnard had encountered only one or two scientists more dedicated to their work, and those people had not been paradigms of mental health.

In fact, a few months after she arrived, Barnard grew concerned over her endless hours in the labs and said something to Casey about her life outside BARDA. Casey shrugged. "What life?" Then he added, "I worried a bit at first, too, Don. But I think Evvie is happiest when she's doing science. I keep an eye on her, but she's fine."

"I envy you," Barnard said now, raising his cup in her direction. "These days, I feel like a slug if I don't get six or seven hours a night. Eight is better."

"Hell, Don, we were the same way when we were young and full of beans like Evvie," Casey said, patting Flemmer's shoulder.

Flemmer blushed. Barnard knew that Casey and his wife, Adell, had never had children and, as devout Catholics, they'd found the barrenness especially painful. So Lew had a tendency to "adopt" some of the younger people who worked under him. His paternal feelings for Evvie Flemmer were right there on his shirtsleeve.

Barnard liked her, too. Not the way he liked Hallie, of course. Hallie was special. She operated on a higher level than other people, and it was pleasantly contagious. Being with her was like being near one of those generators that resembled giant lightbulbs and made your skin tingle. In her presence, Barnard found his brain working more quickly, his speech sharper, his feelings brighter. An old scientist mentor, now long since retired, had once said to Barnard early in his career, "Don, there are two kinds of people in this world: chargers and drainers. The rare ones lift you up; the others suck you down." Hallie was a charger. He missed her every day.

"Were we?" Barnard shook his head. "I'm not sure I ever had your kind of stamina, Evvie."

"You must have, sir." Flemmer shrugged, held both palms up. "Or else you couldn't have accomplished so much."

"You flatter an old man."

"No flattery in truth, sir."

Casey chuckled and patted her shoulder again, and she blushed again. "Evvie has a fine way with words, don't you think? For a scientist, I mean."

Flemmer waved the compliment away, saying, "Oh, stop now, Dr. Casey . . ." She was looking down at her shoes, so Barnard could not see her expression, but in her voice he heard something he could not quite name. The slightest hint of dissonance, it did not sound like the undertones produced by a smile. He had witnessed this kind of interaction before, and always came back to how shy she was. He understood that praise must have felt wonderful at some level but must have been almost painful at another, drawing attention as it did. So he decided to rescue her with a subject change.

"I just came down to . . ." His voice trailed off. He had wanted to get out of his office, be closer to the action, try to help in some meaningful way. But he felt silly saying it out loud.

Casey came to his rescue.

"To get a report on your progress."

Barnard sipped the muddy coffee, swallowed, grunted. "Yes. And with some news. We've just received viable ACE cultures from overseas."

"Devil in a bottle." Casey was listening more intently now.

"Yes. As you know, the other two lab groups are trying to synthesize moonmilk and conjure a new antibiotic."

"Not having much luck, from what I hear."

"That's right. I'd like you and your people to have a go at disrupting ACE's genetic codes."

Casey sat forward. "When can we start?"

"Today."

"We'll go on double shifts. Eight to four, four to twelve, rotating teams through."

Casey looked tired but willing. Flemmer looked suddenly energized, like a dog presented with fresh meat. *Good sign,* Barnard thought. *She's still hanging tough. If you worry about anyone, worry about Lew. The emphysema, last year.* Like Barnard, Casey had been a smoker—unfiltered Camels, a holdover from his Navy days. Unlike Barnard, Casey had smoked until the previous year, when he was diagnosed with emphysema. It was not yet crippling, but it was debilitating.

"We'll get it done, Don." Casey stood up, drained the dregs of his coffee. "Won't we, Evvie?" He patted her affectionately on the forearm. She blushed again, but nodded vigorously.

"We absolutely will, sir." She stood, squared her shoulders, tried to smooth her hair. "When exactly does that ACE get to us, sir?" she asked Barnard.

"Should be down to Four within the hour." Biosafety Level 4, sanctum sanctorum, where only the most lethal pathogens were caged. Barnard hesitated. "Look, I know I don't have to tell either of you this. But please be careful. This is a bacterium like nothing we have ever seen. It might as well have come from Mars. Christ, maybe it *did* come from Mars. You know what it can do."

Casey and Flemmer nodded, said nothing.

"I want every BSL-4 protocol observed *absolutely.* Time is of the essence, but we cannot afford shortcuts."

"We understand. Delta 17 will be tight."

"All right then." Barnard set his cup down, half the coffee still in it. He stood, turned toward the door. Flemmer's voice interrupted him.

"Sir, I just want to say, to you both, thank you. Working on *Acinetobacter* in this crisis is the opportunity of a lifetime. There is no way I can ever thank you enough. For your faith in me."

It was so uncharacteristic of the woman that Barnard stared briefly. Flemmer's eyes were glistening and her voice sounded sincere rather than erratic. Barnard himself might not have put it that way—*the opportunity of a lifetime*—but he understood what she meant. What mattered was her commitment. And that, Barnard knew, was total.

THIRTEEN

BOWMAN HALTED HALLIE AND THE OTHERS JUST INSIDE THE forest tree line, beyond which lay a smooth, green meadow bordered on both sides by towering mountain pines. It was shortly after dawn. They all gathered around Bowman, and Hallie whispered to the team.

"There it is."

The cave mouth was two hundred yards away, at the left end of the meadow as they stood facing it.

"The mouth of that thing is unbelievable," whispered Haight. "You could fly a 747 through it. I have never seen a cave mouth that big."

"As I said earlier, there's nothing normal about this cave," Hallie whispered back.

Between them and the cave, also on the left side of the meadow at the tree line's edge, was a cenote, a circular sinkhole filled with water. From long experience, Hallie knew that such holes were common in cave country, and that sometimes they connected through subterranean chambers to the main cave itself. She had never had the chance to dive this cenote, so she had no way of knowing if this one made such a connection.

Bowman led them along, sheltering inside the tree line, past the cenote's edge. This was a big one, 250 feet in diameter. It resembled a great cistern, with horizontal layers of gray limestone—karst, geologists called it—forming the walls.

"How deep, do you think?" Bowman, voice low.

Hallie answered, "Could be hundreds of feet. Or thousands."

Arguello said, "The ancient Cuicatecs used these as their primary water supplies. Unfortunately, they also dumped human sacrifices into them. They poisoned their own wells. It was one of the things that led to their demise."

Minutes later, they stood far enough inside the cave mouth to be invisible from without. Chilling wind blew from the ancient depths.

"He is breathing." Arguello's voice was reverent, as though he were speaking in a great cathedral. "One reason why Cuicatecs and others believe that caves are alive."

"You could also say that diurnal pressure and temperature changes move air in and out," Haight said. "I'm not sayin' y'all's Cuicatecs are wrong, now. But there is some science to it, too."

"Yes, but there is much more," Arguello said. "For example—"

Bowman had been caching his FAFO weapon and pistol, covering them completely with rocks. He straightened up and detached the NVDs from his helmet. "We won't need these for a while, and every ounce we can take off our backs will help. Let's cache them here."

Five minutes later they were finished. Bowman said, "From now on, we will be observing strict light discipline. That means one helmet light on for travel or tasks. Otherwise, everything off to conserve battery power." He looked at Hallie. "We need to move. We're in a race with that bacterium, and right now ACE has a big head start. Hallie will take the point. She has a map based on notes from the other expedition and she's been in here before. I'll follow her. Next, Al, Rafael, and Ron, in that order. Maintain visual contact at all times with those in front of and behind you. Questions?"

There were none.

"One more thing. When we come to vertical pitches or sections requiring dives, we'll stop, plan, and then move."

"How far do you intend to go today?" asked Al Cahner.

"Until we can't go any farther. Anything else?"

Hallie spoke: "Make sure your suits are zipped all the way up. Make *very* sure the wrist, ankle, and neck seals are secure."

"This early? They're hot. I thought we wouldn't button up until a lot farther in." Arguello sounded worried.

"We'll need them very soon."

Then she led them down terrain steeper than a staircase and experienced, as she always did going into vast caves, not only a sense of descending but of going back in time as well. She knew that a cave like this took tens of millions of years to form. It had already existed for eons when the Egyptians built their pyramids. She knew that when her distant ancestors were knuckle-loping along some African plain, this cave had already been breathing for millennia.

It was both exhilarating and unnerving to enter such a place. What with the wind and rushing water where feeder streams formed rivers, and the heavy wet darkness, she could understand aboriginals' belief that caves *lived*. There was more than just the rock and water and wind. There was unquestionably something else here, a presence that Hallie could feel. She was a scientist, but her mind remained open. It had always seemed to her that what people thought of as possible only revealed the borders of their own fragment of eternity. Two hundred years earlier, flight had been unimaginable, germs were undreamed of, and doctors treated the sick by bleeding them, sometimes to death. For Hallie, the only certainty was that the world and their knowledge of it would keep changing, which made the thing denoted by the word "impossible" itself an impossibility.

She had no way to explain what she felt, nor even a name for it, but it was there. Chi Con Gui-Jao was as good a name as any.

The cave ceiling rose seventy feet over their heads—a big chamber, though Hallie had seen bigger, some vast enough to hold Grand Central Station in its entirety. She led them between rocks as big as cottages—breakdown, cavers called such boulders—which had fallen from that ceiling over the eons, and more of which could fall on them at any moment. It was like walking through a minefield, except that the mines were overhead. The gradient eased, but still they had to take each step with great care, their worlds shrinking to the circles of blue light bouncing along in front of their feet.

Hallie stopped them.

"Check those suit seals again."

She turned and began walking down the moderately sloping floor. After fifty feet, her helmet light revealed a dark, still surface that wasn't solid rock but didn't look exactly like water, either. She waded in. The lake's surface did not ripple like water; it sloshed, heavy and viscous, the consistency of buttermilk but reddish black.

Through clenched teeth, Cahner said, "It smells like rotting corpses and burning crap and year-old garbage."

"I would keep my voice down if I were you," Hallie warned softly. "Look up."

"Mother Mary." Arguello's voice, full of sudden fear. "That is *many*. I do not think I ever have seen so large a colony."

"How many, do you think?" Even Bowman sounded impressed.

"Given the size of this chamber, a million or more."

Fifty feet above them, every square inch of the cave ceiling was covered with roosting vampire bats hanging upside down. It looked as though the rock ceiling had grown a vast gray beard. The bats had furry bodies like rats, but ears like a Chihuahua's. Their faces were pink, and when light from the team's lights touched them, their lips curled back to reveal jagged white teeth.

"It is said that the ancient Incan kings wore cloaks of vampire bat fur." Arguello, awestruck. "How do they, ah, poop upside down like that?"

"They invert momentarily, excrete, and go back to their normal hanging position." Hallie shook her head. "Amazing acrobatics, actually."

"So we are wading through a lake of bat guano," Arguello said.

"The stuff must be *teeming* with viruses and bacteria." Cahner sounded impressed but also horrified.

"It is, Al, but we'll be through soon. It's the only way in."

"Nasty stuff." No curiosity in Bowman's voice, just disgust.

"It could be worse, though," Hallie deadpanned and waited for someone to reply.

Cahner rose to the bait: "How could it get worse?"

"These bats have just come back to roost after a night of feeding. Very soon, their little bowels will go to work. There'll be a cloudburst of bloody bat guano. You don't want to be in here when that happens."

"Let us make great haste, please," said Arguello.

"Yes, but not too much. The footing gets uneven here. You don't want to fall in and get a mouthful of this stuff."

"Sweet Jesus, no. Hurry up, y'all." Even brash Haight sounded concerned.

After another five minutes, Hallie felt the cave floor begin to incline upward, and soon she was standing on the rocky shore of the "lake," watching the others make their way out. Before long they were all together, slathered from the chests down in steaming, stinking, bloody bat excrement.

"We're a rotten lot, y'all." Haight kept moving his nose around, rabbitlike, trying, unsuccessfully, to get it out of the stench.

Cahner didn't laugh. "What do we do now?"

"We take a shower. Follow me." Hallie led them to a small waterfall that shot out from a ledge of sparkling gold-and-ruby-colored flowstone. One by one, keeping their helmets on, they stood under the natural shower while clear, cold water washed their caving suits clean. Hallie showered last. When she rejoined the others, Haight spoke.

"What do y'all call that place?"

"Batshit Lake. What else?"

"Let's go." Bowman's curt tone ended the small talk. "Hallie, move us out."

She looked at him, hesitated a moment, then nodded. Despite his brusque way of going, something about the big man was still attracting her. She recalled the staring contest, the way he had winked at her. If ever something seemed out of character for a black ops kind of guy, that did. And maybe that was part of it, the contradiction such an act implied. Contradiction suggested complexity, and with complexity came surprises. As she had learned, some could be good, some bad, but she knew herself well enough to know that, for her, any were better than none.

The route steepened again and led eventually to a great portal, roughly rectangular, twenty feet high by thirty feet wide, in a rock wall that rose higher than their lights could reach. Here all the air that had been moving up from the cave's unfathomable depths was compressed and blew through the opening with such force that Cahner grabbed a golden stalagmite to steady himself.

"I have been in a good number of caves," Cahner said. "But I have never seen wind this strong moving through an opening this big."

"Y'all know what they say about caves. If she blows, she goes. This is one monster we got us here." Haight, impressed.

"What's on the other side of that?" Bowman was poking his light beam into the void, trying to assess the terrain.

Hallie followed the caver's protocol of keeping her light focused on his chest rather than shining it onto his face, where it would blind him. "A place where a lot of people died."

She led on, down over boulders, past pits with bottoms their lights could not reach, through gardens of varicolored speleothems, white and red and black stalactites and stalagmites. Some were as thick as tree trunks, great columns that rose to the ceiling. Other, younger stalagmites stuck up like short spears from Cueva de Luz's floor.

The darkness down here was the luminal equivalent of absolute zero. It began to have weight, like water on a dive, and it consumed the beams of their lights more quickly than any surface darkness ever could. Hallie felt it pressing her body and her mind. There were other physical manifestations of the cave's presence. Its outblowing breath pushed their chests and faces, filled their noses, had substance and force. There was nothing foul or corrupt in the scent now, but neither was it like any odor ever smelled on the surface. It came up from the cave's ancient heart, carrying a coppery tinge like the smell of fresh blood and other, stranger things unknown to the world of light.

This is the real heart of darkness, Hallie thought. *Watch over us, Chi Con Gui-Jao.*

FOURTEEN

THEY ENTERED A TIGHT, TWISTING PASSAGE, THEN DESCENDED a jagged vertical chute that required them briefly to "chimney"—to press their backs and feet against opposite walls and work their way down foot by foot. They dropped out of that into a room big enough to contain a football field. Near its center, a bus-sized slab of gray stone had peeled off one wall. Following Hallie, they worked their way through boulders and rubble until all were standing beside the giant slab. It rose twenty feet over their heads and was wreathed in mist that boiled up off a small river running down one side of the chamber, an offshoot of the cave's main watercourse.

"Some piece of rock." Haight was playing his light over the slab, examining it in detail.

"This is more interesting." Hallie moved her light down to the floor of the cave, beneath the end of the rock platform.

"Good Lord. Those look like . . ." Cahner didn't finish the sentence.

Bowman did. "Bones. Human bones. Right, Rafael?"

"That is correct. The ancient Cuicatecs believed in many gods. They relied on human sacrifices to stay in good graces with them. *Especially* with Chi Con Gui-Jao."

"Those all're *little* bones." Haight's voice was tight.

"They believed that the most effective sacrifices were children." Arguello sounded sad. "Their souls were thought to be more pure, therefore more powerful."

"How would they get down this deep, though?" Haight had turned professionally curious. "We're two hours past the twilight zone, at least."

"They would line up from the surface all the way down to the places of killing, each holding a torch," said Arguello.

"Why here?"

"That we do not know. But obviously they considered such places to have great power."

Bowman had been shifting from foot to foot. "Let's keep moving. Good people are dying up top."

They started down again, following the bouncing circles of blue-white light. After a while, the descent assumed a rhythm that let Hallie's mind wonder. And what she thought was: *We all change in caves. How will this cave change us?*

Then the down-climbing grew treacherous again. It was not like hiking down a trail on the surface, nor even like clambering over boulders and talus, and not just because of the surrounding darkness. Down here, everything was wet. There was no trail or path, only an endless jumble of steeply sloping rocks and debris. The trick was to stay on top of the boulders as much as possible, moving along without dropping down into the spaces between them. It required both balance and courage, because sometimes the distance between boulders was a jump from the slick round top of one to the slick round top of another, with empty space of unknown depth yawning between them. At other times, the only way to keep going was to down-climb steep or even vertical faces. None was more than twenty-five feet, but such a fall could maim or kill easily enough.

Even in such terrain, Hallie felt the familiar skill coming back as she descended. When she was in a boulder garden, her brain would automatically plot a path several yards ahead that her feet could follow. Climbing down a short face, her hands and feet seemed to find placements on their own, her fingers to become one with the wall's protrusions and hollows. To those behind her, she appeared to be almost floating along, so smooth and even was her progress. Bowman, coming next, stayed close despite his size, though his movement was less fluid. Next in line was Cahner, his experience in caves serving him well. His progress was not as graceful and efficient as Hallie's, but he moved easily and with confidence. Arguello was having the most trouble, and before long, he was sweating hard and swearing. Back at the tail end, Haight could have gone much faster had he not had to stay behind the two older men, but he seemed happy to be easing along, taking in the surroundings, even humming some Appalachian tune to himself as he went.

Hallie came to a huge stalagmite, taller and thicker than one of the Parthenon's columns, colored red and yellow and black by minerals in the dripping water that had created it. The formation rose from the cave floor straight up to the ceiling. Even in this Brobdingnagian cave, such a speleothem was remarkable, and it was the signpost she had been anticipating.

"Let's stop here."

"Why?" Bowman impatient, prodding.

"Because if you keep going you'll fall about five hundred feet straight down."

"The big wall you told us about?"

"None other. Stay beside me, be careful, and I'll show you."

The others waited while she and Bowman stepped closer to the edge of the cliff. Their lights, shining out into the void, revealed the top of a gigantic canyon, deep enough that their beams did not reach the bottom.

"One thousand, seven hundred and eighty-nine feet across to the far wall." Hallie aimed a laser range finder across, then pointed it straight down. "Five hundred and twenty-three feet deep."

"This is a beautiful thing." Cahner eased up and played his light over polished bronze walls so smooth they gleamed. "Think of the water flow it took to carve such an abyss. Unimaginable." There was pure awe in his voice.

"Do we take a break here?" Arguello was already dropping his pack to the floor. "I could use a snack. And some water. It will take you an hour or so to rig the rappel rope here, will it not?"

"We won't be rigging rappel ropes. Remember I mentioned that back at BARDA?" Bowman cast his light around, assessing the area.

"I had forgotten. But I will just grab a snack in any case." Arguello started munching a Hershey bar with almonds. Hallie considered saying something about conserving their rations, not gobbling stuff this early into the expedition, but decided it would be better to mention it to Arguello when she had a chance to be alone with him.

Haight was focused, gleefully, on the down-climb. "*I* hadn't forgotten. I've been dying to find out what y'all have up your sleeve."

"In my pack, actually." Bowman dropped his backpack and began digging through it. "I couldn't release these until we were in the cave, with zero chance of security breach." He handed each of them small bags that resembled zippered toiletry kits. "Otherwise, you would have been carrying them yourselves, believe me. Drop your packs, look at this gear. We'll be here awhile."

Inside her bag, Hallie found two gloves made of what appeared to be thick neoprene, the material used in divers' wet suits, and two other things, made of the same material, that looked like the black rubber overshoes men used, once upon a time, to protect their dress shoes. She slipped her left hand into one of the gloves and jumped back.

"Hey!" she exclaimed. *"Bowman! What's it doing?"*

The glove was moving like a thing alive. Enlarging, molding to her hand. At first, it was like a blood pressure cuff tightening, but then it stopped. It felt to Hallie like she was wearing a new layer of flesh.

"Don't worry." Bowman was smiling, obviously enjoying her discomfiture. "It won't hurt. Performing as designed."

"How in God's name did it do that?"

"The rest of you put on your gloves and I'll explain."

They did, with exclamations ranging from Arguello's *"Madre de Dios"* to Haight's "Unbelievable, y'all."

"These gloves and shoes come to us from DARPA." The ease with which he donned his gloves indicated that Bowman had done this before.

"The supersecret black ops place?" Haight was turning his hands over and over, like a boxer examining a taping job.

"The Defense Advanced Research Projects Agency, yes. They do high-risk, high-reward work."

"Like?" Haight asked.

"Stealth aircraft. An antigravity-force project. Superheal—biotechnology that accelerates the human body's healing process. I could go on for a long time. But you get the idea."

"It sounds rather like science fiction." Arguello was tugging at one of his gloves.

"So about these things here?" Haight was making fists, punching air.

Bowman's helmet light bobbed up and down. "DARPA was asked to develop a system that would enable soldiers to climb and descend vertical surfaces."

"Wait a minute." Arguello sounded worried. "You are not suggesting that we are going to climb down into that pit using these things?"

"How do they work?" asked Hallie, intrigued.

"DARPA calls them z-man tools, but I like gecko gear. Rolls off the tongue better. DARPA first tried suction devices, but they weren't powerful enough. Then they investigated how geckos and spiders climb and stick."

"Magic." Arguello's voice was low.

"No, very much science. They found that certain lizards and spiders use something called van der Waals forces. There's some very sophisticated nanotechnology involved, but I've climbed with these things, and all that matters is that they work."

"Hold on a sec." Now even Haight sounded hesitant. "This pit's walls are wet rock. How're these things ever going to get a seal on that kind of surface?"

"It's not suction, Ron. It's more to do with molecular linearity."

The two scientists, Hallie and Cahner, and the doctor, Haight, were at least somewhat familiar with van der Waals forces, which they had learned about way back in graduate and medical school. Arguello, who was not, looked at the two gloves on his hands like they were snakes.

This is going to be interesting, Hallie thought. *Getting them to trust these things going down a five-hundred-foot wall. Good test of a leader.*

Haight spoke with unusual sharpness, all trace of backwoods Tennessee gone from his voice. "Wil, I've been caving and climbing most of my life. I'm still alive because I am very careful about my equipment. That means not using something I don't understand, especially experimental Buck Rogers stuff."

"Absolutely right." Bowman nodded. "Bear with me for a minute. We're all familiar with how lasers work, I'd guess?"

"They organize random light energy into a coherent, focused beam," Arguello said, sounding distracted. He was trying to remove his gloves, without success.

"These tools work the same way," said Bowman. "They organize random molecular bonding energy—those van der Waal forces—into coherent beams. When they meet other random molecular energy, say from a pane of glass, they pull that energy into coherent attraction."

"Like two magnets?" Hallie was trying to take a glove off, too. It was like trying to peel away her own flesh.

"Yes. But many times more powerful."

"But are they going to work on rock that is slick and wet?" Haight still sounded skeptical.

"Even better. Moisture enhances the van der Waal forces' flow. And a slightly rough surface like rock is better than a smooth one because it presents more total bonding area."

"But how are they able to change themselves to mimic the forms of our hands?" Arguello asked. "And why can't I get them off?"

"Once again, thank DARPA." Hallie could hear impatience creeping into Bowman's voice. But he continued: "It's called 'jamming skin enabled locomotion.' DARPA's molecular engineers made certain substances, including flexible plastics, capable of changing shape to create motion. It could be helpful moving around on other planets with surfaces that might be impassable by conventional vehicles." He moved his light toward Cahner, then Arguello. "They don't come off that way. They meld with, rather than mold to, surfaces."

"So they've literally merged with our bodies?" Haight sounded incredulous.

"More or less. Now watch." Bowman walked to the nearest vertical section of rock, about twenty feet to their right. He slipped the "overshoes" onto his caving boots, where they molded to the shape of the boots as the gloves had to their hands. It was an incredible thing to watch, the inert black material suddenly appearing to come alive, moving and changing, flowing around the caving boots. He pressed the palm of his right hand onto the wall just above his head, then the left. He placed one foot against the wall, then the other. There was a barely audible sound, something between a hiss and a gulp, and suddenly Bowman was attached to the wall.

He started climbing. It was like watching someone crawl along a floor, except Bowman was doing it straight up.

"Dracula," Haight whispered.

Hallie didn't like that comparison. "Spider-Man," she said. Whatever you called it, Bowman's demonstration up there *was* amazing. It wasn't only the Gecko Gear. A climber herself, she knew how much strength it took to go straight up a wall like that, sticky hands and feet or no.

Bowman ascended thirty feet above the cave floor. There he rested briefly in the big spot cast by the light beams of the other four, staring up at him from below. He moved his hands and feet so that they described half of a large circle. He stopped, hanging upside down above them like a giant red lizard in his brightly colored caving suit. He rotated the remaining half of the circle so that he was upright again.

"Now, here's a really cool thing." He peeled his left hand and both feet off the wall and hung by only his right hand. "These things *work*."

He reattached his other hand and both feet, down-climbed, rejoined them.

"Things you should know: You don't need to press hard. And you don't need to have the whole boot sole in contact. A few square inches are enough. It's like front-pointing on ice with crampons. You detach by peeling up and away from the bottom. Which is also how you walk on level ground, if you have to, though it's awkward at best, as you might have noticed."

"So now what, Wil?" Arguello was looking toward the giant pit.

"Now you practice. Let's take . . ." He glanced at his watch. "Ten minutes. Go find a wall."

At the bottom of a vertical section, Hallie put on the overshoes. Then, taking a deep breath, she moved her right hand slowly toward a spot on the wall about a foot higher than her head. When her hand was several inches from the wall, she began to feel a pull, like that of a magnet attracted to steel. *Amazing*. The closer she moved her hand, the stronger that pull became. When the "glove" touched rock, she felt it moving again, changing, joining itself, at the molecular level, with the wall. She tested it carefully, first pulling down on it and then, when it would not move, hanging more and more of her body weight from the hand placement. It was an unbelievably solid connection—as though her hand had become part of the rock. Ascending very carefully, she discovered that the climbing was less physically demanding than she'd expected, once she lost the tension of fear and reverted to good form, using the big muscles in her legs rather than trying to power up with her arms. Before long, she and Haight were moving smoothly around like a pair of giant spiders. Cahner took a bit longer, but eventually he, too, was crawling confidently up and down the wall.

Arguello, however, couldn't seem to get it. Despite working himself into a red-faced sweat, he wasn't able to rise more than a couple of feet. One hand or boot would peel off and he'd lose control of the others, dropping clumsily to the floor. Bowman watched, arms folded. After a while he walked over.

"I think I can help, Rafael. Don't reach so high. You can't use your most powerful leg muscles, and you don't have the right angle to peel off correctly."

Arguello looked skeptical, but he did as Bowman suggested, setting his hands closer to the top of his helmet, then finding his foot placements. He moved tentatively, as though expecting to fall off again, but before long, he was twenty feet above Bowman. He glanced back over his shoulder, grinning.

"It works!" He traversed side to side, went up and down a few more times, then stepped down beside Bowman. "Once you get it, these things are fun."

"Good job, Rafael. You looked strong up there."

Arguello shook his head. "Good job by *you*. If not for you, I would still be flopping around."

"What I'm here for."

"Hey, this place have a name?" It was Haight, calling down from far above.

Hallie answered. "You know cavers give names to everything, Ron. This is Don't Fall Wall."

FIFTEEN

DON BARNARD SAT BEHIND HIS DESK AND TRIED TO REMEMBER when he had slept last. He couldn't recall, but he did know the current day, date, and time—because in a bit less than two minutes he would have a videoconference with the president of the United States and some of his key advisers.

He had put on a fresh white shirt and a new tie, blue with small silver stars. He fiddled a good deal with the knot, getting the dimple just right, and playing with the dimple made him remember the day his father had taught him to tie a tie, more than a half century ago.

"The dimple is everything, Donald," his father had said. "And nothing. Nothing but a tiny detail, but of such details fortunes and tragedies are made." He had been ten at the time, and, though he had dutifully said, "Yes, sir," he'd had little idea what his father was talking about. Now he did.

He ran a comb through his white hair one more time, straightened his suitcoat. His attire was in good order. Not the face, though. The face looked like that of a man who had aged five years in two weeks. Nothing he could do about that. Maybe he would look better when this was all over. Then again, maybe not. Fatigue and fear were cruel sculptors.

He took a sip of water from the glass on the desktop, which was clean except for a fresh legal pad and a pen. He looked at his watch. Twenty-eight seconds.

He watched the red hand climb up toward 12, and just as it passed over that number, a soft chime sounded. The big flat-screen monitor on the wall changed from blue to a bright image of President O'Neil in the White House Situation Room. A tall black man with close-cut hair beginning to show flecks of gray, he was sitting at the head of the room's thirty-foot-long mahogany conference table, wearing a blue shirt with the sleeves rolled up, collar loosened, dark red tie pulled down. He did not look here as he always did in public—calm, collected, quick to flash a dazzling smile. Now he looked tired. The president was flanked by Vice President Eileen Washinsky, Health and Human Services Secretary Nathan Rathor, and Secretary of Homeland Security Hunter Mason.

Barnard cleared his throat. "Good evening, Mr. President, Madam Vice President, Secretary Rathor, Secretary Mason," he said respectfully.

"Hello, Dr. Barnard." A quick flash of the famous presidential smile that, in the early years of his tenure, had lit up an entire country. "I'm sorry that our earlier conference had to be cut short. And for taking too long to reconnect. I need to learn more, and a lot of people say you are the best person to help me do that."

He felt himself blush. "Thank you, sir."

"In our previous discussion, you said that this germ might have the potential to destroy our armed forces from the inside out. Has that proved to be an accurate assessment, Doctor?"

"More accurate than when we last spoke, sir. Its contagion factor appears similar to that of smallpox. Its mortality rate is worse—something like ninety percent thus far."

"Ninety percent?" Eileen Washinsky's eyebrows shot up. "Is that really possible?"

"I'm afraid so, Madame Vice President. No other known pathogen, possibly excepting Ebola, is so deadly. It's too early, and our sample size is too small, to make final determinations, of course."

The president spoke. "Doctor Barnard, we have every CDC lab not otherwise engaged in critical national security at work. We also have the military's biowarfare people involved. We have not brought in any private-sector entities because of security concerns."

"Thank you, sir. I concur that letting the bad news out before we have any good to counter it with could trigger a panic."

"We agree on that, Doctor," rasped Hunter Mason. He was a massive man, not tall but plated with muscle from years of weight lifting, his personal passion. He had a shaved head shaped like an artillery shell, and even in a tailored business suit he looked like he could bench-press a refrigerator. His voice sounded like gravel sliding out of a dump truck. "But when *do* we start to talk about this?"

Barnard took a deep breath. "Sir, we have received cultures of the pathogen from Afghanistan. Our own laboratories are just beginning their work. Until we've had some time with the thing, I would respectfully suggest that it would be best to maintain silence."

The president nodded. "Thank you, Dr. Barnard. We value your opinion highly because, as I understand it, your laboratories were very close to formulating promising new antibiotics. That puts you closer than anyone else to producing something that might be effective against this germ."

"Thank you, sir." Barnard thought, *Rock and hard place. If he keeps it quiet and there's a pandemic, they'll say he should have told the world. If he goes public and there's a panic, they'll say he caused it. Glad I'm not in his seat.*

The president spoke again, bringing that part of their discussion to a close. "Now. Can you brief us quickly on what's being done over there at BARDA?"

"Of course, sir. Since we first learned of the crisis, we've employed a three-pronged approach. One of our lab groups has been trying to synthesize an antibiotic that might prove effective. Another is trying to synthesize moonmilk itself—the extremophile that we had been working with earlier. And a third will now begin looking for a way to disrupt ACE's genetic codes."

Barnard waited for questions. Lathrop had told him and the others that his boss, Hunter Mason, and the president both knew about the moonmilk mission to Cueva de Luz. Barnard assumed that Rathor and Washinsky had been briefed as well. But events had been unfolding very quickly, and no one had verified that fact for him. Because of the Cueva de Luz mission's secrecy and, given its unusual nature, the potential for political backlash, he had decided not to speak of it until the president did.

No one asked him any questions. The president leaned forward, looked down at his notes, then up again. "Doctor, I understand you also have people looking for that extremophile in its natural form."

"Yes, sir."

"How would you estimate their chances of success?"

Barnard had been anticipating this question, but he still wasn't sure how to answer it. The fact that the president and his people were not actually in the room did nothing to lessen Barnard's awareness of their inestimable power. It was like sitting next to explosives that might detonate at any moment without warning. In his whole life, the only comparable experience had been his reaction to combat in Vietnam, an intoxicating brew of fear, awe, and ecstasy. The adrenaline affected heart rate and respiration and, as he well knew, could bend judgment as well. *Always tempting to overpromise. Better to underpromise and overdeliver.* He also recalled Haight's words during their briefing: "a desperate thing." He thought, *Occupy the middle ground.*

"I would say their chances are good, sir."

It was as neutral as he could be without raising false hopes of success or leaving the impression that failure was preordained. O'Neil just nodded. Washinsky and Mason remained expressionless because, Barnard assumed, as nonscientists they placed little stock in what must have sounded something like science fiction to them. Nathan Rathor's eyebrows went up, wrinkling his forehead, and he frowned. The expression was visible only for a millisecond, but long enough to reveal itself as surprise, and that, in turn, surprised Barnard.

"I thought that those people in the cave were a pretty long shot," Rathor said.

Why? Barnard wondered. He had had no direct communication with Rathor about this. *But not yours to question why, old man. A cabinet officer has sources you can't even dream of.*

"They will face—*are* facing—many challenges, Mr. Secretary," Barnard agreed. He hesitated, struggling for some right way to say this, and then found the words. "I can tell you that if any team on earth could accomplish such a mission, it is this one."

Rathor looked as though he were about to ask another question, but then put his flat, cabinet officer face on again and said only, "I understand. That's all from me, Mr. President."

The president, though, was not quite finished. "I have two last questions, and then we will let you go. If your laboratory does come up with a drug that is effective against ACE, won't it take many months to produce enough vaccine? You have to grow it in eggs, don't you?"

"Vaccine you do, yes sir. An antibiotic is different. Once we understand its genetic code, we can produce essentially unlimited amounts relatively quickly. Something like a million doses in two weeks if we involve private-sector assets. Then the real problem would be further down the pipeline. In other words, how do we get the drug quickly to the millions who might need it by then?"

The president looked hugely relieved. "Doctor, I have to tell you, that's the first piece of good news I've heard in a week. Distribution is a problem we can handle. Now my second question: how many casualties are we talking about?"

"Worst case, Mr. President?"

"Of course. There's no other way to plan."

Barnard got up from behind his desk and walked to a whiteboard on the wall. The system's motion-sensitive telecom camera tracked him all the way. David Lathrop moved to stay out of the frame.

"Mr. President, our best information at this point is that ACE's contagion factor is faster than that of smallpox. Here's what that looks like."

With a red marking pen, Barnard drew a numeral:

1

"This scenario assumes that ACE has broken containment. The pathogen appears to reach contagion stage after three to five days. It's about seven to ten with smallpox, by the way—a significant difference between the two. Once contagious, that first person—the index case—will transmit the infection to about twelve people every day in your typical urban setting."

Beneath the 1, Barnard wrote

DAY THREE:
12

"Those twelve will become contagious within the same time period, and each of them will infect another twelve."

DAY SIX:
144

After that he stopped talking and just drew:

DAY NINE:
1,728

DAY TWELVE:
20,736

DAY FIFTEEN:
248,832

DAY EIGHTEEN:
3,257,437

Barnard stepped to one side of the board and waited. Absurdly, he worried for a moment about the dimple in his tie knot. Then that he might have forgotten to raise his zipper after his last trip to the bathroom. *Stress,* he thought. *Stay focused.*

No one spoke. No one in the Situation Room would until the president did. O'Neil stared at the whiteboard for a long time.

"You're telling me," said the president, "that if this thing breaks out, absent some countermeasure, we will have three million infected people in three weeks? And that nine out of ten of them could die?"

"No, sir."

"Then what *are* you telling me?"

"That it's not *if* ACE will break out, sir. It's *when.*"

The president's normally rich skin tone had turned to ashen gray. His mouth opened, closed. He put a hand on his forehead, let it drop. "What in God's name will we do with three million infected corpses?"

For that, Barnard had no answer. Apparently, neither did any of the others.

The screen went blank.

. . .

"The man of the hour," David Lathrop said, pushing off from the wall where he had been leaning, out of camera range, while the teleconference went on. Possibly excepting Lew Casey, Barnard was closer to David Lathrop than he was to any other person in government. Lathrop was younger, but they had much in common, including war. Barnard's had been Vietnam, Lathrop's the First Gulf War, special operations. After the war, Lathrop migrated to the CIA. He completed several tours as a field operative, moved up to running his own stable of agents, and finally came in to serve as CIA's senior liaison with BARDA.

Barnard heaved up from behind his desk and motioned for Lathrop to follow him. They went to the big, comfortable leather chairs where Barnard had sat with Hallie. Barnard stopped at his credenza to pour black coffee for both of them. He handed a mug to Lathrop, who spoke:

"Did you brief Rathor on the moonmilk mission?"

"No. I assumed you had," Barnard said. "But I wondered about it."

Lathrop studied his mug. "I didn't. He seemed familiar with it, though."

"The president must have involved him before the telecon," Barnard said.

"Probably so. Given his contribution to O'Neil's campaign, it wouldn't be politic for the president to keep him in the dark, would it?"

"Fifteen million, wasn't it?" Barnard mused.

"I heard more. And you know what? The same to Steeves. So I heard." Lathrop grinned at Barnard over his coffee mug. Harold Steeves had been O'Neil's Republican opponent in the last presidential election.

"Covering all bases."

"Wish I could cover bases like that. You ever meet him?" Lathrop kept his expression neutral.

"Rathor? Couple of times, official functions, nods and handshakes. He's not known for making nice." Barnard remembered mostly the small man's big head and scrawny neck.

"You hear stories. People calling him 'Rat-whore' and such." Lathrop chuckled, shook his head. "Washington."

"Well, he came from Big Pharma. Not the most popular folks," Barnard said.

Lathrop nodded. "He did bring some of those Big Pharma people into O'Neil's fold. That was probably more important than the money."

Barnard thought about it. "*As* important, maybe."

Lathrop laughed. "Point taken."

"O'Neil's people spun it pretty well, don't you think? 'Another of the president's open-armed attempts to reach across aisles and build bridges between business and government.' Or whatever they said."

"Sure. But we both know O'Neil just wanted to keep a close eye on the bobble-headed little bastard."

Lathrop leaned back in his chair, took in and let out a deep breath.

"I'm guessing you didn't come by just to swap tales about the pols, Late." His friend hated the name David, disliked Dave even more so. Since Phillips Exeter, people had called him Late, which was more than a little ironic because he never was late—was always early, in fact.

"We have a problem, Don."

"What is it?" Barnard tried to brace himself for yet another piece of bad news. But even so, he was not prepared for what he heard.

"Someone tried to send encrypted data out of BARDA."

"What?" Barnard shot forward in his seat. "What was it? How do you know that?"

"I can't answer the second question. As for the first, it was damned good encryption, so we don't know yet. Analysts are trying to break it down now."

"Do we know who sent it?"

"Not specifically. We just know it came out of BARDA."

"So it must have come from a computer here. That should be easy to track."

"That's the thing. It didn't come from a specific BARDA computer. It came directly from the organization's mainframe. Someone was able to get a torpedo into BARDA's central unit."

"You'd better explain that."

"BARDA and other ultrasecure sites use poison-pill comm configurations. The computers can only send to and receive from computers with similar configurations. Alien data, incoming or outgoing, is destroyed at the portal. That keeps unauthorized sources from receiving BARDA information, and also keeps outside sources from penetrating BARDA's systems. But it is possible—theoretically—to get around that by coding to wrap the data in a protective capsule. I'm speaking metaphorically here. It's data hidden inside other data, like explosive inside a torpedo casing. The information can then be received by an outside computer source and will survive while its self-destruct programming is deactivated."

"So we're talking about a security breach. Here at BARDA."

"Yes."

"You know, we had something like this happen over a year ago."

"Sure. Hallie Leland's case. You thought it was all crap. Based on the available facts, I was inclined to agree."

"Right."

"So maybe we were wrong. Have you ever considered that?"

Barnard started to retort, but stopped. "You don't mean to suggest that Hallie was actually selling secrets?"

Lathrop shook his head. "No. I believe, as you do, that somebody set her up, for reasons we don't yet understand. Set *us* up, too. And if that's the case, it's possible the person is still in place. Anyway, she's down in that cave."

"But you think the two incidents are connected."

"I suspect so, but I don't know. And I don't know how to know. But the important thing is to focus on what's happening now."

"Can we get NSA on this?" Barnard could not tolerate the thought of some spy in his labs. It was repulsive, like discovering a cockroach in his morning bowl of oatmeal.

"I would like to say yes. But NSA is brutally overtasked. Has been since 9/11. The Joint Chiefs are convinced this is some kind of bioterror attack and have all their critical assets pointed at AfPak."

"What do you suggest? For here at BARDA, I mean."

"Sometimes the best detection system is the human gut. Think about people. If something twitches when a name comes up, let me know. We can take it from there."

"Jesus, Late. I've got a hundred and fifty scientists and support people working here."

"I didn't say it would be easy. And there's something else. Something I haven't shared with higher-ups or anyone else until just now. Could be very important but needs to stay between us until—" Lathrop's phone vibrated. He pulled it from a vest pocket, looked, touched the screen. "Yes, Mr. Secretary. Yes, sir. I understand, sir. Right away. Yes, sir, I *do* understand that. I'm moving now. Yes, sir. Really, as in *now,* sir."

Lathrop stood up, pocketed the phone, gulped the last of his coffee, and hurried toward the door. "Secretary Mason," he said, by way of explanation.

"Late." Something important had been left unsaid, clipped by an order from Hunter Mason, and Barnard didn't like leaving loose ends. "Just a second."

But Lathrop was already at the door. He stopped, waved. "Gotta go, Don. The secretary is one man you do not *ever* want to keep waiting. I'll brief you on this other thing ASAP, F2F only." *Face to face*. Then he was out the door and Barnard heard him trotting down the hall, the brisk clicking of his steps like small bones cracking.

Barnard went to his desk and took out a yellow legal pad. On his computer he brought up his department's personnel roster. He wrote the first name on the list at the top of the pad:

Abelson, Leonard M. *Leo Abelson*. Very tall, played basketball for Rutgers, amazing hands. Dedicated scientist. Good man. Barnard moved to the next person on the list.

Twenty minutes later he opened his eyes and realized that he had dozed off while staring at the computer screen. He got up, walked around his desk, dropped to the floor, and fired off twenty push-ups. He stood up and slapped himself in the face, twice, hard, then sat down again. This was going to take a while, he knew, because the only way to find a mole was to dig deep.

SIXTEEN

HALLIE WENT DOWN FIRST. SHE WAS AN EXPERIENCED ROCK climber and had been on this wall before, though with standard vertical gear, seat harnesses and rappel racks attached to stout, eleven-millimeter static caving rope. This descent would be very different indeed.

She eased over the edge of the pit, facing toward the cave wall. She attached one foot to the rock, then the other, then both gloves. Five hundred feet of empty space yawned beneath her. If she fell, it would take six seconds to hit bottom, and those would be long seconds indeed unless a wall hit knocked her out. One good thing about such places in caves—the *only* good thing, really—was that she could not see the distant bottoms of pits such as this one. The darkness prevented her brain from lurching immediately into self-preservation mode, with all its tension and fear, which only made the climbing harder, even for one with her experience.

She peeled her right foot off, lowered it twelve inches, and touched it to the wall again. When her boot made contact, it felt as though the rock were opening and closing around it, so secure was the bond between boot and rock. She eased her left foot down beside the right. Same thing. Brought her two hands down, one at a time.

Hanging there without the security of a rope *was* unnerving, seeing bottom or no. A couple of years ago, she had free-soloed some rock climbs, including several challenging 5.12s, doing the routes without belayer or rope for protection, just to see how it felt. She had never been more than a hundred feet off the ground, but that was enough to kill her very dead if she came off. It had required every ounce of effort and concentration not to panic. Easily the most unpleasant experience on rock she had ever had. Some few climbers thrived on free soloing, Hallie knew, but the experience had taught her that she would never be one of them.

Now she did as she had learned to do climbing in the world of light, concentrating on the rock inches in front of her face, breathing deeply and slowly, and using the big muscles in her legs. Foot, foot. Hand, hand. She was about fifty feet down when Bowman called out, "How're you doing, Hallie?"

"Good! These things are unbelievable, thank God."

"Thank DARPA." He was being ironic, but she heard more relief in his voice than she'd expected, and that pleased her. "I'm going to start the others down. They'll be on different lines, so don't worry about rockfall."

The only tricky thing, she found, was peeling the gloves off the wall. If she didn't do it at just the right angle, they wouldn't let go. It was like peeling very sticky Velcro strips apart. After almost an hour, about halfway down, she stopped to catch her breath, hanging straight-armed from the glove attachments to let her skeleton take the weight and her muscles rest. At that moment Haight appeared fifteen feet to her left.

"Hey. I am just plain blown away. Can y'all imagine builderin' with these?"

"I don't think DARPA would be happy about that. But it occurred to me, too."

"Do y'all mind if I go on down?"

"My guest."

Hallie was a good climber and knew it, but she also knew truly artistic work when she saw it. Haight was as smooth as a great ballroom dancer, so effortless did he make the descent seem. It was *not* effortless, she knew, not by a long shot, but the very best could make it look as though it were.

Choosing caution over speed, Hallie took another half hour to cover the remaining 250 vertical feet. Finally, she stepped back onto the cave floor, moved away from the base of the cliff, and found a nice, waist-high boulder with a flat top to rest against. Haight, enthralled, was climbing back up. It was nice to have a few minutes alone here, away from the chatter and distractions of the team.

She said to the cave spirit, *"Chi Con Gui-Jao, es bueno estar con ustedes de nuevo."* It is good to be with you again. *"Rezo por tu bendición y la promesa de no causar daños."* I ask for your blessing and promise no harm. Then she sat and waited.

Fifteen minutes later, Cahner stepped down onto the cave floor. "Unbelievable." Panting but obviously pleased, he came to sit beside her. "It makes one wonder what other things they're doing at DARPA." He paused. "You are an amazing climber."

"Thank you. It helps that I started as a teenager and loved it right away. But for a *real* artist, you have to watch Ron."

"He's something. I caught glimpses of him while I was coming down."

"Hey, Al, does it seem to you like Rafael is taking a long time on the wall?"

"Yes, now that you make mention of it."

"Nothing to do but wait, I guess."

They talked for another ten minutes before Arguello and Bowman dropped down together. Bowman hopped off the wall, then helped Arguello.

When the two of them had joined the others, Haight asked, "How do we get the things off?"

Bowman held up his two open hands in front of his chest, fingers splayed out. "Watch." He touched the tips of his fingers and thumbs together. For a moment nothing happened; then the gloves appeared to inflate slightly. Bowman slipped them easily from his hands. "They neutralize each other's forces when aligned in a certain way, as I just demonstrated. Go on, try it."

It felt to Hallie like the loosening of a blood pressure cuff, and the gloves did slip off easily after that. She watched while Bowman brought his feet together, touching the inside surfaces of his overshoes to each other. They loosed just as the gloves had, and he removed them with a light pull. It made her think of Dorothy, clicking her heels in *The Wizard of Oz*.

"We need to keep moving," Bowman told them. "Hallie, what's the route from here?"

"This level chamber we're in now ends after a couple of hundred yards. There's an exit passage we named Frankenstein's Staircase because that's what it's like—a series of big shelves interrupted by vertical down-climbs. That runs for about a half mile. Then we hit Satan's Anus."

"It *looks* like Satan's Anus," said Arguello when they arrived.

He and the others were standing around a ragged-edged pool twenty feet in diameter through which black water swirled. On the pool's far side, blank cave walls rose straight up, barring any farther progress on the surface.

Bowman unwrapped a chocolate bar, broke off equal sections, and handed one to each of the others. After chewing a bite he looked around and said, "Anybody else feeling it?"

"For sure," Haight said. They two of them looked at the others.

"Yep," Hallie acknowledged.

"Indeed," Cahner said.

"Oh, yes," Arguello said.

Hallie knew what "it" was. A slowly but steadily increasing sense of—how to describe it?—"dread" was the best word she could think of. It was the caving analogue to what climbers called exposure, by which they meant a fear of falling that grew sharper and harder to ignore with every vertical foot climbed. She had felt it before in very big caves and was feeling it now, a gnawing anxiety that kept her looking over one shoulder or the other and intensified with every foot they down-climbed. It was annoying but not a serious hazard—as long as the thing stayed in its cage. Broken free, it could devour sanity in an instant.

"I always think it's best to talk about such things," Bowman said. "Helps defuse them."

"What exactly is happening?" Arguello asked.

"Remember back at BARDA we talked about the Rapture?" Hallie said. "This is how it starts. It's manageable now. But at some point it might not be. And it's different for every person, so you need to pay very close attention to how you're feeling, because once it hits, you go around the bend in two heartbeats and it's really hard to come back. The key is to understand what's going on before that happens."

"But what if one of us does feel it coming on?" Arguello asked. "What can be done?"

"The only thing that helps is going up. So you'd have to ascend on your own until you felt better and wait for the rest of us to pick you up on the way back out."

Arguello shuddered. "I do not know which would be worse," he said. "Losing the mind or spending days alone in here waiting."

"Hobson's choice," Hallie said, and could think of nothing worth adding. Nor, apparently, could the others. They stood around quietly after that, munching snacks, drinking from their poly bottles. After ten minutes, she spoke again:

"Let me brief you on the dive. We go in here. The entrance to the sump is like dropping down into a manhole for about twenty feet. Then the tunnel slopes at forty-five degrees, passing through the underwater face of that wall over there, drops to eighty feet, levels off, and continues straight for about two hundred feet. At that point, it makes a sharp turn to the right and narrows. If we were diving on conventional scuba, we'd have to doff our tanks and push them ahead of us. That's how we got through on my first trip, and it was not fun. But with these new rebreathers, we should be able to pass through."

"Wait a second. How narrow is *narrow*?" Arguello sounded worried.

"After the right turn, the tunnel shrinks to about five feet in diameter. Big enough to pass through with the packs—barely—but not big enough to turn around in. Any problems before the halfway point, you have to back your way out. I don't recommend it. It stays level like that for three hundred feet, then rises at an easy angle for about five hundred feet. That long, slow ascent takes care of any decompression obligation, so you won't want to hurry there. You'll surface in a place we named Grand Central Cavern."

"About the rebreathers." Bowman held up his own. "We briefed in Reynosa, but let's do a quick check again. They have heads-up displays for all critical functions. Self-activating, triggered by submersion. Basically all you have to do is breathe and swim."

"A couple of other things," Hallie said. "The silt in here is really bad. We don't have fins so we'll be pulling with our hands, which means the last to come through are going to have zero viz, or close to it. But I'll be going first and running a safety line, so you can maintain contact with that."

"Actually," said Bowman, "I'll be going through first and running out the line."

She gave him a look. "But I've been through here before."

"I know that. But I'm expendable and you're mission critical. We can't afford to lose you. If there's anything unexpected in the sump, it's best I find it first."

"Okay. You're right." She was annoyed, but could not argue with his logic.

"I've never seen rebreathers this small." Ron Haight was holding his up, turning it over, examining it like some exotic treasure. "Most of 'em are like big suitcases."

"They are. I mentioned that DARPA had a lot of things going. These are another. They're half the size of standard rebreathers."

"Do they use the same scrubbing system?"

"No. These use lithium trioxide to scrub the carbon dioxide from our recycled breathing gas."

Cahner whistled. "Volatile stuff. Explodes if it gets wet."

"But the best carbon dioxide scrubber there is, ounce for ounce."

"I am just curious about one thing," Arguello said. "How much does such a device cost?"

Bowman chuckled. "You don't want to know."

The unit was like no rebreather Hallie had seen or used. It had a full-face mask like those worn by commercial divers. The mask was connected by a short, flexible hose to a chest pack held in place by a webbing harness. The chest pack was about the size of an old Yellow Pages phone book and, with its lemon-colored plastic shell, looked something like one.

"Let's get through this quickly." Any wait longer than thirty seconds had Bowman sounding impatient. "These units do not have voice comm, so we won't be able to talk to each other underwater. The packs' weight should keep us negatively buoyant, so you won't be pinned to the sump's ceiling. I'll dive first. Hallie next. Then Rafael, Al, and, Ron, you will be the sweep diver. Questions?"

Bowman looked around, his helmet light beam swinging from chest to chest. No one spoke. There was only the wind blowing through the cave, and the stream flowing, untold volumes of water folding and rolling down into the rocky throat, and the immense weight of darkness and depth pressing down on them.

Bowman took off his pack and helmet. He put his rebreather face unit on, tightened the black rubber straps behind his head, and snugged the chest pack tight. He grunted back into his pack and replaced his helmet. He took several test breaths, sat on the edge of the pool, and lowered himself carefully down into the water. He turned to face the rock, held the lip momentarily, and then disappeared beneath the surface. His helmet lights grew fainter, like candle flames slowing dying, and then they were gone.

Watching the lights fade, Hallie felt afraid. Not for herself. She had dived many such sumps—the Boneyard being a recent example—and they did not frighten her. But, somewhat to her surprise, the thought of losing Bowman so soon did—more than it should have, her rational side muttered. Then again, what did "should" mean? What needed to pass before she *should* feel that kind of fear for Bowman? Wrestling with such thoughts, she waited for the appointed five minutes to pass, and they passed very slowly indeed. She just wanted to get into the water and have this over with.

After donning her gear, she entered as Bowman had done. The water was cold—about sixty-five to seventy degrees Fahrenheit, she estimated—but not painfully so. They would not be submerged long enough to require wet suits. She lowered herself carefully beneath the surface, took a half dozen test breaths, and then let go of the rock. She sank slowly and her boots touched the sump's silty bottom. She waited, double-checking the rebreather and getting her own respiration under control. Across the top of the glass faceplate, alphanumeric data glowed softly green:

DT	PPO	DIL	DPT	MXD	DIR	BATT	DECO
0.0	1.4	100	13	13	313	100	OK

DT was how much dive time had elapsed. Three hours was the rebreather's maximum. Every minute of use would be depleting that from now on. PPO stood for partial pressure oxygen, the percentage of oxygen in her breathing gas. Anything over 1.8 could induce fatal toxicity. DIL was the amount remaining of diluent, the exotic chemical mix that scrubbed carbon dioxide from the air she breathed. DPT was her current depth. MXD was the maximum depth achieved on the dive. DIR was her compass heading, 313 degrees, or northwest, and BATT showed that the unit's batteries were still at 100 percent capacity. DECO reported any danger of incurring decompression sickness, "the bends." As long as it stayed green, she was good.

She dropped down the twenty-foot manhole, came to rest floating just above the silty bottom, and began pulling herself along. Each helmet had three lights. One was turned on for dry passages. For diving, they used all three. Hers bored luminous tunnels into the milky water. Viz was only about five feet. She knew Bowman would have tried to be very careful, but there was no way to avoid stirring up some silt. The cloudy water scattered her light beams so that it was like driving into thick fog at night. She kept going until the descending passage leveled off. There Bowman had tied off one end of the line from his caving reel to a projection in the rock, and she spotted it on the bottom of the sump right away.

As always, the hardest part had been getting started, and now she was relaxing into the dive. Without fins, she had to pull herself hand over hand along rocks on the sump's floor, which began to incline downward again. No matter how carefully she moved, she stirred up more silt. Bowman had stirred up surprisingly little. The rebreather emitted no bubbles, made only a soft sighing sound as she inhaled and exhaled. She descended gradually, clearing her ears to equalize the pressure every two or three breaths.

She flicked her gaze upward and the HUD was there:

DT	PPO	DIL	DPT	MXD	DIR	BATT	DECO
10:44	1.4	76	63	63	303	88	OK

Arriving at the bend in the tunnel, Hallie knew she was about halfway through. The unstable weight of the big pack on her back and the near-zero visibility made the going awkward, but at least there were no squeezes tight enough to require doffing the pack. The one thing that gave her pause was the awareness that she was doing this dive on a system without redundancy. That violated the cardinal rule of cave diving, which stated that every one of a diver's systems should be triply redundant: lights, reels, cutting tools, computers, air, regulators, everything. And that was just for ordinary cave diving. This was even more extreme.

Finally, the sump began to angle upward. She glanced at her HUD:

DT 18:27	PPO 1.4	DIL 69	DPT 82	MXD 87	DIR 303	BATT 79	DECO OK

She ascended slowly, giving her body plenty of time to off-gas accumulated nitrogen, keeping the decompression light green. Eventually she was able to stand on the gently sloping bottom. Breaking the surface, she turned 360 degrees, orienting herself. It was as she remembered. She was in the middle of a subterranean lake whose smooth surface stretched like black satin far beyond the reach of her lights. Overhead, the cave ceiling rose in a curving dome almost one hundred feet high. The rock here, with heavy iron content, contained bright red strata sandwiched between thicker striations of whitish lime, giving the appearance of a giant layer cake.

Bowman stood at the edge of the sump, waiting. She tapped a fist on top of her head, the diver's signal for "All okay," and slogged toward him, the water growing shallower as the bottom angled up. The sump wall here was vertical and two feet high, almost like being in a swimming pool. She took off her pack, shoved it as far as she could up to Bowman. He set it aside, bent over, and extended both hands. Hallie braced her boots on the rocky face of the sump and grasped his wrists. Bowman popped her out of the water like an angler landing a perch, grabbed her by the waist, and set her on her feet on the cave floor.

When she pulled off the full-face mask, he put his hands on her shoulders. Keeping his light on her chest, he peered straight into her eyes and held his gaze there and, crazy though it seemed, one mile deep in a supercave, on a mission that could save millions of people from horrible deaths—or not, if they failed—Hallie decided he was going to kiss her.

SEVENTEEN

AND, AS CRAZY AS IT SEEMED, SHE REALIZED THAT IT WOULD not be unwelcome. Yes, there was a developing crisis on the surface. Yes, they were on a mission more important than anything she'd ever done. And yes, she and Bowman had known each other for only just over a single day. But if life had taught her anything, it was that messages from her gut could be trusted. More, actually: *should never be ignored*. Her aborted time at BARDA had been a painful object lesson. Even more of one had been her father's early death. It was not that she and he had not had wonderful times together. They had, too many to count, and that was really the sharp end of this death. The future should have held decades more times like that. Except there was no "should" in time's passage or acts of nature. The only things "should" applied to were people, to her, to decisions she could make, actions she could take. It did not require a second lesson like the loss of her father to drive that one home. And last of all, wrapping around everything else, was this: things are different in caves. As the old *curandero* had hinted and as she knew, caves were amplifiers, like great mountains. Mere dislike could quickly curdle into rage. And affection—well, that could turn to something else, too.

But Hallie had learned to recognize the look in a man's eyes before he kissed her for the first time. Some looked hungry, some fearful, others worshipful, and suddenly Bowman didn't look like any of those. Instead, he seemed serious, focused, clinical almost. Then she understood. He was checking for any signs of vertigo or pupillary dilation. Finally he smiled, let his hands drop, and took a step back.

"You look fine. How'd it go?"

She cocked her head, squinted at him. Had he been toying with her? Like winking back at BARDA? She couldn't tell. "No problems. The HUD mask took a little getting used to, but otherwise, okay. How about you?"

He seemed surprised by the question, as though caught off guard by the fact that someone might be caring about *his* welfare.

"Same. I had some time on these rebreathers. It's not your typical cave dive, though. The situational awareness is something you can't simulate."

"You mean the fact that we might as well be on the far side of the moon."

"Right."

"I think the only one we have to be concerned about is Rafael."

At the word "we" Hallie saw him glance at her, but he did not appear to take it as any kind of challenge. "I agree."

"He's just older and doesn't have as much time underground as we do."

"Whose idea was it to bring him?"

"Mostly David Lathrop's. There was concern at his agency about relations with Mexico. Arguello covers that, and the native population as well."

"You have to admire his grit."

That conversation ended, and then it was her turn to look into *his* eyes, and it wasn't for vertigo or disorientation.

"How was I supposed to take that wink back at BARDA, Mr. Bowman?"

"*Doctor* Bowman to you, ma'am." He was smiling. *Great teeth,* Hallie thought. When she was growing up, her mother had told her, countless times, *Pay attention to a man's teeth because they'll tell you a lot about him. You want good breeding teeth when the time comes.* Her mother, the horsewoman.

He appeared to consider her question very seriously. "Well, maybe it was gratitude. I thought we were finished. But then you pulled that group together—a very impressive thing to see."

"Maybe?" She watched his eyes and once again thought of ice in great mountains: Alaska, the Alps and Andes, ancient ice of glaciers and crevasses, night-blue ice only the passage of centuries could create, too deep and cold for any life. But now, so much closer, she saw something that had escaped her before—tiny specks of gold glinting in the blue ice. Or was it a trick of light, reflecting off some odd cave crystal? She moved her head slightly, changing the angle, but those gold flecks stayed.

"Why are you looking at me like that?" he asked.

Why indeed? "I thought there might be something in your eye."

"My eyes feel fine."

"And they look fine." What had they been talking about? *Oh yes.* "So it was about gratitude for some team building."

"I *was* very grateful. We all were."

"Anything else, Dr. Bowman?"

A half smile, the cool blue eyes thawing. "You're a beautiful woman, Hallie."

You're a beautiful woman. She had encountered that approach before, the "open and honest," feigned-neutral-innocence posture. But there had always been something neither open nor honest lurking just below the surface, a dark craving. Bowman's words did not strike her that way. It was her turn to toy.

"But, Dr. Bowman, I might have a husband."

"Nope. You don't." His smile was too satisfied for her liking.

"How would you know?"

"Did you forget what Lathrop said about us?"

Unmarried, live alone, no significant others, and have no children. "I had forgotten that. It works both ways, doesn't it?"

He understood. "Sure does."

Without thinking, she said, "That surprises me. About you, I mean."

Without hesitating, he said, "Don't misunderstand this. But it doesn't surprise me. About you."

It felt like something in what he had just said should offend her, but she wasn't sure what. "Why not?"

"You're not the most approachable woman I've ever met, Hallie. I would imagine not many men have the confidence to storm those walls."

Storm those walls. She wasn't offended. It was hard to be offended by the truth.

She shrugged. "Not many men do. Oh, they try, but—too tall, too assertive, too many degrees, too . . ." She looked for the right word.

"Detached?"

She nodded. But Hallie did not feel detached just then, and she knew her eyes showed it.

"Some might put all those in the plus column."

She waited, wanting to see what would happen, what he sensed. Many men's brains, she had found, dropped into their crotches at moments like this. But for her it was as though a sphere of the thinnest crystal floated between them. A crude movement would shatter it, and such a thing, once lost, could not be retrieved.

Bowman made no move to kiss or grope. He just stood there, his head cocked slightly to one side, a hint of smile flickering on his face. He looked at her from beneath his eyebrows. She realized he was waiting to see what *she* was going to do.

She pulled off her helmet and, standing on tiptoe, which she rarely had to do for this purpose, kissed him lightly on the cheek. He tasted of salt and mineral-tinged cave water. After she kissed him there, she stepped back, smiling like an imp, waiting to see what would happen. He picked up her hand and kissed her fingertips.

She watched him do that, then stood there looking into his eyes. He looked straight back, and for just an instant she saw a flash of pain; then it was gone, his eyes softening again.

She spoke first. "I guess that wasn't very professional."

"I think it was—" Distracted by something, he looked away from her. "Light coming."

"God*damn,*" she said.

"Amen."

They watched Arguello rise dripping from the sump. He handed his pack up to Hallie, and Bowman hoisted him onto the cave floor with not much more difficulty than he had exhibited in lifting her. Shivering, pale, Arguello took off his rebreather.

"Piece of p-pie." His voice shook.

"Piece of *cake*." She patted him on the shoulder.

Arguello grimaced. "Yes. Cake. Of course. I knew that."

"No problems, then?" Bowman was watching Arguello as he had watched Hallie.

"Not really. I have dived, of course, but not much in visibility so low, and once I almost lost the guideline. But I got him back quickly." Arguello's English was excellent, but Hallie understood that the stress of the dive was scrambling his grammar. "It was colder than I had thought it might be." Arguello, whippet-thin, had not an ounce of extra body fat.

"Maybe I'll brew up some hot tea for everybody," Bowman said. "We could all use a bracer."

"Let me do that. You pay attention to the divers." Hallie went to a flat-topped rock nearby, set up one of the little mountaineering stoves they were carrying, and began heating water in an aluminum pot. In the cave, the small stove's hissing formed a steady high note over the wind and the flowing water's bass lines. The burner's circle of flame under the pot cast a sapphire glow.

Before the water boiled, Al Cahner surfaced in the pool, splashed around, and waded to the edge. Arguello took his pack and Bowman reached down to lift him out. They locked hands and Bowman heaved, and Hallie was surprised to hear him grunt with the effort.

"You're heavier than you look," he said to Cahner.

For a second, Cahner just stared. Then, pulling off his rebreather unit, he smiled and said, "Maybe I absorbed some water. Like a sponge?" Bowman chuckled and Cahner continued: "Well, that was really something. I mean, I have done some serious scuba diving, but *that,* my friends, was . . . extraordinary."

"Did your rebreather work okay?" Bowman asked.

"Oh, yes, fine. I loved the heads-up display. Never used one like that before."

"Tea's almost ready," Hallie called.

"In my pack you'll find a bit of medicinal," Bowman said, still standing with Cahner. "I'd say we could all do with a tot. It's in a red flask."

She went to his pack, opened it, and found the flask. Back at the boulder table, she poured a good dollop of liquor into each metal mug of tea, stirred in sugar and a little powdered lemonade, and carried three over to the men, who were standing beside the sump awaiting Haight's arrival.

"Here you go. Service with a smile."

"*Thank* you." Cahner blew on the hot liquid, sipped gingerly, his eyes going wide. "Whooo. Rum."

Arguello took a mug, but Bowman declined the third. "Why don't you have that one?" he told Hallie.

"There's more back there."

"He should have been here by now." Bowman was watching the surface of the lake.

"Haight? No worries about him. He's probably the most experienced cave diver among us." But she understood that Bowman had refused the rum-laced tea in case he might have to dive again. She went ahead and sampled the spiked tea herself. It exploded in her mouth, seared her tongue, and burned all the way down to her stomach. Maybe the best drink she had ever tasted.

"Whew. That's *some* rum."

"One hundred eighty proof," Bowman said. "Real Navy grog."

"If I'd known that, I'd have been a bit lighter with the pours."

"It's absolutely bracing." Cahner, sipping gingerly. "Just what the doctor ordered."

Bowman was looking at his watch. "By my reckoning, he's almost ten minutes overdue."

"Bowman, really, he's . . ." Her reassurance faded. In fact, she, too, was becoming concerned about Haight.

"I know his experience. But it makes his absence more troubling."

That, she had to admit, was true. Still, it had been a relatively straightforward dive, if you could ever say that about a cave dive. Tight passage and poor visibility, sure, but Haight would have dealt with worse many times.

Bowman picked up his rebreather. "I'm going back. I want all of you to stay here. If I don't return, you are not to come looking for me. Hallie will become the mission leader."

"Bowman." Hallie stepped forward. "I'm coming. You should have a buddy."

"Not in a cave rescue. Or recovery. Protocol for those is solo. Two divers doubles the likelihood of problems. You know that."

She did. He was right, and she backed off.

"Is everyone clear?" Bowman's voice was sharper.

Each of them voiced acknowledgment. But Arguello held up a hand. "I understand the mission-critical aspect of what you just described. But I have an unpleasant question. If you do not return, it will presumably be because you have drowned in the tunnel. If that is the case, how will we make the return passage?"

"You will have to pull me out. Ron, too, if it comes to that. Clear?"

They acknowledged the instruction. Bowman geared up and got into the water. They watched him sink beneath the surface, his helmet lights dimming and disappearing quickly as he retraced the route. Hallie felt part of her heart sinking as well.

They sat on nearby rocks and turned off their lights to conserve batteries.

Before long, Al Cahner spoke, his voice tense: "I hope to God that young man is all right. He's a bit rough around the edges, but really quite likable."

"Haight's dived some of the toughest caves in the country," Hallie pointed out. "My guess is he's just taking his time, having fun with a new toy, his rebreather."

No one spoke for a while. Hallie took a Snickers bar from a pocket of her caving suit, unwrapped it, and broke it into three pieces. Without turning on her light, she stood and walked to where Arguello was sitting. She moved lightly, the sound of wind and flowing water covering her footsteps.

"Have some chocolate, Rafael."

"Jesus." Arguello, startled, jumped off his rock seat. "Where did you come from?"

She moved on to Cahner, handed him a piece, and returned to her own place.

"How did you do that?" Arguello asked the question through a mouthful of Snickers.

"I learned it from other cavers a long time ago. You should, too. Before you turn off your light, make a mental snapshot of your surroundings. It's hard at first, but gets to be second nature after a while. You'd be amazed at how much detail you can retain with practice."

"I will try to learn how to do that myself."

"It's a necessary skill down here," Cahner said.

Then they were quiet. Hallie listened to the sound of air moving through the cave, and to flowing water, and she felt the cave enveloping them. Most people thought caves were dead and silent places, she knew, but they were rarely silent and never dead. Life thrived in every cave, often weird life, it was true, but weirdness was really in the eye of the beholder.

And then, almost as if he had been reading her mind, Arguello spoke:

"I was telling you earlier that many native peoples believe caves are alive."

"Tell me—tell *us*—more," Cahner said.

"I am pleased by your interest. Many scientists are quick to dismiss such things."

"These people and their beliefs have survived for thousands of years. That says something," Cahner pointed out.

"Indeed. So, the Cuicatecs say that caves breathe, which we know they do. They have circulatory systems, which is also true. Ours have blood in them; caves' systems have mineral-rich water."

Arguello paused to chew a bit of candy bar, then continued: "There's more. According to Cuicatec beliefs, caves eat and excrete—two more of science's criteria for classifying something as a living organism."

"I'm not sure I get those," Cahner said.

"Think of the earth as a big apple and a cave as a worm eating tunnels through it. And caves do have excretory systems—the rivers that flush waste from them. And they can heal themselves when injured."

Cahner nodded. "All true, when you really think about it."

Hallie had a question of her own. "So those are all the physical characteristics, Rafael. What about the other? The spirit? The thing they call Chi Con Gui-Jao."

"The Cuicatecs believe that the first people were born out of this cave into the light. This cave and a few others. As we saw, they made sacrifices to appease the spirits that live here. For many centuries, also, they buried their dead here, because they felt it brought them closer to the gods who inhabit the cave."

"You said *gods,* plural," Hallie noted. "So it's not just Chi Con Gui-Jao?"

"Oh, no. There are others. Chi Con is like Zeus in the other myths, the god of all gods. But many others exist, some good, some bad. For the ancients who inhabited this region, the cave was like our heaven—but also like our hell."

"So you had demons and angels all living down here together?"

"That is right. In perfect balance. And only the *curanderos* could summon them. But not every *curandero* could summon every god."

"You lost me," Cahner said.

"Like our white magic and black magic. Some *curanderos* could invoke beneficent gods to heal the sick, ensure good crops, bless a marriage. Others could bring up the, as we would say, demons. To curse enemies, defeat invaders, acquire power."

Hallie had another question. "How were *curanderos* chosen?"

"Anyone who wished to follow the path of *curandero* first underwent a trial. Only those who passed could go on."

"What was the trial?" Hallie asked.

"The aspirant was brought deep into a cave by the oldest *curanderos*. He was left alone. Finding his way out proved that he was chosen. Failing to do so proved he was not."

"How did the *curanderos* get in and out? With torches, like you told us about the sacrifices?"

"They needed no torches," Arguello said.

Hallie decided to let that pass for the moment. "So they went back in and brought him out after a certain time?"

"Oh, no. Those who failed remained in the cave forever. That was the trial."

"Come on, Rafael," Cahner said. "If they really did that, there wouldn't have been any *curanderos*. Nobody could get out of a cave like this without light."

"The ancient records abound with accounts of those who did exactly that," Arguello said.

"Sure, but our ancient myths are full of stories about beings who could fly and throw lightning bolts and command the oceans. These things are myths, not to be taken literally."

"The accounts I speak of are not myths, my friend. They are true statements."

Cahner chuckled. "But how could you *know* that, Rafael? You're talking about things that supposedly happened, what, hundreds or even thousands of years ago."

"That's true. But they also happen today." No one spoke for a long moment. Then Arguello said, "They happen, my friends. Believe me. I have *seen* it."

Hallie remembered Lathrop saying that Arguello had undergone shamanic training himself. She and Cahner spoke at the same time, both with the same words:

"What are you—"

Before they could finish, they heard Bowman break the water's surface, back from his rescue dive. All three reached for their light switches.

At first, it appeared that Bowman was alone. But then he placed one arm on the rocky edge of the flooded tunnel, heaved with the other, and Ron Haight came into sight. The blond head flopped loosely, grotesquely, to one side. The faceplate of his diving mask was shattered. Through it, Hallie could see his dull, unfocused brown eyes.

The presence of death tripped a very deep switch in her brain. Later there would be time to cry, but now she needed to act. She, Cahner, and Arguello grabbed the body, hauled it out of the water, and laid it facedown on the cave floor. Hallie ripped off the dive mask, rolled Haight onto his side, cleared his airway with two fingers, then put him on his back and tilted his head to begin CPR.

She breathed and Cahner did chest compressions. Arguello stood to one side, horrified.

Bowman joined her on the body's other side and they performed CPR as a team, taking turns. After ten minutes, Bowman sat back on his heels. "Let's call it. He's not coming back."

Cahner stood up. Hallie stayed on her knees, light-headed and dizzy from the hyperventilating. Through the mental haze she looked at Haight's face, trying to imagine how this could have happened. And then, suddenly, Haight groaned.

"Madre de Dios!" Arguello and Cahner jumped. Hallie and Bowman did not.

"Residual air in his lungs," she said. "The muscles loosen up before they go into rigor, and it escapes." She turned to Bowman. "What happened?"

"I found him about twenty feet beyond where the tunnel makes that sharp right-hand turn."

Arguello breathed a soft prayer in Spanish and did something with his hands over Haight's body. To Hallie it looked like a stage magician's movements, but Arguello was dead serious. He asked, "Where is his pack?"

"I cut it off and left it in the tunnel," Bowman said. "It would have made recovering him much harder."

Arguello moved off to one side and stood there looking at Haight. Hallie saw tears on his cheeks. She went to him and touched him on the shoulder. He put his hand on hers and let out a long breath.

"Look here." Bowman held up the rebreather's shattered faceplate. "That's what killed him. The faceplate cracked, flooded, and drowned him."

"If he had been using standard scuba gear, it would not have happened," said Cahner. "He would have had a regulator mouthpiece in place. Even without the mask, he could have kept going. Visibility was almost zero anyway."

"How did he break his mask?" Arguello asked.

"I don't know." Bowman, still trying to understand, was looking at Cahner, his light making a bright circle on the older man's chest. "The dive plan called for him to come in after you. Did that happen?"

Cahner took a moment before answering, then said, "I suppose so. I went in first, like you instructed. I pulled myself along and just kept going."

"So you didn't see Haight enter the water?"

"No, I was already in, as I just said."

"Were you aware of him behind you? Did he touch your foot or leg to let you know he was there?"

"No, he didn't." Cahner hesitated, considering. "He was probably keeping distance between us, in case there was a cave-in."

Bowman nodded, turned his gaze back toward the body.

"What do you think, Hallie? You've been involved in lots of cave rescues. And recoveries."

She had been sorting scenarios all the while. "I can think of only three possibilities. One is that the faceplate fractured spontaneously. Rare, but it does happen. Two is that in one of the tunnel's wider sections there was rockfall that hit the mask and broke it. Three is that he ran into a sharp outcrop and broke it."

"Ranked by probability?" Bowman asked.

"Collision with rock most likely, rockfall second, defect fracture third."

"I agree. A defect is very unlikely. These things are all mil-spec quality, meaning they went through even more rigorous testing than civilian dive equipment."

"This is awful." There was horror in Cahner's voice, but he was under control. "He was such a good young man. I was getting ready to go in and he could see that I was . . . tense . . . and he double-checked my rebreather and helped me calm down."

Arguello could not seem to stop staring at Haight's body. He stood there, as if mesmerized, and Hallie saw that he had started to tremble. It could have been from the cold, or fear, or both. Bowman saw it, too.

"Al, why don't you two get that stove going and brew us up some tea," Bowman said, nodding toward the area they had used as a kitchen earlier. "I think we could all use another strong one. Hallie and I will join you shortly."

"Good idea," said Cahner. He turned to Arguello and gently took him by the elbow. "Come along. You can help me do it."

When they were out of hearing, Bowman put his light on Hallie's chest.

"Any thoughts?"

"Nothing other than what I already said."

"It would have taken a sharp impact on a pointed object to break this faceplate." Bowman held up Haight's rebreather. "Tempered four-millimeter glass. It's what commercial divers use."

"What are you getting at?"

"I don't think Haight was the kind of diver to go through a tunnel like that in a hurry."

Hallie shook her head briskly. "I don't agree."

"Why not?"

"I liked him very much, don't misunderstand. But he struck me as young, impatient, and impulsive. I can easily see him trying to go too fast, especially since he was the sweep diver. He wouldn't want the rest of us to think he was slow or inept. Ego could have kicked in."

"Did you see or feel any projections that could have broken glass like that?"

"No, but that doesn't mean anything with such bad viz. And as for feeling something, you know we would have come in contact with only a tiny percentage of the tunnel's overall inside surface. There could have been a thousand sharp projections and we'd never know it."

After a while, Bowman nodded. "I think you're right."

"Tea is ready, my friends," Arguello called from the kitchen.

"Haight was fit and strong. He could have been pulling himself along pretty fast," Hallie said.

"True enough."

She waited for Bowman to go on, but he did not. She had been looking at Haight's body just then, but shifted her gaze to Bowman. Her light lit up his chest and showed his face in peripheral glow. To her surprise, there were tears in his eyes.

The big man made no effort to wipe them away or hide them. Hallie was not sure what to say. She felt very bad for Bowman just then. He was the leader, and a good young man had just died on his watch, and that had to hurt terribly. She wanted to reach out and touch him, hug him even, but something stopped her. Her own eyes filled with tears, and her chest felt stuffed.

"We should go back with the others now." Bowman's voice was rough with emotion.

"You go ahead. I'll be along. I just want a few moments with him."

She knelt beside Haight's body. She had grown to like him in the short time they'd known each other; there had been something brotherly about him. She had enjoyed listening to his thick, drawly accent and jokes and had admired his skill on that huge wall they'd descended.

She picked up his hands, one after the other. They felt cold and dead and much too heavy. She turned them over, focusing her helmet light on one palm and then the other, but there was no bruising, no cuts or other signs of struggle there. She examined the rebreather unit on his chest, but it showed no evidence of damage.

She was not unaccustomed to handling dead bodies, given the recoveries she had helped with. Turning Haight's head gently, she examined his eyes. Wide open and staring, they showed no injury. She ran her fingers down his face, closing the eyes. His skin was like cold white wax, and his lips were a livid blue going to gray. There was no sign of struggle or trauma there, either, no cuts or bruises.

In death he looked even younger than he had alive, and tears suddenly filled Hallie's eyes again as she thought of all the years Ron Haight should have had left, the women he would not love, children he would not father, discoveries he would not make. For an instant she hated the cave, but then it passed. The cave was just a cave, a force of nature like mountains and forests, neither benign nor malign but simply there—deadly, to be sure, but indifferent. Then Arguello's words came back to her and she thought, *Or is it?*

Hallie picked up Haight's rebreather, wanting to examine the cracked faceplate, and as she did so a shard of rock fell out and landed on his chest. They had not seen it before. There was the answer, then. It was part of the rock that had shattered his mask. He must have run into it with considerable force to knock a piece of it loose. Her theory had been correct, apparently. Haight, though a veteran cave diver, had made one of the countless mistakes that can get you killed in an environment with zero tolerance for error.

Hallie set the mask down beside Haight. *We ought to cover him with something. It's not right just to leave him here like this.* She stood, meaning to get something out of one of their packs, and bumped into Bowman, who had returned and had been standing behind her. She had not heard him approach. He had a green plastic groundsheet, and together they covered Haight's body, pinning the edges of the sheet down with rocks.

"I'd like to give him a decent burial," Bowman said, "but we can't afford the time. We're behind already."

She took one of Bowman's hands. It felt solid and rough and surprisingly warm. "It wasn't your fault."

He looked straight at her. His fingers closed around hers. She liked how that felt. A little shock sparked in her chest, a windy feeling, something she hadn't experienced for a long time. *Not since Redhorse,* she thought.

"I know," Bowman said. "But it doesn't matter, really."

That, she had to admit, was true. She held his hand tighter.

The cave made its low, unceasing moan, and from a great distance came the crash of vast rock breaking and smashing.

EIGHTEEN

NATHAN RATHOR, A SMALL MAN WHO HAD NEVER BEEN physically strong and who had grown up in a family with servants, disliked doing things for himself. Some tasks, however, could not be delegated. Thus, after the last Sit Room teleconference with Donald Barnard, Rathor had sat in front of his restricted, eyes-only computer for the better part of an hour. Not much caught Nathan Rathor off guard, but Barnard's comment that the team down in Mexico had a good chance of succeeding with its mission had. Knowing little about caves, and less about the team itself, Rathor had assumed it was the longest of long shots. But Barnard obviously knew something he did not—and that was unacceptable. The thing was, though, that Rathor could not delegate any of his sycophantic undersecretaries or special assistants to do this. Only he could tackle this job.

Rathor had told his staff to get dossiers on all the people on the team heading down into that cave. Thick files had come back quickly on every one of them except the security man—Bowman, if that was his real name—about whom not even Rathor's best people had been able to find anything. Bowman aside, the more he learned about those people, the more concerned Rathor became. He was not stupid by any means, and he could see what this unique assemblage might be capable of.

If those people came back with some of that exotic extremophile, and if BARDA's people really could fabricate new antibiotics, Barnard, not Rathor, would be the hero of the day. It would be insulting, but far from the worst possible thing that could come out of this, as Rathor well knew. The worst possible thing would be . . . well, better not to even think about it, given all the planning and money and painstaking preparation he and certain associates had put into this project. Not to mention the level of risk they were all tolerating. Plans, money, groundwork—all those were really only the body of the machine. Risk was the motor that made it run. When he was still quite young, Rathor had experienced the epiphany that avoiding risk meant consignment to the dustbin of life. As he grew older, he understood the epiphany's corollary: that rules were for sporty games and fools. The competitions of life were deadly earnest, and in those, the greatest risk of all was losing.

As a cabinet-level official, Rathor had access to the government's most sophisticated technology. Well, not its *most* sophisticated stuff—that was reserved for the secretaries of defense and state, and he knew it, and it infuriated him. But the things he did have access to still amazed him.

One of them that he had greatly enjoyed was the NSA's version of Google Earth. Actually, Google had replicated the NSA program from cobbled-together bits and pieces of information. Google's version never worried the spooks, whose software was about three generations ahead, and who had access to satellite data the lefty geeks at Google could only dream about. Even Rathor's stepped-down version of the program could let him see, on a clear day, the license plate on a New York City yellow cab.

If people only knew.

Rathor often played with the observation tool. The NSA net collected images not only from orbiting satellites but from countless terrestrial cameras as well. Many were visible to the public—cameras that caught people running red lights and committing burglaries, cameras that monitored prisons and hospitals and government proceedings, on and on. Millions of cameras. People knew about all those and, as sheep always do, had accepted the change in their surroundings without a bleat of protest. Well, maybe a bleat here and there, but nothing the government couldn't handle.

People did *not* know about countless other cameras, for two reasons. One was that their existence came from a top secret DARPA project called DarkEye. The secrecy would be breached eventually, of course—all such veils were, sooner or later—but by the time that happened, those who counted would have already moved on to the next generation. The other reason was that people could not see this network of cameras. They weren't even really cameras. They were energy-transmitting nanobots that could be aggregated into microscopic, crystal-like clusters. These recorded—and transmitted—energy, which could be converted into viewable images. They were easy to place, self-powering, and virtually invulnerable.

Ground and low-elevation images from the nanocams were refreshed every three seconds. With a little canvassing, Rathor could, if he got lucky, look through windows at women in various stages of undress and, if he got even luckier, doing remarkable things to themselves with little machines or big men. In some cases he didn't even have to look through windows. Pulling images from nanocams implanted in cellphones and ceilings put him right in the rooms with the women. Of course, he could—and did—afford beautiful women who performed unbelievable acts in the flesh. But there was something about penetrating the private space of others that excited him, and so he did it.

Given all this, it should have been easy to pull up images of this thing called Cueva de Luz, but he could not. He was able to isolate images of the surrounding region with enough resolution to show individual leaves on trees. But as soon as he moved to within a quarter mile of the cave entrance, the screen broke up into grainy distortion patterns, like gravel tossed onto ice. He tried every method he knew to get real-time images of this cave, with no success. Rathor's temper was never far below the boiling point, and it was hard not to rip the keyboard loose from its cable and smash it against a wall.

He switched over to Google Images and found some stills of the entrance, distant but recognizable. It was immense. *You could drive a train through that,* he thought. *Two trains.* He zoomed in, hoping to get a look inside the cave, but he could get no farther. He saw the dim outlines of huge rocks and, in the center of the screen, blackness that must have been the passage leading down into the cave. It was only a picture, but something about it made him shiver.

You could not pay me enough to go in there.

Later that evening, instead of being taken straight to his mansion in Vienna, Virginia, Rathor dismissed his driver, telling the man he would be working late and would spend the night in his residential suite there at HHS. He did retire to his suite shortly after that, but rather than working, he spent a few hours drinking Beefeater martinis and enjoying YouPorn on a secure laptop computer. Shortly after one in the morning, Rathor changed into casual clothes: khakis, plaid shirt, golf jacket, walking shoes. He left his personal and government cellphones on the dresser in his suite's bedroom, called for his own car, and drove to the Lincoln Memorial. At this hour, the entire mall area, including the Great Emancipator's monument, was always deserted.

Rathor took his time, surveying the area for several minutes. Then he got out and walked toward the memorial, climbing the three sets of triple steps. Golden columns of light glowed between the memorial's thirty-six graying marble Doric columns, one for every state in the Union when Lincoln died. Giant Lincoln, frozen in ice-white Georgia marble, contemplated eternity in the monument's main chamber. Rathor came here not infrequently, sometimes during visiting hours, sometimes after. What could be more natural than a patriotic cabinet member looking to the Great Emancipator for inspiration and guidance?

He climbed the memorial's fifty-eight steps—two for Lincoln's presidential terms, fifty-six for his age when assassinated—and walked to the base of the statue. He moved casually around the memorial's interior, assuring himself that it was empty. Then he went to the far end of the south chamber and stood a few feet in front and to the left of the towering Gettysburg Address carved into the chamber's wall. Rathor reached into his right trouser pocket and thumbed the autodial button on his personal, encrypted sat phone. Buying it from the Israelis had cost what most people would consider a fortune, but the Israelis had also provided the locations of three natural "dead zones" secure from even the NSA's eavesdroppers. It struck Rathor as a kind of ultimate irony that one such zone was right here on the mall, in this south corner of the Lincoln Memorial, surrounded as it was by granite and marble walls several feet thick and screened by the memorial's massive bronze girders overhead.

In the phone's almost invisible earbud transceiver, Rathor listened while the connection was made. Then, gazing at the Gettysburg Address, he murmured the long alphanumeric sequence he had memorized. Anyone watching would have assumed he was simply saying the words of the address to himself, as though repeating a prayer. In this particular spot, though, with his back to the surveillance cameras, he was beyond observation.

Several seconds of clicks and hums followed, the voice recognition software and code acquisition programs processing. Then the soft tone of a connection made.

"We have a need," Rathor said.

"Indeed?" Bernard Adelheid's voice always made Rathor think of an ice pick at work.

"Barnard told O'Neil the cave team might actually do something."

"We have planned for that eventuality."

"Yes, but they have a man named Bowman. Some kind of spook, maybe a former Delta, I don't know. Very big and dangerous, I believe. Were you aware of that?"

"Of course." Silence. Then: "I think you should have known that soldiers were using feminine products."

Rathor's jaw clenched. He would defend himself. "Who could have imagined that soldiers would be sticking *tampons* into bullet wounds?"

"*You* should have. That failure could be very costly. To the plan. And to you."

The plan. Rathor knew Adelheid was right. The plan had been to get contaminated Chinese-made tampons into trailer-trash, welfare women. Tampons were the perfect vector. They were sold unsterilized. Knockoff brands were marketed by the big-box discounters millions of such women frequented. In China, they were ridiculously easy to contaminate. The women, well, they would be like lab rats who sickened and, in some cases, died for the cause, useful but without power to make waves. Spreading infection, they would create a voracious market for the ancient antibiotic colistin, stores of which BioChem had been secretly manufacturing and stockpiling for more than a year.

But then the law of unintended consequences intervened. *Soldiers* using the bacteria-infested tampons began getting sick and dying. That in itself would have been manageable, would in fact have been a good thing, generating even more sales of colistin. But the bacterium killing them was not the standard-issue *Acinetobacter baumannii* that had been introduced into the tampons. It was some mutated microbial monster that sneered at colistin and ate people alive from the inside out.

"The man Bowman is not the problem," Adelheid said.

Rathor's stomach did a little flip. "What else?"

"A man named Lathrop has discovered certain transmissions from BARDA."

"What? *How?*"

Adelheid's silence suggested his contempt for the stupidity of Rathor's question. "How indeed. But *how* is irrelevant now. Something must be done."

"About the transmissions, you mean."

"No. Not about the transmissions. They are part of the irreparable past. That is not all."

Oh, my God, Rathor thought. "What else?"

"One of the laboratories at BARDA has had an unexpected stroke of luck. At this point, full knowledge is restricted to only one individual, a scientist named Casey."

Rathor's mind raced and his legs felt weak. Adelheid said, "We will deal with the second issue ourselves. You will deal with Lathrop. We will take care of the unlucky Casey *and* his lucky discovery."

"But—"

Adelheid said, "Gray," and the line went dead. Rathor stood and stared, unseeing. Then he came back. It was always an immense relief to stop talking to Adelheid. And to turn off the sat phone, which, even with all its safeguards, was dangerous. Some risks felt better than others.

Mostly to maintain his ruse, Rathor continued to stand in front of the Gettysburg Address plaque, pretending to read the words of Lincoln's greatest speech. He wasn't actually reading, but then the word "government" caught his eye and his brain stuck on it. Nathan Rathor hated the government. Few things could make him feel violated and impotent, but the government was one. He would never forget the public humiliations he'd suffered while testifying as Bio-Chem's CEO, groveling at the feet—literally, raised as they were, like false little gods, on their dais—of senators whose performances for the news cameras made them, in his opinion anyway, lower than the women and men who opened themselves for the cameras of porn. One of those senators had been David O'Neil.

That was almost four years ago, of course, a century in Washington political time. He and O'Neil had "buried the hatchet" and "come to terms," as the pandering hacks put it. O'Neil had "recruited him onto the presidential team," and he had "left private enterprise for the greater good of public service." Rathor knew full well that O'Neil had not asked him to serve on the cabinet out of any misguided olive-branch waving. He had asked him in observance of an old adage of war: "Friends close, enemies closer." Rathor understood that there was nothing altruistic in the president's tactic. And Rathor knew that O'Neil knew what Rathor himself knew. That was how the game was played in Washington, like a gladiator match in which both fighters were aware that success depended on seeing one move further through the whirlwind of blows and feints than their opponent. Or on using a poison-smeared spear point.

"Government of the people, by the people, for the people." Rathor hawked, spat. The people. What was it H. L. Mencken had said? "No one ever went broke underestimating the intelligence of the American people." Truer words had never been spoken.

Rathor suddenly felt the need to piss. More than the need—an irresistible urgency, as though someone had inserted hot wire into his penis and stabbed his bladder.

Goddamn, he thought. *The gin.* He had an enlarged prostate and he was old. When he had to go, mild discomfort became searing pain very quickly. So he *really* needed to piss. But the bathrooms here were locked at this time of night. Going to a convenience store or gas station was unthinkable. He would not make it back to his office; that much, from long experience, he knew with certainty. There was only one thing to do. Take another risk.

He glanced over both shoulders. No one else was in the memorial. He was alone. There were security cameras, but they were aimed toward the great statue, not this remote, little-visited corner of the memorial. Casually, he took his right hand out of his pocket, rubbed his face as though brushing away tears, let it drop in front of him. He lowered his zipper, withdrew himself, relaxed, and sighed with relief. A weak stream of yellow urine spattered the marble wall beneath the Gettysburg Address and pooled on the memorial's white floor.

NINETEEN

AS A MAJOR AND TEROK'S SENIOR MEDICAL OFFICER, LENORA Stilwell had her own computer station, and one that was email-enabled, to boot. Command had finally lifted the ban on email, but any mention of ACE was a court-martial offense, with national security implications, et cetera, et cetera. On her desktop she set down the cup of coffee that was now as much a part of her walking-around attire as stethoscope and clinic coat. What time would it be in Tampa? She could send an email home at any time, of course, but there was a better chance of catching Doug and Danny during waking hours, which would allow her to have an actual exchange. She knew the time zone differentials, had done the calculus hundreds of times, so why was she having trouble now figuring out what time it was where Doug and Danny were?

It was Friday. Or was it? She checked the calendar function on her watch. It was Saturday, March 3. Now the time differential. Tampa was eight and a half hours behind the time in her location up in northeast Afghanistan. It was 12:13 A.M. at Terok, so it would be . . . it would be . . . *damn*. She frowned, closed her eyes, forced her brain to kick over. Okay: 3:43 P.M. in Tampa. Doug would be at work, Danny working after school. No way to catch either one of them for real-time commo.

She started to get up, then sat back down. *Wait. Give it a try. No telling when there'll be a chance again*. She flipped her laptop open, keyed in passwords, and opened her email program.

> hey guys its me anybdy there? hw r u gys doing? Ther hs ben sum bad fitng & busy

Whoa. Can't say that. It would suggest that there had been casualties, which could reveal some bit of intelligence with value to some unknown source somewhere. Or, at the very least, bad news for the home front. Start again.

> hey honey its me anybody there? how r u guys doing? is cindy bck frm cmpus visits up north? r u guys gng fshng tmrrow on the boat? Dunno wht ur weather 4cast is. Ours samesame. I miss you both. I love you both.

She hit the Send button and sat back to wait. Doug had an iPhone, so even if he wasn't at a computer, he might receive the email and reply. She watched the computer screen, listened for the little incoming-mail chime. A full minute passed, then two, and she reached to close the laptop, which was when it chimed and the email reply popped up. Doug still wrote like a civilian with all the time in the world, not like a time-poor Army doctor who calculated the half seconds she could save by leaving out punctuation, abbreviating where possible, and butchering normal grammar.

Lenny,

Wow. It had been a while. We were worrying. It is REALLY good to hear from you. I love you. Danny loves you. We miss you. I know you can't say much about much, but from what we see on the news it looks like your area is heating up. Okay, your questions. Danny is nervous. Won't admit it, but he is. Cindy got back yesterday. She visited Pitt, Penn State, Rutgers, and Amherst. She came over to see Danny this morning and said she liked Pitt most of all. We're not going to go fishing tomorrow. And the weather? It's *Florida.* You know how that is. We're really low on groceries so I'm going to the commissary at MacDill this afternoon. I love you. Write me some more.

Cindy was Cynthia Merrit, Danny's steady girlfriend, a beautiful, petite blonde whose voice always sounded to Stilwell like harp strings being softly plucked. She wanted to be a pediatrician and had been away for much of the previous week looking at colleges. Going fishing on the boat was taking their Scout 34 out for some tarpon fishing. MacDill was MacDill Air Force Base, just south of Tampa. National Guard members had access to all facilities of all service branches—commissaries, clinics, pools, everything.

Dnt wrry all gd here major mom gd shape 4 sure. c liked pitt—good P is a great school. no fshng 4 u ☹ tarpon sesn fll swng now dnt waste days bt u gys gtta eat how's ur rnning?

She sent the email, fiddled with her earlobe waiting for the reply, looked around for a Butterfinger, saw none. Reminded herself to tell Doug to send another box. She was one of those fortunate people with a high-rpm metabolism that allowed her to eat anything she wanted and not gain weight. Keeping weight *on* was actually more of a problem. She didn't pig out on Butterfingers, but one a day wouldn't kill anyone.

Honey,

We're not going out because one of the Scout Mercs needs an overhaul and both props need balancing. I'll get my days in, don't worry. I did 12 miles yesterday, still building the long slow distance base. The marathon's not for another four weeks, should be just right by then. Hey, look, if I'm going to get the shopping done and be back in time to make dinner, I have to run. And don't worry. I'll pick up Butterfingers.

She laughed at that. They had been together long enough for them to read each other's minds often, as he had just done. How long before they started to look like each other?

ok go 4 it.
i love you and miss you 247.
Lenny

She was about to hit the Send button when such a shot of adrenaline rushed through her that she gasped out loud. *The commissary.* Oh God. She deleted "Lenny" and typed furiously.

do not repeat not go to commissary. stay away macdill. possible biohazard. shop civilian. Reply please.

She started to hit the Send button again, then stopped herself. *I can't say that. ACE info is top classified, close hold. The censors will pick it up and there will be fobbits all over me. Doug won't get the message that way anyway.*

As a physician, and a surgeon, and one who practiced in a combat area, Stilwell did not lose control easily. But now she recognized the signs of incipient panic in herself: hyperventilating, lightheadedness, shaking from adrenaline overload.

You don't know that there's any problem at MacDill.

But you don't know that there is not, either.

You can't let them go there. It's not worth the risk. Just for groceries.

How to stop them?

She could feel Doug, halfway around the world, waiting for an email from her. If she made him wait too long, he might assume she'd had to break off for some emergency. She closed her eyes, tried to calm herself, forced her thoughts to become orderly. Then she thought of something.

Honey,

I would rather you shopped at Publix. From now on. Until I get home. They are donating 10% of profits to service families in need. Do you copy?

She sent the email, then shook her head. *Do you copy?* Lapsing into Armyspeak.

His reply came in seconds.

Hi Honey,

Sorry, no can do. Got those boat repairs coming and dough is tight. Plus saving for that vacation we're taking when you get back. You know all that. But tell you what. I can shop on base and give 10% myself to that family fund and still come out ahead. Hey . . . have to go. I love you. Will try to call tomorrow. Or email.

LOVE U.

No. *No.* She typed furiously, all caps. Maybe she could catch him.

NO. YOY DINR UNDERSTNND. CANNOT GO TOI THE CONIMA]

She stopped. *More haste, less speed.* It was garbled. Panic was disrupting her motor skills. Doug would be gone already. And in a message like that, or like the one she might revise and send, the Army's censoring software would detect excessive anomalies and route the email to a human reviewer. And then . . . there would be hell to pay. After this was over, there would be a hard sit-down with the fobbits called insects, partly because they came from Internal Security, the Army acronym for which was InSec. Partly, but not completely. The other reason was that they were slimy men roundly detested for a willingness to walk their careers forward over the backs of other soldiers. She could not let that happen. There was too much need here.

But Doug and Danny, going to the commissary? The thought just about cracked her professional discipline. She sat back, wrapped one arm around her chest, and shoved the knuckles of her right hand into her mouth.

A few minutes later, someone knocked, very softly, on the flimsy plywood door to her plywood closet of an office. She composed herself, steadied her voice.

"Come in."

The door opened just wide enough for one of the nurses to poke her head in. A beautiful young black woman from Brooklyn. She remembered that much. But not the nurse's name. She knew it, but could not remember it, and that was a bad sign. So she just smiled and waited.

"Ma'am, there's a call for you." Muffled voice from the Chemturion hood.

"Can you handle it for me, please? I just need a few minutes here to finish up some paperwork."

"Ah, ma'am, I tried to take a message. But it's a colonel, ma'am. Says he spoke to you about coming here. Said to get you ASAP." The nurse's face contracted around the word "ASAP," as though she had just tasted something sour.

The fobbit. Damn. She had forgotten all about their conversation yesterday. No, the day before. Or had it been last week? She could not recall. But she did seem to remember that the colonel had said he would arrive on Thursday, which had come and gone. Today was Saturday. What the hell? Well, colonels didn't make their schedules to suit majors. He was here and had to be dealt with. "All right, I'll speak with him. Is he inside here someplace?"

"No, ma'am. He's outside. I don't think he wants to come in. Even with a suit on."

"He actually has a suit on? Out there? Okay, no problem. Thanks for letting me know."

"Yes, ma'am." The beautiful nurse went away, leaving Stilwell's door ajar. She got up, rubbed her hands over her face in an attempt to scrub away some of the fatigue, and walked to the nurses' station, where the telephones were located.

"Stilwell."

"Major, this is Colonel Ribbesh."

She had forgotten all about him. His voice sounded stiff and formal and distorted by his suit hood. *Pissed off because some general ordered him to come out here,* she thought. *Now he's going to pass it right on down the line.* She wondered why he was wearing a biosafety suit, even though he was outside the unit.

"I had apprised you of my ETA, Major. There were some changes required. Did your staff apprise you?"

"No, Colonel."

"That's too bad. I instructed my staff to do so."

I just bet you did, fobbit. Preemptive strike is called for here.

"Colonel, no disrespect, but I've got four more patients to see stat. Can this wait?"

"I'm afraid not. I understand you've declined to utilize a Bravo Sierra Lima-dash-Four unit."

"Correct."

"I think you should don one ASAP, Major. I know you're aware that NBC regulations specifically state that all medical personnel in Level Four quarantine conditions shall be required to utilize Bravo Sierra Lima-dash-Four units at all times when in the presence of pathogens."

"Thanks for your concern, Colonel, but no. Now I have to—"

"Major Stilwell, that wasn't a request." Colonel Ribbesh sounded like a teacher she'd had in seventh grade, a little man bitter as brine whose life purpose, it seemed, had been to make other people suffer. "It was an order. From a superior officer."

She took a deep breath, fought her temper back down. "Colonel. These boys fight every day without magic suits. I can't take care of them in one. And I'm sure *you're* aware of Army General Order Seventeen, Section Four, Part b, which states that in situations pertaining to the health and welfare of military personnel, medical authority shall prevail over all other considerations. I have to go."

Let it go right there, she told herself, but then it just came bubbling out. "See, a soldier just died and I need to pronounce his death to make his sure his family becomes eligible for what meager benefits the Army sees fit to pay parents for their dead enlisted-men sons, because if one bit of paperwork, just one tiny piece, is missing, well, they can kiss those benefits goodbye. But thank you for your concern."

Stilwell hung up, shook her head. There was, of course, something else.

What's your name, Sergeant?

Daniel, ma'am. Wyman.

Suppose one of these boys had been *her* Danny and it was another doctor? What would she expect of *that* one? The answer was obvious—to her, at least. The others still in here all wore the suits. They were volunteers, sergeants and corporals, nurses and lab techs and a couple of physician's assistants who'd stayed to help, and she was glad they were protected. But for her, not being able to speak directly to these sick kids, to see them and touch them and hear their voices undistorted, was unthinkable.

Not long after Daniel Wyman died, Stilwell herself took up residence in the quarantined hospital, catnapping when she could on a cot, subsisting mostly on coffee and the microwavable meals normally given only to patients. She had been working for more than fifty hours now without really sleeping, and was beginning to feel the red, gritty edge of serious fatigue.

She had encountered that kind of exhaustion before, after medical school when she was interning and then doing her residency. There were times in those days when she had worked ninety hours straight. She was younger then, but she was not old now and knew she still had reserves of energy not yet tapped. She could keep going for quite a while.

But what then? she asked herself, pouring more thick, black coffee from the Bunn at the nurses' station. And what was quite a while, anyway? She couldn't go on forever, and she knew that full well. They could bring other Army doctors, but they would be strangers to the boys in the wards and, working in the space suits, would only make the soldiers feel even more diseased and alone, like dying lepers.

Well, she couldn't do anything about that. But she could keep administering colistin, as long as the supplies kept coming in, and she could provide pain relief, and she could talk to them and hold their hands and reassure them.

And what about you, Dr. Stilwell? Do you really think you've got some kind of miraculous immunity to this thing?

I haven't caught it yet, now have I?

It's just a matter of time. You know that.

I don't know any such thing. I think if I were going to get it, I would have by now.

Get real. It's just taking longer because you're a woman and women have stronger immune systems than men. That was one of the first things you learned in the infectious disease courses. Remember how all the women med students in the classes made faces and thumbed their noses at the men?

Maybe. Maybe not. But you know what? It doesn't really matter. Does it?

No. It doesn't. What matters is them. And no goddamned fobbit is going to get between me and those soldiers.

Roger that, Major.

TWENTY

BARNARD NEVER SLEPT WELL IN THE MOTEL-LIKE ROOMS THAT were now standard issue in all agencies having anything to do with homeland security. Given his seniority, his was comfortable enough—double bed, private bath, color-chip hues—but it wasn't home and there was no Lucianne, slim and warm, beside him.

He showered, shaved, put on fresh clothes, had coffee, and headed downstairs to Delta 17. Lew Casey had called earlier that morning with guardedly good news. Too complicated to explain on the phone, he'd said; Barnard should come down to see for himself.

It was a trip most people would have dreaded, but what Barnard dreaded more were the seemingly endless periods between his all-too-infrequent visits to the BSL-4 labs. He had never stopped feeling the pull of the labs, especially the Fours, where the deadliest pathogens lived. There was nothing on earth like being in a lab with those things. Lion tamers might feel something akin to it, he'd once reflected, but even that would be less intense. You could *see* lions. And train them. You could not see or train monsters like Ebola Zaire . . . or ACE.

He passed through the first air lock and security point, then went to the clothing-and-supply station to pick up a fresh blue lab gown, shoe covers, rubber gloves, and a Level 3 biosafety respirator.

BARDA, like all facilities working with dangerous pathogens, was divided into containment levels. The first, uppermost level, where he now donned his lab attire, contained no dangerous laboratories or research facilities. It was mostly for screening and administration; even laboratories working with the most exotic microbes needed some help from a bureaucracy.

There were only two points of ingress and egress, one of which Barnard had come through today and on the earlier visit with Hallie. In a different elevator, Barnard descended past BARDA Levels 2 and 3 to the lowest, hottest, most tightly restricted area: Biosafety Level 4. Walking toward his final transition point, he felt familiar reactions. His respiration and pulse increased, his spatial awareness became more acute, his eyes and ears more vigilant.

Coming down here always made him think of Winston Churchill's famous statement that nothing focused the mind more wonderfully than being shot at without effect. His own experience in Vietnam had shown that to be true—up to a point. Churchill had spent a few weeks being shot at, Barnard twenty-six months. At first, the exhilaration made it almost easy, but before long it soured into toxic despair.

At the end of his first tour, he had no intention of going back in-country. Stateside it would be, his body in one piece still and his mind, if not in one piece, at least not fragmented beyond reassembly. He spent a few days out-processing in Saigon, sleeping on clean sheets and drinking good Scotch and eating rare steaks with fresh green salads before heading back to the United States. He got sated on red meat by the second day, but the fresh vegetables, crisp lettuce, succulent tomatoes, crunchy carrots—of these he simply could not seem to devour enough. Nor the Scotch. On the third day, he slept late, showered for half an hour, ate a fine breakfast of bacon and five eggs and real toast. By the afternoon, he was sitting at the bar in Saigon's InterContinental Hotel savoring his third double Chivas, neat.

Lined up at the bar on both sides of him were contractors with bodies like sides of beef and plump rear-echelon types who looked like sausages stuffed into their tailored uniforms. Many of the REMFs were with beautiful whores reeking of imitation Chanel No. 5. It was not yet three P.M. but sounded like late on New Year's Eve, all of them drinking and howling and backslapping.

There was a long mirror behind the bar, cracked but still hanging, and he looked at himself in his clean uniform with its edged creases, deeply tanned, emaciated, hollow-eyed and yellow-toothed. At the beginning of his tour he had worn a size 18 collar—big football neck—but now his neck was scrawny, sprouting out of the uniform shirt collar like a straw in a glass. Except for the whores, he was the only underweight person in the bar.

He was surrounded by piggy faces and grinning mouths and jiggling bodies, bartenders shouting and the whores laughing, their voices so high it sounded like screaming, and he suddenly thought he would puke up the Chivas Regal right there on the bar top. His vision misted and it was hard not to draw the .45 Colt—worn against regulations here but the hell with them, he never went *anywhere* unarmed anymore—and start putting red holes in the white faces.

He got himself out of the hotel and to the nearest corner before he did puke. Passersby kept right on going without giving him a second glance. Puking-drunk Americans were as common as Saigon's notorious cat-sized rats then.

The next day, sick but sober, he went to see the DEROS officer and indicated his desire to sign up for another tour in-country. The plump major stared at him for a long time from behind an opulent mahogany desk he had commandeered from a Saigon pol.

"Are you drunk, Brainard?"

He looked at the clock: just past eleven A.M.

"Barnard, sir. No, sir. Not anymore."

"Drugs?"

"No, sir."

The man lit a cigar, offered one to Barnard, who declined with roiling gut. "You're a college grad?"

"Yes, sir."

"Where'd you go?"

"University of Virginia, sir."

"ROTC?"

"Yes, sir."

"What do you want to do? Back in the world?"

"I'm not sure, sir."

"Not a military career, though?"

"No way in hell, sir. No disrespect."

The major sat forward, his belly straining the buttons of his shirt, poked his cigar toward Barnard, and said angrily, "Then why in the hell do you want to go back in there? You don't need to get your ticket punched for promotion. What are you thinking?"

Barnard understood the man's outburst, didn't take it personally—the rear-echelon major being made to feel bad.

"Don't be an idiot, Brainard. You don't have to go back."

He was just twenty-three then and knew that he didn't know many things. But *this* one he did. He could not go home while men he knew and cared about were still back there. *His* men. He might escape a death now by going home, but it would be a bad trade: good death with his men here for bad death at the end of a Smith & Wesson or rope back home.

"Yes, I do." Barnard looked out the office's floor-to-ceiling windows. He could not see the mountains or his men from here, but he could feel them. It was like standing waist-deep in an undertow. "Sir."

Earlier in his career at the CDC, he had spent years in BSL-3 and BSL-4 laboratories dealing with the microbial world's worst demons, group A strep, *Yersinia pestis,* anthrax, Ebola-Z, and others. As time went on and he was promoted out of the labs, he understood that with his experience he could better serve as a supervisor and, later, a director. But he was never entirely free of the same kind of guilt he'd felt that day in Saigon. It was as though he were attached to Four with a long elastic cord that stretched but never let go and relaxed only when he was back in there with his people and the demons.

He went to a small but spotless locker room with stainless steel walls and ceiling. He stripped naked and hung his clothes and the blue lab gown in a locker. He put his rings and watch on the locker's shelf. Then he walked through a door into a shower room and scrubbed himself under 120-degree water with Biodyne disinfectant until, after five full minutes, a timer went off. In the next room he toweled dry and put on sterile green surgical scrubs, including plastic booties and latex gloves. He went through another heavy, stainless steel bulkhead with airtight seals that locked automatically. No two could be open at the same time. The next space was the "weeya," the work and interaction area, a place just outside the suit room, where researchers could sit down and rest, make notes, converse about what went on deeper in. It was deserted now. Then through another airlock into the suit room, where the blue BSL-4 suits hung, like huge blue cadavers, from heavy hooks in the ceiling.

Barnard's name was printed in black letters across the upper back of his Chemturion 3530, as if it were a football uniform. He lifted the bulky, ten-pound suit from its hook, then pulled open the heavy plastic zipper that ran diagonally from its left shoulder down to its right thigh. He stepped into the legs one at a time, got his feet into the attached yellow rubber boots, hitched the suit up, pushed his left arm in and then his right. He drew the zipper head up to its closure point on his left shoulder, folded over the zipper cover, and secured it with Velcro tabs. The clear plastic hood hung down his back. He pulled it up over his head and closed the zipper that ran 180 degrees, left to right, where the hood bottom joined the suit body. He pushed a switch on a control box attached to the suit's left hip and waited while the Chem-Air PLSS unit inflated the suit around him. As long as the air pressure in the suit remained higher than the ambient pressure outside, pathogens could not infiltrate even if the suit was breached. The battery-powered Chem-Air also supplied him with quadruple-HEPA-filtered breathing air from a yellow Accurex ultra-high-pressure bottle that contained 20 cubic feet of compressed air at a pressure of 5,500 psi. The bottle was about the size and shape of a thermos and weighed four pounds. This would be Barnard's air source until he was inside the lab itself, where he would connect an air hose to a fitting on the right shoulder of his suit.

Barnard stood and waited for another two minutes, monitoring air flow and pressurization, to make sure that the suit was intact. Then he went through yet another air lock. This one was what they called a submarine door because its design had been copied from submarines' watertight bulkheads. He pushed a lever from left to right, releasing a locking latch. Then he turned a large steel wheel counterclockwise. He pulled a second latch, opening the bulkhead door, stepped through, and reversed the whole procedure.

He stood in a small room with a grate floor and seamless stainless steel walls from which multiple nozzles protruded. He pushed a doughnut-sized red button—in BSL-4 areas, everything was bigger, to compensate for the reduced manual dexterity—to initiate the chemical-shower decon sequence and stepped onto two white footprints in the middle of the steel-grate floor. High-pressure jets sprayed green Chemex decontamination solution at him from above, both sides, front, and behind. He raised his hands over his head, as though preparing to dive into water, and pirouetted slowly around and around, exposing every square millimeter of surface to the spray, which resembled antifreeze fluid in color and viscosity. He lifted both boots, one at a time, to let the spray hit the soles. Excess liquid drained through the grates into collection reservoirs. After two minutes the jets cut off and powerful fans blew warm air for another three minutes, clearing the suit of decon liquid and drying it.

On the far wall was another big red button, with two lights, one red and one green, beside it. He pressed the button and waited. A stainless steel door slid open, right to left, he stepped through, and the door whisked shut behind him, pneumatic airtight seals inflating once it was closed.

He was now standing in one of the deadliest spots on earth. A pinhole-sized breach in his suit would seem, to any circulating pathogens, like an open barn door. If anything happened to interrupt his suit's positive pressure after such a breach, they would flood in by the millions and he would die one of the most horrible deaths imaginable in less than a week.

BSL-4 labs tended not to be large because they were prohibitively expensive to build and maintain. It was not just the labs themselves but all the safety and containment systems they required, air and fluid collection and disposal, fail-safe redundancies, and ultrasophisticated instruments like scanning electron microscopes. Each square foot of lab space cost $2,000 and required fifteen additional square feet of support facility at the same cost. Thus a one-thousand-square-foot lab needed fifteen thousand square feet of support works, the whole thing costing $32 million altogether. More expensive, foot for foot, than the space shuttle.

Stainless steel counters ran at waist height down both sides of the room. On top of them sat exotic instruments, glass boxes, trays of cultures. Over the counters hung aluminum hoods with ventilator fans that continually drew air out of the lab, maintaining its negative pressure. Evvie Flemmer was working at one counter.

"Took you a while." Casey was smiling, his voice muffled by the plastic hood. "Turn around and I'll hook you up."

"I'm rusty donning the Chemturion," Barnard said, a bit sheepishly. "Don't get down here as often as I would like. Skills deteriorate." He waited while Casey connected the coiled, ceiling-mounted yellow hose that would give him breathing air from the lab's integral supply. With twisting and contortions, one person could do it, but having a partner made it much easier. A self-locking nozzle mated with a circular valve seat on the back of the right shoulder of Barnard's suit. Once it was in place, Casey pushed a butterfly-valve handle that opened the nozzle, delivering air. Finally, Casey rotated the switch on Barnard's Chem-Air PLSS unit, depowering it.

"You said you had something promising."

"Yes. Come over here," Casey said, moving to the electron microscope.

The instrument looked like a white stovepipe eight feet tall and bristling with extensions, controls, and components. At its base were a twelve-by-twelve viewing screen and binocular eyepieces like those found on light microscopes. Barnard bent over the screen. Casey used an oversized mouse and dials as big as cookies to calibrate the settings. They both remained standing. There were no chairs or stools in a BSL-4 lab. Sitting in Chemturions was like trying to sit while wrapped in a stack of inner tubes.

"Okay. Here's our new ACE."

As Casey worked the controls, Barnard saw an image clarifying on the viewing screen. He had looked at thousands of microbes over his career, and their beauty still amazed him. As a child he had had a kaleidoscope, a telescope-like tube that, when rotated, rearranged colored pieces of glass into striking patterns. When he tried to describe the microscopic world to other people, that was the best analogy he could come up with. But the reality was infinitely more astonishing: unearthly beauty, every color of the spectrum, and every shape imaginable. God's artwork—or, really, the

Devil's. *Streptococci,* burning like red suns against a butter-yellow sky. *Neisseria gonorrhoeae,* golden globes with ruby filaments streaming behind like the long red hair of a drowned woman. *Corynebacterium diphtheriae,* graceful green wands with maroon heads, groups of them looking like beds of tulips.

The microbes came into sharp focus and Barnard saw half a dozen oblong-shaped objects. Their smooth perimeters were white, their bodies the rich red of Burgundy wine. The depth of hue increased toward the center, where it finally became black. Magnified a million times, framed, and hung on a wall, the image could have been a painting by de Kooning or, in his wilder moments, van Gogh.

"Now, here's what I wanted to show you."

The image changed to reveal more purple oblongs with white perimeters. The color deepened toward the middle of the organism, but its center had a reddish tint, rather than the solid black Barnard had seen in the previous image. And the white perimeters were jagged and cracked, rather than smooth and intact.

"You got into its genetics." In the suit, Barnard sounded like he was speaking in a closet, but the excitement in his voice was sharp.

"That's right."

"How?"

"We fractured its skull. Withdrew mitochondrial material and breached its defenses to reach the genes."

"Where's the but? There has to be one, or we'd both be dancing around in my office now."

"The but is that we're not exactly sure why it happened. You know what it's like, playing with the genes of these things."

"Like trying to do brain surgery with a jackhammer."

"Yep. The trick is not destroying the whole thing, and it's quite a trick."

"So, what are we looking at for time?"

"Before we do it again? Realistically, two days. Maybe three."

Barnard gaped. He had been the recipient of so much bad news recently that he'd been primed to hear Casey talk about weeks or even months. "By *God,* Lew. That's incredible. Can I take this to the president?"

"Well, I hate to overpromise and underdeliver. But yeah, I think you can go with it. That good enough for you?"

"More than good enough."

"We're not all the way there, Don. Not by a long shot."

"No, but based on what you just reported, we have taken a huge step closer."

"Yeah, I think we can say that." Casey suppressed a grin, but the smile in his eyes was a mile wide. They stood there gazing at each other through the plastic hoods. Barnard felt an affection for Casey not unlike what he had felt for his men in Vietnam. He could happily stay down here for the rest of this shift and the next one, as well. But he had news to deliver, and he was aware that at best he was a director-level distraction. Still, he did not want to leave. When he was up in his office with his three-piece suit and secretary and windows showing daylight, it felt wrong. Down here, it felt right. Deadly, but right.

He smiled and patted Casey on the shoulder, his heavy rubber-gloved hand thumping on Casey's biosuit. Clumsy, but Casey got the idea.

"I gotta go make some calls, Lew. Find me when something more happens."

"Damn right. Now go on, give the powers that be some good news. Turn around and I'll disconnect you."

Barnard started to leave, then stopped. "One more thing. Who did it?"

Casey looked embarrassed.

"I thought so. Nice going, Dr. Casey. Keep it up and you may make a scientist yet."

TWENTY-ONE

THEY TRAVELED FOR TWELVE HOURS AFTER HALLIE AND Bowman secured Haight's body. No two steps were alike. There were crashing waterfalls, glistening slopes slick as tilted ice, vertical faces, rubble fields, wormhole crawls. At the shorter drops, they rappelled on their only rope, a ninety-meter PMI Classic that Bowman was carrying. Where the vertical distance was too great, they donned their Gecko Gear and down-climbed. In other places the cave floor dipped below the surface of lakes so vast their lights could find no shores, and these had to be waded or swum, Bowman going first, rigging a line where he could, and the others hauling themselves along the line to join him. There were long passages where the space between the cave's floor and its ceiling was so small that they could move forward only by taking off their packs and shoving them in front or pulling them behind. They had to pass through acres of boulder gardens, sections where, over the course of eons, huge fragments of ceiling had broken off and fallen. The trick here, as it had been earlier in the entrance chamber, was to avoid dropping between the rocks. But walking along their wet tops, which were never flat but always jagged or rounded, took immense concentration and was physically exhausting.

By three P.M. the next day, even Bowman was beginning to falter. He halted them at the only potential site for a camp, and it was a poor one. The floor sloped downward and there was no one place big enough for all of them to deploy their sleeping bags together. There was one spot where the four of them could stand. It was about eight feet square, walled by giant breakdown rubble. A narrow slot between two of these boulders gave exit, and from there each found a place on the boulder-littered floor with room for a sleeping bag. Now Hallie and the others were standing in the little clearing, spooning MRE chicken and dumplings out of foil pouches.

"This is very bad." Arguello listlessly stirred his glop. *"Muy malo."*

At first, Hallie thought he was talking about the food, but those last two words signaled something else. Not very bad. Very *evil.* Food was not evil.

"What do you mean?"

"I mean the thing that happened to Dr. Haight. To Ron."

"He had an accident."

Arguello looked up, careful to avoid shining his light in her eyes. "You think so?"

"Don't you?"

"There is evil in this cave, and I can feel it."

Cahner spoke first.

"What does it feel like, Rafael?" He was looking at Arguello intently. The light was on Arguello's chest, but Hallie could see the seriousness of his expression.

"Excuse me?"

"You said that you could feel evil in the cave. I was asking what that felt like."

"Oh, yes. I see now. It feels like nausea, but not only in the stomach. Everywhere. A sick and weak feeling. Like maybe the flu. But worse."

"You believe the *cave* is evil." There was no hint of mockery or sarcasm in Cahner's question.

"*No*. Not the cave. But there is evil in the cave. There is a difference."

"There is *danger* in the cave," said Cahner. "Danger's not good or evil. It's just danger. In the mountains we talk about objective dangers, things like weather and avalanches over which we have no control. Same in a cave. Isn't that right, Hallie?"

Arguello spoke before Hallie could. "I am thinking about the two men who were lost in here, during your other expedition. What happened to them? Why did they not return?"

"As I said, we never found out."

"That is a great pity." She waited for Arguello to go on, but he said nothing more.

"We all need some rest." Bowman, more gently than Hallie would have expected, was telling them it was bedtime. "We haven't gone as far as I'd planned, but given the circumstances, I think it would be dangerous to keep moving. Let's plan to sleep for four hours, and then head out again."

"You will have no argument from me," said Arguello. "I can surely use the rest."

"Sleeping in caves is such fun," Cahner sighed.

Bowman waved an arm. "Welcome to the Cueva de Luz Hilton, my friends. I hope you find the accommodations to your liking."

Hallie's spot was a hundred feet from where they had eaten. Back there, she took from her pack an airtight red capsule about the size of a flashlight. She unscrewed the container's top and removed its contents, a super-compressed, waterproof sleeping bag with an integral bottom pad. On contact with air it began to expand like a dry sponge absorbing water. Unlike a sponge, it kept on growing as though it were being inflated, which, in fact, was exactly what was happening as the nanopolymer filling's affinity for nitrogen molecules drew them in. In less than two minutes, the thing had grown to resemble a conventional, puffy mummy bag.

She took off her boots and set them just to the left of her bag. She stripped off her filthy caving suit, folded it, and put it on top of the boots. Wearing her damp but clean red polypro long underwear, she slipped into her bag. But for a long time she lay awake, staring at false light images. It never failed. The times when she needed to sleep most were inevitably the times when she could not sleep at all. She lay there, watching the fireworks that the dark tricked her eyes into producing, feeling more impatient as the seconds passed—which, of course, made it even harder to fall asleep. Before long, she heard snoring from the direction of Cahner's sleeping spot. Then Arguello, whose snoring was slower and more deeply pitched than Cahner's. She waited, expecting to hear Bowman next, but did not.

One reason she could not sleep was that her mind kept returning to Haight's death, seeing the young man's body, which lay, unburied, under the green plastic groundsheet. By now, she knew, it would be stiffened by rigor mortis. Tomorrow decomposition would set in, if it had not already. Another thing holding sleep at bay was her own body's soreness. She knew from experience that no matter how good her conditioning was when she came into a cave like this, it would still take several days to get acclimated.

But there was a third reason why she could not sleep. She waited half an hour, listening to Cahner and Arguello snoring, waiting for them to work their way down into REMs. Finally, she slipped out of her bag and, navigating from her mental snapshot, started moving.

Hallie moved through the dark softly, smoothly, going by sense of touch and memory, looking not so much like a blind person groping through unfamiliar rooms as a dancer in slow motion. After two minutes she caught a trace of scent, a minute later picked up the sound of soft breathing. She kept moving forward, working her way between boulders, until, without warning, a hand clamped her ankle.

"Hallie." Bowman's voice, whispering.

"You heard me coming. But how'd you know it was me?"

"Scent. You're quiet, though. I'll give you that."

"Don't you ever sleep?"

"Not much. You?" He released her ankle.

"Now and then. But I wasn't having any luck."

"Cahner and Arguello don't seem to be having trouble."

"Exhausted, both of them."

"Yes. Long, hard day."

Neither of them spoke for a while, Bowman lying down, Hallie standing over him, both listening to the cave talking: water flowing, wind soughing, every once in a while the sharper, cracking sound of rock breaking from the ceiling of some distant chamber. There would be silences of varying lengths and then another sound, explosive, as rock hit the cave floor. Some impacts were so distant that they sounded like small bags being popped, but others, closer, were louder and made the floor shake. It was a process that never stopped, like a human body continually sloughing off dead skin cells. And where the rocks landed was purely the luck of the draw. Hallie knew that a rock, pebble sized or big as a house, could hit any of them at any time.

Cahner had been right about objective dangers in the mountains. Caves had plenty of those as well. Rockfall was one, roughly analogous to avalanches. Up top, you could at least see and avoid avalanche-prone terrain. Down here, the only thing you could do was not dwell on the danger. If you were in the wrong place at the wrong time, well, you had to hope it would be big enough to kill you quickly.

"Are you just going to stand there?" She could hear the smile in Bowman's voice.

"I don't know. Is there room down there?"

"Plenty. Come on down and stay awhile, why don't you?"

Hallie eased down to her knees, felt for the cave floor, and sat down beside Bowman. Or tried to. There wasn't enough room between his body and the rock wall for her to sit. She squeezed down beside him on the cave floor. She couldn't even lie on her back, but had to turn onto one side, facing Bowman.

"See? Tons of room."

Hallie could tell he was still smiling. "For you, maybe," she said.

"For us."

"Oh, roomy as hell."

She was lying on her left side and he on his right, their faces separated by a foot of darkness. She could feel the warmth of his body and smell the scent that had led her here, a salty, leathery smell with traces of something like burnt honey. Not a bad smell at all, she had to admit. *Wonder what I smell like?* But she quickly scratched that thought.

Hallie's critical distance—the minimum space between her and another person before she began to feel uncomfortable—was greater than most people's. But here, squeezed together with Bowman like two sardines in a tin, she felt safe and relaxed. She wasn't *making* herself relax, it simply was what it was.

"I'm curious about you," she said.

"I can understand that."

"What is Wil short for?"

"Might not be short for anything. You've heard of Will Rogers? He was just Will."

"Are you just Wil?"

"No. It's short for Willem."

"Sounds Scandinavian."

"Middle English, actually."

"How do you know?"

"My twenty-sixth great-grandfather was a soldier in the English army at Agincourt. An archer. Bowmen, they were called then."

"So that's where the name came from. Bowman."

"Yep."

"You're serious about all this?"

"Very. My mother was obsessive about family history."

"She got back that far?"

"Just a bit further. But the records start to fade beyond the eleventh century."

"Where are you from?"

"Colorado. A little town called Arago. How about you?"

"Near Charlottesville, Virginia. But that's not what I meant. We're Washington, after all. I meant, where do you work?"

"I know. No place important. You wouldn't have heard of it."

"Try me."

She heard him sigh. "Say you go out to dinner. They want to know what I do. I say I can't say. Okay. They drop it. But they can't *really*. It's *Washington*. You are what you do. They keep picking, through the soup, the salad. Halfway into the main course, they're still picking. Not funny now. They get irritated. Think I'm weird, or just pretending, trying to get over on them. Man, woman, doesn't matter. About dessert, I see them get down behind their eyes, the *hell with that arrogant jerk* look."

"Wow."

"Why wow?"

"That's the most I've heard you say since we met."

"Oh. Well, you asked."

"So are you like, a black ops guy, doing clandestine things all the time? CIA? DIA? Delta Force?"

"I don't talk about what I do. Didn't I just say that?"

"Sure. I just wanted to see how you handled it."

"Oh. Well?"

"A little testy. But not a deal breaker."

"That's good."

"Why don't you just make something up? Create a fantasy life?"

"Never works. 'Fantasy' is another word for 'lie.' You make

mistakes. Somebody close finds out you've misled them about a huge chunk of your life . . . I mean, how would you feel?"

"Used. Abused. Betrayed."

"Well, then."

"Are you really from Colorado?"

"Yep. My mom is dead. My dad runs our cattle ranch."

"Like, a *working* ranch?"

"Very working. About three thousand acres in Gunnison County. He's a cattleman, through and through. A vanishing breed, but it's all he knows. He'll die in a saddle one day."

Horses, she thought. "Are you a dog person or a cat person?"

"Not much for cats. Some dogs are okay. Really, I'm a horse person."

Yes. "You know what? Me, too."

"Really?"

"Yep. I grew up on a horse farm down in Virginia. My mom raises horses and trains them. I was riding before I could walk, almost."

"What breeds? Quarter horses?"

"Quarters are kind of like Goofy, don't you think? We have Morgans and Trakehners. They're rocket scientists with four legs."

"Ever worked cattle on a really good cutting horse?"

"No."

"Then you can't know much about quarter horses. Maybe not about riding, either."

"Ever gone over a six-foot jump?"

"No."

"Then *you* don't know anything about horses. You've never ridden until you've jumped."

He laughed.

"What's so funny?"

"How about this? I'll get you on a great cutter if you'll get me on a jumper. Deal?"

She could sense him reaching for her hand. She took his and they shook. "Deal."

"You can ask some things about me." She left her hand where it was.

"I already know some things about you."

"How?"

"They put together files on all of the team members."

"Who's they?"

"Just they."

"Okay, okay. What was in them?"

"A lot."

"Example?"

"Stephen Redhorse."

"He was in there?"

"Him and a few others. Not as many as I would have guessed, though. But from the volume of data, I'd peg him as *the* one. What happened?"

"Wasn't that in the file?"

"It was in the file that you haven't seen him for a few years. Not why."

"We met at Hopkins. He was a physics PhD. And a full-blooded Native American. Comanche."

"Complicated?"

"No. We got on well. The thing was, his parents hated me. All whites, really. We tried, but couldn't get past that."

"I'm sorry."

"Are you really?"

"No," he said.

"Me, neither. Not now, anyway. With hindsight, I can see it was for the best."

"What happened with you and BARDA?"

"So we're really going deep here?"

"We're already deep." No smile in the voice now.

"In more ways than one. Didn't my file talk about that?"

"There were odd redactions."

"Somebody wanted me out, and they made it look like I was selling secret research for big bucks."

"But you weren't?"

"*Of course not*. That's the first asshole thing you've said."

He ignored that. "Who would want you out? And why?"

"I asked myself that a million times and haven't come up with a good answer. My turn. Do you kill people?"

"Rarely. And only those who really do need killing."

Wow, she thought. *That's something you don't get in every conversation*. "Tell me about your family."

"I'm an only child. My mother died of brain cancer six years ago. Glioblastoma. At least it was fast. She was diagnosed and was gone six weeks later. My father is one tough customer. He's sixty-four. Served in Vietnam, a LRRP." He pronounced it "lurp." "Works sixteen hours a day, most of it horseback."

"A LRRP. Those were tough men."

"You know about LRRPs?"

"Told you, my dad was career Army. He was in Vietnam, too. Airborne Ranger. You have a wife? Kids?"

"Neither."

"I didn't think so, but I needed to ask."

"Sure."

She waited for another question, but an instant later her head snapped up and her eyes opened. "What?"

"I didn't say anything. You dozed off."

"I did? Yeah, I did. 'S funny . . . couldn't sleep over there." Her brain was sluggish with lactic acid and fatigue. Making it all the way back to her own spot felt just about impossible. "D'you mind if I sleep here a while." More a statement than question.

"Do you snore?"

"Been known to. Jus' elbow me."

"Fair enough."

"Wha' about you?" She could feel her eyes drooping.

"What about me?" Bowman tilted his head.

"Do you snore?"

"Never."

"*Never?* Come on. Ever'body snores."

"True. There's a surgical procedure. Reduces the uvula, tightens up surrounding tissue."

That woke her up a bit. "You're not kidding."

"No."

"Why in hell would anyone do that?"

"There are places where snoring can get you killed."

Yeah. There must be. Her eyes were beginning to fall shut again. She was easing into the misty, unfocused place between here and there. *There's something else I want to ask,* she thought, but for the life of her she could not remember what it was. "I think I'm going to sleep."

"Good idea."

He turned over onto his back. She shifted her position and their bodies settled and softened, molding against each other. She lay with her head on his shoulder, his arm around her. She folded one arm against his side and lay the other across his chest. His breathing was slower and deeper than hers, but every once in a while they would breathe together and she liked the unison. He felt solid next to her, but warm and yielding at the same time. And he smelled even better close up.

The last thing she remembered was him kissing the top of her head, and then she was asleep. She snored softly a few times, but Bowman didn't elbow her. He lay awake for a while, listening, feeling her chest and belly move against him as she breathed. When he knew she was deep in REM sleep, he drifted off himself. Or as much to sleep as he ever went. She dreamed of swimming in cool, blue water. He dreamed of black mountains and red muzzle flashes.

TWENTY-TWO

THE NEXT DAY, HALLIE WAS LEADING THEM ALONG AN AIRY spine of whitish rock, a natural catwalk that looked like frozen milk. It was two feet wide, its surface slightly convex, and glistening-slick with moisture. Mountaineers would have roped up before crossing such terrain. They had been moving for fourteen hours.

"How deep are those drops beside us?" Cahner was playing his light down into the darkness. The beams disappeared into a yellowish fog before hitting anything solid.

"About two hundred feet on the right, two-fifty the left." Hallie had laser-ranged them the last time. "Not as big as Don't Fall Wall, but nothing you want to go down."

"I am not enjoying this part." Arguello was shuffling along in baby steps, barely picking up his boots, his arms raised and outstretched like a wire walker's.

"Put your weight in your feet." Hallie shone her light on his boots.

"My weight *is* on my feet."

"Not on. *In*. Think like all your weight, all your thoughts, and all your energy are dropping into your feet. Make them part of the rock."

"Aikido," said Bowman, right behind her.

"Yep. A master can plant himself like that and you couldn't move him with a tractor."

"Seen it."

"That is better, yes," said Arguello, his arms coming down a little.

"Keep your eyes focused on the trail three feet ahead. The rest of you will go where you look."

Half an hour later, Hallie held up one hand. "Stop here." She had been watching a yellow Sirius atmosphere analyzer, about the size of a deck of cards, which showed an increasing concentration of hydrogen sulfide. They had all been able to smell the rotten-egg odor, too. "Rebreather time." Because the rebreathers were closed-circuit systems that did not draw in external air, they could function as gas masks like those used by firefighters. They all retrieved the rebreathers from their packs, put them on, and checked their functions. Doing that made Hallie think of Haight.

Too good a man to have died like that.

Hallie realized the others were all looking at her. She raised her voice to be heard through the mask: "Let's go. Be especially careful with these things on. They'll restrict your peripheral vision. You'll lose some view of the footing."

After another quarter mile, Hallie's skin began to tingle inside her caving suit. She looked at the Sirius and saw its red warning LED illuminated. The concentration of hydrogen sulfide here was now lethal. If any of them had a mask leak or failure, they would die like the soldiers gassed in the trenches of World War I.

They passed through a stadium-sized chamber with a domed ceiling fifty feet overhead and walls striped red and white like a barber pole from alternating layers of iron sulfide and calcite. The air filled with a yellow-green fog that diffused their light beams and, in low places, collected into a gaseous soup so thick it hid their feet.

After another five minutes, Hallie stopped. The others came up beside her.

"Holy Mary, Mother of God." The rebreather did nothing to muffle the horror and awe in Arguello's voice.

"Welcome to the Acid Bath." Hallie played her light beam back and forth, out in front of them. "Pure, industrial-grade sulfuric acid." The light reflected off the surface of a subterranean lake filled with shining liquid about the consistency of kerosene, glistening and oily. Even though there was not enough air movement to create wave action, the liquid had a life of its own, colors changing on its surface in a slow, endless upwelling of iridescent reds and yellows and greens. Vapor floated over the liquid and collected in a urine-colored fog.

"Without rebreathers, standing here you'd be dead in five seconds." Hallie picked up a rock and tossed it far enough out into the lake that no liquid would splash on them. When the rock hit the lake's surface, there was an instantaneous boiling, accompanied by a sound like sharp static electricity. And that was it. The lake had eaten the rock that quickly.

Bowman stepped closer, using a stronger hand light to see farther. "We can't go through it, so we must be able to go around it. Right?"

"Yes." Hallie led them to the right, following the acid lake's shore, and came to the place where the cave floor met vertical wall. Two feet above the floor there was a ledge no more than twelve inches wide, like those that ringed older buildings in cities.

"A section of wall peeled off, leaving that ledge. It'll take us around to the lake's far side. No other way."

"How far?" Bowman asked.

"A thousand feet, give or take. The ledge isn't wide, but it's dead flat all the way. Like a traverse on a rock climb."

"I have not climbed rock as much as you," said Arguello, tense but under control. "What is the best way to do this?"

"Keep as much boot sole on the ledge as you can. Hands shoulder height. Never move both hands at the same time. Left hand moves forward, finds a hold, secures, then right hand follows. Then left foot, then right. Don't overreach. You want to stay balanced on this thing."

"That will not be so easy with such packs." Arguello, again.

"It's doable. We made it before. Just cinch your shoulder straps and waist belts as tight as you can get them."

"Why don't we use the Gecko Gear?" asked Cahner.

"The atmosphere here is toxic, so all the moisture on the rocks will be, too. It could damage those tools. I don't know that for sure, but I don't know that it won't, either. Without those, we won't get out of the cave. We'll have to go with our regular caving gloves."

"I understand."

"I have one question," Arguello said.

"Shoot," Hallie said.

"If that acid dissolved the rock you threw, why does it not eat through the rock at its bottom and just seep away someplace?"

"Good question. The acid is lighter than water, so it floats on top of an aqueous layer—it's called a lens—that protects the bottom." Hallie turned to Bowman. "How do you want to go? What order, I mean?"

"I'll lead off. Then you, Al, and Rafael. Let's do it."

Bowman stepped up onto the ledge and found secure holds for both hands. He stood there for a moment, checking his balance. Then he started traversing along the ledge, sliding his feet and relocating his hands in small, smooth movements, the fluid rhythm of an experienced climber.

Hallie waited until he was fifty feet ahead, then clambered up to the ledge herself. Standing on it was, right away, an exercise in battling vertigo. Her whole body was pressed against the cave wall, breasts and belly and thighs. The pack was not much of a problem, but the ledge was narrow enough that she had to lean her head back to change the direction in which she was looking.

"Let's keep separation!" she called back. If anyone came off, better not to have him grab someone else and take them along. She started moving to her left, sliding her feet one after the other, letting her hands find their own placements. She went foot by foot and could not help seeing the oily, roiling surface of the lake two feet below.

After Hallie had traversed fifty feet she stopped, rested briefly, and watched Al clamber onto the ledge. *If we're going to lose Arguello,* she thought, *this will be the place.*

But there was nothing she could do, so she started off again. Left hand ahead, right hand, left foot, right foot. After a few minutes, the sequence became almost automatic, and that, she knew, was the greatest danger. *Got to stay sharp.* Their one bit of good luck here was the cave wall. If it had been smooth, they would have had serious problems. This one was rough and pocked, offering good hand placements—"jugs," climbers called them, because they resembled jug handles.

She had gone perhaps three hundred feet when she realized that she could not see Bowman, in front of her, or Cahner, behind. Bowman had been moving faster, Cahner slower, and the cave wall here had become convex, bulging outward enough to block her view past twenty feet either way. She had not remembered that from before. Bowman could take care of himself, in any case. Arguello she worried about, but his fate was out of her hands.

She was more than halfway when she got sewing-machine legs: her exhausted calf muscles starting to spasm, heels jerking up and down like the needles of sewing machines. The next thing, she knew, would be a searing cramp—a charley horse, they used to call them—and her calf muscles would contract into agonizing knots.

She stopped, stretched one carefully, pulling her toes up toward her knees, breathing deeply, letting her system flush out the lactic acid, giving the muscles time to rejuvenate.

That let her mind, which had been focusing so hard on traversing the ledge, flutter off to think of other things. It landed on Bowman. The idea of him, anyway. And the next thing she thought of was how it would feel to kiss him, and then how it would feel to . . .

She returned her attention to the wall, her calves feeling better now. She moved off, more slowly this time, trying to make her shuffle-and-clutch sequence of movements as smooth and fluid as possible. After a while she finally found her rhythm and it became almost like a slow dance, her feet and hands making their own decisions. The curve of the cave wall became more pronounced, a true bulge, so that she could see even less of the ledge in front of and behind her.

She kept going, developing the incredible intimacy with a surface known only by climbers and the blind. Sliding her hands slowly over the wall, she felt every crack, crevice, and protuberance. Tiny flakes of rock no thicker than a guitar pick seemed huge to her hypersensitized fingertips.

Just as it seemed the ledge would never end, with her calves on fire again, her light revealed the surface underfoot beginning to tilt downward. She recognized this from her last time here. She moved carefully down the slope until she was over solid cave floor. A bit farther along, the ledge dropped enough that she was able to step off. Her legs were so tired that she stumbled, knees buckling. Moving faster than she would have thought possible for a man his size, Bowman was suddenly in front of her, grabbing her under the arms, lifting her to her feet. They stood like that for just a moment, his arms around her, her hands clasping the backs of his shoulders, separated by the rebreathers on their chests, faces averted so as not to blind each other with their lights. She did not often feel small in the presence of a man, but in the expanse of this one's arms, she did.

"You good now?" His voice was muffled by the rebreather, but she could hear the concern.

"Real good. You?" She pulled him a little closer, but the goddamned rebreathers . . . it was like trying to hold someone with two briefcases squeezed between them. Still, it was better than nothing, and she held on.

"Yeah."

"Bowman?"

"Yes?"

"What are we doing?"

"Sharing body warmth. Very common in potentially hypothermic situations."

"Right. That's what I thought."

"You warm yet?"

"Not yet."

"Me neither."

So they stood like that, pulling together but pushed apart by the chest units, arms around each other, unable to kiss or even to look into each other's eyes.

"Lights," he said, and let her go.

Hallie and Bowman watched Cahner inching along carefully, stopping once to lean against the wall and rest. Through the faceplate of his rebreather Hallie could see that he was pale, his face streaming with sweat.

"You okay, Al?"

He waved a hand. "Yeah, fine. Just need to catch my breath."

"Why don't you dump the pack and rest over on that flat boulder."

"Okay. How long before Rafael shows up, do you think?"

"Five minutes, maybe ten," Bowman said.

They waited. Cahner sat on the boulder, elbows on knees, saying nothing. Hallie and Bowman dropped their packs, too, and sat on them. Ten minutes passed, then twenty.

"He should be here." Bowman stood.

"Give it a while." Hallie, looking toward the ledge.

They gave it another ten minutes.

"I'm going back. He may be stuck somewhere along there." Leaving his pack, Bowman climbed back up onto the ledge and started off. In several minutes he disappeared around the curve in the wall. Hallie stood there, watching. Cahner came up beside her.

"He's an amazing man."

"Bowman?"

"Yes. Never hesitated. Just jumped right back up on that ledge. I'd rather poke sticks in my eyes than do that again."

"It's different for him, Al. He does things like this for a living."

"For a living." He shook his head. "Imagine that."

After twenty minutes, Hallie began to feel crawly inside. She touched Cahner's shoulder. "Al, I'm worried."

"*You're* worried? I'm terrified. If we lose both of them, I don't know how much help I'll be for you."

"You're doing just fine. No worries on that count. But goddamn it. Arguello has caved. He knows how to do something like this."

"What was that you said a while back about objective dangers, though? Maybe a piece of ledge collapsed. Or some of the wall peeled away. He could even—"

They saw a light beam flickering through the gloom, and then Bowman appeared at the apex of the curve. Soon he was standing with them.

"Nothing."

"Can't be." Cahner said. "He *has* to be here somewhere."

Bowman shook his head. "He must have fallen. There's no other explanation." His voice was dead calm now. "He's not on the wall or on the other side. I went all the way back. So he must be in the lake."

Hallie pushed her mind away from what it would be like to die after falling into pure sulfuric acid.

"We have to get out of this toxic area," said Bowman. "These rebreathers have a limited capacity." The big man hefted his pack. "Let's go."

The other two shouldered their packs and moved off, Hallie leading, Cahner in the middle, Bowman last. From here the cave floor formed a great ramp that rose gently upward for about 150 vertical feet. The gain in elevation lifted them out of the sulfur fog. When the Sirius analyzer showed green, they stopped long enough to remove and stow their rebreathers, then kept going to put more distance between them and the sump of poison gas.

Near the top of the ramp, the chamber narrowed, and the exit passage was not much bigger than a subway tunnel. Soon they were going downward again, at first gently, then more and more steeply until they had to turn and face inward, descending like rock climbers on technical terrain—which is exactly what they were, just a vertical mile beneath the surface. Hallie led them on. Fatigue blunted her concentration, and several times she realized that she had just stopped without meaning to, her body turning itself off and her mind going blank.

She began to feel something close to panic, not from fear of injury but from fear of failing. The loss of Haight and Arguello, her exhaustion, the distance remaining to the moonmilk, and then the long, killing climb back to the surface. The thoughts themselves had weight and almost pushed her down, off the face into the black air.

That rock there. Focus on that rock. Then the next one. See it? Just keep doing that. One step at a time. That's how you do these things. You've been here before. This tired, this wrung out. Remember?

But try as she might, she couldn't remember such a time.

TWENTY-THREE

"I DON'T KNOW WHY THEY CALL THESE THINGS 'COOL SUITS,' " Dempsey whispered. "I'm sweating my ass off."

Stikes had been with Dempsey and Kathan for less than twenty-four hours and he was already tired of hearing Dempsey complain. He whined about the heat, his hemorrhoids, their gear, the short notice for this run. *Wee, wee, wee,* Stikes thought. *Just like the little piggy, all the way home*. In the many years he had been a SEAL, Stikes had never heard such whining. But Dempsey and Kathan had been Army Special Forces, where, apparently, whining was a trainable skill. He was not a SEAL now, nor were they SF. All three were ex-military and part of a reaction team assembled very quickly by their current employer, GFM—Global Force Multiplier. GFM was a private security contractor whose main customers were men with reason to fear for their lives and enough money to do something about it. The company also took on missions like this one, some government, some private, the prime criterion being compensation level; in Stikes's experience, they were usually on short notice. Thus he had ended up with these two mission partners, both ex-SF, rather than the former SEALs he usually joined.

"It's not about heat. It's because they don't reflect anything, little buddy." Kathan kept his voice down, too. He did not look at Dempsey or Stikes while speaking, but monitored the 120-degree arc of their surroundings that was his responsibility. Dempsey and Stikes had their own thirds of the circle.

"Hey, you think I don't know that? I was just saying."

"Yeah. But it was worse in Iraq. Down in the valleys, anyway."

Stikes was glad, at least, that they had the good sense to whisper, given the kind of country they were in here, triple Indian country, crawling with *narcotraficantes* and Mexican *federales* and natives with some unpronounceable name. He knew that, Dempsey's whining aside, the three of them could give a good account of themselves against any ordinary military force of up to thirty men, but this mission had to be slick—in and out clean. No fuss, no muss. Those were the orders, and to Stikes's way of thinking it was stupid arguing over the heat—about which none of them could do a damned thing—even if they whispered.

"All right," Dempsey said. "I'll give you that. But it was dry. There's nothing like this wet bean-eater heat."

Enough, Stikes thought. "You should have gone with the SEALs, my men. It's always cool in the water."

"I hate the water," Kathan said. He was huge, easily six-six, with a neck like a professional football player's. His accent was Georgia redneck and his voice was like a bass drum, so that even when he whispered Stikes winced at how the sound might carry here. Kathan's answer befuddled him. How could anyone, even infantry pukes like SFs, hate being in the water? Now, *ground*—that was something to hate, all right. Ground was hard and painful rock, or soft and sucking mud, or some other nightmare like this infernal thorny forest they were fighting through. The military talked a lot about good ground but, as far as Stikes was concerned, that was an oxymoron. Water was different. Water was cool and soothing, and once you knew how to relax, it folded around you like a woman. *Moved* like a woman, too.

Kathan was the team leader. He made a single motion with an index finger and they moved off again. The three had done a night HALO drop from fifteen thousand feet, right about the time Hallie and her team had been approaching the Acid Bath. Their intention had been to land in the clear meadow near the cave mouth. But as so often happened with high-altitude, low-opening night jumps, they touched down somewhere else. Now they were trying to find their way to the meadow and the cave, at night, through the forest of *mala mujer.*

They were all very fit. Even with the altitude and heavy packs they weren't breathing hard. Under the camouflage paint, their faces were sharp-featured, their bodies distilled to bone and muscle. They all had noses that had been broken but nicely even, white teeth, the products of expensive reconstruction after battle damage. They carried silenced M4 carbines with eight thirty-round magazines in chest packs, Beretta 9mm pistols in thigh holsters, big fighting knives in belt sheaths. They were dressed identically in the "cool suits"—green-and-tan camo, one-piece Gore-Tex suits coated with a nanopolymer that protected them from infrared, UV, and short-phase radar scans. To anyone looking through NVDs, they were invisible.

But, as Dempsey had noted, the suits were hot and not so good at protecting them from the *mala mujer* plants. The pain of getting stuck by those poisonous spikes was such that Stikes found it hard not to curse out loud. But he had been on many missions that were, if not identical to this one in details, just like it in purpose, which was to kill some people, and Stikes had long since accepted that pain was part of the price you paid for the privilege of killing.

Dempsey, following Kathan at the prescribed fifteen-foot interval, was a foot shorter and fifty pounds lighter than the other man.

His voice was high and rough, like that of a boxer who had been punched too many times in the throat. As he had explained to Stikes earlier, that damage had actually been done by shrapnel from an IED north of Fallujah. Dempsey wore his brown hair shoulder length, kept in place by a headband of velvet-soft suede that, he'd bragged to Stikes, he had made from the skin of an Iraqi woman's breast.

Stikes was good-looking enough to have been on a recruiting poster, though the Navy would never have allowed that. He was last on the trail but the middle man in height and weight. Stikes was normally languid in movement and soft-voiced, and he was the best hand-to-hand fighter of the three, with black belts in jujitsu, tae kwon do, and Krav Maga. This would almost certainly be his last mission, though. At thirty-six he was pushing the far edge of the envelope for work like this, and knew it. Old and slow got you killed doing these things, and it was they who were supposed to be doing the killing. He moved along fifteen feet behind Dempsey, making sure to maintain visual contact. This was no place to be wandering around alone.

Nor was it any place to be letting thoughts wander, but he could not keep himself from picturing Keyana. They had met six months earlier in San Diego after connecting on Facebook. They made a stunning couple, everybody said. She was a model and every bit as beautiful as the pictures he could see after she friended him. Almost six feet tall, slim in the right places and full where it counted, almond-eyed, with skin as flawless and smooth as porcelain.

Right away she had wanted to know what he did for a living, of course, and over dinner at a wharfside seafood restaurant, he'd said, "I do high-end security work."

"You mean like guarding CEOs and movie stars, that kind of thing?" she had asked.

"Yeah, that kind of thing." Keeping his voice a little vague, mysterious, but holding her gaze.

"It must be exciting." She had sounded impressed. But what had impressed *him* was how she'd picked right up on the fact that he wasn't eager to talk about it in more detail and didn't push him.

"It can be, at times." Stikes had let her go on believing that he guarded CEOs and movie stars and that kind of thing, telling himself it was not a complete and deliberate lie. Once in a while Gray did have an executive-protection assignment to offer. For every one of those, there were half a dozen like this one, but that didn't cancel out the others.

At any rate, it would be different from now on, because he was getting out. They were being paid handsomely for this run, as they called the things they did, $100,000 apiece, $20,000 for each of the five removals, $300,000 altogether. That was getting-out money for sure. You could marry, start a little business, maybe even have some kids, and stop dipping your hands in blood. It wasn't that he minded the killing now. War and the SEALs had taken care of that, had taught him to shave away all the moral tangles and leave just the hard, clean fact of his craft. He knew how dangerous and difficult the jobs he did were, and he knew how well he did them, and satisfaction flowed from such awareness. So at this point, it wasn't so much the killing as it was Stikes's sense that every bullet and RPG he dodged brought him that much closer to the next one, and at some point there would not be enough room or time to dodge.

They kept moving for another two hours and Kathan held up a closed fist, time for the prescribed five-minute break. Dempsey came up and knelt near Kathan, and then Stikes joined them. On one knee, they drank electrolyte-replacement fluid from plastic tubes connected to hydration packs. They had added powdered coca leaves and ginseng to their ERF, providing a stimulant solution that could keep them moving for several days without rest, if the need arose. It was the same ancient pharmaceutical mix that had allowed Inca messengers to run a hundred miles a day.

Nobody spoke. They had about two minutes remaining, and Stikes was beginning to think they might make it through another stop without breaking noise discipline. No such luck.

"The blonde is a hot little puss." Kathan was referring to pictures of Hallie Leland and the others they had viewed as part of their pre-mission briefing.

"Not so little, from what I could see," Dempsey said, appraisingly. "You can't really tell from a picture, though. The camera do lie. I had this girl in Anbar, like a beauty queen in person. But she couldn't take a picture. Looked like a truck ran over her face."

"Yeah." Kathan reflected for a moment. "But some ugly girls are great in the sack. Butterfaces. They're so grateful, I think is what it is."

"They should be grateful. It's not like dudes are lining up to do them."

"Nah." Kathan giggled softly, the childlike sound eerie coming from such a huge man. "They did for that little haji in Nasiriyah, though? You remember her, Demp?"

"Roger that. The whole team had a taste."

"Those were good days." Kathan's voice went bitter.

"Finest kind." So did Dempsey's.

If you liked it that much, why'd you get out? Stikes could not help but wonder as he listened to them mourn the passing of their good old SF days. Reading between the lines of their stories led him to believe that theirs might not have been voluntary separations. References to three prisoners and the phrase "extraordinary measures," or its abbreviation, "EM," kept popping up, as in *Hey, we were just emming those hajis, you know?*

Stikes had come to suspect that their good old days consisted mostly of violating prisoners and women. Kathan, in particular, reminded him of certain SEAL trainees, crackers from Alabama and Georgia who'd talked about the Civil War, their voices going all soft and stupid over the Lost Cause, moaning in prayerful tones about Robert E. Lee like he was some kind of saint instead of a slave-owning, butchering old bastard. For Stikes, a black man, such things did not sit well at all. He said, "Hey, my men, you want to stay focused here. Can't let anything derail this mission."

"Be cool, Stikes," Kathan said. "This a mission with benefits. What the contract said, recall, bro?" "With benefits" meant that they were free to take whatever ancillary proceeds the mission might deliver: money, jewels, precious metal, drugs—or women.

Stikes hated being called "bro" by someone like Kathan. "I can read contracts as well as you. But we don't want to be in here one minute longer than we have to. With what you're getting paid, you can buy yourself Pamela Anderson."

"She's old, man. I *could* go for Rihanna, though. *Whoeee*. You know what they say about colored girls, Stikes."

"Yeah. Say they can't find your tiny little peckers."

Kathan blinked, as though he could not believe Stikes had spoken to him like that. Stikes stared back, and the longer the moment lasted, the calmer he became. *You want it, I got it,* he thought. *Come on.* Time stretched like a hot thing nobody wanted to touch until Dempsey said, "We need to roll." He stood, and after a moment's hesitation, the others followed suit.

But Stikes couldn't quite let it go. He said to Kathan, "Hey, man."

"What?"

"You got good waypoints? Feels to me like we might have lost the track."

"You think I started doing this yesterday? Course the waypoints are good. Gray's intel is always A-grade, man."

TWENTY-FOUR

LENORA STILWELL STOOD TO ONE SIDE, HER UNIFORM SPOTTED with dried blood, shivering in the chill. Two biosuited nurses slid the long, stainless steel platform bearing Sergeant Marshell Dillon's body into a refrigerated locker and closed the door. Dillon had died several hours earlier, but they had not autopsied the body; the cause of death had been all too obvious. Dillon had died like all the others: a mass of oozing red tissue, his face a bloody horror, screaming in pain that, near the end, massive doses of morphine did nothing to blunt.

Stilwell said a silent prayer for the young soldier, then turned to walk back to the wards. In the morgue's doorway she had to stop and steady herself, placing one hand on the wall.

"Major? Are you okay?" One of the nurses, concerned, watching.

She straightened up. "All good here. Good to go." She walked out into the hall, followed by the nurses, who closed the morgue door behind them. Out here, Stilwell was once again struck by the smell. She had been a physician for two decades and had smelled just about every awful stench sickness and death could produce. But even all that experience had not included anything like the smell produced by ACE eating the flesh of living bodies. It was a sharp, nauseating stink, with elements of blood and decaying meat and fecal matter, as the bacterium ate through intestinal walls and abdominal muscles. That *would* be one advantage to a biosuit, with its rebreather filters, she thought.

Her life had settled into a rhythm of sorts. She worked until the numbers on the charts and instruments started to blur, excused herself and slept for an hour or two, got up, poured more coffee into an already sour stomach, gobbled junk food, went back to work.

No new cases were being admitted, of course, but more than a dozen remained from the time when wounded were still being brought in before they understood that ACE was rampant in the hospital unit. She was experimenting with adding other antibiotics to the colistin, creating "cocktails" of various combinations, hoping that one might be more effective than the colistin by itself. So far, none had been. The last regimen was purely palliative, trying to alleviate pain as the ACE infections moved into their advanced stages.

Miraculously, she had not been infected. By this time it amazed even Stilwell herself, given how beat-up her immune system must have been from all the stress and fatigue. But she knew there really was something to the idea that doctors developed immunities over career-long periods of exposure to bacteria and viruses, and it was a proven fact that the female immune system was more powerful. Maybe those advantages would carry her through after all.

In her tiny, cluttered office she sat down, opened her laptop computer, and wrote an email to her husband:

> Hi majormom here how things w u? I'm swmped here. How Danny? ? tackles did he mk lst gm? Hv 2 go doc work nevr dun. I love you and miss you. Give my love to Danny. Talk soon. Lenny.

She read over the note and clicked on the Close button on her email program.

Do you want to save changes to this message?

She clicked on the Save button.

This message has been saved in your Drafts folder.

That folder contained many messages by now, They had shut down the outgoing comm again. She had been writing emails and saving them anyway. It made her feel a little better. And if she didn't make it, they would at least give Doug and Danny a sense of what she had been doing.

A Chemturion-clad soldier leaned into the doorway to her office. "Major, we need you on Ward B, please."

"Is it urgent?"

"No, ma'am. Private Cheney died a few minutes ago, is all. You need to pronounce."

"Give me a moment." She nodded at the door to her tiny washroom. "I'll be right with you."

"Yes, ma'am."

She went into the lavatory, lowered the lid on the toilet, and sat on it. She took a digital thermometer out of her camo shirt's chest pocket and put it under her tongue. Ten seconds passed and the thermometer beeped. She removed it from her mouth and looked at the readout: 100.2.

She sanitized the thermometer with an alcohol wipe, put it back into her pocket, and headed for the ward. Before she had gone five steps past her office, another Chemturion-suited nurse stopped her.

"Major, we need you on Ward A."

She halted, trying to remember where she had been going in the first place. Oh yeah: Private Cheney. She needed to pronounce his death to make it official.

"What is it there?"

"Sergeant Clintock just died, ma'am. We need you to pronounce."

She nodded. How many did that leave? Eleven? Ten? At this

rate, they would all be gone by the end of the week. And then what? Can't worry about that now. *Then what* would take care of itself.

"Is Captain Franch available? Could he help you on Ward A?"

The nurse looked shocked. "Oh God. I'm sorry, ma'am. Didn't someone tell you?"

"Tell me what?"

"Captain Franch overheated in his suit and collapsed. Dehydration and hyperthermia. They took him outside. His temperature was a hundred and six and spiking. They think he might have suffered some neurological damage."

That left her and one physician's assistant, plus the nurses.

"Thank you. I'll be with you in A as soon as I can. B called me first."

"I understand, ma'am. Thank you."

TWENTY-FIVE

THEY CAME TO A SLOPING, OPEN SPACE BETWEEN GIANT boulders where the three could all stand together. There was not enough room to sit.

"We need to talk about what's next," said Hallie, watching the others.

"What've we got?" Bowman actually looked tired. Cahner was panting, bent over.

"It's a siphon. A narrow slot about two hundred yards long. Widest at the bottom, two feet or so, but narrowing at the top to less than shoulder width, so we have to pass through sideways in places."

"Why couldn't we just crawl along the bottom, where it's wider?" Fatigue made Cahner's voice faint, as though he were speaking to them from a distance.

"Part of the cave's main watercourse diverts into this passageway, which siphons it off from the primary flow. Thus the name."

"You said it's filled with water. How full?" Bowman, curious.

"It all depends on the year's surface rainfall."

"So let's just put on our rebreathers," said Cahner.

"I don't think we should." Bowman shook his head, his light beam slicing the darkness sideways. "We still have that long sump to recross on the way out. And the Acid Bath before that. We've breathed them down too much already, because of that acid lake."

"So how do we do it, then?"

"We can't wear our packs because they're too big to fit through the siphon's narrow top," Hallie said. "We can't push them ahead because the floor of the siphon is submerged. So we drag them along behind us."

She led them down for another few hundred yards to a waist-deep stream that flowed into a vertical, wedge-shaped opening in the cave wall. They paused long enough to tie haul ropes fashioned from parachute cord to their packs. Bowman said, "I'll lead off. Al, you take the middle. Hallie can be our sweep."

Cahner spoke with unusual firmness. "I don't think that's the best way to do this. If something should happen to me, I could block her passage. From Hallie's description, it sounds like a hellish place to have to drag a body out of. So I'd best go last."

Hallie and Bowman looked at each other, then at Cahner.

"Are you sure?" Bowman asked.

"I'm sure."

"All right, then." Bowman turned and walked down an easy sand slope to the stream bank. Hallie waited several minutes, then pulled her pack into the water behind her and started off. At first it was easy passage. The water was chest-deep, cold but not painful, and the siphon had the rich, bright smell of pure water tumbling over clean rocks, just like a brook in sunlight on the surface. The haul rope was snug around her waist and buoyancy reduced her pack's weight, so pulling it along the sandy bottom was not that hard. She sloshed forward, her helmet light illuminating the passage's walls: red from iron deposits, blue and green from veins of copper.

As she waded farther the water gradually deepened, rising to the middle of her neck, which meant that the floor was sloping down. Now that she had been in it for a while, she began to feel the water's chill. Sixty-five degrees Fahrenheit didn't sound all that cold, but it was thirty-three degrees below normal body temperature. With that differential, you lost heat very quickly, and water sucked it away seven times faster than air.

There was no perceptible current here. The walls were less than shoulder width apart. The siphon's ceiling started sloping downward, so that after a while she had to stoop slightly to clear the top of her helmet. Hunching down dropped her chin to the water's surface. Occasionally an off-balance step dipped her mouth and nose under, but she was prepared for that. The greater problem was having to move sideways in a modified duck waddle, knees bent, unable to stand fully erect. That, and dragging the pack along, was tiring her more quickly than she had anticipated.

About halfway through she stopped to rest. By then the ceiling had dropped more, forcing her to remove her helmet and carry it. While resting, she unclipped one of the helmet's lights and held it above the water with her left hand, hanging on to the helmet with her right. Now there was about four inches of space between the water's surface and the passage's ceiling. She could breathe only by tilting her head back to keep her nose and mouth out of the water.

Stooped, knees bent, head thrown back, she started off again. *If this thing keeps dropping, I'll be breathing good old H_2O before long.* Presently the ceiling did exactly that, dropping another three inches, leaving a space about the width of three fingers between water and rock.

Easy now. You've done it before, this is no different, just breathe easy and go slow.

She had forgotten how awful it was negotiating this kind of passage. It was worse than diving, worse than dropping down vertical walls, worse even than acid lakes. It required the utmost control to keep moving along like that, nose and lips scraping the siphon's rough ceiling, rock fragments falling into her eyes, water lapping into her mouth every so often, and the passage so narrow that she could move forward only by turning her body and edging along sideways.

She inched along—*step . . . breathe . . . step . . . breathe*—and only when she was stationary and could straighten her knees ever so slightly was she able to bring her nose and mouth out of the water. Then the ceiling dropped more and only her two nostrils were clear of the water's surface. There was perhaps an inch of space between the water and the rock, no more, so that she was moving with both mouth and eyes underwater. It was hellish. Try as she might, she could not avoid inhaling water, which made her throat constrict. But she could not afford to gasp or cough, because that would have sucked more water into her breathing passages, and it would take only a few teaspoonfuls to trigger involuntary spasms, and those would drown her.

She had passed a point of no return. If she got into trouble here, even with her tremendous breath-hold capacity, she would not make it back to clear space before drowning.

Her right boot toe caught on a rock. She stumbled forward, smacked her forehead against the siphon's spiky wall, dropped both her hand light and helmet. The impact set off red flashes in her vision and for just a second she was off somewhere else. She came back quickly, on her knees underwater, left hand on one cave wall, right hand on the floor.

She thought she should be able to spot the lights and pick them up, but there was nothing. Either the lights had been damaged or the visibility was so bad that she could not see them. That, she realized, was entirely possible, given how much silt she would have just stirred up.

She would look for the helmet later. And the other light. Right now she needed to breathe. Gently she pushed herself upright, going up inch by inch, feeling along the wall with her left hand, careful to keep her feet in place and steady. Finally she felt the top of her head touch the cave ceiling. She tilted her face upward to get her nose above water and take a breath, but she ended up kissing the rock ceiling. There was no space between it and the rock. The siphon was completely flooded, floor to ceiling. She had fallen away from the air space. When she'd gone down and struck her head, she had lost her orientation, and now, submerged in black water with no perceptible flow, she wasn't certain which way to go.

Then she remembered her pack. She was tethered to it, and all she had to do was follow the short rope back to the pack, stand up, and find the air space that she knew would be there. She put her hands on her waist, feeling for the rope, but her fingers found nothing.

Must have slipped into a fold in the fabric. She used her fingertips to explore with more pressure. Nothing. She reached behind her, groping for the section of rope that led back to the pack, but it was gone. Her knife, worn on a belt clip when diving, was now in her pack.

She began to feel the first burning in her chest, oxygen depleting, carbon dioxide building.

The pack can't be more than six or eight feet away. Which way? Don't know. Go one way. If you don't find it, go the other. Where the pack is you can stand and breathe.

She felt for clear space, found it, took a step that way—and fell, thrashing, onto the bottom of the siphon. The rope had somehow dropped down from her waist and become wrapped around her ankles. When she tried to move, it tripped her.

The burning in her chest was worse, bigger, hotter. Underwater, she felt for the rope, found it, tried to push it down over her boots, but it would not pass their tops. Tangled or knotted. She found the snag, explored it with her fingers. Not soft and loose. A hard little lump. The force of her stumble had cinched it tight. If it had been big, eleven-mil rope, such a knot would have been easier to loosen.

But this was three-millimeter parachute cord. Picking tight knots out of that was hard enough on the surface, in good light.

The burning was spreading out into the rest of her body, heat in her throat, face starting to tingle, eyes twitching. Soon her brain would slow and her muscles would grow clumsy. She picked furiously at the knot. It was no bigger than a pencil eraser and felt hard as a pebble. It was not going to come loose. With the last of her remaining strength she grabbed the bottom wrap of the rope and tried to force it down over her boots, but there was not enough slack for that.

Her diaphragm began the involuntary jerking that signaled the end. Very soon the carbon dioxide level in her system would trip the autonomic breathing reflex. Back arched, she would throw her mouth open wide and suck in a great draft of water, and a few seconds after that, her consciousness would fade and she would drift down to the bottom of the sump, eyes open and staring, hands no longer flailing, feet tied together. They would find her and she would be like Ron Haight, white skin, gray lips, a dead, sodden thing.

So much pain.

A relief. Her eyes had not been able to see for some time. Now the light in her brain began to dim as well.

Soon.

TWENTY-SIX

"WE SHOULD HAVE SIGHTED THAT CAVE HOURS AGO," STIKES, down on one knee, whispered to the others. The previous night they had kept going while it was still dark, fighting uphill through the vines and brambles and *mala mujer,* expecting to come out of the forest and spot the cave anytime. Then the sky began to glow and they went into a hide. A person could have walked within ten feet and not seen them. Two slept while one watched, the shifts rotating. It was after eight P.M. when Kathan judged it dark enough to move again.

Now it was getting close to their second dawn. "The GPS coordinates are bad," Dempsey said. "Got to be."

"Never happened before." Kathan sounded disgusted. "Gray's intel's always been good."

"You said that already," Stikes pointed out. "We can't keep wandering around out here. Get them up on comm and ask for some decent intel." His patience was exhausted.

"Can't risk that." Kathan, adamant. "The *narcos* or Feds or both will be running energy scans. Even on the IR bands. Gotta solve this one our own selves."

"Here's something else I gotta solve. I need to take a crap," said Dempsey.

"Hold it, little buddy," Kathan said.

"I *been* holding it. See you boys in a few minutes."

Stikes and Kathan waited, seated back to back, M4s held across their chests. Stikes was feeling guilty about needling Kathan. Plus, it could turn into a long mission. So he reached out with a whispered question.

"How come you hate water, man? Me, I'm like a fish."

Kathan was silent for a moment, then said, "I drowned when I was a kid."

"You mean, almost drowned?"

"No, I mean drowned. Dead."

"What the hell happened?"

"My old man took me fishing for bullheads in this creek. He called it fishing, anyway. Mostly it was about drinking whiskey and smoking weed. So he got drunk and stoned and fell asleep on the bank. I waded in. Five years old, you know? Creek just sucked me away, man. A guy downstream pulled me out. I wasn't breathing. He did CPR and I came around."

"Oh." A story like that was pretty much a conversation stopper. But then Kathan continued.

"You know how people have dreams? So now I have this dream where I drown. It's not a good way to go, trust me. There's a reason we used waterboarding to get intel out of the hajis. People who think it's all quiet and peaceful, they need to try it for themselves. Take it from one who's been there. It feels like somebody's pouring acid into your chest."

"You have that dream often?"

"Often enough."

Stikes started to say something about a dream he had, but Kathan spoke first: "He's been gone too long."

"Maybe it was a huge dump."

"No. We need to look. Leave everything here except your M4. Let's go."

Fifteen minutes later, Stikes found him. "Kathan. Here."

Dempsey's body had fallen backward and lay with its legs stuck out stiffly, frozen in the spasm of death. Around his shoulders, blood had pooled into a shape that reminded Stikes of those thought balloons over cartoon characters' heads. But Dempsey had no head. It was lying five feet away, face up, on top of its own small blood pond, still warm enough to appear bright green in the NVDs. Stikes had seen plenty of decapitations, most of them haji-done. Usually the cut edges were ragged, like steak hacked with a dull knife. Not Dempsey's.

"Look at his neck," Stikes said. "A scalpel could have done that. You ever seen anything like it?"

"No."

"What the hell, Kathan? We were twenty-five mikes away. I didn't hear a thing."

"Me, neither. I'll tell you this. Whoever killed him knew what they were doing. Dempsey was good at this work."

"There's no way anybody could sneak up on him through undergrowth like this. All those thorns and brambles scratching at your clothing, I mean," Stikes said.

"Maybe somebody was waiting here for him," Kathan said.

"I don't see it. How would they know where he would be?"

"Something else, Stikes. There aren't any tracks."

The forest floor here was damp and soft. Their own tracks, and Dempsey's, were clearly visible. And those three sets, with the distinctive Vibram patterns of their boot soles, were the only ones to be seen.

"This feels bad. Something's not right here."

They were down on one knee, facing away from each other, surveying. Through his NVDs Stikes saw the shimmering green columns of tree trunks with darker green empty space between them. Nothing moved. He listened for any sound, but except for their controlled breathing, there was nothing to hear. He sniffed the air for any dissonant scent, but nothing came.

"What do you think?" he whispered. "Narcos?"

"Could have been the *federales* or those Indians just as easily," Kathan said. "My money's on the *narcos,* but it doesn't really matter, does it?"

"What do we do with him?" Stikes asked.

"The body stays. We'll take his comm gear and weapons," Kathan said. Stikes thought he detected a hint of emotion in the big man's voice, but he couldn't be sure. It might have been fatigue.

TWENTY-SEVEN

PULLING INTO A PARKING SPACE IN HER APARTMENT BUILD-ing's lot, Evvie Flemmer stabbed the brakes so sharply the old Camry's tires screeched. She was never especially happy to be coming home, and with so much at stake now at the lab, she was especially *un*happy. But after her fourth sixteen-hour day in a row, Dr. Casey had finally *told* her to take time off.

"And since I am aware that our definitions of 'time off' may vary considerably, let's be clear that I mean sixteen hours, minimum, Evvie Flemmer. Sixteen. Do you read me?" Dr. Casey had delivered his little lecture in mock-stern tones, laying his hand on her shoulder for emphasis, but his fatherly smile never wavered as he spoke and she knew he thought he was doing a good thing.

It was after eight P.M., full dark, the parking lot washed in sodium-vapor sepia. She turned the engine off and just sat there. She *was* tired; he had been right about that. Not too tired to work properly, of course, but the thought of making it all the way to her apartment on the third floor was a bit daunting.

Flemmer passed through the small lobby, with its stainless steel mailboxes and blue barrels for recycling. She glanced briefly at the bulletin board where the property manager posted notices—time for parking sticker renewals, elevator maintenance, changing days for trash pickup—but there was nothing new.

She thought briefly about taking the stairs, but it was too late and she was too tired. To save money they had installed energy-saving bulbs that made riding the elevator like standing in a cube of dusk. The third-floor hallway itself was completely dark when she stepped out, but motion sensors detected her presence and turned on the lights—more dim energy savers. The hall smelled faintly of fried fish and cigarette smoke. The whole place was supposed to be nonsmoking, but of late new kinds of people had begun infiltrating the building. Sullen women with red dots on their foreheads. Hand-holding men who conversed in shouts. Pierced and tattooed families of astonishing corpulence that made her think of sideshows. Flemmer gladly would have moved, but Washington-area rents were exorbitant, and even this place stretched her $65,000 salary.

Inside her apartment, Flemmer closed the door, double-checked the locks, and hung her brown coat in the closet. She set her pocketbook on a table and stood waiting for her mind to issue some direction. At the lab she never hesitated like that because the work told her where to go and what to do; her mind broke big projects down into smaller tasks, and the tasks took her to certain places where she had to do specific things very precisely. *Orchestrated,* was how she thought of it, and how she liked it.

Finally she asked, out loud, "Are you hungry?" Like many who lived alone, she had acquired the habit of speaking to herself.

"Not really."

"What, then?"

"Maybe a glass of wine would be nice."

"Yes. Let's have some wine." From a box of Chablis in the refrigerator she filled a water glass halfway. She carried the glass of wine into the living-dining room, turned on a table lamp, sat on the sofa, and looked at the red paper poppies in the white vase on the coffee table. There was no television or radio—cracks in the wall of hell, was how she thought of those things. She watched the poppies and sipped wine and her mind whirred.

She thought of her parents, still out there in Oklahoma. What time would it be? About nine. Her father would be in bed already, snoring, sleep drool collecting into a dark stain on his pillow. She drank some more wine, swallowing it like water in audible gulps. She hummed "La Marsellaise" all the way through, and then halfway through again. She started to drink more wine but the glass was empty, so she filled it from the box in the refrigerator and came back to the couch.

She did not like being away from the lab. Being away from the lab made her angry. As the wine worked, she felt the anger more, and then her stomach growled. In the kitchen she heated a Stouffer's frozen chicken à la king dinner, warmed three Parker House rolls, and slathered all with real butter. For years she had tried without success to lose weight. Finally she had seen a doctor, hoping to get some diet pills. Instead, he had told her to find out *why* she wanted to lose weight. Core motive, the doctor called it. If she could identify her core motive, it would empower her, the doctor said. It wasn't easy. For an hour every day for a week, she sat with blank paper and pen, staring into space, thinking, waiting for her core motive to show itself.

It never did. The best she could manage was that it might have something to do with wanting to look good for men, and she laughed out loud at that. She wrote the word in the middle of the blank sheet of paper:

MEN

After staring at it for some minutes, she drew a line though it:

~~MEN~~

It felt good to do that, so she drew more lines and more and more until she could see only a jagged clot of lines that looked like a ball of fishhooks and no word. She had never visited that doctor again and had not tried to lose weight since.

She set her plate and glass and silverware on the coffee table. The living-dining room had a beige couch, end tables with matching lamps, and two matching white chairs. A large bookcase stood against one wall. The shelves were filled with big hardcover books arranged alphabetically by the single word that appeared on the spine of each book: Argentina, Australia, Brazil, England, France, Germany, Greece, Italy, twenty-nine in all.

She decided to read the book about France again and went to retrieve it. On the shelf above the books sat two framed pictures, black and whites, her mother and father. Her mother had straight dark hair, three deep creases in her forehead, and full, swollen-looking lips. Her face was tilted slightly to the left and her eyes were soft and unfocused. Her father wore a T-shirt that emphasized his thick and muscular neck. Black chest hair curled over its collar. Her father was the hairiest man she had ever seen. The hair swathed him like an animal's coat of fur. She remembered running her fingers over the mat of hair on his back and being surprised by how stiff it was, not soft and pliant like her own hair but more like the bristles of a brush.

She talked to them as well as to herself. "Hello," she said. "How are things where you are?"

She brought the book back to the coffee table and paged through it as she ate the soft chicken and mushrooms and peppers over white rice, careful not to spill any on the beautiful pictures. There was an entire section titled "Paris, City of Light." She lingered over those pages, pausing to put herself in one photo, savoring a glass of fine Bordeaux at Café Constant on Rue St. Dominique, watching the Tour Eiffel throw off shards of light as night overflowed the day.

But it was the sun of Provence she loved most, and that was her favorite part of the book. Every photograph of Provence seemed to radiate light. There were times when she felt a physical hunger for light, especially in gray, overcast Washington, D.C. She had spent too many years in dark places. There had been no choice about some—the trailer in Oklahoma, dark dorm rooms in college, the dingy studio in graduate school. Then, after earning her doctorate, she had searched for apartments that would be filled with light. She had looked at a good many. But every time she stood in one, empty and echoing, the white walls and white ceilings bright with light that poured through curtainless windows, she had begun to feel anxious for no reason she could understand. The longer she stayed, the more anxious she became, until the urge to *get out* became a breed of panic. And so somehow she always ended up in places like this one, apartments that were clean and dark, and in which she felt safe.

She hand-washed her dishes and set them in the drainer, replaced the book on its shelf between England and Germany. In the bedroom she locked the door, undressed, and put on her white terry-cloth bathrobe. She stepped into the bathroom, locked that door, and took the robe off again. She turned on the shower to let hot water run in. From the medicine cabinet she took two sleeping pills and swallowed them with a handful of water she cupped in her palm under the faucet. She closed the medicine cabinet door, over the mirror of which she had taped thick brown wrapping paper, and stepped into the shower. Flemmer showered twice every day, once in the morning before going to the lab and again after dinner.

The white wire basket hanging from the showerhead held three bars of soap, white, green, and blue. She washed her face with the white one and her body with the green one. With the blue soap she washed her buttocks and groin area three times, using the handheld sprayer to rinse with very hot water after each soaping.

Toweled dry, she put on her nightgown and robe and went back to check the apartment locks a last time before going to bed. On the tan carpet lay a white envelope someone had slipped under the door. They must have done it while she was showering. She picked up the envelope and took it back to the brighter light of the kitchen. She tore one end of the envelope open and shook out a single sheet of stationery on which was written,

PLEASE TAKE OUT THE TRASH BEFORE FRIDAY.

She stood in front of the stainless steel kitchen sink, looking at the paper for a long time. She found some matches from a drawer, lit the envelope and paper on fire, and let them burn to ashes in the sink. She used the sprayer to flush the ashes down the drain and then ran the disposal for a full minute.

Back in her bedroom, Flemmer went to a second closet, which did not contain clothes. In it were scores of true-crime paperbacks, a library of murders committed by husbands and wives, bosses and workers, friends and strangers, parents and children. She ran her index finger along the spines of the books on the top shelf, dropped to the second, and stopped at one with a yellow cover and red title: *Home of the Devil: A Grisly Tale of Torture and Murder in Small-Town America*. It was one of her favorites.

She read until she became drowsy and put the book on top of the Bible on her bedside table. She looked at the framed photos of her mother and father, the same photos as those on her bookshelf, just in different frames.

"Good night," she said, and turned off the light.

TWENTY-EIGHT

HALLIE'S BRAIN FLARED WITH ONE LAST BRIGHT THOUGHT: *Go left*. She pushed off in that direction, legs still bound together, stumbling, clawing the cave walls with her bare hands.

She bumped the pack.

She lurched up so fast that she hit her head again, but felt no pain, felt only the inrush of cool air into burning lungs, felt the agony begin to recede from her belly and chest and groin, felt her throat begin to loosen and her eyes to settle back into their sockets.

There were only two inches of air space here, but that was more than enough for her to fill her lungs over and over again, flushing the carbon dioxide out of her system, oxygenating her brain and muscles.

"Cave almost got you, Hallie Leland," she said.

It was as close as she had ever come to dying in a cave, and she knew it. But something strange had happened, that last flaring thought, and she was alive.

"Thank you," she said to Chi Con Gui-Jao. "Thank you."

When she felt able, she freed her legs from the rope. Instead of retying the rope around her waist, from then on she would haul it along with one hand or the other, so that she could break free instantly if she needed to. She retrieved a backup light from one of the thigh pockets on her caving suit and used it to find her helmet and the other light.

Half an hour later she came out the siphon's far end. She stood knee-deep in a black lake of still water. On her right, the beams of her lights revealed a sheer gold-colored rock wall rising up to the ceiling fifty feet overhead. She thanked the cave god again and walked out onto dry cave floor. Bowman was waiting.

"That was a bitch," he said, sounding really challenged for the first time.

"Tell me about it. I almost bought it back there."

He looked up quickly. "What happened?"

She saw that Bowman had taken off his pack. She shucked out of hers, too. "I stumbled, fell underwater, and got my legs tangled up with the pack tow rope. Damned stupid and clumsy."

He didn't speak for a moment. Then he walked over, put a hand on one of her shoulders, drew her closer to him. He put a hand on her other shoulder. His jaw was clenched, brow furrowed. The air around him felt electric. It was the first time she had seen him like this. He started to speak, stopped, shook his head. Got control, then spoke.

"Hallie. *You have to be careful.*" His eyes were filled with concern, but his voice was sharp. "If anything happens to you, all of this will be for nothing."

She had never taken well to being scolded. She reached up, grasped his wrists, and took his hands off her shoulders. "Who's talking here?" she asked. "Secret Agent or Horse Man?"

She was confused. The eyes looking down at her were the eyes she knew she would have seen, had there been light, when she and Bowman had slept down in the boulder garden. But the voice had a crackling energy that made her feel afraid. It took her back to the first time they had seen each other at BARDA.

He hesitated, and she could tell that he was trying hard to find the right—the true—answer. He held his hands out, palms up, the first time she had seen him evidence anything even close to helplessness. "Both. I care about you, Hallie. You know that. You feel that, like I do. And I need *you,* Dr. Leland. You know that, too. *You are the mission.* You need to understand that. To understand both."

Her anger dissolved. *Oh hell.* She pulled off her helmet, stood on tiptoe, took his face in her hands, and kissed him. Not on the cheek. Kissed him for real, sliding her arms around his neck, holding on. *In for a penny, in for a pound.* She felt the tension of surprise for just a millisecond, and then he softened. He put his arms around her, gathered her in, and the kiss went from her lips down her neck into her chest past her waist to her toes and all the way back up again. A breathless, giddy spinning like the first moments of a skydive free fall.

It lasted until both had to come up for breath. She laid her head on his chest, the top of it just touching his chin. *What a hell of a place to fall for somebody,* she thought.

She pulled back just enough to look toward his eyes, which she could see, dimly, in light reflecting from their helmet lamps, both of which had fallen to the cave floor.

"Roger that, ma'am."

He leaned down and they kissed again, and they were more relaxed than ravenous this time, savoring rather than devouring. After a while they both leaned back and looked at each other, wide-eyed, panting.

"Roger *that,* sir."

He shook his head as if to clear it, then set his jaw. "Al will be showing up pretty soon.

She took a deep breath, let it out, touched his face with one hand. "You're right."

They separated. He got some water from his pack and shared it with her. She peeled the wrappers off two energy bars and gave him one. They sat on the cave floor, leaning against some rocks, waiting in the dark, lights turned off. A smooth wind flowed over their skin, rockfall clicked and boomed, the river fought its way on down into the cave. Ten minutes passed, then fifteen. She could feel Bowman starting to worry. Five minutes later he stood up.

"I know he moves slowly, but not that slowly. I'm going back."

"No." It escaped before she could stop it.

He turned. "What?"

"Maybe wait just a little. Al gets through, in his own poky way."

He hesitated, torn between two responsibilities, one old, the other new.

"Five more minutes."

"If you go back, I come along."

Bowman didn't respond. He shut his eyes, rubbed his face, breathed.

Five minutes came and went. *The cave killed him,* Hallie thought. *Three down, two to go. At this rate, we won't even make it to the moonmilk.* She suddenly felt a depression so crushing she pushed out with her arms, in the dark, as though warding off a living thing. Bowman took a backup light from his pack. He turned to face her.

"Hallie, if you had trouble in there, it'll be worse for him." He glanced at the luminous face of his watch. "Look. If anything . . . if I'm not back in fifteen minutes, just go on."

She thought, *If you don't come back, I won't be able to get out of the cave because your body will block the passage. Maybe I could haul you all the way out. But maybe not. So we'd end up staying down here together.*

But she said nothing. She helped him cinch the ankle and wrist seals to keep as much water out of his suit as possible. Checked the mounts on his three helmet lights to make sure they were secure. Made sure his diver's knife was tight in the scabbard he wore strapped to the inside of his left calf. Then there was nothing else to do, nothing more to check.

When he looked at her, there was no mistaking with which eyes. "Fifteen minutes."

She nodded. "Be careful. For God's sake."

"Always. The soul of caution."

He turned and started wading back down toward the siphon. He was three feet from it when Al Cahner stepped out. They had been so intent on each other that they had somehow missed the telltale flickering of his light as he approached. He and Bowman almost ran into each other.

"Hi!" Cahner sounded almost chipper.

Hallie was dumbstruck. Cahner made his way toward her.

"Al! We thought you were . . ." Hallie couldn't bring herself to say "dead." Some deep cautionary reflex stopped her. *Bad luck, don't do that*. "We were worried about you, goddamnit!"

He hung his head like a chastened boy. "I . . . look, this is embarrassing, but I had to go to the bathroom."

"In the siphon?"

"Well, I had drunk a lot of water between camp and the siphon. Should have gone before we went in, but it didn't feel so bad. I think all that flowing water was what did it."

"So you . . . peed in the siphon?"

"I got to that place where the water was just about thigh-high. Whew. I was about to explode. Can't tell you how much better I feel."

"But . . . it took all this time?"

"Well, I kind of got messed up. See, I had to pull down the zipper on the front of the cave suit, but it got stuck. So I worked and worked and finally got it down. I went ahead and did my business, but then it stuck again on the way *up*. I yanked it so hard that my helmet came off. Guess I forgot to fasten the chin strap. I got the zipper back up, and fished for my helmet, and put it back on. Then I was ready to go again. I guess it did take a while." He looked back and forth between them. "I'm sorry if I worried you." Then he brightened. "But I'm glad you cared about old Al Cahner!"

"Of course we care, you jerk." Hallie walked over and gave him a hug so strong his eyes bulged slightly.

"Do you want to have a rest, Al?" Hallie could tell from the sound of his voice that Bowman very much did not want to have a rest, but she admired him for resisting the need for haste.

"You know, I'm feeling pretty good. Why don't we just mosey right on. I'll let you know if I start to get really tired."

"Okay," said Hallie. "And let us know if you need to pee, for God's sake."

They headed on down.

Seven hours later they were all beginning to stumble from exhaustion. Cahner had fallen once, fortunately suffering nothing worse than skinned knees and cut palms. Hallie's own knees were screaming from the constant pounding of descent. Her thighs were on fire as well, and her back felt like someone had been smacking it with a hammer. They agreed to keep going until they found a place where they could camp. It took another two hours.

"I think this is as good as it's going to get!" Hallie yelled. She was only a few feet from Bowman and Cahner, but the watercourse here was a full-fledged river, booming and boiling and frothing, so powerful that the cave floor throbbed under their feet. "There is no other place to camp between here and the moonmilk chamber. It's another ten hours, at least."

They had passed nothing remotely suitable for a camp during their last hours of descent. It had been one vertical drop after another, interspersed with short, steep connecting passages. They could have hung portaledges, like climbers use, from the cave walls if they had brought any, but the weight of those things was prohibitive, which left them with no choice; they had descended until they simply could go no farther.

"It will have to do," said Bowman, shrugging.

Once again, there was no one open area big enough for all three of them to camp together. But after hunting for half an hour, each managed to find an adequate sleeping spot. Bowman's was between the other two, about a hundred feet from Cahner's and half that distance from Hallie's.

Alone in the dark, Hallie switched off her light and removed her boots and filthy caving suit. She repeated her ritual placement of suit and boots by her shoulder, so that even if all light failed she could still find them. Then she lay down on top of her bag.

Caves make luxuries of the simplest things. One cup of tea, better than champagne. One damp bag, better than a Plaza suite. What else do you need, girl? Well, okay, that would be nice, too. Been a while for you. But it's not going to happen here. After, maybe. I really could see us doing something together if we get out of this cave. That kind of thing doesn't do much for mission focus, like he said. But it's fun to think about, just for a minute.

Her sore muscles began to relax, inducing a sense of cozy security. She knew it wasn't real, knew that the camp couldn't protect her from any of the cave's dangers—flooding, falling rock, bad air. She knew that there were still hazards between them and the moonmilk and that every one would have to be faced all over again on the way out. But just for a few minutes she surrendered to the luxury, false though it might have been, of allowing herself to feel safe.

Hallie thought of the farm down near Charlottesville, the best and safest place she had ever known. She saw green pasture washed by light, the breeze stirring summer hay in great slow waves, black horses grazing, their necks stretched down, muzzles working in the smooth green grass, tails flicking the air. She thought of all that, and especially of the sun, felt its warmth on her face and arms and neck. She fell asleep.

She dreamed of Bowman. Of his scent, that salty, citric tang with a hint of warm honey. She dreamed, as well, of the touch of his hand when it had brushed her face, the palm and fingers rough but the touch somehow light. And how it felt to kiss him. He would be a man who knew how to touch horses, and that said a great deal, because horses could tell in an instant what kind of person was laying hands on them, even if it was just fingertips. She dreamed of his voice, too. It was soft, softer than most of the men's voices she had ever heard, but it made your attention snap to.

"Hallie."

Her eyes opened and she realized it was no dream. Here was Bowman, his face inches from hers in the dark, close enough for her to feel his breath on her forehead and smell that lovely scent. One of his hands was touching her shoulder. "Wil." Her voice was rough with sleep.

"I thought you might be lonesome." His lips brushed her ear. "No, that's not true. I wanted to see you."

An honest man, she thought. *Truly rare in this day and age.*

"Well . . ." She yawned, despite herself. *Now, what message does that send?* she thought. *Stupid girl.*

"Do you want me to go?"

"No."

Then she knew he would kiss her, but he did not. Instead, he pulled her closer to him, wrapped one long arm around her, and settled her head against his shoulder. She put her arm across his chest. Their legs touched all along their length. He kissed her ear. She kissed his neck. Together like that, wrapped around each other, they fell asleep.

Later, half dreaming and half awake, she thought she felt Bowman moving beside her, rising to an elbow, saying, "I'm just going to the river, Hallie. I won't be long," and she nodded and said, "Take a light," and he said, "No need. I've got it pictured," and she said, "Too far. *Take* it," shoving her backup light into his hand, squeezing his fist around it, saying, *"Take it,"* and he finally did. Then she felt him standing up, she thought she felt that, anyway, or maybe she dreamed it, and listened to him moving off, all sound torn away by the crashing river, and then she dropped back down into the darkness of her own sleep.

. . .

When Hallie woke, she was alone. She looked at her glowing watch dial. She had slept almost four hours. She lay there in the dark, breathing, feeling her heartbeat, coming back to herself. She listened hard for the hiss of a stove, but there was nothing to hear but the river, nothing to see but red and silver bursts of false-light images swarming before her eyes.

She stood up, dressed, turned on her light, and headed toward Bowman's spot. His gigantic red pack was there, leaning against a rock. His green sleeping bag was there, too, spread out flat on the cave floor, but it looked neat and smooth, like it had just been deployed. His one-piece red suit had been rolled into a compact tube and placed at the head of the sleeping bag. His boots and socks sat beside his pack.

A touch on the back of her shoulder made her cry out and spin around.

"*Al!* You scared the hell out of me."

"Sorry! Where's Bowman?"

"I don't know."

She used her light to slash the darkness up and down, again and again, the signal divers used to alert each other, but saw no flashing in return. She began to feel the first nibble of fear in her belly. She stopped moving, took several deep breaths, let them out slowly.

She turned toward Cahner. He held his hands out, palms up, eyebrows raised. He looked afraid. Hoping to calm him, she put her hand on his forearm.

"We need to search."

"How?"

"Cardinal directions first. You go north. Three hundred steps. I go south. We meet back here. Primary light and backups."

They retrieved all the lights from their packs and started out from camp, walking away from each other's backs as if they were duelists. It took her almost ten minutes to complete the three hundred steps, the terrain was that rugged and broken. As she went, Hallie searched on both sides slowly and carefully with her light, yelling Bowman's name all the while. *We are using way too much light,* she thought, *but there's nothing else do to. We have to find Bowman.*

Hallie reached the end of her search line and came back to their starting point. She was surprised to find that Cahner had beaten her there.

"Hallie, you've got to come see something."

Her heart jumped. "Did you find him?"

"No. Maybe. I don't know. Come on."

Cahner headed back in the direction of his search route and she followed close behind, so anxious it was hard not to step on his heels. She expected them to walk for a long time, but they didn't. Thirty feet at most.

"Stop!" Cahner's voice was a bark, unusually sharp. She looked past his shoulder. There was a hole in the cave floor about twenty feet in diameter. "It's deep, Hallie. Very deep."

"How do you know?"

He stooped, picked up a baseball-sized rock, and tossed it into the hole. They waited. And waited. Nothing. But there was always the river's roar covering everything else, so she picked up a larger rock herself and tossed it in and listened. Again, nothing.

"How deep would it have to be for us not to hear those rocks hitting bottom?" Cahner asked.

"A thousand feet, at least. Probably more."

"Is that possible?"

"Anything's possible in a cave like this."

"If he fell in here . . ."

If he fell in here, he's gone, Hallie thought. "I don't think he fell in here."

"Why not?"

"Why would he come over this way? Even if he did, Bowman was too experienced to just fall in. Not possible."

"You just said anything is possible down here."

She opened her mouth, shut it again. He was right about both. She had said that. And anything *was* possible. Motioning for him to stay where he was, she inched closer to the edge of the pit. The perimeters of shafts like this were often rotten and unstable, like big cornices on mountains. Stopping five feet from the lip, she played her light down into the darkness. The walls were dead vertical. Twenty feet down, a layer of thick mist ate her light. She glanced back at Cahner. "Too much fog. Can't see."

Standing there with her light on his chest, Hallie could see that Cahner looked used up. His eyes were bloodshot, the circles beneath them were almost black, the flesh of his face sagged, his body curved beneath unseen weight, even without the pack. He seemed to be having trouble holding his head up. Fatigue? Neck injury? *He's keeping it together with sheer willpower. Have to admire that.*

Then a thought struck her: *Do I look like that?* She knew the answer, but there was nothing to do about it other than keep going. She pulled up the image she had seen in Don Barnard's office, that soldier who had died so horribly, and it gave her strength.

"Now we do east and west. You go east."

They started off again. Hallie headed west and made her three hundred steps more quickly this time, the route presenting fewer obstructions. She got back to their starting point first. Cahner returned five minutes later, held up his hands. They stared at each other.

Hallie shook her head, slumped against a boulder. *You will not cry. You cannot afford that luxury here.* Cahner came closer and patted her shoulder. Thoughts began to fly around in her mind like bats, darting, uncontrolled. A second later, she slapped herself hard, startling Cahner. *Get yourself together. You have to find Bowman,* she thought.

They could keep going out, following more points of the compass, northeast and southwest, northwest and southeast. But she was beginning to think the unthinkable, that they just might *not* find Bowman. She recalled the two scientists who had simply vanished when she had last been in this cave.

How had the cave done that? Those men were experienced cavers, and there were two of them. One, you could imagine dying by a fluke fall or getting hit by breakdown. But two? That stretched the limits of the imagination. And now Bowman. Not just anybody, but *Bowman*. The least likely man she had ever met to come to grief in a cave. Or anywhere, for that matter. And yet it was appearing more probable with each passing minute that that was exactly what had happened.

Cahner pointed toward the river. "I think we need to look down there. Maybe he went to pee, fell, and hurt himself. Maybe he can't move."

"That *is* where he went!" Hallie suddenly remembered. She regretted revealing the knowledge to Cahner because of what it would tell him, but the hell with it. She had been half asleep when Bowman had told her he was going to the river. She had given him her light. But Bowman being Bowman, he might not have turned it on, relying instead on his snapshot. Or he might have turned it on and still gotten too close to the rushing water and slipped.

It was, she realized, one of the easiest places to die in the whole cave. *When did you need to pee? Middle of the night. Where did you go? To the river. What shape are you in? Half asleep. Jesus Christ.*

"Let's go see." She pointed at his feet. "Be careful."

They walked toward the river, and it was like walking down a wet, steeply pitched slate roof. Closer to it, the rocks became smooth, almost glassy, scoured by the action of grit-carrying water over countless eons. And right down close to the foaming water itself, Hallie could see that the rocks had an eerie shine, covered with a greenish algal growth that was almost invisible. She stood where she was. They played their lights up and down the riverbank, over and over. The river down here was so powerful that they felt it as much as heard it, their bodies vibrating with the energy that came up from the rocks, through their feet, and into their legs.

Flashing their lights, they walked back and forth both ways along the river, staying above the slippery algal sheen, for half an hour. Finally, she turned to Cahner and motioned for them to head back. There was no point in trying to make herself heard here.

They returned to their camp area and Hallie struggled to steady her voice. "He's gone. Don't know how, but gone. Probably the river."

But her mind was filled with a simple, terrible question: *How could he make such a mistake? He was tired, and exhaustion makes you careless, but still. How?*

For a second, Cahner's face looked like a pane of glass, pushed out of shape by great wind, in the moment just before it shattered. Hallie could sense the struggle going on within him, the urge for self-preservation warring with his conscious desire to help. Sometimes people lost that struggle and went berserk. She put her hands on his shoulders and looked into his eyes. "Al. I can't do this alone. *I need you.*"

The words seemed to hit him like a slap. His head came up, his eyes clearing. He focused on her. She saw his jaw working, watched as the muscles of his face appeared to rearrange themselves, regaining tone and strength. He stood erect, swallowed, nodded. It was the first time she had ever seen him stand up really straight, and she realized that he was almost as tall as she. He took her hands from his shoulders and held them.

"You have me." His voice was firm and certain. "Whatever it takes, we will do this." He looked at her for another moment, then released her hands and turned toward his pack.

"Let's go," he said.

TWENTY-NINE

SIX HOURS AFTER LEAVING DEMPSEY'S BODY, STIKES AND Kathan finally located the meadow and sighted the mouth of Cueva de Luz. The mission had never called for them to actually go into the cave. Rather, they would wait for whoever came out and deal with them on the surface. They made a camp fifty yards back from the tree line. Then they created a hide, just inside the tree line at the meadow's edge, from which one of them could watch the cave mouth constantly. One man slept or rested, one kept watch. Four on, four off. If Dempsey had been alive it would have been four on, eight off. This two-man rotation was punishing, but Stikes had endured worse.

He had just finished one of his fours and was rousing Kathan—carefully. It was unwise to startle a man like Kathan from sleep.

"Kathan. *Kathan,*" Stikes whispered.

The big man's eyes snapped open. "My turn?"

"Yeah."

Kathan sat up and rubbed his face. He gazed around the campsite with a puzzled look and for just a moment he seemed to Stikes like a huge child. But then Kathan focused and Stikes thought, *No eyes like that in any child.*

"I was about to ask you where the hell Dempsey is," Kathan said. He shook his head. "Jesus."

"It's tough about Dempsey," Stikes said. "I know you two went back a way."

"Yeah, we did." Stikes waited for more, but then Kathan started assembling gear for his turn in the hide.

"This place is crawling with bad actors," Stikes said. "You can't afford to get careless for a second."

"Dempsey never got careless. I served with the man a long time. Something else happened."

"Like what?"

"I don't know what. But trust me—Dempsey was not the careless type."

Stikes saw no reason to argue the point. "I guess we'll never know."

"The real question is, why didn't they come for us? They must have been watching, waiting for an opening, like Dempsey moving off to take a crap."

"Two of us together, they probably figured too much for them," Stikes said.

"Yeah, probably so." Kathan paused. "We lost a guy like that in Iraq."

"Like what?"

"The hajis cut his head off," Kathan said. "His name was Stanton. They put spikes through his eyes and hung his head from a road sign. There was so much blood, you could tell they put the spikes in before they killed him."

"A buddy?"

"Closest kind," Kathan said. "Him and me and Dempsey were on our third deployment together."

"Why'd you get out? You and Dempsey, I mean."

Kathan hawked, spat. "It wasn't our choice, you want to know the truth. After we lost Stanton, we had some problems interrogating hajis near Fallujah." Kathan's eyes went vague, then refocused. "It wasn't like we did a My Lai. Just three hard-core hajis. And we got good intel, too." He took in a long breath, exhaled, gazed toward the cave mouth. "But then, look how it's all turned out. We're making five times the money, and the benefits definitely don't suck."

"Plus which," Stikes said, "as much as it pains me to say this, the benefits just got better."

Kathan nodded. "Yeah. We'll split ol' Demp's share. It would have been the same if they'd got you or me."

"The way it works."

"Sure enough. And those other benefits, too."

"Other benefits?"

"Come on, man. The tall blonde. Honest to God, Stikes, I can't stop thinking about that one." Kathan winked, grinned, but Stikes saw no trace of humor in the other man's face. More like hunger. *She's gotten into his brain and there's only one way to get her out.*

"No?" Stikes said.

Kathan glanced at him. "Hey, don't worry, man. There's plenty for two there, count on it."

Stikes saw that Kathan had misunderstood. "She's all yours."

"You don't want some of that?"

"It's not my thing, Kathan."

"Not your *thing*? What's that supposed to mean?" Kathan's gaze suddenly hardened, turned suspicious. Stikes saw that he was going to have to talk this through.

"It's my last run. I've been doing this long enough. I'm getting out."

"Getting *out*?"

"Give it another ten years or so, see how you feel then. Yeah, I'm getting out."

"Getting out." Kathan repeated the words as though they were in some foreign tongue.

"Come on. Don't you ever think about it?"

Kathan rubbed a hand over his eyes, looked out at the forest. "What the hell would I do?"

Stikes shrugged. "Anything you wanted to."

"I don't want to do anything else. I *like* this work. What are you thinking about doing?"

"Starting a business. Boxing gym, or maybe a martial arts academy. For kids in the 'hoods."

"Jesus Christ." Kathan studied him for a few moments, as though sensing that he was missing something. Then he grinned. "You have a woman back there, don't you?"

"Yeah. I do."

"What's her name?"

"Keyana."

Kathan repeated the name slowly, enunciating each syllable. "Nice name, the sound of it."

"What about you? Who do you have back there?"

"You mean, like wife or girlfriend?"

"Yeah."

"Nah. I got the work, is all. And you know what? I like it, man. Don't tell me you don't get off on it."

"Sometimes, some part of it. But not like it was once."

"You really getting out?"

"Absolutely."

"Told Gray yet?"

"I gave that some thought. I figured the best time is after we're back and I have my money."

"Good call." For just a moment Kathan's eyes changed and he looked like he might say more, but then they hardened again. He finished collecting his gear and moved off toward the hide.

THIRTY

HALLIE, HOLDING UP HER HAND, WHISPERED, "AL . . . TURN YOUR light off."

"What's the matter?" His voice, like hers, was thick with fatigue.

"Turn off your light." She had turned hers off already. Cahner did as he was told, and the darkness rushed over them like black water closing around two drowning people.

"What are we hiding from?" He kept one hand in contact with her pack.

"We're not hiding. Look past my right shoulder."

He did. Gasped. "My God, Hallie."

"I know. Amazing, isn't it?"

A faint blue glow. Fifty yards ahead, the route turned right, and the glow was coming from beyond that turn.

"That's it, then? The moonmilk chamber?"

"That's it."

Five minutes later they stood in a roughly circular chamber fifty feet in diameter. The floor was gravel and sand, sloping gently downward toward an exit passage, the ceiling about thirty feet overhead. The chamber's walls were vertically fluted yellow-and-white flowstone. Off to their left glowed the moonmilk colony. It was a microbial mat, five feet square, six inches thick. It looked like a big, glowing blue-green brain hanging from the cave wall.

The glow was bright enough here that they could see without their lights. It felt like being under azure Caribbean water. It was not a steady glow but instead wavered and flowed like the northern lights.

"How in God's name does it survive down here?" Cahner was still whispering. It was like being in a cathedral, somehow. They had moved away from the watercourse, its sound now distant and faint. There was nothing but the softly pulsing blue light. The air in this chamber felt different, drier and slightly warmer.

"We don't know." Hallie's voice was reverent, tinged with awe. "But it does. Has for eons, apparently."

"I could stand here and look at it for hours." Cahner sounded mesmerized. "It's like staring into a fire."

"I know. There's a feel to it, too, Al. Are you getting that?"

"Yes, a little. It's like warmth."

They dropped their packs. Still operating in the light given off by the moonmilk colony, Hallie retrieved an Envirotainer, an aluminum cylinder eighteen inches long and six inches in diameter. Inside were four test-tube-sized stainless steel containers. In the Envirotainer's base was a battery-powered EMU—environment maintenance unit. Moonmilk, she had learned the hard way, had a very narrow range of survivability: plus or minus about four degrees in temperature, plus or minus 5 percent in humidity. It had zero tolerance for light, natural or artificial. Not that any of those things were surprising, given that it had evolved in an environment where the conditions were hyperstable and absolutely dark.

"Now comes the hard part." Hallie set the four containers on the cave floor beneath the moonmilk colony. As she did so, the biomass's colors changed subtly, a hint of pink flowing in.

"My God. Look at that." Cahner stopped moving.

"I know. Amazing, isn't it?"

"Changes colors. Like an octopus."

"Probably more like chameleons." Hallie had investigated the color shifting. "Cephalopods use muscles to control their color changes. Moonmilk doesn't have muscles, so it must be cell signaling, which is how chameleons do it. They can change color in response to temperature fluctuations. Mood. Stress. So this is probably chromatophores responding to hormone releases."

She put on a high-filtration, isolation surgical mask with a 0.1 micron barrier capability. She donned sterile, elbow-length surgical gloves and removed from sterile packaging a Bard-Parker No. 60 straight-blade scalpel and a stainless steel dissection scoop. She turned to Cahner.

"Okay, here's where it gets tricky. Once we separate a sample, we have about ten seconds to isolate it in the Envirotainer capsule before it loses viability. I need you to position the containers while I deposit samples. Put on a mask and gloves first."

Cahner did as he was told. Then he picked up one of the sample-collection cylinders, unscrewed the top, and held it for Hallie. With the scalpel, she made an incision in the biomass slightly smaller than the cylinder. Using the dissection scoop, she excavated beneath and behind the incisions and gently worked the sample free. For the first few seconds, it glowed and pulsed in consonance with the primary biomass. Then its luminescence began to dim and the color pulses slowed. It gave off a peculiar scent that reminded Hallie of crushed grapes.

"Quick, now," she whispered, more to herself than Cahner, who was standing there with the cylinder ready. She deposited the sample.

"Secure it!"

The words came out more sharply than she'd intended, but Cahner seemed not to notice. He put the cap in place, screwed it down tightly, inserted the cylinder into the Envirotainer. "Good job," she said. "That one ought to be fine. Let's do another."

They obtained two more samples and sealed them into the Envirotainer. They were working on the last one when the scalpel slipped in Hallie's fingers. The stainless steel handle had a scored surface for better purchase, but it had been designed for use in the controlled conditions of a surgical theater, not the bottom of a supercave. The handle had become wet and slick with biomatter as Hallie worked. She was making a vertical incision in the body of the moonmilk, her left hand holding the mass steady as the blade passed through. Though visually it appeared to resemble brain matter, the moonmilk's tissue was tougher. Cutting it, even with the surgical-grade scalpel, was more like cutting through the skin of a grapefruit, requiring considerable, steady pressure. Before she could stop it, the scalpel blade slipped and jumped sideways, slicing a deep gash that ran through the web between her thumb and forefinger and halfway across her palm.

She screamed, dropped the scalpel, grabbed her left wrist. The pain hit instantly, like someone laying a red-hot blade on her palm, running all the way up her elbow into her shoulder and neck. She was off balance anyway, and the explosion of pain caused her to stumble, shoving her bleeding hand into the body of moonmilk. When she pulled her hand free it was smeared with blue-green matter, which mixed with the blood flowing heavily from her wound. The pain flared, as though someone had poured pure alcohol into the gash.

Cahner was already tearing through the contents of his pack for the first aid kit. Hallie pulled the surgical gloves off, held her left hand up, and squeezed her left wrist fiercely with her right, compressing the ulnar and radial arteries—the deep ones that suicidal wrist slitters had to cut to be successful. Those both lay deep, however, and blood kept welling from the wound, running down her forearm, dripping and pooling on the cave floor at her feet.

"Al!"

"I'm looking, Hallie! Hang on!" He was buried in his pack up to the shoulders, digging its contents out, socks and toilet paper and MREs flying out behind him. Hallie was watching, and then suddenly she was sitting down, feeling dizzy, nauseous.

"Got it!" Cahner ripped the paper wrapping from a sterile compress and hurried to kneel beside Hallie, dressing in one hand, poly bottle canteen in the other. "You hold your wrist, keep that pressure on, and I'll flush this cut out."

She held on, gasping from the pain when Al sloshed water over the wound. It wasn't sterile, but it might wash out fragments of rock and moonmilk. He emptied his canteen onto her hand, then put the compress on her palm and cinched its gauze straps tight.

She yelped.

"I'm *sorry,* Hallie!" He sounded horrified.

"No worries." She forced herself to relax, breathe deeply. "It has to be tight."

When he was finished, Hallie sat, letting her head clear. Cahner knelt, one hand on her shoulder. "That is a nasty cut. What else should I do?"

"I don't think anything, right now. It'll need stitches for sure when we get out, but the bandage should hold it together until we do."

"Climbing isn't going to be fun with that."

"Tell me about it."

"Does it hurt like hell?"

"It did. But not so much, now."

"Probably mild shock. You were looking wobbly there."

"Better now." She started to stand up, but Cahner pushed her gently back down.

"You just stay there for a few minutes. We'll rest a bit and have something to drink and a bite to eat."

"We need to get more moonmilk," she said.

"What we need now is to get *you* fixed up." Cahner took off his mask, and removed his rubber gloves. They ate energy bars, drank what remained of Hallie's water, and napped for two hours on the cave floor. Then it was time to start the long trip out.

THIRTY-ONE

LENORA STILWELL WAS DREAMING OF A TIME AT A SMALL island in the Gulf, called Delfín. Spanish for "dolphin." She and Doug and Danny were swimming out past the low, white curl of surf, slicing through blue ocean strewn with sun glitter, when a group of bottlenose dolphins came toward them, making silvery arcs in the air with their leaps. They stopped, treaded water, watched the dolphins on a feeding run, chasing schools of mackerel, which, herded to the surface, made it swirl and bubble like water boiling in a vast pot. Then she looked around and Doug and Danny were gone and someone was calling her name, someone she could hear but could not see, and she could not keep her head above the water.

"How are you feeling, Major?" Stilwell opened her eyes. The nurse, a young woman in a blue Chemturion suit, had one gloved hand on the rail of her bed. Stilwell turned her head. "I'm sorry to bother you, ma'am," the nurse said. "Just a vital check and I'm out of here."

"No problem. Doing your job." The clear plastic cannula, inserted into her nostrils, made her sound like she had a bad cold, but they were delivering four liters per hour of 100 percent oxygen.

"How you doing, ma'am?"

"All things considered, not so bad."

The nurse smiled, nodded, but, to Lenora's amazement, she saw the other woman's eyes well up with tears. A lot of people seemed very concerned about her here at CENMEDFAC. She knew it was because word had gotten around about her work with the troopers back at COP Terok. They were calling her a hero, Major Angel, things like that. She had no patience for such things. The heroes were those boys fighting every day.

"I *hate* this. Excuse me, Major."

She smiled back. Could still do that. Only had three lesions so far: right thigh, abdomen, left arm.

"Ma'am, why don't you let us give you a little something to make you more comfortable?"

"I may just do that in a bit. Right now, I'm good. But I appreciate your concern." She reached out and gave the nurse's gloved hand a squeeze, managed a wink.

"All right, ma'am. You know I'm close as that button there." A large woman, she nodded at the call button safety-pinned to Stilwell's sheet, and her forehead bumped against the blurry plastic of the suit's helmet. She squeezed Stilwell's hand back and headed off to the nurses' station.

Stilwell was in an isolation ward with four beds. There was another woman, an ACE sufferer, drugged to sleep. There would come a time, Stilwell knew, when morphine would not be enough, when nothing would be enough, and then it would be truly bad. The other woman's case was not as advanced, but in her, asymptomatically, ACE had emerged through the tissues of her face first, rather than eating its way out of the body cavity. There were so many nerves in the face, so much pain there just waiting to be set free. She needed morphine, and a lot of it.

It won't be long for you, girl, Stilwell thought. *You're steady at level seven now. Yesterday was level five. So a couple of days at most. You can probably handle up to eight without the morphine.* She had often asked patients to rank their pain on a scale of one to ten, one being pain-free and ten being unendurable agony. Now, for the first time ever, she was giving herself the same quiz.

She didn't want meds yet. For one thing, they made her constipated. They also muddled her thinking. The pain did that, too, of course, but she found that she could take "vacations" from the pain, going to other places and times in her mind. And when she came back from vacation to the hospital room, she could think clearly for a while. She was thinking about ACE, reviewing all she knew about it, trying to create a virtual laboratory in her mind to work out some protocol to counter it. Having contracted it herself put her at a disadvantage. But looked at another way, it gave her the advantage of being a physician and scientist who could analyze the symptoms and progression firsthand.

Just now, though, the pain interrupted her thoughts. The spots on her leg, abdomen, and arm were red and raw, leaking blood and pungent fluids, the products of putrefaction. The spots felt like someone had poured gasoline on her body there and set it afire. Bad. Very bad. But so far the spots were a relatively small part of her body's entire surface, and none of them were in a nerve-dense zone. So she could manage, at least for periods of time. Now, though, she knew it was time to go on vacation.

She closed her eyes, breathed deeply and slowly, and thought back to the day she had graduated from Vanderbilt University's School of Medicine. She went there, felt the green-edged black cap with gold tassel on her head, the weight of the black gown on her shoulders, saw the black toes of her low-heeled pumps peeking out. Felt the graduates in front of her and behind shuffling forward.

Smelled the aftershave and perfume and sweat on that hot Tennessee day. Felt her heart beating more quickly as she approached the steps to the outdoor stage—

"Major?"

It was the young nurse. Stilwell pulled herself back to the world of pain.

"Hi."

"Major, ma'am, you have a visitor." The young woman grimaced, blew air through her nose in an indignant snort. "I told him you shouldn't be disturbed, but . . . he's an officer."

That brought her awake. "Really? Who?"

"Um, I didn't catch his name, ma'am. Can't see the name tag through his suit. He's an officer, though, made sure I knew that. You feel up to it?"

This was a surprise. She had not had any visitors, save routine calls from the doctors and the nurses' regular checks. "Yes, I can do it. Tell him to come in."

"All right, ma'am."

"Wait . . . I'm sorry, I've forgotten your name."

"Artwell, ma'am. Sergeant Artwell."

"Your first name."

"Oh. Yes, ma'am. It's Regina. People call me Reggie."

"Thanks. Reggie, would you please raise the bed so I can sit up?"

"Sure enough, ma'am." She did that and left, and presently a short, stout man in a Chemturion shuffled in. His face was obscured behind the suit's scratched, wrinkled plastic faceplate. In one black-gloved hand he held a bulging yellow envelope with the word CONFIDENTIAL stamped on it in fat red letters.

"You don't look so good, Major." She recognized the stuffy voice. Ribbesh the fobbit. *What the hell is he doing here?* "Sorry to see that. Anything I can get you?" Some kind of adenoidal hypertrophy, probably, his voice.

"I'm all good, Colonel."

"Hm. Is it . . . very painful?"

"Not so bad." No way she would admit hurting to this fobbit.

"I'm glad to hear that." He came around the foot of her bed, took a cautious step closer. She could see his face more clearly. Some people had facial features that made them look piggish—round, pink cheeks, upturned nose, tiny eyes, plump chin. Colonel Ribbesh was one. Overweight, he was perspiring heavily inside the suit.

"I'm sorry about that little business with the suit, Colonel," she said. "I was under a lot of stress."

"No doubt. It's regrettable. But I would be remiss if I didn't point out that if you'd obeyed my order, you wouldn't be here like this."

"And young soldiers would have suffered a hell of a lot more. Not a good trade-off, Colonel. May I ask why you're here?"

"Of course. As a matter of fact, it's about that . . . incident." His eyes flicked around the room. He touched the side of his hood, cleared his throat. "You see, I had you on speakerphone to hear you through the suit. So our conversation was witnessed by a number of other personnel. A major who is my adjutant and quite a few enlisted people. That created a problem."

"What kind of problem?"

"If it had been a direct, unobserved communication just between you and me, it could perhaps have been resolved differently. But the presence of other personnel made it . . . unavoidable."

"Made what unavoidable?"

"I had no choice but to report your action to higher authority. I'm sure you're familiar with the military Code of Conduct. Any failure to report a violation of the code is a violation in itself." He reached up as though to wipe the sweat from his forehead, remembered, let his hand drop. "Hot in these things, isn't it? You'd think they'd air-condition them or something."

"Go on, Colonel, please."

"Yes. Well, I had no choice, don't you see? I would have risked my career by turning a blind eye to that exchange. It wasn't something I really wanted to do, I can assure you."

I bet not, fobbit, she thought. Ribbesh was not only a fobbit, he was a purveyor of chickenshit, which had a very special definition in the Army. She knew officers like Ribbesh, miserable people with small minds and great buzzing swarms of resentments. They lived to dole out chickenshit—unnecessary punishment for trivial infractions, the punishment bearing no appropriate relationship to the offense, the purpose being nothing more than making life worse for someone of lower rank. She also knew that the Army, which welcomed all and fired none, bore an inordinate number of chickenshitters.

"Shouldn't I have been notified? Served with a paper or something?"

"That's what I'm doing now, Major."

"Oh. Took you a while, then, didn't it?"

His pink face got pinker. "It was necessary for the document to move through proper channels."

"Of course," she said. *So there'll be a letter in my Guard file. Big deal.*

As if he had read her mind, he said, "I had a need to review your personnel file. Unfortunately, this was not the first occurrence of insubordination."

"That's true. Sometimes orders and good medicine don't mix. From where I sit, medicine always trumps."

"Yes, that was clear from your responses to the previous charges. Frankly, I was surprised. No ordinary officer could have gotten off so lightly. But then, you're a *doctor.* Obviously exceptions were made."

"Colonel, is there anything else? I'm tired and—"

"If you'll allow me, I will complete this conference and leave. Because this was a subsequent incident, rather than an initial occurrence, the severity escalated. In addition to disciplinary action, it appears that there will be DOB as well."

Denial of benefits. Her tired heart wrenched. "What are you saying?"

"From the Army's point of view, Major, it is no different than shooting your toe off to escape combat. Your intention might have been noble, but, to paraphrase your words, orders always trump intention. In essence, you inflicted this infection on yourself."

"So you're saying that I will bear the expenses for all of my medical care."

"That is correct, I'm afraid."

"Stateside as well as here?"

"Yes."

She experienced a new dread so intense it made her dizzy and even more nauseous. Her civilian, private health insurance provided zero coverage when she was on active duty. That was when the military Tricare program kicked in, and, as a physician, she knew the regulation verbatim: "When on military duty, members are covered for any injury, illness or disease incurred or aggravated in the line of duty."

She also knew, however, that Tricare had exclusions, including—as Ribbesh the fobbit had pointed out—self-inflicted injuries. If she lived, the expenses could be hundreds of thousands of dollars. It would bankrupt them. The house, the cars, their savings . . . everything would be consumed. Because of this fat little fobbit.

But then she realized it wasn't as bad as the fobbit obviously thought it would be, because she was not going to need a lot of medical treatment. She knew the odds. So if she died . . . no, *when* she died, Doug and Danny would receive the payout from her military life insurance. Five hundred thousand dollars. They could take care of the mortgage and be secure for the rest of their lives, if they invested wisely. So the fobbit was not getting over on her, as he assumed. She wanted him out.

"Colonel, I respectfully request that you exit my room and leave me alone. I will summon medical staff if I have to."

"I was just leaving, Major," he said. "But there is one more thing I am required to communicate."

She waited, glaring, one hand holding the call button.

"DOB cases involve not only denial of medical benefits, but of death benefits as well. We can't very well be paying huge life insurance dividends for people who cause their own deaths, can we? Army regulations, I'm afraid. I'm sure you're familiar with General Order Nineteen, Section B3, Subsections r and s."

"Get out! *Now.*"

"Goodbye, Major." He dropped the heavy envelope on the foot of her bed. "I imagine someone here can help you review the documentation." Colonel Ribbesh waddled out, buttocks pushing against the Chemturion's heavy plastic.

THIRTY-TWO

IT WAS SHORTLY AFTER THREE A.M. AND DAVID LATHROP had been moving fast, running between the secretary's office and BARDA and half a dozen other places, nonstop, since six that morning. His eyes felt like someone had thrown sand in them, his mouth tasted like spoiled meat, and his brain was grinding up thoughts before he could finish them.

"Time to call it." He pushed up from his chair too quickly, felt light-headed, leaned over with both hands on his desk until he steadied. Whenever he was on duty, Lathrop kept his vest buttoned and tie snug around his collar. Discipline was the key to the universe, and if you built it one small step at a time, the big things took care of themselves. *We are our habits*. He loved that saying, though just now he could not have told you its source to save his life.

Lathrop did allow himself to hang up his suit jacket after six P.M., however. Walking to the closet in his office, he shrugged into the jacket, concealing the SIG Sauer he carried in a fine leather shoulder holster. He could have carried, compliments of Uncle Sam, a standard-issue Glock 9mm, but he preferred the extra power of the big .40-cal load and the greater reliability of the SIG. He had heard too many stories about Glocks jamming at inopportune times. Or he could have carried no weapon at all. The likelihood of him getting into a firefight now was about the same as his getting hit by lightning. His rock-and-roll field days were years behind him. But once upon a time, when he ran agents in Iraq and Pakistan, the need to carry a weapon had been real and ever-present. After all those years of going armed, being without a gun made him as uncomfortable as walking around without pants. And he reasoned that if one chose to carry a handgun, one should provide oneself with the very best, and that was a SIG Sauer. They were built like Swiss watches and never, ever malfunctioned. They cost an arm and a leg, true, but that was a fair price for life insurance.

As a GS-15, the highest nonappointed federal employment grade, Lathrop had an assigned space on the parking garage's blue level, beneath the Homeland Security headquarters building. A year earlier, the department had moved from its temporary offices over on Nebraska Avenue to this new $6 billion complex, which held no fewer than seven major federal agencies, in addition to the Domestic Nuclear Detection Office and the National Cyber Security Division. It was not a little ironic, Lathrop often reflected, that the gigantic new headquarters facility was located on the former grounds of Washington's infamous St. Elizabeths Hospital, a psychiatric facility that had treated, or at least housed, the legally and criminally insane since 1852. After all, if 9/11's perpetrators and consequences were not insane, then who and what on earth was?

The official address of the new Homeland Security complex was 1100 Alabama Avenue SE. Lathrop drove up out of the parking garage and headed for the Alabama Avenue exit. He stopped in front of massive gates bristling with razor wire and security cameras.

Presently two uniformed Homeland Security guards came out of the small-windowed concrete gatehouse and approached Lathrop's car. The screening for outgoing personnel was no less intense than that for incoming. Lathrop knew one of the guards, a young man named Jermayn Foster. During Lathrop's countless comings and goings, he had encountered Foster often, and now and then they chatted. Foster had come over from Washington's Metropolitan Police Department, where he had been stuck at sergeant grade, hoping for better promotion possibilities in the vast federal system. A tall, thin man, he moved to the driver's side while his partner—a man Lathrop did not know—walked to the passenger side and illuminated the interior of Lathrop's vehicle with a million-candlepower spotlight. Lathrop knew that closed-circuit cameras and NBC—Nuclear, Biological, and Chemical—detectors were scanning the underside of his car at the same time.

He had already lowered his window. "Evening, Jermayn. How's the shift?"

"Good evening, Mr. Lathrop. Slow and slower. Not many folks work the hours you do, sir."

"Just a tired spook with nothing to go home for." It was true, and made something inside him wince as he said it. But he winked, and Foster smiled, taking it as light self-deprecation.

Lathrop handed out his ID folder. Foster scanned it with an infrared barcode reader that he took from a leather holster in front of his Glock. He handed the ID folder back and, from another belt holster, took a device that looked like a small flashlight.

"Sorry, Mr. Lathrop."

"No problem. Rules are rules." Lathrop knew the drill for iris detection. He turned his head so that Jermayn could see his eyes. The guard positioned the biometric scanner a foot from Lathrop's right eye, touched a button, and waited. Lathrop knew that a soft, musical voice would say, "Approved" in Foster's earpiece.

"Thank you, Mr. Lathrop." Foster started to move away, then hesitated. He put his hand on top of the car. "Mr. Lathrop, I hope you won't take this wrong, but you look really tired, sir. I can call you a department car, you know? Take you home, leave your car here?"

Lathrop actually considered that for a moment. He knew how dangerous exhausted drivers who dropped into microsleeps could be. But it was only twenty minutes to his condo in Rose Hill, Maryland. He would keep the window down and the radio turned up. "I appreciate that. I do. But I'll be okay. I'm going straight home and then to bed. Long day." He forced a chuckle. "Correction: long *days*."

"All right, sir. Drive carefully." Foster stepped back, smiled, and gave Lathrop a crisp military salute.

Lathrop headed west on Alabama Avenue, turned south on Fourth Street, and picked up Indian Head Highway southbound. There were few other cars on the road at this time of night, but he lowered both front windows halfway, just to ward off drowsiness. He was only half a mile west of the Potomac, enjoying the water's fertile scent that the wind carried to him. He kept going for several miles before turning east on Palmer Road. As he made the turn he glanced at his gas gauge and saw that the empty warning light was blinking.

There was a twenty-four-hour 7-Eleven and Mobil station in an otherwise deserted mile between Tucker and Bock roads, about halfway to his condo. He turned in and stopped by one of the pumps. A black Ford Expedition with tinted glass pulled up on the other side of the pump island. It looked like the kind of vehicle driven by upper-crust Washingtonians, and normally Lathrop might have glanced over in case a shapely leg emerged, but now he was too tired to care.

He took out his wallet to remove a credit card. He heard car doors open, and in less time than it took him to draw his next breath, two men were five feet from him, one in front and one to his right side. The Expedition was between them and the 7-Eleven. They both wore baggy Levi's low on their hips, new Timberland boots, shiny Redskins jackets, and black ski masks. Gangbangers. Both held guns—Beretta 9mms. Thumb-sized silencers extended from the muzzles of both pistols.

Muggers must be doing better these days, he thought. Berettas cost as much as his SIG. And silencers? Another thousand per gun on the street, easy. Lathrop kept eye contact with them. He was not all that alarmed. For one thing, he was too tired for this. For another, he had been in many worse situations.

"Give me the wallet." The man in front spoke calmly, no tension in his voice. *Doesn't sound like a gangbanger,* Lathrop thought. The robber held out his left hand, palm up. He had brown leather gloves on, but between jacket cuff and glove Lathrop glimpsed black skin and the gleam of a blade-thin gold watch. Lathrop saw the man glance up at the security camera that covered this section of pump island. With any luck, Lathrop thought, the clerk inside would see what was happening and call 911. On the other hand, with the way things had been going lately, such a clerk was more likely to be mesmerized by iPhone porn.

"Relax, guys." Lathrop still wasn't particularly upset. "This isn't the first time I've had guns pointed at me. Let's do this the easy way. I'm going to hand over my wallet to you slowly. Is that all right?"

"Give it up." The man's calm was the third strange thing Lathrop noted. The first had been the expensive Berettas. The second had been the robber looking straight at the security camera. Why on earth would he do that, even with a mask on? And now, third, was how this man talked. From his days in intelligence Lathrop knew that you could tell a great many things from the way someone spoke, even a single sentence.

Holding the wallet between his thumb and forefinger, Lathrop extended his right arm slowly. The man in front of him didn't move, but the man off to one side reached in and took the wallet.

"There. See—no muss, no fuss." Lathrop's voice remained calm, easy. He had no thought of reaching for his own SIG. For one thing, they could shoot him ten times each before he cleared the holster.

No, a wallet was not worth getting shot for. It was just a typical D.C. mugging, like dozens or maybe even scores that happened every day in the beleaguered city. A bit unusual out here, but this was an isolated store with easy getaway routes. Nothing special, so don't make anything special of it. Though why these guys would choose to do it under the bright lights of the gas pump island, with surveillance cameras watching their every move, was beyond him. But then, armed robbers were not generally known for their intellectual prowess.

"You good?" one said to the other.

"All good."

The first one turned back to Lathrop. "Your cellphone."

"Excuse me?"

"Give me your cellphone." The man still spoke slowly and clearly, as if he had all the time in the world. They might have been chatting at a cocktail party, so relaxed was his voice. Lathrop had heard such a voice before. People who worked for him in the field, the ones who did the wet work, often had such voices. They could crush skulls and slit throats and feel not one flicker of remorse. In a way it was not their fault. Their brains were wired wrong. No true feelings of any kind, in fact. They inhabited an emotional wasteland where only two colors existed: black and red.

"You want my *cellphone*?" Lathrop pretended to sound astonished, but that was just a play for time. The wallet meant nothing. The cellphone meant a great deal, a mother lode of data that could confer tremendous power on anyone who knew what it was and how to use it.

The man smacked the butt of his Beretta into Lathrop's face, gashing his right cheek to the bone. The impact stunned Lathrop but did not knock him out.

"I hate repeating myself, Mr. Lathrop. Give me the phone. Like you said, easy or hard. It's all the same to us."

They know my name. And they said my name. From the confrontation's first moment, a part of Lathrop's brain had detached itself and begun calculating odds, probabilities, and permutations. Until now, this whole meeting had been nothing serious. In an instant that had changed and, at last, Lathrop's pulse rate went up and he felt the hot surge of adrenaline through his body.

"All right, all right." Lathrop let his eyes go vague and wavered on his feet, pretending to be more concussed than he was. "It's in the car."

He watched the other man's eyes flick sideways just once, as Lathrop had known they would. It wasn't much, but it was the only opening he was going to get. He ducked and wrapped his left hand around the other man's gun, covering the cocked trigger so that it could not drop and fire a round. He shoved up and pivoted to put that man between him and the other one. At the same time he drew his own weapon from the shoulder holster under his left armpit. He always kept a round in the chamber, and a SIG Sauer has no safety to release. All he had to do was point and pull the trigger. His index finger found it and he was an instant from firing when the man head-butted him so viciously that he lost consciousness for several seconds. When he came back, he was sitting on the pavement, leaning against his Accord's rear quarter panel. Blood was pouring from his shattered nose and now he saw four men instead of two, but two were twin images and he knew it was a real concussion this time.

Still not hurrying, not moving like someone who wanted to do damage unnecessarily, the man leaned down and removed Lathrop's cellphone from his inside pocket.

"Any more in the car?" Asking his partner.

"No."

"You good, then?"

"All good."

The man who had butted him looked down and Lathrop's vision cleared. He was watching the other man's eyes, which showed nothing more than the attention of a craftsman doing a job of work, as he fired two times into the center of Lathrop's chest, the silenced Beretta making small sounds, like a child's hands clapping. But the impacts: punches of a giant fist. Then pain, and then astonishment. *They have the wallet. And phone. Why shoot*?

But then, why not? In certain circles, murder had long since ceased being the greatest sin. *Why* didn't matter anymore. Killing might be for fun, or to satisfy curiosity, or to pass a gang initiation, or for no more reason than a sneeze or a random thought. *But not gangbangers, these.* He kept his eyes on the other man's, settling deeper into shock, a slow falling away, numb, his visual field graying, contracting. His brain produced no coherent thoughts but there were feelings too fast even for the shock to intercept, neurons firing and synapses sparking, and still the astonishment, blended now with an oceanic sadness as though watching the departure of a loved one who would never be seen again, but not regret, not one hint of it. David Lathrop had long since made his peace with death, and had tried to live each day of his life in such a way that when death came he would be able to greet it, if not with open arms, then at least without fear. The only thing he had always known about this moment was that he would never know when it would come.

The man then aimed his gun at Lathrop's forehead, slightly left of center, and pulled the trigger. The last thing Lathrop saw was the Expedition's license plate. The car was as immaculate as if it had just rolled off a showroom floor, but the license plate's numbers were completely obscured by a layer of what looked like dried mud. They had done things like that in Baghdad and Kabul and Karachi. He understood.

THIRTY-THREE

Dr. Casey—it's just after midnight. If you get this message before you go home, could you please come down to 4? There's something I think you should see before tomorrow.

Lew Casey stared at the handwritten note on his desk. It was 2:17 A.M. He had been at BARDA since 6:30 the previous morning and, except for two catnaps, had been working the whole time. He always came in earlier than those who worked for him, and he never left until all of them had gone home for the day. He would not go home now until he'd answered Evvie Flemmer's request for him to visit BSL-4 one more time. Her tone seemed bright with the promise of good news.

He picked up the note, put it back down, went into the small bathroom that adjoined his office, and splashed cold water on his face and neck. Drying off, he caught a glimpse of himself in the mirror. He looked so ghastly that he laughed out loud. His pale skin was sheet-white, making the dark circles under his eyes look almost black. He hadn't shaved since the night before last, and his cheeks bristled with wiry red stubble.

"You look like the living dead." He made a face, went, "Boooooo," laughed, shook his head.

Fatigue does strange things to the human brain, Lewis.

Especially to one not exceptionally sharp to begin with.

Knock it off. You do that when you're tired. Your brain is still goddamned fine.

Then why haven't you cracked this thing wide open? It's not like those soldiers don't need a cure.

You're close, though.

Yeah. Big deal. What's that old saying about close? Horseshoes and hand grenades? Close doesn't cut it, Lewis.

He would just have to work more, work harder. As Evvie Flemmer was doing. He'd lost track of the last time she had been out of the building. If she could stay at it, so could he.

Forty-five minutes later, he stood in the decon shower, blowers drying his suit after their chemical bath. The fans stopped and the lights on the ingress panel turned green. Casey punched the big red button, the automatic doors slid open, he stepped through, and they closed again. Evvie turned from the lab bench where she had been working.

"Hello, Evvie. Don't you ever go home?"

"I prefer it here, sir. Turn around and I'll connect you."

Casey turned, felt her connect the lab's air hose, felt her depower his PLSS unit, felt her pull him over to the EM. He had wanted to tell her something, but through his fog of fatigue he could not remember what. No matter; it would come back to him.

"What's so exciting that it couldn't wait until tomorrow?"

"You have to see for yourself, sir. Just stand by while I get the viewing field calibrated."

He waited, half asleep on his feet, while Evvie bent over the instrument, twisting dials, adjusting settings with the big dials. It seemed to be taking longer than usual.

"Damn." Evvie's voice sounded edgy with fatigue. "I'm sorry, sir. I messed it up. I'll have to recalibrate. Just . . . bear with me. It'll be worth it, I promise."

"No problem, Evvie. We have all night." He yawned, swayed, the need for sleep pulling him down like weight in water. He tried to focus on what she was doing, but her big suit blocked his view and there wasn't room to stand beside her. So he remained where he was and . . .

Casey's head snapped up. He had fallen asleep on his feet. But something else was happening. His vision was blurring and he was having difficulty breathing. Evvie Flemmer wasn't bent over the electron microscope. He turned quickly, but his balance was off and he almost fell over. *Careful. You breach this suit, you're a dead man.*

There she was, over by the air lock's door.

"Evvie?" It seemed to take immense effort to say that one word. The exertion left him panting like a sprinter. His vision blurred again, graying. His heart was starting to race. "Evvie!"

She stood there, arms hanging loosely at her sides, watching him without expression. Studying him, as one might study a lab specimen. He began to gasp, hyperventilating, his heart going tachycardic, pushing up past 180 beats per minute.

Suddenly, he understood. His air supply had failed. He reached for the hose behind his shoulder, but the effort knocked him off balance and he nearly fell again. Then he grabbed at the PLSS unit on the waist belt of his suit, found the on/off switch, but nothing happened. His vision was contracting, his accelerated breathing burning up what little oxygen was left in his Chemturion. The carbon dioxide levels in the suit and in his body spiked and the laboratory began to spin around him. He lost his balance, fell, hit the floor hard on his back.

Stunned, he lay where he had fallen, arms waving feebly beside his body. He saw Evvie Flemmer come to stand beside him. She bent over slightly and he could see her face, calm, in her eyes only the pure curiosity of a scientist witnessing a mildly interesting event. Then Evvie did the strangest thing.

She smiled.

His lips began to turn blue and his pupils dilated. He could still think, but his feet and hands and lips were numb and his vision was failing, dimming, as though he were sinking deeper and deeper into darkening water.

"Evvie."

He was not even sure he had spoken aloud.

She watched Casey dying, but the dual distortions of their plastic hoods made his face blurry and indistinct. It could have been the face of another man, thick-necked and hairy as an ape, who did unspeakable things to her year after year in a scorching Oklahoma trailer while her mother watched. She looked at their pictures every day, to keep fresh in her mind the horror of her father's life in McAlester, Oklahoma's maximum-security penitentiary. "Short eyes," the other prisoners called despised child molesters, and she had researched in great detail the things those other prisoners did to such deviants. She kept her mother's picture, too, the morgue photo, so that she could relish the horror of that woman's existence as well, not in prison but in hell, where she had surely gone after hanging herself before their child-abuse trial was over.

Casey said something. She saw his lips move but could not hear him. Over the years she had come to dread every minute they spent together, what with all his touching and petting, stroking and pressing and cooing. Her revulsion was sometimes so violent that she barely made it to the bathroom before vomiting. It had taken almost unimaginable strength not to scream and claw the old devil's eyes out, but she had managed it. *Had* to, really. No other choice. There was too much at stake. And oh, how she had laughed inside when the code finally came to go forward: *Take out the trash*.

After a while she walked to the lab's primary incubator, a stainless steel box the size of a refrigerator. The unit had an exterior glass door and four separate interior chambers with their own hermetic glass doors. The chambers allowed microenvironment management. In each one, the type and intensity of light, mixture of atmospheric gases, temperature, humidity, ionization, electromagnetic fields, pressure, and other factors could be precisely controlled.

All the chambers contained petri dishes in which bacteria were growing—these were the colonies of ACE that Lew Casey had been working with. The genetically disrupted bacteria showed as bright red and green and orange splotches on the tea-colored agar growth medium in the dishes. Flemmer removed from her biosuit's thigh pocket a slim, three-inch-long, battery-powered bulb capable of emitting intense ultraviolet radiation.

She pushed a button on the unit's base and it glowed with harsh blue light. She opened the door to the top incubator chamber, passed the UV wand over the cultures, and closed the door. She repeated the action in the other chambers. She closed the incubator's main door, pocketed the wand, and looked around the lab. Nothing appeared out of order, other than Lew Casey lying on the floor. She left him in the lab, deconned, went up to his office, and retrieved the note she had left for him earlier; given the hour, she was confident no one else would have seen it. They would find him tomorrow and it would be an obvious accident, stress and exhaustion and the debilitating emphysema all combining to produce tragedy.

For too much of her life Evvie Flemmer had lived alone in places without light, small dark rooms and apartments with alley views. Now she would change her appearance and her fingerprints with the best plastic surgery money could buy. Slim and beautified, she would purchase a villa in the south of France—Provence, nothing splashy, but spacious and very old. It would have thick stone walls covered with stucco the color of cream, laced with green ivy. The orchard trees would be heavy with pears hanging like great drops of gold. Best of all, there would be light. The villa would have tall windows through which pure light would stream and collect in bright pools on floors of ancient oak. She would never live in darkness again. And this she knew: there would be no fear of the purifying light of Provence. Jocelene Alameda Tremaine would never fear anything. That was the name she had given Mr. Adelheid for her new identity. So Jocelene, not Evvie, would soon be enjoying Dom Pérignon in the master suite of a superyacht named *Lebens Leben,* sailing east into the sunrise of a new life.

THIRTY-FOUR

HALLIE AND CAHNER MADE IT BACK TO ROARING RIVER CAMP, the place they had last seen Bowman; both of them were staggering with fatigue. Without even speaking, too tired to fix food, they found sleeping spots and collapsed into their bags.

Hours later, she was dreaming of Bowman again. He was leaning over her face, fingertips brushing her cheek, whispering something, his lips touching hers. His hand moved down along her neck, slipped under the sleeping bag, and settled on her chest, cupping her breast. She moved under his hand, moaning, as his fingertips caressed.

Please, she said in her dream. *Please yes.*

But his hand slid away and she dropped back down into sleep.

"Hallie."

Bowman?

"Hallie, wake up, I have something for you."

Groggy, she opened her eyes. Her sleeping area was illuminated by the glow from a helmet light, but it wasn't Bowman's. It was Al Cahner's. He was down on one knee beside her sleeping bag, holding a steaming mug. "I thought you might like some tea," he said, putting his face close to hers so that he didn't have to shout.

She came fully awake, pushed the sleeping bag down, and sat up. She took the proffered mug and sipped.

"Careful, it's hot," Cahner warned.

It was, but it was strong and thick with sugar and powdered milk and she thought she had never tasted anything better. She blew over the tea's surface, drank, felt energy surge through her.

"This is wonderful. Thank you."

"My pleasure." He sat close beside her, cross-legged, smiling as she drank and came fully awake. "You slept a long time."

"Have you been up long?"

"Oh, a while. How's your hand?"

She flexed it very gently, grimaced. "Sore as hell. But nothing life-threatening. It'll heal. How are you holding up?"

"I'm good," he said. "Really good."

She looked at him. "You sound almost cheerful."

He heard the surprise in her voice. "Well, we've got the moonmilk, we're alive, we're on our way out. What's not to like about that?"

Not much, except for the fact that three good people are dead, she thought, but she didn't say it. She knew that in one sense he was correct. The moonmilk was the mission, and they were close to completing it now. That was the most important thing. The three deaths had been horrible, but they might well prevent hundreds of thousands—*millions,* maybe—of more agonizing deaths. And all of them had come into this thing with their eyes wide open. "You're right," she said. "I'm sorry, Al. I'm tired. And we've lost a lot down here."

He nodded gravely. "We have indeed." Sighed, looked away,

then back at her. "I've got some MREs ready to heat up over at the kitchen," he said. "Scrambled eggs and bacon. Are you hungry?"

She *was*. "I'll be right over. Give me a minute."

"Sure."

He moved off. She shucked out of the bag, pulled on her suit, boots, and helmet, and made her way over to the kitchen. Cahner was already there with the hot MREs. He refilled her mug with steaming black tea, handed her a foil pouch. They stood spooning up the food. The eggs actually tasted like eggs, and the bacon bits were crisp and smoky-flavored. The tea and the warm food began reviving her. She was about to thank Cahner for making breakfast when he bent down to retrieve something from his pack.

It was Bowman's red flask of rum. She watched, surprised, as he unscrewed the top and poured a healthy dollop into his own mug. He started to add rum to her tea, but she put her hand over the mug to stop him.

"That's Bowman's," she called to him. "How did you get it?"

"I took it from his pack before we left this camp the last time." He shrugged. "I mean, it's not as if he was going to need it anymore."

That was obviously true, but the matter-of-fact way Cahner said it bothered her.

"Really, you should have some," Cahner persisted. "I don't think he would have wanted it to go to waste. There's nothing wrong with enjoying ourselves a little bit now, is there?"

"We're a long way from being finished with this mission." Despite herself, Hallie's voice was taking on an edge. "It's way too early to celebrate."

Cahner regarded her neutrally, then drank again and set the mug down. He took a few steps closer, until they were standing at arm's length. "You're not often wrong, Hallie, but this time you are. It's not too early to celebrate at all."

He opened his arms wide, signaling that he was going to give her a hug. *What the hell,* she thought. *He's done his part*. She stepped forward and wrapped her arms around him. "You're right, Al. We do have reason to feel good."

She started to disengage, but his arms remained around her. *Okay, I get that you're happy.* She leaned her head back to speak, and, to her astonishment, he kissed her on the lips. His helmet hit hers and knocked it off. She put her arms on his shoulders and pushed, but he pressed his mouth against hers more tightly, scratching her with his rough stubble of a beard. She felt his right hand settle onto her breast, cupping it, rubbing with his thumb.

"Al!" She shoved with all her strength and peeled him off her. She could not have been more astonished. In all their time together at BARDA, she had not seen him give her so much as a suggestive glance. What the hell was the matter with him? And then she remembered: *People change in caves.*

She moved back to put space between them. Before she could speak, he said, "I like you, Hallie. Very, very much. I always have."

"I like you, too. You once said you were glad to have a friend you could trust. That goes for me, too. But that's as far as it goes."

For a moment she thought that he was going to come at her again, but he stood where he was, holding her gaze, apparently pondering some kind of decision. She thought, *If he loses it down here, we're in trouble.* Her biggest concern was not for herself, but for the moonmilk. They had to get it to the surface, no matter what it took. She would not let anything come between her and that end. Not fatigue, nor danger, nor the others' deaths, even Bowman's—and not Al Cahner.

"Where to begin?" Cahner said.

"What?" She had no idea what he meant.

"Okay. I think it's time for straight talk. I know how you looked at me back in the lab, Hallie. I wanted to return those looks more than I can tell you. But I just couldn't."

She had once stood on a steep snow slope on Denali and in the moment just before it avalanched the world had shivered. That's what it felt like now.

"How I looked at you? I don't know what you mean."

"Don't lie, Hallie. It doesn't become you. And it is not necessary anymore."

"I thought of you as a good friend. With affection and trust. But that was all."

"You're *lying.*" He spat out the word, and it was the first time she had ever seen him really angry. His face reddened and his features contracted. "Why are you doing this? Don't you remember our lunches together? All the things we talked about?"

She did remember the lunches. Sandwiches and coffee in the grubby little canteen. They had talked about the weather, politics, co-workers, and baseball. Period. Then, suddenly, she understood what was happening and mentally slapped herself for not having figured it out before, but fatigue had dulled her brain. This was not the first time a man had conjured up a fantasy romance with her. Misinterpreting casual remarks, reading too much into smiles and accidental touches, investing meetings and phone calls and emails with imagined meaning.

She also knew how to dispel such fantasy once and for all.

"Of course I remember the lunches," she said. "And our talks. I *don't* remember talking about anything romantic. But it doesn't matter. Perception is reality. So if I gave you the wrong impression, or misled you in any way, even unintentionally, I apologize. It was certainly not my intention. I thought of you as my friend, and just that. Still do, in fact."

As she'd been speaking, he had been moving toward her. Slowly, not threateningly, listening carefully to her words. She was about to hold up her hands when he stopped a couple of feet away from her. He nodded at the rum-laced cups of tea. His expression had changed, leaving the kind of pained sadness she had seen on the faces of people at funerals. Sadness mixed with anger.

"Are you sure you don't want to have a drink with me, Hallie?"

"I already said no. Now let's put this behind us and get going."

"I am sorry, Hallie," he said. "I really, truly am."

His right hand came up from beside his thigh, holding a small black flashlight. Except that it was not a flashlight. She heard a crack like a live wire arcing, saw a sparking blue flash. Something bit her in the neck, like cobra's fangs lancing her flesh, and suddenly a million wasps were stinging her all at one time, inside and out, her whole body erupting with more pain than she had thought could exist in any world, enough pain to kill her many times over. Explosions of light seared her brain. She tried to scream, but her muscles were frozen.

And then she was gone.

THIRTY-FIVE

THE FIRST THING HALLIE HEARD WAS THE MELODY OF "SWEET Caroline." Cahner was bent over his pack, putting in odds and ends, whistling cheerfully all the while.

Her whole body hurt. She understood that Cahner had used a Taser on her. He must have been carrying it the whole time. *Everybody changes in caves*. She had known that coming in. She had seen it before, seen cavers panic, lose heart, even attack teammates, becoming so deranged that their partners had to tie them up with climbing rope. But Cahner had been carrying a Taser. That implied premeditation.

Hallie was lying on her back, on top of her bound hands, an uncomfortable position. When she rolled to one side, the pain was such that she made a small, involuntary scream. Coming fully awake, she felt like someone had beaten her all over. There was an unpleasant, coppery taste in her mouth, and it was painful to swallow. From the smell, she could tell that she had vomited at some point. She was shivering from the cold. How long had she been out?

"Finally waking up?" Cahner's voice was pleasant, but not like before. "You slept longer than I'd expected. But I think I had that thing set a bit too high. Live and learn."

She started to speak, found her throat muscles paralyzed. Swallowed, coughed, spit bile, tried again. "Al. Why are you doing this? You have to let me go."

He looked up from his packing chores, and now his voice was not so pleasant. "You're quite wrong about that. I don't have to let you go. In fact, from now on there will not be one thing in the world that I will ever *have* to do."

It was hard enough to think through the shock-induced fog in her brain. Now Cahner seemed determined to speak in riddles. She forced herself to focus, and the effort made her face and head hurt. "Why do you have me tied up? We're partners, for Christ's sake."

"We *were* partners. I had honestly thought there was a future for us. Hoped and prayed there was. With this thing, the life we could have made together—you cannot imagine."

"What thing? I don't understand you, Al."

"Such a life it could have been. But it isn't what you want. I understand, really I do. Beautiful young woman, plain old man. Is my heart broken? Of course." His voice turned colder. "But broken hearts mend, don't they? And ten million dollars can do a lot of mending, believe me."

"What are you talking about?" Despite the pain, she struggled to a sitting position, leaning against a boulder.

"I'm talking about the money I will be paid when I give them the moonmilk."

"What?" If the pain throughout her body had not been so real, Hallie might have assumed she was still dreaming. Finished with the pack, Cahner cinched its top and came over to squat on his heels in front of her. He let his light shine straight into her eyes.

"Of course. It must have occurred to you at some point how valuable that extremophile would be to certain people."

"We have to give it to BARDA. The new antibiotics—"

"No, that's not the plan anymore. It never was, actually. We—well, *I*—will give the moonmilk to my friends, who have already deposited half of my fee. Have you ever seen a bank statement showing a balance of five *million* dollars? Unbelievable. When I give them the material, they give me the rest."

It wasn't possible. She could not believe that Al Cahner could do such a thing. She had worked with the man every day for two years. He had nearly wept when they threw her out. One of the nicest men she had ever known. All during this expedition he had been steady, kind, ready to help.

And yet . . .

Of *course* it was possible. Failure warped people in unknowable ways.

Still, Al Cahner was no psychopathic demon. She knew there were better angels in him. And they could be reasoned with.

"Al. You can't do that. Think about what you're saying."

"I have been thinking about it, Hallie. Believe me. For a very long time. Do you know how long I've worked for the government?"

"I think you said once it was almost twenty years."

"Nineteen going on twenty, to be exact. Do you know how much money I make?"

"Of course not."

"Eighty-seven thousand, four hundred and seventy-six dollars a year."

"I'm not talking about the money."

"No, but I am. *Any third-year biologist at Merck makes more than that*."

Hallie's head hurt, her body hurt, her thoughts kept turning into wisps of fog, but she had to focus. There must be some way to get through to him.

"It's never been about the money for people like us, Al. It's about doing the science. To help those who need it."

"The science, yes. Forgive me if I point out that such fine sentiments are easier to entertain in your thirties than in your fifties. Truthfully, Hallie, when I was your age, I said the same kinds of things you did just now."

"And I know you still feel them. We spent too much time together for me not to believe that."

He inhaled, let out a long breath. There was genuine pain in his voice when he spoke. "I will always cherish that time. I need for you to believe that. Even if it wasn't exactly . . . what I thought it was."

"I *do* believe you. And for that very reason, I need for you to tell me exactly what is going on, Al. You owe us that. This is not how friends treat each other."

He hesitated, and Hallie could see the struggle. *A tormented man,* she thought. *All those years. Needing so much, having so little. Like a thirst with no way to slake it.*

Finally he said, in a voice that sounded more exhausted than exultant, "I don't suppose there's any harm in it now."

"In what?"

"Telling you what was really going on." He paused, and she watched his expression change again. It was like seeing the tumblers move in a lock after the key had been inserted and turned. "It began not long after you came back with that first sample of moonmilk. Do you remember?"

"Sort of."

"At first it was no big deal. Then your work with moonmilk began to attract a lot of attention."

She waited for him to go on.

"I'd been unhappy with . . . call it a lack of proper recognition at BARDA, for some time. Did I mention that they passed me over for promotion three times?"

He had mentioned it fairly often, actually, but she thought better of saying so.

"At some point I put out feelers to private enterprise. I was thinking about making a move, but in my fifties, I wasn't the most marketable prospect. I needed something special, a bargaining chip. And then the moonmilk came along."

They had been conversing casually for a while now, so Hallie decided to test the water. "These ropes are really hurting my wrists. Do you think you could take them off? Or maybe just loosen them. It's not like there's any place for me to run to."

"No, I'm afraid that's not going to happen. We've gone beyond such niceties, unfortunately."

His answer infuriated her, but she knew it was important not to show it. *Build rapport in every way possible.* "Okay, I can understand that. I just thought I'd ask."

"So the moonmilk was my bargaining chip. Not just for a job, though. A job, they can take away from you. No, this was for a future. Something no one could ever take away."

"What did you do, Al?"

He reddened. At first she thought it was anger. Then, as he spoke, she understood that it was something else: *shame*. He was almost whispering. "I had to get you out of the way, first. You were leading the research. I needed to get closer to it myself."

"What did you *do*?"

"I hacked into your home computer and made it send messages to a man from BioChem. Offering to sell certain proprietary information related to moonmilk."

"That was *you*?"

"I know—amazing, isn't it? Nobody suspected shy, quirky old Al Cahner."

"But . . . they must have investigated your BioChem connection. Why didn't they blow your cover?"

"They couldn't find him because he didn't exist. He was an avatar. BioChem, of course, denied everything. They really were as mystified as BARDA. Neither side wanted scandal, so they just let it drop. Well, that's not entirely right. They got rid of you."

He hesitated, then went on: "It's amazing how easy computer systems are to manipulate, Hallie. Pimply high school dropouts compromise Department of Defense computers all the time. It's no big thing, if you have a certain level of knowledge and sufficient interest."

"So you got me fired?" She was still having trouble believing it.

"Well, technically it was BARDA's doing, but I maneuvered them into a position where they had no choice. They weren't very nice about it, were they?"

"How could you *do* that?"

"It wasn't the easiest decision, believe me, given how I felt about you. Of course, I had no way of knowing we would come together again. When I learned that Barnard was planning this expedition, I made sure that he put me on the team. I would get the moonmilk. And you. Or so I thought."

Hallie had been exaggerating before about the discomfort of her bonds, but now they really were becoming painful. She shifted, pushed herself to a standing position, where she could move her arms just enough to relieve some of the pressure.

"Sit down!" Suddenly he had the Taser in his hand. She lowered herself quickly to the cave floor, the boulder's rough surface cutting into her back. Cahner said, "Do you know, that's the first time I've ever seen you look really afraid, Hallie."

"So you got me fired. Thinking you would take over the research work."

"Exactly right. And so I did. But watching you do it was one thing. Tackling it myself turned out to be quite another."

"It was some of the most complex work I'd ever done."

"Indeed. At first I tried using your initial hypothesis. But that turned out to be a dead end, I'm sorry to report. I had to come up with new experimental directions, and I did. Some were more promising than others. But they all failed in the end. Every single one."

"And you ran out of moonmilk."

"Yes. And Barnard didn't think I'd showed enough progress to justify another expedition to retrieve more moonmilk. Goddamn him. If he had had the vision to see how close I was, all of this could have been avoided."

"But then the ACE emergency came along."

"Thank God for small favors." He put his hands together in mock prayer, the Taser pressed between them. "Not that an ACE pandemic will be a small thing. But the bacteria that cause it certainly are."

She understood that the ACE mutation, wherever it had come from, antigenic shift or enemy biowar, had given him exactly the opportunity he'd needed.

"What did you mean when you said 'all of this could have been avoided'?"

For several seconds he hesitated. Then, finally: "Well, those men would still be alive, for one thing."

"Would still be—did you have something to do with their deaths?"

He nodded absently. "Honestly, I didn't know if I could do such things. But they turned out to be easier than I'd expected. I think it has something to do with the darkness, and being so isolated from everything else on earth. As you said back at the river camp, anything is possible in a cave like this."

"How?"

"In the sump I waited around that sharp turn. When Haight came along, I smashed his faceplate with a rock. Arguello was easier. I pretended to be frozen with fear on that ledge above the acid lake. I reached out a hand and asked for help, and he responded like the good man he was. I just gave a little yank and off he went."

"My God."

"And as for your big friend . . ."

"Bowman?"

"I knew that when the two of you had finished . . . doing what you were doing . . . he would go to the river. He was far too proper a man to piss right there at the sleeping spots. There was so much noise from the river it was easy to follow him. I went right down to where he was. He said, 'You too, eh?' And I said, 'Yes, me, too,' and moved off as though finding a little privacy. One quick shove from behind was all it took."

Hallie's mind shuddered. For a moment, she could form no response. Then, her voice steady: "I'm alive, Al."

He remained silent for a while, then said, "Do those ropes still hurt?"

"A lot."

"Stand up and I'll take them off. But please do remember the Taser."

"I'll never forget that thing."

"All right. Stand up and don't move."

She struggled to her feet, saw him holding the Taser in his right hand. He came very close to her then, so close that she could feel his breath on her face.

"You understand that I could do anything I want with you now, don't you?"

He stared into her eyes and she held his gaze, saying nothing. The moment stretched.

"You're not that kind of man," Hallie said.

Cahner inhaled, let out a long breath. "No," he said. "I'm not."

Then, in one swift motion, he bent over, wrapped his arms around Hallie's thighs, and picked her up in a fireman's carry. With her draped over his shoulder like a sack of grain, he walked forward. Bent over his back, she could not see where they were going. She managed to sink her teeth into his flesh and bite hard enough to make him yell in pain. He swung an elbow around and hit her in the face.

She was about to bite him again when he stopped.

He pitched her over the edge of the bottomless pit.

"I loved you, Hallie" were the last words she heard, and she could not tell if he was laughing or crying.

THIRTY-SIX

KATHAN AND STIKES WERE SITTING IN THE DARK. KATHAN had just come back from the hide. It was Stikes's turn, but he had a question first.

"Hey. I been thinking. If all of them come out, what do we do with five bodies?"

"I've been thinking about that, too. What if we weighed them down with rocks and put them right here in this lake?" Kathan scratched the side of his face. Something, Stikes saw, some vicious bug or plant, was giving him a bad rash.

"They're going to bloat and float sooner or later, though," Stikes said. "Unless we do a lot of cutting. You know how messy that gets."

"Okay. But I think burning is out of the question, wouldn't you agree?"

"Yeah. Slow, messy, leaves identifiable residue. Plus which, we don't want to be advertising our presence here with a big barbecue."

"I don't like dismemberment much, either," Kathan said. "Animals will take care of the meat, but there'll be bones and that's too many loose ends." He frowned, considering. The details were always messy. People like Gray never worried about the details.

"Agree again. We could blow them up with grenades."

"We have six, with the two we took off Dempsey. But way too much noise."

"Yeah. What about dropping them into a pit somewhere?" Stikes so far had escaped the facial rash, but his groin had become a playground for bugs that were no less vicious for being invisible.

"Probably the easiest," Kathan said. "But not if we have to haul them far. That big one's gonna be heavy. Another thing: you know how long it takes a body to decompose. *Really* decompose."

"For the bones, you're talking years."

"Centuries. Especially when you don't have the usual insects and bacteria and such. Hey, maybe we could make them eat each other."

It was hard to tell from the tone of his voice whether Kathan was making a joke. But they were having a serious discussion, so Stikes gave a serious answer. "Do you know how long that would take?"

"I'm just tossing out options here."

"*You* should eat something." Stikes had been growing concerned.

"Not really hungry." Kathan showed an eerie little smile.

"You go too long on that stuff without eating, it'll drop you right in your tracks."

Kathan snorted. "Not me, it won't."

"Suit yourself." Stikes knew that Kathan had been taking microdoses of the blue meth to keep his edge. Stikes stayed away from the stuff. He was eating his second chocolate and peanut butter bar, washing it down with the coca-laced water. They were sitting side by side with their backs against the rock face.

"I guess I'm leaning toward putting them in the lake here after all." Kathan sounded resigned.

"It does seem like the best option, all things considered. Lot of cutting, though. Can't have them floating back up."

"Concur."

"Suppose they find another way out of the cave?" Stikes asked.

"Then we're screwed. But they won't."

"How can you say that for sure?"

"We were told there was only one way into this cave. That means there's only one way out. Gray's intel has never been bad before."

"Yeah, but how would he really know? And what about those GPS coordinates?"

"There is that, you're right. But it doesn't change anything. What else can we do?"

"We could go in after them."

"Knock yourself out, Stikes. You ever been in a cave? Like this, I mean."

"No. You?"

"One time and one time only. Caves are very weird places, man. There's no way I'm going in that thing."

Stikes thought, *If it was bad enough to make a man like Kathan afraid . . .* It was hard for him to imagine *anything* that could frighten Kathan. But clearly a cave had. "Okay, I hear you," he said.

Kathan, obviously wanting to change the subject, said, "Where do you think we should start first? With the blonde, I mean." It was as though he had forgotten their earlier conversation about Hallie's fate and Stikes's plans to get out. Keyana's image came to Stikes, as if conjured by Kathan's words. She seemed to be frowning. *Don't you worry, girl,* Stikes thought. *Your man doesn't do those things.* "I hadn't really thought about it," he said indifferently.

"*I* been thinking about it. But I worry about teeth, man. There was a girl in Kabul, if I hadn't shot her, she'd have bit it off."

Stikes forced a grin. "That must have been something to see."

"She was clamped on me like a snapping turtle. I hurt for a month."

"You're lucky you didn't shoot your own self."

"Wasn't like it was a tough shot. The range was pretty close." That seemed to strike Kathan as hilarious, and he began to laugh so hard tears ran down his cheeks.

The meth, Stikes thought.

Kathan clamped both skillet-sized hands over his mouth. He sat there rocking back and forth, holding the laughter in, until finally the fit subsided. Gasping for air and wiping his cheeks dry, Kathan said, "That one won't be doing any more biting. But I don't think I want to risk it again. What do you like?"

Keyana was still there, glaring at Stikes in his mind. He shook his head. "It doesn't matter what I like, Kathan. I'm not into that. I *told* you."

Kathan went on talking about Hallie as if he had not heard. It seemed to Stikes that the other man might be slowly detaching from their reality, the forest and campsite and hide, and slipping into another one that only he could see. "She's no simple country puss, that's for sure. One good looker."

"Except for that nose."

"Yeah, except for that. Someone must have laid one on her."

"Probably a pissed-off boyfriend," Stikes said. "Or maybe a girlfriend. Always a possibility these days."

"I don't know about you, but I think that's sexy as hell," Kathan said.

"What, girls on girls?"

"Oh, yeah. Gets me really hot." Kathan made an ecstasy face, stuck out his tongue. "You know what I always wonder, though?"

"What?"

"Why do each other when you could be doing the real thing? You know what I'm saying? It just doesn't make sense." Kathan scowled.

"Lot of stuff in this world doesn't make any sense."

"You got that right. Like us hanging around in this bean-eater Pancho Villa sad excuse for a country waiting for those fools to come out and get dead."

"Roger that."

Kathan seemed to have run out of words. Stikes geared up and made his way to the hide at the tree line. The rock face two hundred yards away reflected enough starlight to glow softly green in his NVDs. The cave mouth was a black oblong at the face's bottom. Stikes settled down, sitting cross-legged, to watch that dark space and wait for the moment when luminous shapes would appear to float from it.

To pass the time, Stikes disassembled his Beretta and then started putting it back together. He could do it easily blindfolded and now he did it in the dark, keeping his eyes trained on the cave mouth. His hands took on lives of their own, moving over the pieces like a piano player's lightly touching keys. Then he imagined touching Keyana, and while Stikes's hands worked, his mind played with her astonishing body.

Eventually, though, his thoughts were pulled back to Kathan. There was something wrong with the man. Objectively, Stikes knew you had to be a little off to do this kind of work. But Kathan was *way* off. Stikes had met such men before, and he felt that Kathan's mind, like the others', must have been dismantled by some horror and never properly reassembled. Earlier, during the daylight, Stikes had returned from the hide to find Kathan playing with some of the orange, white-spotted lizards that were about the size of a cigar and slow enough to be caught bare-handed. Kathan had made a small track framed with rocks to contain the lizards and was staging races.

"Need to do a little handicapping," Kathan said. As Stikes watched, he pulled a hind leg off the next two contestants. He looked up to see Stikes staring at him. "I got bored." Grinning. "I used to do stuff like this when I was a kid."

"With lizards?"

"Cats, mostly. My old man's metal shears worked great. But they bled out too quick. Big veins in their legs."

"So what'd you do?"

"Well. You make them run around without *eyes,* now that was a hoot, take my word for it, bro."

"How in the hell did you do that?"

"Welder's gloves." Kathan chuckled. "Like steel mesh. You can't drive a nail through them. And they come up to your elbows."

"You are one sick bastard," Stikes said, flat-voiced, but Kathan laughed, appearing to take it as a huge compliment.

THIRTY-SEVEN

STILWELL'S BERTH IN THE MEDICAL BAY OF THE C-5A GALAXY transport was surprisingly comfortable. The self-leveling bed was affixed to a set of stainless steel pillars with oil-filled shock absorbers. Instead of a mattress, she was cradled in a red elastopolymeric cocoon that molded to her body, insulating her from turbulence and the aircraft's vibrations. She was receiving oxygen through a nasal cannula. A baby-blue, IMED Genie-R1 intravenous pump, hung from a stanchion beside Stilwell's berth, kept a steady ketamine drip flowing into her right arm. Every sixty seconds, it beeped softly.

Stilwell was one of six ACE patients being transported back to the United States for admission to Walter Reed Army Medical Center. The doctors and nurses on board were all garbed in full Chemturions with self-contained ventilation units. There were three doctors and twelve nurses for the twelve-hour flight. When they rotated off-shift, they went to eat, rest, and sleep in a secure, biosafe section of the plane.

When it came time for her next half-hour check, a nurse trundled over in the ungainly suit and stood beside the bed.

"Hey there," Stilwell whispered. "Don't you people ever sit down?" One of ACE's many gifts, she was learning, was a sore throat that made strep seem mild.

"When the aircraft lands and we roll you off, then we sit, ma'am," the nurse said. This one, the shift supervisor, was a female lieutenant named Gauthier, a young woman with short-cropped blond hair.

"Where are you from, Lieutenant?"

"Vermont, ma'am. Northern part of the state."

"Vermont. I've never been there. What's it like?"

"Quiet. My parents run a dairy farm. They milk three hundred cows." Stilwell could see the pride in her eyes, but then she added, "I couldn't wait to get out of Vermont. All the kids are like that."

"Did you?"

"Oh yes. I wanted to go to a *city* where it was *warm*. Those were the only two criteria. Well, and a good nursing school."

"Where?"

"Rice, ma'am. In Houston."

"Great school. Expensive, though."

"Yes, ma'am. But my uncle paid for it."

"Lucky you. He's not a dairy farmer, I'd guess."

"Uncle Sam, ma'am."

"Ah. Did you like Houston?" She could talk for a while, until her throat hurt too much. It took her mind off things.

"At first it was incredible. So many places to go and things to do—restaurants, clubs, malls. Wow. But you know what? By my junior year, I couldn't wait to come home. You don't know what you've got till you lose it," Lieutenant Gauthier said. "Houston was great for a while, but there was dirt, and crime, and people were rude, always in a hurry. Nothing like Vermont."

"How long till you get out?" Stilwell assumed that the woman would do "five and fly," as they called it. The Army paid for college educations, but got five years of service in exchange. Most recipients, especially medical professionals, put in their time and jumped back into civilian life.

"I'm thinking of staying in, ma'am," she said.

"Really?"

"Yes, ma'am. I kind of like the Army."

"Army can use people like you." Stilwell's voice was a raw croak, her throat beginning to hurt too much.

As if sensing it, Lieutenant Gauthier said, "I'll let you rest now, ma'am. But you know how close I am."

"Two things before you go, Lieutenant."

"Yes, ma'am?"

"Please turn off that IV pump beeper."

The nurse tapped a red touch-pad button on the pump's front panel. "What else, ma'am?"

"What mode is the ketamine pump in?"

"Auto, ma'am."

"Reset it to PC mode, please." *Patient control.*

The nurse hesitated for just an instant. "The doctors like to keep them on auto mode, ma'am, when they're dispensing pain meds."

"I am a doctor, Lieutenant," Stilwell said, locking eyes with the younger woman.

"Yes, ma'am, you sure are." The nurse tapped an orange touch pad on the pump twice. "There you are. All set, ma'am."

"Lieutenant?"

"Ma'am?"

"This stays with you and me. Clear?"

"Yes, ma'am. Clear."

"Thank you. I think I'll sleep a little now."

It had felt good talking to the young lieutenant, had taken her mind to the green beauty of Vermont. Maybe she would go the Guard route, as Stilwell herself had. Or maybe she really would stay in. God knew the Army could use kids with degrees from places like Rice.

The phrase came back into her mind, as she had known it would. *You don't know what you've got till you lose it*. But she had no guilt on that account. She had always known how precious Doug and Danny were, how infinitely lucky she was to have met such a man and had such a child. She knew that she had never taken either of them for granted, not for one second. Maybe it was because, as a doctor, she saw so much loss, but for whatever reason, having Doug and Danny had never become dull and ordinary, the way some things do after you've had them for a long time and grown accustomed to them.

As Stilwell lay there in the C-5A's dim bay, tears began streaming down her face. It should have made her feel better, thinking of them, but now it did not. She thought of Ribbesh. *Why are there such people?* She had asked herself that question a hundred times. *People who live to cause other people pain?* She wrestled with the question through the ketamine fog, striving for some answer that made sense. Stilwell wasn't a religious woman in the conventional sense, didn't go to church every Sunday, didn't take the Bible literally, couldn't understand the minds of people who thought the world had been created—*snap!*—six thousand years ago, or whatever it was they believed. But she was spiritual, did believe in some kind of ordering higher power, and that faith in something larger than herself had been very valuable to a physician who often dealt with seriously damaged people.

Every once in a while, however, she ran up against something she could not reconcile with a loving higher power, and people like Ribbesh were the most troubling. He had actually seemed to take pleasure in making her suffering worse. She didn't want to die, of course, but was fairly certain that she was going to. Before, at least there had been the comfort of knowing that Doug and Danny would be taken care of. Now she didn't even have that.

Stilwell turned her head to look at the IMED Genie-R1. Just

beneath the green LED screens showing dose level and drip frequency were two yellow touch pads, one with an arrow pointing up, the other with one pointing down. It would be so easy. She could just tap the up arrow over and over and the Genie would send her into a sleep from which she would never wake.

THIRTY-EIGHT

PAIN.

Terrible, blessed pain.

You don't feel pain when you're dead.

That thought blinked in Hallie's brain like a firefly on a moonless night. Then it flicked out again and she was gone.

She came to again. Pain indescribable. But her brain flickered to life and the small light in the darkness grew brighter.

I'm alive.

How can I be alive?

She was lying on her back in the absolute darkness. Her wrists were still bound, but Cahner had tied her with lengths of parachute cord. It was dynamic—had a lot of stretch under load—and Cahner had not taken great care with her bonds. No reason to, really, since he had the Taser. Just enough to keep her from running away. Five minutes of stretching and wrenching, though painful, was enough for Hallie to work her hands free.

She took stock. Both hands worked, and arms and legs. She was not paralyzed, obviously, but her head hurt as though someone had been hitting it with bricks. How long had she been unconscious down here? She looked at her watch, which Cahner had not bothered to remove. Why would he have? He expected her to drop a thousand feet. But the fall had done what Cahner did not, and the watch was broken. No way to know how long she had been out. She might have suffered a serious head injury, concussion, subdural bleeding. Nothing to do about that now, though. Just try to ignore the pain and think.

She moved to hands and knees, groaned from the pain in her head and back, then cursed herself. For all she knew, Cahner might still be up there, listening to make sure she had died. She could see absolutely nothing, but she could feel, and the palms of her hands were touching something that felt like a thick, wet blanket. She moved to one side, gasping again with pain, and when she did the surface under her hands and knees moved. Terrified, she froze. What the hell was going on here? Experimentally, she pressed down gently with one hand. The surface gave beneath the pressure and then the rest of it undulated gently, almost like a huge water bed.

Then she understood. It was a microbial mat. A thick, living colony of photophobic bacteria sometimes formed atop a body of mineral-rich water. Such mats metabolized the elements in that water, primarily calcium, iron, and carbon. They could grow to be two feet thick. Beneath the mat would lie another, foot-thick gelatinous layer of metabolizing matter and, beneath that, water. Together, the mat and that subsurface layer had absorbed the shock of her fall. They also explained why the rocks she and Cahner had dropped earlier had made no sound.

So the biomass had broken her fall, like those giant cushions stuntmen landed on after dropping ten stories. Though from the way she felt, this mat may not have been as yielding as those Hollywood cushions. She lay back down, trying to still the pain in her head, breathing quietly, listening. She could hear, very faintly, the flowing water of the river that ran near the camp. She waited. When she judged that an hour, at least, had passed and she'd heard nothing but flowing water from above, she decided to try moving.

Her first concern was inadvertently punching through the mat. But then she reasoned that if the thing had been thick enough to break her fall from who knew how many feet, it could stand her moving around on it. She crawled in one direction for about fifteen feet, until she found the pit wall. Then, keeping her left hand in contact with the wall for balance, she stood up very slowly. The mat moved under her, and when she took a step it moved more. But she found that she could stand well enough, and began working her way around the circumference of the shaft. It was smaller than she remembered the surface opening being, and that was a very good thing, because it meant the walls would slant away from the floor rather than overhanging it. Climbing out was going to be hard enough, but if the walls had been overhanging it would have been impossible.

Having located the pit walls, she got down on all fours and began crawling back and forth in as close to a grid pattern as she could manage in absolute darkness, looking for anything Cahner might have tossed in after her. But there was nothing.

Can I climb out of this thing without the Gecko Gear?

Stupid question. You either do that or you lie down and die.

So that was settled. The question was, how? She could see nothing at all. But she knew that blind people climbed, and that some of them were among the best pure rock climbers on earth. For one thing, their hypersensitive fingers and feet found holds where sighted people could not. For another, being blind, they were immune to exposure, the inescapable sense of dread that got worse the higher you went on a wall and, after a time, began to feel like a dead weight pulling you over backward.

If they can do it, you can do it.

With the decision made, she never looked back. Once committed to the climb, she could only hope that features in the rock would constitute a route she could climb to the top, wherever that was. It was remotely possible that the top was hundreds of feet above her, but she did not think so. For one thing, she could still hear the faint sound of flowing water. But equally, even with a cushion like the thick microbial mat, there was a limit to the vertical distance a human body could fall without sustaining fatal injuries on landing. That was why the stuntmen who specialized in high falls topped out at about ten stories, or one hundred feet. Drop farther than that, and no net or cushioning system in the world could save you. It wasn't always broken bones that did the damage so much as injuries to the brain and internal organs, slung around inside the skull and body cavity by the sudden impact.

She walked around the circumference of the pit again, this time more slowly, feeling for the best place to begin. It turned out to be at about three o'clock from her starting position. There, the wall offered two good handholds and one good foothold. It wasn't perfect, but it was the best this wall was going to give.

The handholds were protrusions, the foothold a shallow hole in the wall at about knee height. Hallie put her right boot toe into that, grasped the two handholds, and stood up. In rock climbing on the surface, where you could see the route and plan your way up it, the best way to go involved maintaining continual upward momentum, so that very good climbers looked as though they were flowing right up the wall. In the dark, though, where the route remained invisible, there would be none of that. Her climb would be a series of starts and stops, and going up that way would be both more tiring and more dangerous.

Her first task was to find a placement for her left foot, now hanging free. She searched with the boot toe, running it up and down systematically, as though she were painting the wall with brushstrokes.

Lucky, she thought, when half of that boot slipped into a smooth-edged hole two feet above her other foot. *You won't be that lucky twice.* Hallie stood up straight, weighting that foot, looked for and found a ledge over which she could hook the fingers of her left hand, and locked her right fingers over the lateral continuation of that ledge. She had braced for an explosion of pain in her bandaged left hand, but it wasn't as bad as she had expected. Nothing she couldn't handle. She repeated the search with her right foot, looking for a new placement for it. At first she thought there was none to be found, but eventually she felt a rounded nubbin about the size of a grapefruit. If the wall had not angled away from her slightly, making it a few degrees from dead vertical, she would not have been able to support her weight on that round, slick surface. She placed the boot carefully and pushed herself up another two feet.

When she had climbed what she judged to be about thirty feet, she found four holds secure enough to allow her to rest. Her left leg had started doing the sewing machine, and her ungloved fingers were raw and bleeding. Every once in a while her head spun, inducing vertigo, and she could only cling to the wall and hope it would pass.

As she had been climbing, the sound of the river above had been growing steadily stronger. Hallie had no way of knowing for sure, but she estimated that the top was still another forty or fifty feet away. Though it was nothing but a wild guess, she settled on that distance. It felt manageable, yet not overly optimistic.

She understood that this was a rock climb with a margin of safety afforded by the microbial mat below, which had saved her earlier. But she also knew that she had been very lucky to survive that fall. Cahner had thrown her over with enough force to propel her away from the walls of the pit. If she had hit those jagged rock walls on her way down, that probably would have been the end of it. And if she felt herself starting to fall from the wall where she clung, it was possible she would have time to push off and fall free all the way to the bottom. But climbing falls did not usually give you fair warning to get yourself together. Most of the time you were in the air before you knew it. If that happened here, she would hit the wall all the way down, and if the impact did not kill her it would certainly cause serious injury. And would she be able to try the climb out a second time, hurt even worse than she was now?

As she hung there, her left leg jerking up and down, her fingers burning, her side stabbed with pain, a tiny thought sprang up deep in her mind.

Let go.

It would be so easy.

Just let go.

She could let herself fall over backward, making sure that her head hit the rock, and there would be just that one blinding impact, so quick that she would probably not even feel any pain, and that would be it. Her mind played with the thought briefly, like a tongue cautiously tasting some new and exotic morsel.

But then her father's face flared up from memory, and his voice, and, in quick flashing succession, her mothers and brothers and Mary . . . When she focused again she was already climbing, and now she started to become one with the rock. Her hands and feet felt the wall in slow but continuous motions, seeking and finding placements, gaining a foot here, six inches there, two inches somewhere else. The wall smelled like cold, wet metal tinged with a faint hint of rotten eggs, the cave's sulfur lending that scent. At about sixty feet, the wall's outward slant increased, making the climbing a bit easier.

It also made a mistake easier to make, and she climbed with even greater caution than before. Sooner than she expected, her right hand reached up and felt no more wall, just space. She reached farther, felt the pit's edge and then cave floor. She got her other hand on the flat surface, pulled herself up, and flopped down onto her stomach, gasping.

THIRTY-NINE

AFTER RIDDING HIMSELF OF HALLIE, CAHNER BROKE CAMP and started up, taking his time, no need to hurry now. He traversed the ledge above the Acid Bath and worked his way back to clear air. Cahner had taken Hallie's map from her pack and had traveled the same route, but following her lead and finding the way himself proved to be two very different things. Fatigue slowed him and wrong turns forced him to retrace his steps several times, wasting precious energy. As it turned out, exhaustion stopped him sooner than he'd expected. His legs simply would not move anymore.

He dropped his pack at the first clear space he could find, not much bigger than a one-car garage but with a soft, sandy floor. The ceiling above this area of the cave was exceptionally wet, and so much mineral-rich water dripping over the eons had created a forest of stalagmites about his campsite. Some were no bigger than scallions, some were as high as a man's waist, and a few massive columns rose all the way to the ceiling. He liked being in the midst of so many stalagmites. It gave his camp a safe, secure feel, like a stockade of stone.

A watercourse flowed close by, loud enough to fill Cahner's camp with the sound of the stream jumping over rocks, tangling in currents, flowing and bubbling down into the depths. He ate a dinner of MRE beef Stroganoff, then set about brewing tea. As he was trying to light the little stove, he dropped his yellow butane lighter. Locating it in the spot of his light, he bent over to pick it up. Just as he started his downward motion, something smacked the back of his helmet, knocking it off. It felt like someone had hit him with a baseball bat. Then something smashed him squarely in the back.

He was down on his belly and the something was on top of him. A forearm closed around his throat, cutting off his air. He flailed back wildly with his fists, felt one connect hard with his assailant's face, heard a grunt of pain. He bucked with his hips and rolled and got out from under the attacker. Instinctively he dropped to his hands and knees and felt for his helmet, which, by sheer luck, he grasped almost immediately. Without putting it back on his head, he flashed the light around, trying to spot the person who had come after him. When his light found its target, he could not believe his eyes.

"Hallie!"

He tried to blind her with his light but she was on him in a second, hauling him to his feet, shaking him, slapping his face. He reached for the Taser, but, with nothing to fear after disposing of her, he had stuffed it into his pack. She hit him on the side of the neck with a rock, smacking the brachial nerve bundle, stunning him. His legs collapsed and he fell, dropping the helmet, kicking it inadvertently and sending it spinning out of reach. It came to rest twenty feet away, the light broken. They were plunged into complete darkness. He scrambled away from her, scuttling like a crab.

"You can't be here!" he yelled.

Her reply was a rock the size of a grapefruit that whisked past his head, missing by inches, crashing into a stalagmite on the other side of the clearing. Cahner rolled onto his belly and crawled to the right, trying to make no sound, stifling his breathing. He wanted to find a rock, stalagmite, anything to hide behind and let him gather his wits. Another rock struck the cave floor just inches from his face, spraying him with sand and gravel. He rolled left, slid backward, covered his head with his hands and just lay there, trying to become part of the cave.

Hallie's attack had been fired by rage and adrenaline, but the fighting had burned through those and now she was winded and nauseous. Her intent was not to kill Cahner but to render him helpless and bring him out of the cave as a prisoner, to answer for his actions. Or maybe she would leave him in the cave and let somebody else come back for him. She really hadn't thought through the possibilities by the time she had caught up with him, the sounds of her approach covered by those of the river flowing nearby.

She had lost her own helmet in the scuffle, so now they were both blind. She heard Cahner roll off to her left, but then soft sand muffled the sound of his movements and she no longer had any idea of his location. He could be standing right behind her, for all she knew. Instinctively she waved her arms all around, felt nothing, dropped to her hands and knees, and scuttled several feet to one side. Then she stayed absolutely still, listening for any sound that would reveal Cahner's location.

So we are reduced to this, she thought, *crawling around in the dark and trying to kill each other with rocks*. Cahner might not need a rock if he had the Taser. But if he had it, he would almost certainly have used it already. So why hadn't he? The only possible reason was that he did not have it in his possession. That meant either he had lost it or, more likely, had stowed it in his pack. Did he carry a knife? She could not remember seeing one on his belt, but that did not rule out a pocketknife. He wouldn't need either one of those to kill her, though. A rock would do that just as well. He could even break off a sharp stalagmite and use it like a spear. Suddenly she heard a grunt, a half second of silence, and a rock smashed against the cave wall off to her left, not even close to where she lay. But she understood that Cahner was trying to frighten her into revealing her position. Another rock struck a few feet closer. He was working his way around the clearing like the sweep hand of a clock, hoping either to hit her at random or to frighten her into making noise. Moving very slowly, she began searching the cave floor with her right hand, looking for a rock to use as a weapon. She moved her hand and arm through a full arc, from shoulder to waist, but felt only soft sand. She repeated the motion with her left arm, but again found nothing.

Another rock hit the cave wall directly behind her. Whatever his location, Cahner's throws were surprisingly precise, the rock impacts moving from left to right with about five feet between them. Without knowing where he stood, she could do nothing but wait for him to find and attack her. Furious with herself for not having planned her own assault more carefully, she could only lie in the sand and stare into the darkness.

Then she began to see, not with her eyes but with her mind, the snapshot that her brain, out of long habit, had taken when Cahner's helmet had gone spinning away into the darkness. She closed her eyes and began to perceive images, outlines, shadows. Judging from the sounds he had made while throwing the rocks, Cahner was sidling from her left to her right, picking up rocks as he went, pausing to throw and hoping to hit her without really knowing where she was. That was all helpful, but still did not tell her where Cahner was at that moment, which was the one thing she needed to know.

Then Cahner told her himself. Not with his voice, but she heard him pick up a rock. It was just the slightest scraping noise, like one fingernail brushing a desktop, but it was enough. She did not hesitate, because she knew that it would take only a second or two for him to throw the rock and move again. She came up out of the sand and launched herself toward the sound Cahner had made, thinking to run into him with her shoulder and knock him down.

Her snapshot was not detailed enough to show every feature of the cave where they were, and so halfway to Cahner, her right foot twisted in a small hole in the floor and she went down, falling hard on her chest. Cahner was on her in an instant, straddling her back, grabbing her forehead with both hands and pulling up, trying to break her neck, but she was slick with water and sweat and his hands slipped off. She flipped onto her back, clawed at his groin, squeezed with strong rock climber's hands.

He screamed in pain, twisted out of her grasp. She heard him stumbling to his feet and jumped up herself, remaining in a crouch, hands up defensively.

"Goddamn you!" Cahner rushed toward her in the dark. She jumped to one side, felt him brush past, shoved him that way, turned to face the direction in which he had gone, fully expecting him to spin around and come for her again.

Instead, there was a gasp and then sudden silence. Terrified, she crouched down in the dark, felt around her for a rock, found one, clutched it. She knelt there like a Neanderthal, defenseless except for her rock and muscles and brain, her face twisted into a snarl, waiting for the attack of whatever horror might come at her out of the dark.

Nothing came. She knelt and waited, listening, trying to feel the dark for motion, but there was nothing.

After a while she said, "Cahner?"

No answer.

"Al?"

Still no answer.

She tossed the rock ten feet to her left, waited for him to throw one of his own at the sound. Nothing happened.

"Cahner."

He did not answer.

She decided to search for the helmets and their lights. Dividing the chamber into quadrants in her mind, she moved back and forth on her hands and knees as if she were mowing a lawn. By sheer luck she found her helmet in less than a minute. The impact on the cave's floor could have broken its lights. Holding her breath, Hallie turned one on. Blue-white light flared from the LED bulbs.

"Thank you," she said softly. "Thank you, Chi Con Gui-Jao." She put the helmet on and stood up cautiously, scanning for danger.

And then she screamed.

Cahner was lying facedown, legs splayed and arms thrown out like those of a skydiver, held several inches above the cave floor by the base of the waist-high stalagmite onto which he had fallen. The impact of his body had broken off the stalagmite's slender tip, but the thicker shaft at its base had pierced his body and he lay now, impaled, the bloody stone spear protruding from his back.

Unbelievably, he was still alive. She saw that the shaft must have missed his heart by inches. One of his feet was twitching. Blood dripped from his nose and mouth, gathering in a dark red pool on the cave floor inches beneath his face. He turned his head slowly toward her, and she saw in his face the agony of hell, so horrible she had to look away. He tried to speak but made only a guttural, animal groan. His blood gave off a ferrous, rusty smell, the iron in it reacting with oxygen molecules.

Her stomach clenched at the sight of him like that. She felt not hate but horror. She watched, transfixed, as Cahner managed to bring both hands together under his chest, wild-eyed and shrieking with agony as he did so. He grasped the bottom of the stalagmite where it joined the cave floor. She saw his knuckles go white as he squeezed with all his strength. Then his whole body tensed, legs jerking out straight, as he tried to push up and off the spike. He managed to lift himself a few inches, screaming, bloody froth foaming from his mouth and nose. He stopped, unable to do more. She heard him moan something that might have been "air" or "Eric," but it was a guttural, animal sound and she could not understand. Then a gout of blood erupted from his mouth and his hands fell free. He dropped back down, quivered, and was dead.

She took a few steps closer. Hallie had seen the results of violent death before: climbers who had fallen, divers who had drowned, cavers who had been crushed by rockfall. She had not actually watched people die from their tragedies. She felt inexpressible relief that Cahner would no longer be trying to kill her. And, in another realm of her heart, some grief. Despite everything that had happened, everything he had told her about his treachery, during their years of working together she had come to like Cahner. Those feelings had been genuine then, and she recognized them within her now.

She looked around for a place to sit, and the only place was Cahner's pack, so she walked unsteadily to it and dropped down. Sure that he had killed her, Cahner had not bothered to dispose of Hallie's pack back at the river camp. After she'd climbed out of the pit, an hour's careful searching had brought her back to the sleeping spot and her pack, right where she'd left it. Before attempting to subdue Cahner, she had taken it off and cached it near this clearing, and she would retrieve it shortly. For now, she just wanted to rest. Her hands and knees were bloody, and the eye where Cahner had caught her with a punch was swelling. She was sore from shoulders to butt from the hard landing on the microbial mat in the pit, and the hand she had sliced throbbed painfully. Worst of all, she was alone. Then she thought of Bowman, and her skin tingled and her chest tightened.

You will not cry. There is still too much to be done.

But she did cry then, long and hard. For the soldiers, and Haight, and Arguello, and Bowman. And then, finally, for herself and everything she had lost along the way to this place.

Hallie awoke and realized that she had curled up in the sand and gone to sleep, but had no memory of doing so. She had not turned her light off first, and its glow was now noticeably dimmer. Hurrying, she found her pack and brought it back to the camp. She was carrying only the bare minimum now: a rebreather unit for the dive through Satan's Anus, the Gecko Gear, a poly bottle of water, the few remaining PowerBars, her sleeping bag, her helmet with its lights, and her last backup light. Even if the headlight batteries failed, the one hand light with fresh batteries might be enough to get her out of the cave, though she did not relish the thought of diving through Satan's Anus without light.

She dumped the contents of Cahner's pack on the floor and found the Envirotainer. He was dead and could never threaten her again, but his corpse, impaled on the stalagmite, was only fifteen feet away. She could not see it unless she looked in that direction, but that barely lessened the horror of its presence and she wanted to get away from that place as fast as she possibly could. From Cahner's gear she took only the flask of rum. She picked up the butane lighter from the cave floor and thought about bringing his rebreather and Gecko Gear as backups, but her strength was failing and even those fifteen extra pounds would be too much.

Hallie organized the objects in her pack, shrugged into the harness, and started back up. She had to walk by Cahner's corpse on the way out, but she did not look at him. She was ten steps past when she remembered the map. It had not been in his pack, which, when she thought about it, was not surprising, given how often he would have had to check it.

She had traveled the route three times already and she felt fairly sure that it was inscribed in her memory. But she knew that "fairly sure" was not good enough here. With weakening batteries and failing strength, she had no room for errors on this climb out. So, though the thought revolted her, there was no choice. She walked to Cahner's body, took a deep breath, and searched the left hip pocket of his suit, then the right. It was too soon for rigor to have set in, and through the fabric his flesh felt like cold dough. Both pockets were empty. She would have to go through his front pockets then, and if neither of them held the map, she would be forced to reach into the blood-drenched chest pockets.

Bending over the corpse, she could not keep from recalling the last frames of so many horror movies in which the supposedly dead monster suddenly exploded to life and leapt upon a lulled victim. But she pulled herself back to reality and worked her hand to the bottom of Cahner's left front pocket. There was no way to avoid making contact with his dead thigh as she searched. The map was not there. She moved to his right side, bent over, and said a silent prayer. *Please let it be here.*

It was. Carefully, so as not to tear the map, she eased it out of his pocket. When it came free, she put it into one of her own chest pockets and walked quickly away.

The wonderful thing about mountain climbing was that the second half of every expedition was all downhill. The terrible thing about caving was that it worked the other way around. After two hours she had slowed to a crawl. But she kept going in a daze, one hand in front of the other, one foot after the other, wading chest-deep ponds, clambering up rock faces, squirming through squeeze tunnels, going on hands and knees and pushing her pack in front where the cave ceiling dropped to within two feet of the floor. She came out of one long, low-ceilinged passage like that, staggered to her feet, and then sat back down as her legs gave way. She rolled onto her side and passed out.

She awoke after she knew not how long. Shucking the pack, she sat up and looked around.

I don't remember this place.

She took out the map and studied it in the light's weak glow. She examined the cave around her, at least as far as her light beams would reach, but nothing resembled what the map showed. She made short forays in four directions, looking for features that she could match to the map or to mental images. She found none. After half an hour of searching, she went back and sat beside her pack.

She had lost the route. She had the map, but without the route, it was useless.

How long had she been plodding along, lost without even knowing it? How long since she had checked her location against the map? She could not remember. Hallie was so tired that she felt no panic, not even much fear. Just a dull astonishment and disappointment that she could have done something so stupid. And deadly. Fatal for her, of course, but not her alone. So many others. That was not going to be an easy thing to die with.

But dying would have to wait. She was too tired to die. First, she would have to sleep some more.

FORTY

KATHAN WAS STANDING AT THE WEST EDGE OF THE CENOTE, his camoflouage suit all but invisible in the brush. They still had not seen *narcos, federales,* or savage Indians, but several times they had heard the sounds of firefights, long, ripping bursts of weapons on full auto, the heavier *whoomf whoomf* of rocket-propelled grenades and mortars. Once the fighting noise had come very close, no more than a half mile, but eventually it had faded and they'd relaxed as much as they ever did on missions like this.

Stiff and sore from sitting so long in the hide, and needing to urinate, he had made his way to the cenote. Finished, he was watching his reflection in the water. He saw a man dressed in camo, rugged face, body like a tree trunk, eyes invisible behind the dark glasses, shaved head rough now with stubble, cigarette dangling from full lips. The Marlboro was about down to the filter, so he shook a fresh one from the pack and lit it with the stub of the old one. He tossed the butt into the water, where it hissed and went out, floating on the surface. He was smoking more now, and Stikes had been saying it could tip off people a long way away. But Kathan had not smoked at all until that day and it had about driven him crazy. He rubbed his cheeks, feeling the scruff of beard that had grown in while he and Stikes had been holed up here, waiting for whatever came out of the cave.

The waiting was starting to get to him, and that made him think of more unpleasant things to do to whoever the cave disgorged. They had eventually agreed that the best disposal would be to shoot, gut, and sink everybody except the blonde, for whom Kathan had elaborate plans. But now Kathan was not so sure he wanted to do any of them the great favor of a quick and easy death. One of his assets—given his line of work—was an ability to enjoy making other people hurt badly. In Kathan, it went beyond simply extracting information, which all special ops people had to do from time to time. It sprang from a fondness for the activity, which he anticipated the way other men might anticipate a round of golf or a good steak dinner.

So maybe we'll do a little knife work first, he thought, looking down at his reflection, the tip of his cigarette a red glowing dot in the water. He had never been big on gross dissection, stuff like cutting off body parts or removing eyes—in living people, anyway. It was messy and put subjects into shock. That way, they became useless, because they could feel less pain and could not communicate well. He much preferred refined techniques that he had developed himself. He knew, for instance, that the ulnar nerve on the inside of the elbow could be stimulated with something no more menacing than a hatpin. But the return on investment was immense. Penetrated, the ulnar nerve created indescribable agony without doing serious damage to the body. Another good one was the optic nerve; one ran from behind each eyeball to the brain. Those you could reach with a piece of stiff wire, going up through the nose and behind the eye socket.

He would not do those things to the woman, of course, at least not before he had taken his time exploring her in other ways, with other instruments. After that, well, it would depend on what kind of mood he was in.

He smoked the second cigarette down, tossed it into the cenote, heard the hiss as it died. Then he looked up. His mouth dropped open. He whirled and disappeared into the forest.

Stikes had been napping on top of his sleeping bag when Kathan came rushing back.

"Move your ass. We're on."

Stikes stood, rubbing his eyes. "What'd you see?"

"Lights."

"Lights?"

"Yeah. Light beams bouncing around inside the entrance to the cave. Somebody's coming up."

"About time," Stikes said. "Full rig?"

"Full rig. We don't know who's coming out of there. Might be the big guy. Can't take chances with that one."

"The one who was Delta?"

"They said he was beyond Delta. Plus, this place is still crawling with *federales* and *narcos*. If we get compromised out in the open like that, we'll need everything we have. Come on, gear up."

They both donned full mission gear: utility belts with Beretta 9mm semiautomatic pistols and four extra twenty-round clips, tactical knives, backup switchblades, one frag grenade and one white phosphorus grenade each, Kevlar helmets with integral commo systems. They put on full-torso body armor, secured it with Velcro straps, and hung over it their chest harnesses with eight thirty-round magazines for their M4 carbines.

Grabbing their rifles, they slipped back through the forest to the tree-line hide. They settled down on their bellies and slid into the hide, an oval depression covered with a selection of branches and foliage that made it all but indistinguishable from the surrounding forest floor. From their positions, with binoculars they could watch the cave entrance as though they were lying just twenty yards instead of two hundred from it.

They watched. And waited. And watched. "What the hell are they doing?" Stikes asked. "I'm sweating like a pig, man."

"Here we go." Kathan's eyes were pressed to his binoculars. "It's *her.*"

Stikes brought up his own binoculars. "How many others?"

"Hang on."

They waited. They watched Hallie come out of the cave, cover her eyes from the blinding sunlight, stumble around like a drunk. They saw her drop her pack and scan the meadow and tree line. She looked right at them, and her eyes kept on going.

"Can't tell much with that suit on." Kathan, frustrated.

"Looks like she's eating a candy bar or something," Stikes said. "She's drinking out of a red flask. They carry that kind of stuff in caves? Should we snatch her now?"

"No. We're two hundred mikes away. She sees us, bang, she's back in the cave. Or into the forest. Either way makes a lot more work for us, exposed. Bad way to roll around here, you know?" Kathan was quiet, considering.

"So . . . what then? Suppose she calls in an evac team or something."

"I been thinking about that, too. She couldn't do that from inside the cave. Only out here. And she'll have to use a radio. Can't let that happen. She picks up anything that looks like a radio, we'll have to take her out. Can you line her up and stay on her?"

"Roger that." Stikes brought his M4 forward and settled it onto the rocks he had earlier arranged into a shooting rest.

"You got her?" Kathan asked.

"I have her," Stikes said, not moving his eye from the telescopic sight.

"Head shot, if you have to take it."

"I said I have her. Two hundred mikes is nothing."

"I'll spot for you, stay on her with the binocs. Keep those crosshairs centered."

"I can put one in her ear from here."

They waited, sweating in the heat, besieged by biting insects from the air and crawling ones from the forest floor. As hides went, it was turning out to be unusually hellish.

Minutes passed. Stikes watched through the scope, crosshairs centered on Hallie's head, the pad of his index finger putting two pounds of pressure on the M4's trigger, which would fire with four pounds. Sweat burned his eyes. "I don't see any others. You?"

"No."

"You think *she* did all of them? Left them in the cave?" Stikes sounded skeptical, but he knew stranger things had happened.

"No. I think the cave did them."

Out of the corner of his eye, Stikes saw Kathan lick his lips, massage his crotch. "I hope to hell we don't have to shoot her." He turned to Stikes. "Send the signal."

"Not good. We don't have it yet. The stuff from the cave."

Kathan spat. "What do you think, she's gonna kill us and take that stuff back herself? I don't think so. Send the signal."

"Kathan . . ."

"The sooner we let them know we have the stuff, the sooner they get our money flowing to the right places. I want it waiting for me when I get back."

Stikes still didn't think it was the right thing to do, but Kathan was the mission leader. From a uniform pocket Stikes took a sat transmitter. It was black, the size of a pack of cigarettes, and had a telescoping antenna, which Stikes pulled out to full extension.

"You sure about this?" he said one last time.

"Do it."

The device had one purpose only: to send an encrypted data burst to a certain satellite, which would relay it to an intended recipient on earth. In this case, that was Gray. Stikes lifted a hinged cover, exposing a red button the size of a dime. He hesitated briefly, then depressed the button and held it for five seconds.

"Done," he said.

"Done *deal*," Kathan said.

FORTY-ONE

STAGGERING FROM EXHAUSTION, EYES POURING TEARS FROM the sudden glare, face bruised and swollen and with several cuts oozing blood, Hallie came out of the cave into the world of light. She had no idea how long she had been moving since the encounter with Cahner. Many, many hours, more than she could remember. It was daylight—that was all she knew and all she needed to know.

Her body hummed with pain. But she was out. She was out and she had the moonmilk. Her eyes would gradually calm down, the cuts would heal, the bruises would fade, the bumps and sprains would ease. Normally, when she came out of a cave, she felt a mixture of exhilaration and sadness, thrilled by the adventure and sad that it was ending. But not this time.

Stepping through the mouth of the cave had been like crossing the finish line of a marathon, squared. She had focused so hard, and for so long, on reaching the goal that when she finally made it, everything fell apart. It was all she could to do shrug off her pack, let it fall, and drop down beside it.

For a while she just sat in a fog of exhaustion and pain, eyes blinking against the light, unfocused, unseeing. After a long time, thoughts began to coalesce. She thought of the EPIRB in her pack, an emergency signaling device, employing a secure frequency similar to those downed military pilots used to call for rescue. She had a radio, too. Bowman had given one to each team member. He had said to first activate the EPIRB, alert the extrication team, then wait for comm on the radio. She opened her pack and started rooting around, trying to find the EPIRB. Then she stopped. It was daylight. They would not come in daylight. There was no point in risking detection now, when they could not come. She would have to hide until nightfall.

Back into the cave. Oh God.

But she did not move. She had become little more than the collection of her primal needs, hunger and thirst chief among them just now. She leaned toward her pack again and rummaged in it for something to eat or drink. She found a crushed energy bar and an empty water bottle. Bowman's flask caught her eye, so she took that out. *Little early for a drink, but what the hell.*

She munched some of the energy bar and washed it down with a sip from the flask. The fiery rum burned taken straight like this, but it was better than anything she had ever tasted, good enough to cut through some of the fatigue like a light beam through fog and kindle a little spark in her brain.

Easy, girl. Won't take much to get you stumbling drunk. Can't have that.

She put the flask away, stood, hefted her pack, and turned toward the cave. Then a glint caught her eye, all the way across the meadow, sunlight glancing off the cenote's still, shining surface. She looked at the water, kept looking, and felt something like great thirst arising in her. She was thirsty and would drink, but this was an urge of another kind: to feel water's cleaning, healing touch all over her body. Hallie was filthy. "Disgusting" was the word that came to her mind. She had not bathed for more than a week. She couldn't remember when she had run out of toilet paper, but it had been some time ago. After she had passed through Batshit Lake on the way out, there'd been no waterfall to shower beneath, so the stuff was drying and caking, giving off an unholy stink, layered over all the accumulated dirt and sweat and mud from the previous week. Some of her cuts had crusted and scabbed, and each one of those felt like a nail stuck through her flesh. She looked at the cenote and thought of all that cool, clear water. Thought of how good, no, how *exquisite* it would feel to wash again in pure water, to be *clean,* to actually see her own skin, to have the searing pains cooled and soothed.

"It will only take ten minutes." She said this out loud and headed for the cenote. At its edge she dropped her pack, removed her boots and socks, stripped off the filthy caving suit. She took off her red long underwear and, wearing only a sport bra and panties, walked to the pool's rocky lip, and dove straight in, entering with barely a splash.

It felt every bit as good as she had imagined it would. *Better.* She could not think of a word powerful enough to describe the feeling, in fact. The water was cool but not cold, caressing, cleansing, and she swam easily, relishing the smooth flow against her skin. She stroked out to the middle of the cenote and floated there, rubbing her face and pulling fingers through her hair. She turned over on her back and let the water hold her up, moving her legs and arms in great arcs, as though making a snow angel, limbering stiff muscles, relishing the water's lovely touch.

She did a quick surface dive and swam straight down for twenty feet, then thirty, the light dimming, feeling the pressure. She equalized her ears continually, the action automatic from having done so much scuba diving. She turned toward the surface and pulled up as fast as she could, bursting out of the water and falling back with a loud splash and a barely stifled cry of joy.

God, it felt good. And it felt good to move in water. She knew of no better therapy for a sore body. She also knew that she was going to have to get out and carry on soon. But just a couple more minutes wouldn't hurt. She turned over on her belly and began swimming with a slow, graceful crawl, gulping a bite of air over her shoulder with every other stroke, long arms pulling at the water. Ten feet short of the cenote's far wall, with unbroken forest looming up just beyond the edge, she pulled up and treaded water.

And then she saw the floating cigarette butts.

FORTY-TWO

"PULL!" SAID BERNARD ADELHEID.

A steward pushed a button and the cage's spring-loaded top flew open. A ruffed grouse exploded out of the cage, soared up and away from the yacht's fantail, a dark slash across white clouds. Adelheid swung his Purdey shotgun right to left, smooth as an artist stroking paint on a canvas. The shotgun roared once and the grouse's flight ended in a red burst of feathers and blood. Adelheid broke the Purdey, withdrew the spent shell from its smoking breech, reloaded. "Your shot," he said to Nathan Rathor.

Nathan Rathor had no love of yachts or oceans. He wasn't prone to seasickness, had always been blessed with a strong stomach. What he found nearly unendurable was being at the mercy of an uncontrollable force like the sea. But he also knew that there was nothing like a boat and vast expanses of open water for communications security. Unless someone managed to bug your vessel, of course, but no one was likely to get a bug into any boat that carried Bernard Adelheid.

Standing next to Adelheid while the man was holding a loaded shotgun would not have been one of Rathor's first choices of places on earth to be. But when the man called, you came, and when he wanted to shoot, you shot. Rathor had shot skeet before, of course, though always with clay pigeons, and that was what he had expected to be shooting at this sunny afternoon on the Atlantic, twenty miles east of Cape May, New Jersey. But Adelheid had said, "There is little sport in shooting dead things, would you not agree? These grouse are legendary, one of the most difficult wing shots on earth."

Rathor had done a little upland hunting himself, so he knew that grouse had advantages in the field they did not enjoy here. Hunting without dogs once in Maine, he had walked within ten feet of a grouse and had not seen it, so perfectly did the bird blend with its surroundings. Then he took another step and the grouse flushed, bursting twenty feet straight up from cover, its wings drumming so loudly that he started and nearly fired his gun by accident. At the height of its rise the bird hurtled off into the darkness of the far woods and he did not have time even to raise his shotgun, let alone make a decent shot. It was very different here, but he said nothing about that to Adelheid. Rathor was curious about something, however. "What happens to the ones we miss?" he had asked.

"They fly until they cannot fly anymore. They fall into the ocean and die. Fish eat them." He'd shrugged. "Better than polluting the sea with toxic ceramics, don't you think?" he'd added, referring to clay pigeons.

Now Rathor stood holding a Purdey over-and-under that was the matching twin to Adelheid's, who had said there must be no advantage to either gunner. The Purdey's stock was Turkish walnut. Its gold side plates were the background for scenes of mounted knights carved from solid silver. Rathor was not a gun lover, but he knew the price of wealth's trappings. Adelheid—or whoever owned this boat, which might or might not belong to Adelheid—would have paid $300,000 for this pair, maybe more.

The yacht was a 164-foot oceangoing Benetti, but the deck still moved beneath Rathor. He shouldered his gun, bent his knees, and braced his feet. Finger on the Purdey's front trigger, he shouted, "Pull!"

The game cage went *spang!* and another grouse flew out, rising on a right-to-left trajectory. Rathor knew what he was supposed to do to hit the thing—*don't aim, just point and swing like you're sweeping the sky*. He tried to imitate Adelheid's effortless technique, done so quickly that the leading and firing seemed to happen almost in the same instant.

Rathor pulled the gun's brass trigger and its stock punched his shoulder. The grouse flew on, intact. Rathor found the rear trigger and discharged the gun's lower barrel and missed with that one, too. Shooting like this was hard enough on steady dry land. Trying to hit a moving target from the rising and falling deck of a yacht—an impossible thing. Yet Adelheid had shot a dozen times and had hit each bird with the first barrel. Rathor had hit one bird and knew he had been lucky to do even that.

"Oh, my," Adelheid said, though Rathor thought he detected more irritation at Rathor's inept shooting than sympathy in the other's voice. "Perhaps enough of this for now. Let us go forward." An attendant materialized and took the shotguns. Another appeared with flutes of Dom Pérignon. Rathor followed Adelheid through the yacht's interior to its foredeck, with white leather banquettes and mahogany tables. They had made a slow turn and were now heading for the mainland at a stately pace. They would not be back until after dark, but that suited Rathor quite well.

They stood at the bow, warm in sweaters and jackets, and drank the icy champagne without talking for a few moments. Then Adelheid said, "I am beginning to feel good about our venture. Cautiously so, but good."

That surprised Rathor. In his experience, Adelheid was almost invariably gloomy. Rathor himself was not feeling so confident. "We're a long way from the goal line, I'm afraid."

Adelheid smiled thinly, shook his head. "The goal line. You Americans and your athletics. But, you see, I know something that you do not."

"And what might that be?"

"Not long ago I heard from Gray. He believes that our team in Mexico has met with success."

"He does? What happened?"

"I am not in possession of full details yet. Apparently the environment there is not secure for lengthy transmissions. But there was a prearranged signal that could be sent as a single data burst. Gray's people received that signal."

"I don't know," Rathor said. "I won't be comfortable until we have that substance from the cave in our hands."

"Gray's people do not make mistakes," Adelheid said, and Rathor detected another trace of irritation in his voice.

"I understand that. But all the same—"

Adelheid fixed Rathor in his stare. "With the other two problems accounted for, there is less cause for concern, would you not agree?"

Rathor wasn't sure, but he did know that differing too often with Adelheid was unwise. "I suppose you're right," he said. "I can be overly pessimistic at times." He tipped his flute and finished the champagne. In an instant a white-jacketed waiter appeared with a full glass. When Rathor turned halfway around to accept his new drink, he said, "Where did they come from?"

Seated on a banquette were two of the most beautiful women he had ever seen. They must have come out while he and Adelheid were facing forward, talking. Both looked to be in their mid-twenties. One had shining, shoulder-length red hair. The other was blond, her hair in a shorter blunt cut. Their faces were different in details but alike in the beauty those details combined to create. Adelheid turned around then.

"Magic," he said.

"Magic indeed," Rathor agreed. Both women wore silk blouses, one pale blue and the other lime green, and white linen walking shorts. They were barefoot, and Rathor noted that their perfect tans extended all the way to the tips of their toes. He was struck by how perfectly the tailored blouses revealed the contours of their breasts, neither hanging loose nor stretched lewdly tight. Rathor thought himself a connoisseur of women, and these two, he knew, were rare jewels. His heart quickened just looking at them. Taking his elbow, Adelheid guided him to the table, where the women sat drinking champagne and nibbling sashimi.

"Erika and Aimée, may I present our guest for the evening."

"Hello," Erika, the woman with red hair, said.

"Enchantée." Aimée's accent was heavily French.

The touch of their cool hands, one after the other, set off a buzzing in Rathor's chest.

"Erika and Aimée will be joining us for dinner," Adelheid said.

Nathan Rathor was not often at a loss for words, but just now he could not find the right ones. Finally he said, "You are a man of many surprises."

"Indeed? It is good to be surprised, would you not agree? Otherwise life becomes"—he shrugged, appearing to search for just the right word—"unlivable." He raised his glass in a toast. The women raised theirs, and so did Rathor. They settled deeper into the banquette's cushions, sipping champagne, Adelheid doing most of the talking, the yacht rolling along with agreeable small swells that eased its landward passage.

Astern, the sun became a shimmering red globe sinking into the edge of the darkening ocean. The light began to go blue, and attendants placed candles in windproof crystal holders on the table. They were served oysters on beds of crushed ice with crescents of lemon. Rathor noted that Adelheid and the women ate noisily and with great relish.

Adelheid seemed to have no desire to talk more about their venture. Instead, he led them into discussions about medieval art, the planets, evolution. To Rathor's surprise, Erika and Aimée held their own, and it must have shown on his face because Adelheid said, "Erika and Aimée are both graduates of excellent colleges." He looked at Erika.

"Kiev University," she said.

"Sorbonne," Aimée said.

"Without intelligence, we do as the animals do," Adelheid remarked. "For the greatest reward, we must bring intelligence to all in our lives. Including the taking of pleasure."

"Of course," Rathor said. "Otherwise we're just like . . . like a bunch of rutting hogs."

Adelheid blinked, coughed. "Perhaps not how I would have phrased it, but the thrust is correct." Adelheid glanced over his shoulder at the sunset, just then completing. "I believe we will have dinner now, but let us move inside."

They all got up and went into the yacht's saloon, a glittering cave of leather and marble. The two women excused themselves. "To dress for dinner," Erika said.

"Just so." Adelheid nodded.

Rathor needed to use the bathroom—the head, as Adelheid called it out here—and went there. It took him a while to get things working with the deck moving underfoot, but finally he did. When he returned to the yacht's dining salon, Adelheid and the two women were already seated at a rosewood table long enough for twenty. Adelheid had donned a black blazer and put on a pale rose ascot for the occasion. Erika and Aimée, Rathor saw, had also changed for dinner, though not as he might have expected. Both had removed their blouses and now sat across the table from him bare from the waist up, shoulders back, sipping champagne with insouciance. Their tans, he noticed, were complete. Both smiled when he caught their eyes, but they might have been fully clothed, for all their poise. He swallowed. *What promises here?*

"Is there anything more exciting," Adelheid said, "than anticipation? I think not. And what is anticipation but the sweet pain of self-denial? To be in the presence of great reward and endure an ordeal of delay. It is"—he gazed at the women—"an exquisite thing."

Teasing, was how Rathor put it to himself. But he had to agree with Adelheid that by the end of a leisurely dinner with Erika and Aimée displayed this way, his pent need would be like the water held behind a great dam.

Adelheid raised his glass of champagne and said something—a grace or benediction, perhaps. Rathor had heard him say it before, had thought it sounded somewhat—but not exactly—like German. He had never asked what it meant, and Adelheid had never offered to explain.

Adelheid picked up a fork, but before starting to eat he said, "In case you were wondering, they are both for you. I have my own."

FORTY-THREE

"WELL, HEL*LO* THERE."

One of the men spoke, the huge one. They had not been there seconds earlier. For a moment she thought they were *narcotraficantes*. But the man did not sound Mexican. His accent was distinctly American South, red-clay, redneck cracker. The other man, standing to his left, was black, not quite as large. They wore camouflage uniforms, helmets, giant knives, sidearms, even grenades. They certainly looked like warriors, but they were too neat and their uniforms were too complete for them to be *narcos*. They wore no insignia of unit or rank. And their helmets were not U.S. mil-spec gear.

"You're Americans?" Hallie thought perhaps they were part of some special operations unit sent to retrieve and protect the team. She had seen pictures of such fighters, and they often looked less than spit-and-polish. The two men exchanged glances and the big man snickered. She sank lower in the water, right up to her chin.

"We sure are, honey," the big one said. "Patriotic Americans, both of us. Retired veterans, too. Hey, let me ask you a question: any of your friends coming out behind you?"

"Did BARDA send you?"

The huge man looked puzzled. He glanced at his partner, who shrugged.

"Well, no, as a matter of fact." The giant was grinning, and she could not help noticing that he had amazing teeth, as even and white as a news anchor's. "We work for the competition, you might say."

"The what?"

"Never mind. Why don't you come on out of there and we'll get you a blanket and some hot chow. I bet you're hungry after all that time down in that cave. We got some great stuff. Delta rations. None of that MRE junk."

"How did you know how long I've been in the cave?" Hallie was feeling more afraid with each passing second. The two men radiated threat like heat. Watching them, she started to swim away on her back, sculling with both arms.

"Whoa now, that's not very friendly. Come here so we can talk." The giant was still grinning, but his mouth was tight around the white teeth.

She flipped onto her stomach and started swimming as fast as she could toward the other shore. Then she heard a short, sharp noise that sounded like *puppuppuppuppuppup* as the man squeezed off a six-round burst from the silenced rifle and the cenote's surface erupted three feet in front of her face. She stopped, turned, treaded water, unsure of what to do. There was no way she could dive deep enough quickly enough to escape if they fired again. She was a good swimmer, but not faster than rifle bullets.

The big man held his rifle at the hip. Looking down, she saw the red laser aiming dot centered on her exposed breastbone. *Twenty feet away. He can't miss.*

"Now why don't you just swim your beautiful self on over here and let's talk." No more nice, the voice raw and frightening.

"We don't have time for this, man," the other said, standing with one hip cocked, his rifle stock tucked against his waist, muzzle pointing skyward. He sounded like someone who just wanted to get on with a piece of business. The big man ignored him.

There was no option. She swam slowly to the rim of the cenote, put her hands on the rocky edge, and pulled herself out, first to her knees, then up to stand in front of them in her underwear. She sluiced the water back out of her hair. The bigger man had the strangest expression on his face, mouth open, eyes glazed, breath coming in short, sharp little pants. *Like a starving animal who sees food,* she thought.

"Let me tell you something." She tried to sound commanding. "I am on a special assignment for the United States government. Many people up to and including the White House know exactly where I am and what I'm doing. Do you understand that? If you interfere with me in any way you will—"

The giant cut her off. "What we *understand* is that you are here all by your own self. And we are here with you."

"But I radioed for evac ten minutes ago, right after I came out of the cave. A serious military presence will arrive here in minutes."

"No, you didn't, as a matter of fact. We've been watching you every second."

"All right, look." She maintained eye contact with the big man, who stood six-six if he was an inch. "I'm going to tell you why I'm here. I think when you understand the nature of my mission—"

"Honey, you could be on a mission to save Jesus Christ himself and it wouldn't matter to us."

The other man spoke, his voice sharper: "Kathan—we need to *move*."

He used the other one's name, she thought. *A very bad sign.*

"You need to shut up and let me do my thing," the one called Kathan said to the other in a voice heavy with warning. He never took his eyes off Hallie. "Honey, I got a question for you."

"Like what?" She immediately regretted saying that, because the giant's question had to do with what variety of sexual activity she preferred. He shifted his rifle to his left hand, then lowered the zipper of his camo suit.

"Here's how we're gonna start. You get down on your knees and I think you know what comes after that."

"No."

He moved more quickly than she would have thought possible for a man so huge, slapping the barrel of his rifle against the right side of Hallie's neck, just below her ear. It wasn't a hard blow but it hit the brachial nexus, the same spot where she had hit Cahner with a rock. Her legs collapsed and suddenly she was on her knees, trying to blink away bright sparks of light.

"Do it," he said.

"No."

Kathan sighed. He set his rifle on the ground. With his right hand, he pulled the combat knife from its belt scabbard and held it poised over her head. His left hand wrapped around her neck. He lowered the point of his knife onto her scalp, letting her see how it felt. He wasn't even pressing, but just the weight of the knife itself made her gasp, and a small rivulet of blood ran down her forehead. She flicked her eyes sideways at the other man, who stood as he had before, hip cocked, rifle propped, watching. For a split second their eyes met and she thought she saw a flicker of something human, but then he blinked and looked away. Hallie thought of lunging at the rifle where it lay on the ground, but as if he had read her mind, her tormentor applied pressure and the knife point dug deeper and she grunted, her vision blurring into a red mist.

"I'm hoping we can all be nice about this, blondie," he said.

"Kathan, goddamnit, we—" the other one said.

"Hey, bro? You need to shut the fuck up now, hear?"

Kathan dug the knife point in so hard she almost fainted. Then he eased the pressure off and lifted it a centimeter above her scalp. He put his other hand behind Hallie's head and pulled her toward his crotch.

In her peripheral vision, Hallie saw the other man take a step sideways. He said, "Hey, *bro*."

His aiming laser's red dot appeared in the center of the big man's throat, just above the top of his body armor. "Throw the knife in the water. Let her go."

The grip on Hallie's neck did not loosen, but the big one turned his head toward the other. "You really do not want to do this, Stikes," he said.

Kathan and Stikes, she thought. *Do not forget those names.*

Stikes sighed. Hallie heard the sharp double click as he thumbed his M4's safety lever from "safe" past "semi" to "burst." He said, "It won't take two of us to get that stuff home, and I can really use another share. You know what else? This world could use one less racist psycho cracker."

"Wait, Stikes—" Kathan said.

Stikes braced the rifle's stock against his side, locking it in tight with his right elbow. Turning her head an inch, Hallie saw the tip of his index finger starting to pale as he applied pressure to the trigger.

A small hole appeared just in front of Stikes's right ear and a dark red fountain blossomed out the other side of his skull. Hallie heard the sharp report of a rifle, the sound coming a millisecond after the bullet. Stikes stood upright for a second. Then he jerked, collapsed to his knees, and flopped onto his face.

More rifle fire, short, full-auto bursts. Bullets spattered the rocks around them, threw up geysers of water and spurts of soil. The giant named Kathan dropped the knife and snatched his rifle off the ground. Hallie jumped to her feet, readying for a sprint into the protective forest. With his rifle in one hand, Kathan lunged and grabbed her upper right arm with the other.

Reaching for her like that put him off balance, so that he was leaning sharply toward the cenote. Her mind did the necessary calculations in a microsecond. Whoever had fired the shot might be as bad as the man named Kathan. Or they might be help. It was at least possible. With Kathan, there was only one possibility.

Hallie spun behind Kathan and wrapped both arms around him in a bear hug, pinning his own arms momentarily to his sides. She pulled back and Kathan began to tilt like a great column, slowly at first, then more quickly, accelerating toward the water. As they landed, she wound both legs around his waist and just before going under she sucked in a huge breath.

Kathan let go of his rifle as soon as they hit the water, but with all the weight of metal and body armor he was wearing, they sank like an anchor. Hallie kept her arms and legs tight around him. She could not risk having him get free to drop the rest of his gear and make it back to the surface. She locked her ankles, one over the other, heels in his crotch. She grasped her left wrist with her right hand and her right wrist with her left. The double grip gave her twice the holding power. Twined together front to back like lovers, turning slowly, they plunged deeper, and the deeper they went, as pressure squeezed buoyancy from the man's gear and their bodies, the faster they sank.

In two seconds they were twenty feet down. Kathan struggled frantically, kicking his legs, working his arms free to pull Hallie's wrists and hands. Then panic took over and he began flailing in the water, trying to claw his way back to the surface.

At thirty feet he reached back and grabbed a handful of Hallie's hair, but it was short and very fine, wet and greasy, and it was like trying to hold on to oiled monofilament. Then he went after her face, clawing for her eyes, but she kept them pressed tightly against the soft place where his neck and shoulder joined. At forty feet, his eardrums burst. Hallie actually heard the two sharp pops and knew that it felt like ice picks had just been driven deep into both sides of his skull. He opened his mouth in a silent scream and his head whipped back and forth with a will of its own, trying to throw out the agony.

At fifty feet he began to jerk and dance with the involuntary spasms of near drowning as his immense body went to war with itself. His diaphragm and breathing muscles struggled to suck in air as the levels of carbon dioxide in his blood rose. His mouth and throat, controlled by the voluntary nervous system—which understood that to inhale meant death—fought those efforts.

A few seconds later his blood's carbon dioxide level won the battle, tripping that irresistible switch in his brain, and the reflex designed by evolution to save his life took it instead. His body arched in one violent spasm. His head stretched back and his mouth opened wide, water flooded his lungs, and Hallie knew it would feel like someone had poured acid into his chest.

Her own vision was starting to dim. She pushed him away and he rolled over, turning his front to her. The cenote water was so clear that there was still light even at this depth. Without a mask everything underwater had a blurred, ghostly look, but for an instant their faces were so close that she could see his eyes. There was a second of life in them yet, agony and horror, the look of one in a nightmare from which there was no waking. Then he rolled over again and sank out of sight.

Hallie looked up. The small silver circle far above shone like a full moon in a dark sky. Her arms and legs felt as light and useless as featherless wings. There was no pain, and some dim remnant of consciousness knew that was bad. Then clouds began to tarnish the silver moon and the sky grew darker. When she was a child in Virginia, on summer nights Hallie had stood in the pasture among their grazing horses, touching stars with the tips of her fingers. Now she saw the stars beginning to come out, more and more tiny white sparks flickering against the black, and she stretched her fingertips up and up, trying to touch those stars one last time.

FORTY-FOUR

EVVIE FLEMMER AWOKE FROM A DREAM THAT LEFT HER WITH clenched fists. She sat up in bed, breathing very carefully, and waited for the nausea. *Mal de mer,* the yacht's steward had called it with a sympathetic tongue clucking. She knew it as seasickness, but whatever you called it, the puking horror had made every minute of the first days of her new life miserable. She had never spent time on the ocean before, and no one had warned her that seasickness might be a problem even on a boat the size of this superyacht with the peculiar name, *Lebens Leben*. To make things worse, they had put out from Cape May at night—no steadying horizon to stare at—and she had started throwing up within an hour. The steward had given her some blue pills that did nothing for the nausea but made her so drowsy she could barely talk, so she'd quit taking them. Flemmer had been told that this oceangoing yacht carried a chef lured away from La Tour d'Argent, the most famous restaurant in all of France, but she had been able to keep down nothing more substantial than weak tea and chicken broth.

So now she breathed deeply and sat quite still in the bed, while the ship rolled slowly under her like a colossal thing stretching and waking. She kept her eyes fixed on one spot on the far wall of this suite done in red and gold, the colors of an ocean sunset. Once during the night she had come awake and been surprised by a constellation of glints and sparkles, moonlight flowing in through portholes and caught by the chamber's mirrors and ornate gilt fixtures. Now she waited, breathing and staring, and after some minutes realized that her stomach felt better. Not fully normal, but better.

She wondered what time it might be, and then dismissed the thought. *Time doesn't matter anymore.*

She had wanted to do something for a day now, but the seasickness had kept her from it. She got up, perused the half dozen outfits that had been waiting for her on board, and dressed in white linen slacks and a burgundy blouse, both of which fit perfectly. She started to slip on a pair of delicate gold sandals, but decided instead to go barefoot. Shoes were no longer required. Many things would no longer be required.

There was a discreet double knock on her suite's door.

"Yes?"

The steward, a different one this morning, made a single, deferential step into the room. He was slim and dark-skinned, wearing black slacks, a starched white shirt with black studs, and white waistcoat. His black hair was slicked back so perfectly it looked as though someone might have painted his skull.

"Would mademoiselle care for coffee and breakfast now?" His accent was French, but his complexion and heavy features suggested some other nationality, she thought. Algerian, perhaps, or Egyptian.

The thought of coffee made her stomach lurch, and she shook her head quickly. It would be some time before she would feel no unease while conversing with servants. But she knew that this man expected her to feel superior, and that to act otherwise would discomfit him. She sensed that people of true quality would be neither haughty nor familiar with servants. Neutral, rather, but firm. So she said, in a tone she might have used addressing an Oklahoma horse, "I will have breakfast. How is the weather?"

"The weather is lovely, especially warm for March. A few clouds, bright sun, breezes light from the west."

"Then I will have breakfast on the sundeck."

"Very well. What would mademoiselle prefer for breakfast this morning?"

She almost asked him what her options were, but stopped. She no longer had to worry about options. *I can have what I want. Whatever that might be.*

"Freshly squeezed juice from blood oranges. Two freshly baked croissants. Unsalted butter. Fresh strawberries in champagne. Swiss chocolate. And Earl Grey tea."

"Very well. Thank you, mademoiselle." The steward half-bowed and backed out of her room.

The sundeck was the uppermost of the yacht's four decks, an expanse of brown teak and chrome and white leather nearly as big as her entire apartment had been. Flemmer sat at a table placed for her in the middle of the deck, facing aft. She ate breakfast slowly and carefully, waiting for her stomach to reply to each bite before taking the next. The chocolate had been a mistake, and she left it alone after a tiny nibble. The croissants and strawberries, though, were delicious.

She knew that it must take a good-sized crew to operate a yacht like this, but they were so expert at performing their duties invisibly that she might as well have been alone on the boat. The steward had been right about the weather; it was as perfect a day as she was likely to see in the middle of the Atlantic this time of year. The bracing air and skin-warming sun complemented each other perfectly, and with the addition of a cream-colored cashmere sweater and navy windbreaker she was quite comfortable. She sat there excited and a little breathless from champagne so early, queen of a new realm, watching the white scar left by the boat's screws hacking through dark water.

A leather bag the color of burnished brass, from some Italian designer whose name she could not pronounce, sat on the deck beside her chair. From it she took a brush with an onyx handle and brushed her hair over and over, something she had not done since she was a child. She put the brush back into her bag and pulled from it two framed photos of her parents. Other than the clothes on her back and her wallet, they were the only things she had taken from the apartment. Flemmer got up and walked as far aft as she could go on the sundeck. She stood there, thirty feet above the water. One after the other she dropped the pictures into the violent wake.

"Jocelene," she said out loud, and the syllables tasted as sweet as the plump strawberries she had just eaten.

Flemmer spent the day reading and napping and jotting little entries into the black leather diary she had begun keeping. She liked the sense of suspension that stately travel induced, feeling weightless in time without needs or shoulds. She explored the yacht's vast interior, ambling through passage after passage, peering into its guest suites, grand saloon, library, bars and lounges. She found no fewer than three huge Jacuzzis, their still water making them look like giant blue jewels. Here and there she encountered doors that were locked. No indiscreet "Do Not Enter" signs. Just locked. In all her wanderings she encountered not another person, nor saw evidence of any other. There were only the constant, subtle vibrations pushed by the engines through the vessel's steel skeleton. She could not see those engines, but imagined they must be as big as buses to drive so huge a vessel as fast as this one was traveling.

She called for dinner when her stomach told her to. After dark, it was too cool on the aft sundeck, so she told the steward to serve her in the dining salon. The room's floor—*deck,* she reminded herself as she entered—was some shining exotic wood from, she guessed, Africa. The walls were an elegant pearl white. Vases held fresh pink tulips, red roses, yellow chrysanthemums. The long table could have seated twenty, but only one place had been set, for her, at its head. There were no lights—the entire ceiling glowed—and mirrors ran the length of each wall. She had avoided looking into those mirrors when she'd entered. There would come a time when she would have no fear of mirrors, but not yet.

"Would mademoiselle care for a cocktail before dinner?" Yet a third steward was attending her this evening. Or was he the first one she had met when coming aboard? She couldn't be sure.

"Yes." Flemmer thought about that. What would she drink? "I will have a martini," she said, and he turned to go. She stopped him. "Wait. With *two* olives."

"Immediately, mademoiselle." He reappeared in two minutes, white-gloved, with her drink on a silver tray.

"I have a question," she said, when he had put the long-stemmed glass in front of her.

"Yes, mademoiselle?"

"Where are we? I mean, how long until we get to where we're going?"

The steward looked at her as though she had said something that was funny without realizing it. But when he answered, she understood.

"We are almost exactly halfway, mademoiselle." He half-bowed and left her.

The gin was so cold it stung her lips. She had never drunk a martini before, and couldn't make up her mind whether she liked this one or not. The juniper's perfume scent appealed, and she felt warm through and through after the first few sips. But the liquor did something strange in her throat, making it feel taut and a little numb. The suffusing warmth soon overwhelmed that, however, and before she knew it, she had finished the martini and ordered another.

The nausea began when she was halfway through the second cocktail. Right after came a headache, swift, sharp pain like a blow to the front of her skull. Her stomach moved.

I need to go to the bathroom, she thought, and tried to stand, and found that she could not. For just an instant she thought that she had imagined it, but then she tried to stand again and nothing happened. She opened her mouth to call the steward, tried to raise her hand to signal for help, tried to scream. Nothing happened. She was conscious, breathing, could feel the chair pressing against her buttocks and clothing touching her skin, but that was all. Panic flared. It felt as though she had been buried alive.

Where was the steward? What was happening to her? Then she heard movement from behind and four of them appeared, two on each side of her chair. She recognized the Algerian and one other. Two more she had not encountered.

Thank God. They must have seen I was having trouble.

They lifted her out of the chair, their hands careless and rough. She could still feel pain where they squeezed her flesh. They supported her under both shoulders because she would have crashed to the floor without them.

They tilted her backward, as though her heels were affixed to a hinge on the floor. Two of them held her under the arms and the others lifted her legs, gripping them at the ankles and knees. She could feel their hands tightening like manacles. None tried to touch her improperly, and she thought that they might be carrying her to a clinic or infirmary. But the stewards who had bowed and called her mademoiselle now bore her through those locked doors and along shadowed, diesel-smelling passageways as though she were a side of beef. They neither rushed nor lagged but moved purposefully and without speaking. At one corner, her head swung on its limp neck and smacked into the steel bulkhead. For a time she saw nothing but red, and when she came back, she knew they were not taking her to a clinic. She tried again and again to scream at them but managed not even a squeak.

They carried her to the ultimate end of the ship's pointed bow. Working smoothly in unison, they lifted her over the chrome rail and dropped her into the ocean. She disappeared beneath the centerline of the onrushing prow. The yacht was making sixteen knots and she did not have time to drown before her body met the hacking screws.

FORTY-FIVE

SHE BROKE THE SURFACE GASPING AND FOR A SECOND thought she was hallucinating. The last time she had come up there were two men. Now there were more.

"Buenos días, señorita."

The speaker was ragged-toothed, leering. They wore patched jeans and odds and ends of scavenged military garments, sleeveless camo shirts, ragged straw hats, cowboy boots. Each one held an AK-47 and they all had pistols holstered on web belts. One, the biggest, carried crossed bandoliers of ammunition that gleamed like a golden X on his chest. He wore an oversized red ball cap with a huge bill cocked at an angle.

Narcotraficantes.

Holding his rifle in his left hand, the man who had spoken reached down with his right.

"Ven!"

No options to analyze this time. She reached up, took his hand, and he pulled her out. Once again she stood barefoot, dripping—now with *four* men leering at her. Two were obviously drunk, weaving on their feet, mouths slack, half-mast eyes. The big man with the bandoliers of ammunition appeared sober. He had a hard slab of a face, a beard like steel wool. A hand-rolled cigarette, or maybe a joint, dangled from his lips. He had huge feet and his shoes were black sneakers with the toes cut out.

The two drunk men, saying something in rapid-fire Spanish to the one who had pulled her out, started toward her. The big man remained where he was, watching the leader, who barked at the drunks. They scowled, mumbled slurred curses, but stepped back.

"Hablas español?" The leader was talking to her.

"Sí, un poco. Inglés, por favor."

"*Ah. Norteamericano. Me llamo Carlos.* Been Laredo, Houston, big cities. Some English, me. *Them* . . . no English. Brains *here.*" He grasped his crotch, shook his head. "Want you for bad things. But no. You I take to Comandante. A gift. From me to him." He smacked his chest, grinned.

The two drunks were passing a clear bottle back and forth, swigging yellowish liquor that, even from where she was, smelled like kerosene and formaldehyde. *Aguardiente,* the local sugarcane moonshine. As they drank and passed the bottle, their eyes, red as crushed strawberries, never strayed from her breasts.

Negotiate. "If you let me go, I can get you money. Millions."

He shook his head, looked genuinely regretful. "No good. No use to man with no hands. Feet. Head. Dick."

Each time he named a body part, he made a chopping motion with the edge of his hand as though hacking with a machete, and she understood: *Jungle justice.*

He gave the big man orders, and Hallie caught enough of it to understand that he was to search the dead body, take anything of value from the camp, throw everything else, including the corpse, into the cenote, and then catch up with them.

"So. We go get your pack."

He snapped at the other two, and they all walked around the cenote. She picked up her long underwear, not even bothering to glance at Carlos.

"Stop."

His snapped command did stop her, and she stood, glaring. He looked back, expression neutral, considering. Pursed his lips, shook his head. One of the drunks muttered something guttural and obscene, and Carlos laughed so hard spit flew from his lips. But then he waved at her. "Okay. Put on. Is better for Comandante to undress you."

Carlos said something to the men and one of the drunks led off. The other shouldered her pack and stood next to her.

"You now." Carlos poked her in the side with the muzzle of his rifle and she started walking. The heels of the leading *narco*'s cowboy boots, she saw, were worn almost flat. She remembered her own bare feet.

"My boots." She pointed at her feet. *"Botas."*

Carlos smiled. "I think no. Is better to run. I go behind, protect you." He pointed. They marched across the meadow and into the forest. They used no maps or compasses but clearly knew exactly where they were going. She tried to focus, to plan an escape. They had not bound her hands, either because they had nothing to tie her with or, more likely, because they could not imagine how she could be a threat. Once they got to the *narcos'* camp, wherever that might be, she knew she'd be lost. The head man would rape her and then let his lieutenants like Carlos rape her. They might keep her for days and days, making her do whatever they wanted, handing her down to the lower ranks, torturing her if she balked. Eventually she would weaken, get sick, and die. Raped to death. That might take a long time, though.

"Carlos." She looked back, spoke over her shoulder.

"Eh?"

"When we get to the camp, your *comandante* will take me. We could do something first. You and me. Here."

"Cómo?"

"Send these others on ahead. Then we can . . ." What was the word? *"Relaciones sexuales."* His face lit up. *That* he recognized. *"Yo soy muy buena,"* she said, thinking, *If I can separate them, I have more of a chance. Not much, but better than three against one.*

"Sí?" Carlos grinned, tongue slipping over cracked lips and yellow teeth. "But Comandante no like used. Fresh, he like. You see?"

She didn't bother to answer, and they walked on. The forest floor, littered with pinecones and fallen *mala mujer* leaves, cut her feet, which left spots of blood where she stepped.

"Carlos!"

"Eh?"

"I need to go . . . to *piss*. Right now."

He laughed, but there was no humor in his eyes. "My English bad. But I am no stupid. Go on, *puta*."

She marched, dazed and despairing. Even with all the risky things she had done, not once in her life had Hallie known, beyond doubt, that she was going to die. She did, now. Part of her looked forward to it. She was so exhausted, and hurt so much in so many places, that relief would be welcome, even if it was permanent. She began to think of all the things she would miss: her brothers, her mother, the horses, the water in Ginnie Springs, the ocean . . . The list went on and on and she just let it keep playing, and tears began to run down her cheeks at last.

"Eh!" Carlos grunted and threw a quick glance over his shoulder, but did not stop.

She turned to look. The big *narco* was a hundred feet behind them, lumbering head-down through the deep forest gloom to catch up, bandoliers like a cross of gold on his chest, the AK-47 a toy in his huge hand. The drunk *narco* in front and the one beside her didn't even turn around. "Keep moving," Carlos said. "He catch us."

She walked again, uncaring. Something would happen, some opening, and she would seize it. Or not. Maybe she would just have to run. They would shoot and she would die, but she was going to die anyway, so she might as well do something, anything, that would give her even one-half of one percent of a chance. Better quick and painful than slow and painful. But not now, not just yet.

She plodded on. The thud of the big *narco*'s feet grew closer, his jingling bandoliers reminding her of the bells on the sleighs when they hitched the Morgans up in one of Virginia's rare snowfalls. She heard an odd, soft, high sound, a yelp like a small dog might make when kicked, and turned in time to see Carlos fall on his face, the handle of a knife sticking from the soft place where skull and spine met at the back of his head. The *narco* carrying her pack was also facedown on the ground, a knife handle sticking out of the side of his skull.

In his left hand, the big *narco* held a third knife, one with a stainless steel hilt and a vicious serrated blade, the kind divers used. She had seen that knife before, strapped to Bowman's lower left leg in the black plastic scabbard.

They killed him, she thought, *or found him dead and took his knife. But why . . .*

The other drunk *narco,* the one in front of her, was spinning around, the muzzle of his AK-47 coming up. Small details began to take on immense significance and clarity for Hallie. She could see his finger, like a fat white worm, searching for the trigger.

She did not understand what was happening here, but she knew that dealing with one of these men would be easier than fighting two. So just as the *narco*'s finger found the trigger, her hands found his eyes. She dug, felt her thumbs go in, heard him scream. She smashed her body against his, driving one knee into his groin, trying to wrench the rifle away. He pulled the trigger and the AK-47 fired on full auto, the recoil making the barrel writhe and jump like a crazed snake. Reports from the big 7.62-millimeter rounds sounded like dynamite blasts so close to her ears. Muzzle flashes burned her side, but she was not hit. The *narco* stumbled backward under the impact of her rush, blinded, doubled over by the pain in his groin. He dropped the rifle and clawed at his eyes. She scrabbled for the gun, found its forestock with one hand, its pistol grip with the other, and spun to shoot the big one. The wound on her palm had opened and was bleeding, but she ignored it.

He wasn't there. A forearm that felt like a steel bar closed over her throat. Somehow the huge man had moved quickly enough to get behind her. She threw her head back, hoping to butt him, but hit only air. She tried to swing the gun around to fire back at him over her shoulder. He grabbed it just above the magazine and ripped it out of her grasp as though taking a rattle away from a baby. But that freed her hands and she clawed at the forearm, scratching it, drawing blood, snarling and biting, fighting now with the last of her strength for the last of her life.

"Hallie."

It took several moments for the word to punch through her rage and terror. But then she came back to herself.

"Bowman?"

The forearm loosened, fell away. She sucked in cool air, turned.

"I really thought you were going to shoot me." Bowman, grinning, rubbed his bleeding forearm.

"Bowman!" She put her arms around him, dragged him toward her. "Bowman, god*damn* you. I thought you were dead."

They held each other tightly, her head against his shoulder, his arms completely around her, both of them panting, not talking. Suddenly she remembered the third *narco,* the one whose eyes she had gouged but who was still alive and could kill them with a pistol or machete. But she saw that he would never kill anyone again. He lay on his belly with the third knife, the diver's knife, driven into his skull up to its hilt.

"Bowman. How did you . . . ?" she started to ask, but felt a wetness against her chest, looked at him, saw his right sleeve darkening with blood.

"You're shot!"

"Spraying and praying. Just one." Through his right pectoral muscle, between his shoulder and nipple. He touched it, looked down without expression, shrugged. "Through and through. It's okay. Missed the important stuff. Arm's no good, though."

"We have to do something for that." She reached to take the shirt off, examine the wound.

He pushed her away, both hands on her shoulders. "Leave it. We—"

They both heard it then: a cacophony of shouts, men yelling, running, equipment clanking. Somebody fired off half a clip on full auto, a signal perhaps.

"That must be their main camp. It's why I didn't want to shoot these three and alert anyone else close by. Can't be more than two hundred yards away. They heard that man's AK for sure. We need to get back to the meadow. Do you have the moonmilk?"

"In the pack there."

He retrieved the stainless steel cylinder, shoved it into her good hand, picked up Carlos's rifle. "Run!" he yelled.

They took off back the way Hallie and the *narcos* had come. Bowman carried the AK-47 in his left hand, keeping his right arm tight against his belly. Louder shouts came now, mixed with the pounding thuds of booted feet.

"Run!" Bowman yelled.

They ran. Hallie's soles were cut, her body slashed and bruised, and she was so tired that she had been able to doze while walking with the *narcos*. None of that mattered now. She sprinted, cradling the steel cylinder in her right arm like a football, gasping, looking over her shoulder to make sure Bowman was still there. He could have run much faster, she knew, but would go no faster than she could.

A burst of automatic rifle fire, then another. Bullets snapped past, hissing and cracking. Others clipped leaves and branches, thunked into tree trunks. She looked over her shoulder to make sure Bowman was not hit again. More rifle fire. Rounds kicked up spurts of dirt.

She felt herself going anaerobic, chest burning, muscles flooding with lactic acid, and it was as if she were running through mud, but there was no possibility of stopping. She heard a long burst of fire,

Bowman shooting left-handed from the hip as he ran backward. Through the forest ahead she could see the meadow, then ran toward the light, pain blossoming in her chest.

She looked back at him again. He was clutching the AK-47's pistol grip in his right hand, pressed against his body. In his left he held a black, softball-sized grenade, one of several that had been hanging from the big mercenary's harness.

"Pull the pin!"

Without breaking stride, she reached back with her left hand, grabbed the ring, yanked. The pain in her hand almost knocked her down. He opened his fingers, letting the spoon fly loose, turned, threw the grenade underhanded without missing a step.

"Go left!" he shouted, and she veered in that direction. She heard the grenade blast, heard screams, curses. The meadow had to be close. A hard blow in the middle of her back slapped Hallie down. For an instant she thought she had been shot. She hit the ground face-first, so hard that it knocked the breath out of her and made her vision blur, but she did not lose her grip on the canister. She felt no pain in her back, felt no blood pouring out of her.

"Don't move!" Bowman was yelling, moving, pressing her down all the while. Fifty feet farther on, between them and the meadow, two *narcos* materialized out of the forest gloom. One was having problems with his AK-47. The other was not. He fired off a short burst on full automatic—*spraying and praying*—and bullets cracked the air around them. Bowman threw himself on top of Hallie. The *narco* fired again, correcting his aim, coming closer, bullets kicking up spouts of soil on the trail as he walked his rounds toward them. It was happening in microseconds, too fast for Bowman to fire back.

Though Bowman had his arms over her head, she had a slice of vision between them and could see the *narcos*. And then she saw the strangest thing. A quick silvery glint, like light flashing off a mirror, and the *narco* stopped firing. The barrel of his rifle drooped, slow and easy as a dying flower, until its muzzle was pointing at the ground. Another flash of light, and the second *narco* dropped his rifle.

She watched as the two fell slowly forward, like men who had suddenly gone to sleep standing up. Before their bodies hit the ground, both heads toppled from their shoulders, fell to the trail, bounced, and rolled away. Then the bodies flopped down onto their chests, spouting blood from their headless necks.

She glimpsed something white slipping from the trail into the forest. Then nothing except the two headless corpses and one small, white dog with eyes like red coals. He walked to one of the decapitated heads, sniffed, and disappeared into the forest.

Running again, they broke out of the trees, into the meadow. The cave mouth was two hundred yards away. She was running harder and harder but moving slower and slower, her muscles tying up, face contorted with the pain flooding her body.

Bullets snapped and crackled around them, whined off rocks. It was not easy to shoot accurately at a dead run, she knew: the only reason the *narcos* had not brought them down already. That and *aguardiente* and God only knew what kind of drugs they'd taken. Bowman must have thrown another grenade, because she heard the explosion, closer this time, felt pieces of soil and rock pelt her head and back.

Halfway across the meadow, Hallie realized that Bowman wasn't behind her. She stopped, turned, saw him kneeling, firing single shots from the AK-47, hitting men with every one. He yelled, "Keep going! To the cave!"

The *narcos* had come running out of the tree line into the open meadow, exposing themselves, and Bowman had six of them down in three seconds. There were a dozen others at least, but they understood what was happening, spun on their heels, and fled back toward the trees. Bowman got two more, fired the rest of that magazine in one long, ripping burst, and sprinted toward the cave's mouth.

A line of boulders formed a natural wall a hundred feet from the cave, and Hallie was there, on hands and knees, gasping, when Bowman jumped over the rocks and landed beside her. "Stay here!"

He ran, crouching, back into the cave mouth, bullets spanging off boulders, spraying chips and splinters of rock. Hallie could see that his right side was soaked with blood, which was now running down over his pants as well. He disappeared into the cave, and for a few horrible moments Hallie was alone there. She inched her head out to look across the meadow, but the *narcos* were holding in cover, sheltering behind trees, spraying and praying, the bright muzzle flashes of their rifles reminding her of Fourth of July sparklers. Their wild firing made one continuous, ragged, wavering blast.

Bowman returned, carrying in his left hand both the odd weapon she had seen on the stealth flight in and the SIG Sauer.

There was something she did not understand. "Why are they coming after us like this?"

"We must have been approaching a secret camp. They can't afford to let us get away now that we know its location." He paused, checked the weapons. "Looks like you'll get to shoot this sooner than we thought. It's heavier than an AK and I'm not going to be any good one-handed. Twenty-four rounds. Look through the scope, put the pipper on your target, and squeeze."

"Pipper?"

"Red dot. It's the laser that tells the projectile where to go. For now just put out some suppressing fire."

"What's suppressing fire?"

Bowman actually grinned. "Just point it and shoot."

"Give me the thing."

Bowman handed her the weapon. It was much heavier than she had expected. She settled the stock into her shoulder, wrapped her right hand around the pistol grip, cradled the forestock in her bloody left palm, found the trigger. Her cut hand was on fire with pain, but she could manage it.

"Wait for them to shoot." Bowman was getting his breath back. "The moment they stop, you pop up. Don't linger. They can't aim worth a damn, but they have a lot of bullets."

"Okay." She took a long breath, let it out, waited for a burst of automatic fire to end. When it did, she rose up, rested her elbows on top of the boulder, pointed the weapon's muzzle at the tree line, and squeezed the trigger.

The next thing she knew she was sitting on the ground. Her butt hurt from the impact, but she still had hold of the weapon. Bowman hauled her up with his good arm. "Sorry. It was set on full auto." He moved the fire-selector switch to its semiautomatic position. "One round for every trigger pull now. It's got quite a kick on full auto."

The recoil had been worse than that of the 12-gauge shotgun she'd used to hunt geese on the Chesapeake, but the second time she was ready for it, leaning into the weapon, back leg braced. She rose up, fired four rounds, each a half second apart, saw them rip the air with yellow bursts at the tree line, dropped down again.

"Don't fire from the same position twice." Bowman was sitting with his back against a boulder, cradling his right arm with his left, his voice getting a little sloppy, his tan face starting to whiten. She looked, saw blood on his other side, just above his waist. He had been hit again while out in the open.

"Bowman."

"Nothing to worry about. Stay on those guys. They'll have your last spot presighted."

Hallie moved ten feet to her left, popped up, fired three times, took cover again. The *narcos* were staying in the cover of the trees, but she had seen several edging out from behind trunks, hesitating, thinking about making a rush, then fading back.

"Bowman, what do we do when this thing is out of ammunition?"

"Fourteen rounds in the SIG. But before then, we should be on our way back to Reynosa."

"You tripped an EPIRB?"

"Yes. It was a backup I carried in a suit pocket. Before I started after you."

"How did you get out of the cave?"

He gave her an odd look. "Tell you later. Hell of a story."

Bursts of fire from the *narcos*. "Wait." She moved to the left ten paces, popped up, shot four rounds, dropped down, and came back to Bowman. "They're getting ready to do something." She knelt on one knee, the weapon's stock on the ground.

"What do you mean?"

"They've separated into two groups behind the tree line. I can see them moving back in there."

"They can't outflank us." Bowman pointed behind them, where the cliff with the cave mouth rose two hundred feet straight up. "Ha. I wouldn't have thought they knew enough to do it right."

"What?"

"They'll come in rushes. One group will fire to suppress you while the other advances. Then that group will go to ground and fire while the other advances. Pretty soon they'll be close enough to use grenades."

"I'll shoot them as they come closer."

"You'll try. And you'll get some. But it all comes down to math. I'm guessing there are twenty or thirty of them out there. Every one with an AK. Sooner or later, one will get you when you pop up to fire."

"Not if I'm careful."

Despite himself, he laughed. "You've got guts. But careful's got nothing to do with it. Give me the weapon."

She pulled back. "No. You can't shoot it." She moved out of reach. "Forget it." There was an explosion, much louder than the AK-47s' reports, out in front of their rocky parapet.

"Grenade," he said. "Too far for them to throw all the way just yet. *Give me the weapon*."

"No!"

Hallie had thought the first time she'd laid eyes on him that Bowman was not the kind of man you wanted to have angry at you. Now she realized how right she had been. The look in his eyes was like nothing she had ever seen. It made her think of an arcing high-voltage line. But then it faded.

"Stay here." He crawled a few yards to his left, where there was a tiny space between two adjacent boulders. He passed his hand quickly over it and there was a flurry of automatic rifle fire, bullets smacking and whining off the rocks in front of them, showering them with dust and fragments. "They had that one figured."

He moved back to the right and lobbed two grapefruit-sized sized rocks out toward the *narcos*. *"Now!"*

While the *narcos* were distracted by Bowman's "grenades," she stood, fired five quick rounds, sweeping the muzzle from left to right, then dropped again just as a dozen AKs replied with long bursts.

"Those boys have a lot of ammo. We've been shooting off some ourselves. By my count, we have six left."

Bowman looked at the weapon, then in the direction of the *narcos,* then back toward the cave. Another grenade blast, closer. "Hallie. I want you to go back in the cave. Take this." He extended the SIG.

"And leave you here? Never happen."

His face tightened. "*Listen to me*. I can hold off one rush. Maybe two. But then . . . There's no sense them getting both of us. And you can take the moonmilk with you." He stopped and they both listened. The *narcos* were shouting back and forth, their voices clearly coming from two different directions, moving closer all the time.

"They've got their groups sorted out." Hallie stared at Bowman as she said this.

"You have to go into the cave." Bowman's voice was urgent, angry again. "When the team arrives, they'll blow these guys to hell and get you out."

"I'm not going anywhere, Bowman. So stop asking."

"Do you know what you're doing?"

"Of course I do."

She did, and she didn't. On the one hand, nothing had prepared her for this. But on the other, it felt strangely as if her whole life had been lived between two invisible converging lines that were about to intersect at a bright point she had always been able to see. It was the oddest brew of feelings. She was afraid, flushed with adrenaline, angry, sad. A thought flashed through: *Dad would be proud of me*. Hallie heard a flurry of shots from in front.

"They're coming." She slid right, popped up, fired two rounds at the rushing group and another at the one covering their advance. Screams, curses. While their heads were down, Bowman rose and, shooting left-handed, fired the SIG so fast it sounded more like a machine gun than a pistol.

Hallie looked at Bowman. An idea: "Why don't we both run for the cave?"

"Without one of us laying down suppressing fire, they'd shoot us dead before we made it halfway."

Then, for a moment, it was quiet. After so much noise for so long, the silence felt queer, more alien and threatening than the gunfire. She crawled over to Bowman, put the weapon down, locked her arms around him, and kissed him hard. Not much of a goodbye, but it would have to do.

"Where are the goddamned soldiers?" Hallie, a shout of fury and frustration. It was not supposed to end like this.

"They should have been here by now," Bowman said, and Hallie heard the sadness of one who had waited too many times for help that never came. He gazed up at the empty sky.

"Wil." She gestured helplessly, the right words lost somewhere beyond rage and grief.

He touched her face, his eyes full of pain as ancient as death, but his expression calm.

Then he turned to the front. "They're close. They'll be off balance coming over these boulders. Shoot as many as you can." He got up on one knee, the Sig ready in his left hand. "Four rounds here," he said.

She got to one knee also, weapon shouldered, ready for the final shots. She looked at Bowman's face, awed by the peace she saw there, then past him and beyond the boulders and up to the sharp tops of the pines that were like spears, their green points touching the polished sky. A single bird, red as a new ruby, rose from the trees, and she watched it fly up and disappear into the sun.

They waited for the coming tide.

FORTY-SIX

"MAJOR? YOU ASLEEP?"

Lenora Stilwell opened her eyes, shook her head, focused. It was Jeran, one of the night-shift nurses at Reed.

"No," she rasped, her throat on fire.

"I brought the tape recorder, like you asked for." The BSL-4 suit muffled his voice, but she could see the concern in his eyes.

"Thank you, Jeran. I think I'm going to need your help."

"Yes, ma'am. Anything at all."

"I want to make a message for my family." She had thought about asking for a video camera, but, given the way she looked, discarded that idea immediately. "Only I don't think I can hold the recorder. My hands . . ."

"Yes, ma'am, I understand."

"Could you turn it on for me and just put it on my chest?"

"Yes, ma'am." Jeran did that. "I set it on voice activation," he said. "When you talk, it'll run. When you stop, it'll stop. I'll go now, leave you with it. Check back in an hour or so."

"Thank you, Jeran." He nodded and left her alone. Stilwell took a deep breath, let it out, took another. She wanted to do this right, to keep the pain out of her voice, to tell them that it had not been bad.

"Hey, you guys. Doug and Danny." She saw the little red light flicker when she spoke. "It's me. I'm not in Afghanistan now. I know you haven't heard from me for a while, but I also know that's happened before, so hopefully you're not too concerned. I'm okay. There have been some things going on that we couldn't talk about. But don't be worried. I'm good.

"I just wanted to tell you how much I love you both and how much joy you bring me. I honestly don't know what I did to deserve you two, but . . ."

She paused, thinking where she wanted this to go. It was not about her. It was about them. What they meant to her.

"Do you guys remember the time when we went to that dude ranch in Wyoming? You were ten, Danny. On the first day, the wranglers were matching up all the guests with horses and they brought out this little pony for you. And you got mad and said, 'I'm not gonna ride that midget thing. I want a real horse.' So they brought you one, a mare named Sophy—remember?—and you rode her the whole time. That was so much fun. I will never forget the look on your face when they walked that pony out of the corral and brought Sophy in."

She stopped, exhausted. She was up to about seven and a half, still managing, but knew it would not be long before she had to ask for serious meds. It was important that she get this done before then.

FORTY-SEVEN

HALLIE'S FACE WAS TURNED UP TO THE SKY, WATCHING. THE blasts of gunfire and grenade detonations continued, but she heard them as from a great distance. A soft, light breeze touched her face. There were no more thoughts, only a vast stillness enveloping her like mist in the mountains.

Suddenly a new sound, the whole world exploding. She looked at Bowman and knew. A barrage of grenades before their rush. In a moment the *narcos* would flood over their wall, shooting, killing them. She peeked over the rocks, watching the entire far meadow and tree line erupt in one long, roaring burst. But the *narcos* were not attacking. They were dying.

"Thirty-millimeter cannons." Bowman was grinning. "Did you ever hear sweeter music?"

Two Apache attack helicopters were destroying the *narcos*. The black Osprey was hovering behind them, waiting for them to finish their work.

Most of the *narcos* were trapped in the open space between the tree line and Bowman and Hallie. The Apaches fired Hellfire missiles and the *narcos* simply disappeared in red fountains of flame and earth. In less than sixty seconds, nothing was moving, in the trees or the meadow. The Apaches kept watch, circling while the Osprey settled down. A ramp dropped and troopers in jungle-green camo sprinted out and set up a perimeter around the aircraft.

"Go!" Bowman pulled her up with his good arm. They left the shelter of their rocks and crossed the fifty yards to the Osprey at a dead run, Hallie carrying the moonmilk, Bowman the FAFO weapon. She was dimly aware of short bursts of fire from the troopers and the immense ripping roar of the Apaches' cannons hosing down the forest. She ran up the ramp, its hard metal hurting her bare feet, and blundered straight into the arms of a sergeant, big as a wall, grinning.

"Go easy, ma'am," he said. "You with us. Safe now."

He deposited her gently onto one of the bench seats that ran the length of both sides of the fuselage interior. Bowman dropped down beside her. The team rushed back aboard and the ramp door closed with a hiss. Acceleration shoved her down as the Osprey shot up and away from the meadow.

Two medics went to work on Bowman, laying him flat on the deck. The men watched, mildly interested. They had seen wounds before. These were not the killing type. When the medics cut away Bowman's shirt, she saw the two surprisingly small red holes, one in his right upper chest, the other through the muscle just above his left hip bone. They irrigated the wounds, infused them with antibiotics and coagulants, and gave him a handful of capsules, which he swallowed dry-throated. One of them started an IV transfusion in his right arm. "You want a little something for the pain, sir? We can put it in that other arm there."

"All good, Sergeant, but thanks."

Bowman got up and came to sit beside Hallie on the bench again. The medic hung the IV bag from a hook on the fuselage. There were a lot of things she wanted to say, questions she needed to ask, events she had to tell Bowman about. But inside, the Osprey wasn't so quiet, and she would have had to shout. There were all those troopers, too, at ease now, the day's work done, sitting on the benches, rifles between their legs like hockey players with their sticks. They were all, to a man, looking at her and grinning.

She grinned back at them, then stood up, stepped across the fuselage, pulled one young trooper to his feet, kissed him on both cheeks. He sat back down, grinning even wider and looking slightly dazed. To the rest of them, standing in the middle of the aircraft bay, she gave a double okay sign, thumbs and forefingers circled. They understood her gratitude and answered: every right arm came up, fist extended, thumb upraised, and they let fly a thunderous *"OOH-RAH!"*

Hallie sat back down beside Bowman, who had been watching the whole thing with undisguised amusement.

What the hell, she thought. She wrapped her arms around him, careful with the shoulder, looked into his eyes, and kissed him long and hard. The troopers gave another cheer, even louder than the first.

PART THREE

SALVATION

FORTY-EIGHT

"SO THE NARCOTICS TRAFFICKERS SHOT THE BLACK MAN, AND the big man fell into the water. He might have been shot, too. You're not sure. But you believe he drowned." The Homeland Security debriefer glanced down at notes she had been taking. She was a petite woman who'd introduced herself as Rosalind Gurwitz. She had brown hair that framed her face in clusters of natural curls, an apple-cheeked face, and a surprisingly sympathetic, unlawyerly manner. The living, breathing opposite of Rhodes and Rivers.

Hallie thought, *No, he did not fall in and he was not shot. I pulled him in*. But instead, she nodded and said, as Don Barnard had instructed earlier, "That's correct."

Gurwitz, in a navy blue pantsuit, was standing by Hallie's bedside in the room at Walter Reed. A wallet-sized digital video recorder mounted on a tripod at the foot of the bed was capturing the interview. Barnard, looking official and very directorial in a dark gray three-piece suit, hovered around the room, a glowering presence making sure the debriefer did not overstay her welcome.

"And the drug traffickers who attacked the two men took you prisoner."

"Yes."

"And it was when they were taking you back to their camp that you managed to escape."

"What?" They had given her meds. Her head felt weird, filled with a soft buzzing that would not stop, and thoughts floated around, wispy, hard to grasp. *What had Barnard said to say about that?*

The lawyer appeared to sense her confusion. She repeated, "The drug traffickers were taking you back to their camp. But you got loose and escaped them. And signaled for the recovery team to pick you up."

She blinked, rubbed her face, looked at Don Barnard, behind the lawyer. He nodded almost imperceptibly.

"That's right."

"How were you able to do that?"

"They were drunk and high on drugs. It wasn't so hard."

"Really?" Gurwitz looked at her with admiration and astonishment and, just maybe, a hint of disbelief. "Incredible. No—wrong word. I *believe* you, of course. It's just . . . fantastic."

"Tell me about it." Hallie took a sip of ginger ale. She thought the hospital straw with its little flexible joint was one of the funniest things she had ever seen, and laughed out loud.

Rosalind Gurwitz stared.

"Sorry. It's the meds." Hallie blinked, grinned.

Hallie looked bad, but the meds were helping. The extraction team had lifted her and Bowman out of the meadow two days earlier. At the Reynosa airfield they'd both been transferred to a government jet. Accompanied by a medical team, they'd flown to Washington and had been airlifted to WRAMC. She and Bowman had been separated then, and she had not seen him since.

The doctors here had sutured the cut in her eyebrow from when

Cahner punched her, or maybe when he'd kicked her. There was a stitched cut above her right ear, but she couldn't recall when that one had happened. One eye was plum-colored and swollen half shut. She had to squint through the other eye, because she had still not fully adjusted to bright surface light, let alone the light in a hospital. That would take several more days. They had also sutured the gash in her left hand, the worst wound of all, requiring twenty stitches. It was wrapped in a sterile bandage. Her back was covered with wine-colored bruises from hitting the microbial mat. She had suffered a mild concussion and had lost nine pounds. But she was alive and, as Barnard had assured her, every BARDA lab and a number of others at the CDC were working with the moonmilk she had retrieved.

"Is there anything you'd like to add to your statement, Dr. Leland?"

"No. But if you'll turn that off, I have a couple of questions."

"Of course." The little red light on the camera winked out.

She tried hard to focus. "First, who were those two paramilitary types working for?"

"I'm sorry, Dr. Leland. I don't have that information."

Hallie asked several more questions, but it became obvious that Gurwitz either didn't know or wasn't going to talk about what had happened in Mexico. Then the lawyer said, "One thing I *can* address: it appears that you may have been the victim of a very sophisticated subterfuge, Dr. Leland. Dr. Barnard will provide full details. I am authorized to tell you that everything possible will be done to make things right, including full reinstatement with back pay and benefits."

Barnard cleared his throat.

"Oh, yes. And a promotion as well."

Barnard looked a degree less disturbed, but he clearly wanted the lawyer gone.

"Have you worked in Washington long, Ms. Gurwitz?" Hallie struggled to focus.

The lawyer frowned, puzzled. "Thirteen years, actually."

"Ah. Then you understand how much this could cost the government, both in dollars and publicity, not to mention rolling heads."

Gurwitz turned pale. "Dr. Leland . . ." she began, then just stopped. She was a good enough lawyer to know when the best thing to say was nothing.

Thinking of that time with Rhodes and Rivers, Hallie let the silence linger, feeling the air in the room getting tighter and tighter, watching Gurwitz suffer. But Hallie took no real pleasure in that. Gurwitz had had nothing to do with any of it. She finished the ginger ale, set the glass aside.

"Why don't you turn that thing back on." Hallie nodded at the camera.

Gurwitz hesitated but then touched her remote, and the red light glowed.

"For the record, I'm not going to sue the government. And I have no plans to call the *Washington Post* or *60 Minutes*. Al Cahner was very good at what he did. He fooled some very smart people here. Including me, right up to the end. What's done is done. Case closed."

Gurwitz regarded Hallie for a moment longer, appeared to realize that her mouth was hanging open, and closed it. This was clearly not the D.C. denouement she was used to seeing. "That seems like a good place to end our interview. Thank you for your time and cooperation, Dr. Leland."

She clicked the remote, and the red light winked out. When she had packed up and put her coat on, Gurwitz walked to Hallie's bedside and touched her shoulder.

"Off the record. You got screwed, honey. I'm not sure I could be as forgiving. But I do admire you for it." She paused, considering, then continued: "I have no children, but my only nephew is in Afghanistan. We are all in your debt, Dr. Leland."

Hallie gave the lawyer's small hand on her shoulder a squeeze. "Thank you. But we don't have the magic bullet just yet."

"No, but from everything I've been told, we will. Thanks in large part to you. Goodbye—and get better soon."

When she had gone, Barnard moved close to Hallie's bed. "Can I get you anything, Hallie? A sandwich? Some ice cream?"

She considered, shook her head. "I'm good. But thanks."

He nodded, but now, with the lawyer gone, she saw something in his face that pulled her back from the medication haze. "What's wrong, Don?"

"Some things happened while you were away. I didn't want to say anything until you'd gotten some rest. But you have a right to know."

"What?"

He told her about David Lathrop and Lew Casey.

For a few moments she was too stunned to speak. "Dead? Both?"

"Yes. Late's might have been a robbery gone wrong. We're not sure about that just yet. Lew's appeared to be an accident."

"You don't believe it."

"No. He would never have messed up his air-supply connections."

"I am so sorry, Don. I know you were close to both of them."

Barnard took in a long breath, let it out. He started to reach for his pipe, but his hand stopped halfway to the vest pocket and he let it drop. "I was. I'd almost forgotten how much it hurts to lose men like that." She saw his eyes go vague. A big hand came up, rubbed his chest, fell again. "Good men." He blinked, came back to the room, rearranged his face. "That was the very bad news. I also have some very good news."

"Glad to hear it. I can use some of that just now."

And then, as if he had been listening just outside the door, it opened and in walked Wil Bowman. He wore jeans and running shoes and a long-sleeved tan shirt with the tail out. A slight bulge was visible under the right sleeve just below his shoulder, where they had bandaged the bullet wound. His right arm was in a sling. The loose shirttail made the bandage on the left side of his waist unnoticeable. Other than the loss of a few pounds, Hallie kept thinking, he looked good. Very good. *Better* than good.

"Hello there," he said, grinning. She had not seen him look so happy.

"Hello there, yourself. You look pretty good for a man who got shot twice."

"Amazing powers of recovery. We Colorado boys are tough as nails." He walked to the bed, picked up the unbandaged hand, closed it within his own. "You don't look too bad yourself, all things considered."

Barnard cleared his throat. "I was just telling Hallie about Lew and Late."

Bowman nodded, his face hardening for a second. "Any movement in the investigations?"

"Not with Late's killing. But with Lew, possibly. When something like this happens, they look at any anomaly, no matter how small."

"Sure."

"Well, we have an unexplained staff absence."

"Who?" Hallie and Bowman said at the same time.

"Evelyn Flemmer."

It meant nothing to Bowman, but Hallie's eyes widened. "Evvie Flemmer? You don't think *she* was involved with this, do you?"

"We can't be sure of anything at this point, of course. But she hasn't reported for work since Lew died. Agents went to her apartment yesterday, but she wasn't there."

"They can get records of all enplanements," Bowman said.

"Easily. Already done. She did not leave on a plane, train, bus, or rental car. And her personal vehicle was in the lot at her apartment building."

"My God, Don," Hallie said. "If you'd asked me to pick the one person at BARDA *least* likely to be involved with something like that, I would have named Evvie Flemmer."

"You know what? Me, too," Barnard said. "And we don't really know if she was. But it's the only blip in our operational procedures we've detected."

Hallie remembered the soldiers, their families. "How have containment efforts been working?"

"We've just about run through our colistin stockpile. The more cases we find, the faster we have to use it."

"How many cases reported so far?"

"Almost seven hundred."

"Mortality rate?"

"Right around ninety percent. A few survivors. But so disfigured . . ." He shook his head.

"Any other developments?"

"Fox News sniffed out the story. They've agreed to embargo it until noon tomorrow. When it breaks . . ." He shrugged. "Very bad."

"If we could at least say a new drug works, it might stave off panic."

"It could." Barnard nodded. "If we had one." There was a clock on the wall, but he pulled out his pocket watch. "I need to get back to BARDA, and you need to rest."

"Don, before you go . . ."

"Yes?"

"Whatever happened to the people from the COP? The Z point."

"Fourteen soldiers dead at this point. And three nurses."

"What about that doctor?"

"She contracted ACE herself. It was a virtual certainty, with her not wearing a biosuit. But she refused. Said she couldn't treat the soldiers with one on. For five days she was the only physician at the COP. All the others were dealing with battle casualties. That's a brave woman."

"What's her name?"

"Lenora Stilwell."

"Say again?"

"Lenora Stilwell. She's a major with the Florida—"

"I know who she is, Don. Mary's older sister."

"Mary who runs the dive shop? Your college friend?"

"My *best* friend. My God. Don, is Lenora dead?"

"Not yet. Soon, though. She got bad enough that they had to bring her stateside. She's here at Reed, as a matter of fact."

"Why would they bring her all this way?"

"Better palliative care, basically. And with an outbreak, you have two options. Contain each cluster individually—put out the small fires. Or aggregate cases. There's a tipping point after which aggregation becomes safer."

"Are there others here?"

"About fifty. The worst cases. All in the big iso ward downstairs."

She yawned, despite herself. Barnard headed for the door.

"I'll come back tomorrow. I hung a fresh change of clothes in your closet."

Barnard left, closing the door behind himself, and Hallie and Bowman were alone. The meds were reaching for her, pulling her down, but she would not leave him again.

"How is your arm? And your side?"

He stepped back and took his right arm out of the sling. He snapped off three fast jabs, took a quarter out of his jeans pocket, tossed it in the air, and caught it.

She could do nothing but gape. "How did you do that? I saw your bullet wounds."

He grinned. "Recall I mentioned that DARPA was working on a way to speed up the body's healing process? Something called Superheal?"

"Yes. Okay. But why the sling?"

"It's just for show. DARPA's not ready to go public with this yet." He was smiling down at her, eyes alight. He touched her face, just his fingertips, careful of her injuries. "You're a sight, Doctor."

"We almost died back there."

"As close as I've ever come."

"Given what you do, I'd guess that's saying something."

"Yes, ma'am. It is. You know, I would have kissed you already except for the bruises. I know love can hurt, but kissing shouldn't."

Love? A blossoming in her chest, hot and beautiful.

"Get me some of that fast-healing stuff. Then . . ."

"Would if I could, believe me. I only got it because . . ." He trailed off.

"Because?"

"They like to keep me functional."

"Wil, I have so many questions."

"You deserve answers. Shoot."

"Were those paramilitaries working for the same people as Al Cahner?"

"Unclear."

"Did we find out who Cahner was working for?"

"Possibly. A very shadowy network, multinational, no discernible tracks. But good people are working hard on it right now."

She yawned again, could feel herself drifting. "I want to hear how you got out. Of the cave. You said you'd tell me later."

He hesitated, and she saw something behind his eyes, quickly there and gone but sharp enough to wake her up. "What?"

Bowman shifted on his feet, then sat on the edge of her bed. She could tell he was having an internal debate of some kind, and wondered if he had used more DARPA black magic to get himself out. He sighed, pursed his lips, rubbed his face. Made some kind of decision.

"Okay. Cahner shoved me into the river. You know about that." Shook his head. "I still cannot believe he suckered me so badly."

"Suckered *us*. I worked with the man for almost two years, Wil. And he had me fooled completely. You can't blame yourself for not suspecting him. None of us did. Not even Don Barnard."

"Yeah. The guy could act, I'll give him that. So anyway, the river flowed down into a sump for about a hundred yards. There was some air space in the middle where I got a couple of breaths. Then it spit me out like a watermelon seed into a huge room."

"But you were still by yourself, without a light, no food . . ."

"I had a light, thanks to you." He reached out for her hand, held it gently. "Without that, I was a dead man."

"So that room you were in reconnected with the main route we had followed the whole time?"

"Well, no."

"But if not, how did you get out? Were you able to follow some air currents?"

"No." He rubbed his nose, looked perplexed, more uncertain than she had ever seen him.

"Well, what then?"

"The watercourse had a nice, sandy beach in that big chamber. It looked so inviting. Near drowning can beat you up. I basically passed out."

"And?"

"And I had the strangest dream."

She stared. "What kind of dream?"

"There was nothing in it but light. As if I had been awake, seeing this incredible light. Nothing else. Just light." He shook his head, continued. "By my watch, I slept for a couple of hours."

"And?"

"When I woke up, I knew how to get out of the cave."

She stared, open-mouthed.

"Why are you looking at me like that? I know it sounds crazy, but . . . I got out. So something happened." He glanced over his shoulder to make sure the door was still closed. She could see that he was disturbed by the way she was staring at him, as if afraid that she suspected him of lying to cover up for DARPA—or for some other, unsuspected reason. He backtracked: "Look, I'm sorry I said anything. But you have to promise me you won't mention this to *anyone*. Okay? Promise?"

She was laughing by then. He frowned. She held up her good hand. "I'm not laughing at you, Wil." And then she told him: "I got lost. I still don't know how, but completely lost. I was going to try to relocate the route, but it would have been impossible, really. I needed to rest, first. So I curled up and slept. And I had the same dream. As though I were floating in a cloud of light. And when I woke up . . . I knew how to get out."

He stared at her as she had been staring at him a moment earlier. "What in God's name?"

"I think it was in Chi Con Gui-Jao's name."

"Arguello's cave spirit." Disdain in his voice, disbelief on his face. "No. There must have been some moving air we followed. Or . . ." His words trailed off. Out of ideas.

"You said, 'I knew how to get out of the cave.' When you woke up. It wasn't moving air, Wil."

"It was like there was a map in my brain."

"Exactly." She thought of something. "Is it still there?"

He concentrated for a moment. "No. Gone. You?"

"No."

"But . . . you believe me?"

"Yes." She nodded, squeezed his hand. "Absolutely."

"And I believe you. I think I do, anyway. But I also think we might be better off keeping it between ourselves. People who haven't experienced something like this . . ."

"Exactly right. We know the truth. That's enough for me."

"Me, too."

She had one more question. "How did you manage to find me and those *narcos*?"

"I didn't come out of the cave at the main entrance. Another, a mile or so west. I made it back to the meadow just as they were marching you away. Watched the big one for a while and then dealt with him. You know the rest."

"I know you saved my life."

"And you saved mine. We're even there." He paused, smiled. "I have never met anyone like you, Hallie."

That feels good, she thought. Now tell him how you feel about him. "Wil . . . I . . ." Her mind lunged, grabbing for the words, but they eluded her like bubbles blown on the wind. She felt the sleep closing over her. She looked up, saw him watching her, grinning. *He knows. I can see it. Don't need words.*

She dropped off, came back. "Know wha'?" She was starting to mumble, heard herself, but the best she could do.

"What?"

"I like the way you smell."

He laughed. "I'm glad you do. It'd be a hell of a thing if you didn't."

"Do you like the way I smell?" She giggled, the sleep pulling her.

"That and a whole lot more."

"Like what?"

"I'll tell you all of them, every single one, and that will take a long time. But you need to sleep now."

He leaned down and kissed her softly on the unbruised cheek, then on her forehead, careful, tender, then on the lips, his touch soft as light. He straightened up, still holding her hand, and the last thing she remembered before dropping off was him standing there, towering over her, looking down from what appeared to be a great height, the air around him seeming to glow, and her feeling not only safe, but saved.

FORTY-NINE

SPENDING SO LONG IN THE CAVE HAD DISRUPTED HALLIE'S biorhythms, which would take days to restabilize. She slept for twelve hours after Bowman left and awoke in the middle of the night. The floor was dark. Somewhere down the hall a patient was snoring softly, but that was the only sound.

She tossed and turned and tried to go back to sleep, but her body was still in midday mode. At three A.M. she was still awake, trying to make her mind stop revisiting the things that had happened, when a nurse padded in silently with a stethoscope, digital thermometer, and sphygmomanometer.

"Hey. I'm awake. You don't need to tiptoe. But if you could leave the light off, I'd appreciate it. Still hurts my eyes."

"Of course. The night-light is plenty. I'm really sorry to disturb you, Dr. Leland." The nurse was a short, plump woman in her thirties wearing white pants and a floral-patterned hospital top. Her name tag said, "Placida Dominguez, RN."

"I can get you something to help you sleep if you like." She had a slight Latin accent and a velvet-soft voice. Hallie wanted no more befuddling pain meds.

"Thanks. I'll count sheep or something."

"Warm milk? That really does work. Tryptophan, you know."

"No, but I appreciate your concern."

Hallie sat up and had to be quiet for ten seconds while the nurse took her temperature with the digital thermometer, read it, and said, "Ninety-eight point four." She took Hallie's blood pressure, listened to her lungs.

"It's quiet here tonight," Hallie said.

"Here, yes. Not so much in other wards, though."

"No?"

"No. They have activated the Biosecurity Isolation Area. Down in Sublevel Two. We have not been told what is there." She paused, frowned. "People are thinking maybe smallpox. It's all soldiers from Afghanistan. You know, germ warfare maybe."

It's ACE, Hallie thought. *They don't know yet*. "Have they confirmed smallpox?"

The nurse shrugged. "No. It's just what people are saying. Nobody knows, really."

Hallie nodded, but did not add anything.

"Your vitals are looking very good, Dr. Leland," the nurse said. "I think they will discharge you tomorrow."

"That will be nice. To sleep in my own bed. Yum."

"Good night, Doctor. Please use your call button for anything at all. Even if you should only want to talk. I am just at the nurses' station."

Hallie eased down, then turned onto one side because her bruised back hurt. They had raised the safety bars on her bed, and now she lay there staring through them. She was not thinking about her expedition into the cave. She was thinking, instead, of the footage of the soldier Don Barnard had shown her in his office, back before this all started. The things she'd seen were like the afterimages caused by staring into a bright light, but these would not fade. She closed her eyes, tried to think about other things, to squeeze the horror out of her mind. Then she stopped doing that. Turning away struck her as cowardice. Turning away from the people themselves struck her as worse. Especially from one person. What would she tell Mary, knowing that her sister was right here in the same hospital, and that she could have seen her, and did not? She dropped the safety bars and swung her legs over the side of the bed.

Because it was so late, the halls were deserted. It was not hard for Hallie to find a supply closet and exchange her hospital johnny for green doctor's scrubs. She pulled white Tyvek covers over the running shoes Don Barnard had brought and put a hair cover on, just for good measure.

"I'm Dr. Leland," she said as she approached the desk by the elevator. She had expected that access to the elevators and stairways would be restricted. The young corporal looked at her, then looked again, transfixed by her damaged face. "Car accident," she said. "The stupid Beltway. You know how it is. I need to get down to the iso unit to see a patient."

He examined a clipboard on the desk, running his index finger down a printout with a list of names, the finger stopping beneath each one. His lips moved while he read the names silently. Finally he looked up.

"Uh, I'm sorry, ma'am . . ."

"Doctor."

He blushed. "Yes, ma'am, I mean, Doctor, but I don't got your name here." He held up the clipboard.

She grabbed it, laid it on the table, picked up one of his pens, and wrote her name between two others. Eyes flashing, she pushed the clipboard toward him.

"Now you do. Open that elevator, soldier."

After passing into the iso unit's air lock system, Hallie performed all the BSL-4 procedures, donned a Chemturion suit, and finally walked through an inner air lock into the unit itself, as quiet and dim as the area she had left. Ultraviolet germicidal lights on the ceiling and walls glowed an eerie, radioactive-looking blue, and even with the Chemturion's filtration system running the air smelled of a chlorine-based aerosol disinfectant.

The nurses' station was deserted—no surprise with a ward full of critical cases. She turned right and started down the long hall. Most of the rooms had their doors open, privacy curtains drawn around the beds inside. When she was halfway to the corridor's end, she passed a room where the curtain was not drawn and she could see the person lying in bed. She was sleeping or, more likely, knocked out on meds, on her back. Some of the flesh on the right side of her head had been eaten away, exposing white patches of skull. There was a plum-sized hole in her left cheek, through which Hallie could see jawbone and teeth. There was no eye on this side, just a suppurating empty socket.

Hallie's stomach churned. It was one thing to look at pictures of this horror, another to actually see—and smell—it. She started down the white corridor again. At its end, she turned left and kept walking. She passed five rooms and then stopped at the door to one. The rectangular metal frame on the wall beside the door held a paper name label: STILWELL, L. MAJ. FLNG.

It was a private room, just the one bed, a perk of rank. Night-lights at the baseboards and wall switches illuminated the room softly. Hallie could see a woman with short brown hair lying in the bed. She had met Lenora only once, at Mary's parents' home in Louisiana. Now an oxygen-supplying cannula was inserted into

Stilwell's nostrils. A sheet was pulled up to her chin. Her arms rested on top of the sheet. Both hands were bandaged. And then, as Hallie watched, one came up and waved her in. She walked to the bedside.

"Hey." Stilwell's voice was a raw whisper, roughened by pain and throat inflammation. "What's up, Doc?"

My kind of gal. "Lenora?" she said very softly. Then, remembering the suit, she repeated her question more loudly.

"Yes. You're early."

"I'm sorry. I didn't mean to wake you."

Stilwell chuckled. "Not much sleeping going on here, Doc."

"I'm not a doctor. Not a medical doctor. I'm a microbiologist."

"I see." Stilwell did not sound happy to hear that. "Do you really need another biopsy? They've already taken about a pound of flesh for tests."

"No, it's not that. I . . ." Now that she was here, she found it difficult to explain to this woman *why*.

"Take your time, Doctor," Stilwell rasped. "I'm not going anywhere."

"I'm not supposed to be here."

"Neither am I. What's your name, Doctor?"

"Um, it's Leland. Hallie Leland. I know your sister, Mary."

Stilwell did not sit up—could not—but the surprise was clear in her voice. "Hallie Leland. I remember meeting you at our home. What on earth brings you here?"

"I . . ." What *had* brought her here? Should she tell Stilwell about the whole Cueva de Luz effort? No. Too complicated. "I learned you were in here yesterday." Leave it at that.

"So if you're here, you must know about ACE?"

"Yes. A lot."

"That surprises me. They've been working hard to keep this contained."

"I work in a government facility that's been researching countermeasures. For ACE, I mean."

"What facility?"

"BARDA. Biomedical Advanced Research and Development Authority."

"Never heard of it."

"Most people haven't." She hesitated. "What you did. Over there. Incredible."

Stilwell let out an exasperated sigh. "No big deal. It's war. Those boys get shot and die every day. I'm going to leave them when things finally get dangerous in my house? Not likely." She winced, groaned, obviously in sudden pain.

"Should I call someone?" Hallie could see a small area of infection on the left side of Stilwell's neck, and one the size of a half dollar on her forehead. They looked like third-degree burns, red and raw and oozing.

"No. It passed. Nerve endings flare up when they die, but just for a few seconds." She got her breath back. "Of course, there are billions of nerve endings, so I have plenty to look forward to."

"Lenora, maybe I should go. I don't want to make this worse." Hallie was damning herself, feeling selfish now, for having interrupted this good woman's rest.

Stilwell waved a bandaged hand. "Lenny. My friends call me. Stay. Good to talk."

"All right. I feel stupid in the suit, though."

"You'd feel stupider if you came down with this stuff. So don't even think about taking that off. But you can come closer."

Hallie stepped to the side of the bed.

"How is Mary? She won't answer my emails or phone calls," Stilwell said.

"I know. She's . . ." Was this the time to tell her big sister about the drinking? No. "She's doing okay. I've spent some time with her recently, down in Florida."

"She really okay?"

Then again, was this a time to lie? "Not really."

"The Army treated her like dirt."

"I know."

Stilwell did not speak for a while. Then: "Husband know you're down here?"

"I'm not married."

"Sorry. Shouldn't assume. Can't see your hand, though. Is news about this stuff getting out?"

"Not yet. They fear there will be a panic."

"My family doesn't know anything, either." Real pain of a different kind came into Stilwell's voice.

Hallie couldn't believe that. "They haven't been notified?"

Stilwell shrugged, winced. "Two things you learn about the military. Follow orders. And often they suck."

"Do you want me to call them? I'll do it right now."

"Not just yet, thanks. They couldn't visit now, anyway. I think it will be easier to wait until I'm a little better."

The ACE mortality rate thus far was 90 percent. So there was at least a chance. But Stilwell did not look like she was on the road to recovery.

"Tell me about your family."

"Tampa. Husband's name is Doug. We met in college. Tall. Looks like Jimmy Stewart. Great dancer. Son Danny. Fifteen. Plays football. Boyfriend?"

Hallie realized it was a question.

"Not just now. Well, maybe." She smiled at her own confusion. "Time will tell. Danny plays football, you said?"

"Varsity already. Wrestling team, too."

"College plans?"

"No. Wants to enlist. Day he turns eighteen."

"Jesus." Hallie regretted that the moment she said it.

"Exactly." Stilwell started to say more but coughed violently. At one point she raised a bandaged hand and pointed at the vomit pan on her bedside table. Hallie held it, clumsily with the thick gloves. When the bout finally subsided, Stilwell spit out a volume of red-and-black mucus dotted with solid yellow bits of tissue.

"Should I call someone now?" Hallie put the pan aside.

"Nothing they can do." Stilwell was gasping, struggling for air. "Pulmonary edema. Body trying to flush itself. Feels like drowning."

They waited until Stilwell's breathing settled. She said, "Danny. Terrifies me. But how to discourage? Wants to do his part."

"A military academy," Hallie said. "In four years, the war might be over. Or at least winding down."

Stilwell shook her head. "No. Afghans don't know anything but war. They *need* it. Go on forever." She paused, coughed. "It's like their baseball."

They sat in silence for a while. Stilwell's eyes were closed, her breathing shallow and rapid. Then her eyes opened wide. Her back arched, her mouth stretched, as though readying to scream, but no sound came out. Her body convulsed twice, violently, and she collapsed onto the bed. She did not move. Her chest did not rise and fall. There was no pulse visible in her neck.

It took Hallie a second to react. She searched for the nurse-call button. Because Stilwell could not use it with her bandaged hands, they had secured it on a hook near the top of her bed, on the other side, and Hallie could not see it. She looked at Stilwell, lying there, not breathing, in arrest. She yelled for help, then screamed for it, but the biosuit hood trapped her voice. Hallie grabbed Stilwell's wrist to check for a pulse, but the heavy gloves kept her from feeling anything.

She could run to the nurses' station, alert someone. But she could not really run in the damned suit. Without oxygen, Stilwell's brain was dying right now. That would take too long. Hallie's mind made a flash calculation, like the one when she had been standing with Kathan by the cenote. Odds and probabilities. *This woman has ACE. If I help her, I might get ACE. If I don't help her, she* will *die. If I do get ACE, we* may *be able to kill it.*

She ripped the zipper open, threw the hood back over her head, screamed "HELP!" twice as loudly as she could. She pulled back the sheet and did fifteen fast chest compressions, expecting an explosion of pain in her sutured hand, but felt none. *Adrenaline,* she thought.

Then she tilted Stilwell's head back, made sure her airway was clear, and blew three breaths into the unconscious woman. Fifteen more compressions, three more breaths. Hallie tasted the blood in Stilwell's mouth, sour fluid coming from her nose, ignored them, kept compressing and ventilating.

A nurse appeared at the door, saw what was happening, rushed back toward the floor's main station. The biosuits made running nightmare-slow. Hallie kept working, compressions and breaths, compressions and breaths. She lost track of how much time elapsed before the biosuited code blue team came race-waddling into the room. Someone in a suit pushed her out of the way. More suits kept squeezing in, and soon she was pressed back out into the hall.

No point in putting this back on now. Hallie walked away from Stilwell's room without resecuring the hood. Presently she came to the nurses' station. With most of the shift team down in Stilwell's room, there were only two nurses there, both in biosuits. One was in the dispensary, back turned to Hallie, inventorying the drug stocks. The other was looking down at a stack of paperwork. She heard Hallie approach but did not look up at first. When she did, and saw the tall woman with the white blond hair and stitched-up, blood-smeared face standing in front of her wearing a biosuit but no hood, she dropped her pen.

"Hey," Hallie said. "I need a room."

FIFTY

FOR THIS VISIT, DON BARNARD WAS CLOAKED IN A FULL biosuit. She tried to think of a joke about it, but could not.

"I'm told you saved her life." The hood and faceplate made him sound like he was talking to her from inside a closet.

"I'm glad to hear that." Hallie was in a bed herself now in the iso ward. "She deserves to live."

"How do you feel?"

"I feel fine." He appeared skeptical. "Really, Don. Look . . ." She pointed at her lunch tray, where only crumbs remained from the cheeseburger, French fries, and chocolate sundae she had devoured. "Appetite good, no fever, no pains, pulse, BP, respiration, all good."

He just nodded.

"I know. Incubation period, three to five days. This is just day one."

He nodded again. Looked at the floor, at the wall, at the ceiling. Through the faceplate, she could see that something was wrong.

"Don, talk to me. Did Lenora die?"

"She's hanging on. It's not that."

"What then?"

He looked directly at her. She could see only his eyes through the faceplate, but they frightened her.

"*What,* Don?"

"It isn't working, Hallie." Strange voice, dead-sounding, flat.

"What isn't working?"

"The moonmilk. It isn't working."

Her body felt as if it had just taken a hard electric shock. *Can't be. He has to be wrong.*

"No way, Don. We gave them my research results. And Lew's work. With the new moonmilk, they can't miss. We were *this* close. They have to . . ." Her voice trailed off as she watched his face.

"No. Not that. We have seven laboratories working on this. They all got the same response. Either this material is different or the samples were contaminated."

"Tell me exactly what happened."

"The protein-sequencing conformations—the ones you developed, as a matter of fact—aren't aligning properly. There's nothing wrong with the work you did. It's the new material. It's as if the keys you've always used in a lock suddenly don't fit. As I said, every lab has encountered the same problem at the same point in their enzyme transfections. It may be that the moonmilk can mutate just as quickly as ACE."

"Jesus. If you can't engineer the transfections, the door stays locked. You can't get in to arrange the furniture."

"Exactly." Barnard sounded devastated. "Given time, we may be able to do resequencing—some kind of work-arounds, the computer guys would call it. But what we don't have is time."

Neither of them spoke as Barnard's news settled in her mind. Hallie was off the meds now, her mind sharper, and she understood instantly that she had just received a death sentence. And then she was not seeing Don, or the room, feeling as though she had been hit by a giant wave and was being washed away, pulled deeper and deeper, light fading, sound dying, until nothing was left but a rushing in her ears.

She came back, pulled herself out of the bed, walked around, utterly dazed. "I wish there were some windows in this goddamned room," she snapped. "It would be nice to see the sun."

Barnard could only shake his head. "I'm sorry, Hallie. I am *so very sorry.*" He hesitated. "I suppose now you'll be wanting to call your family."

She dreaded doing that more than she had ever dreaded anything in her life. Barnard walked to her and wrapped her in a hug. The suit made it feel like she was being squeezed by a man made of beach balls, but she could see his face through the plastic and that made it feel good. Something let go deep inside her and suddenly she was sobbing so hard her ribs hurt. Barnard held her tight, letting her cry, tears pouring down his own cheeks. A passing nurse paused by the door, saw what was happening, moved on.

Two hours after Barnard left, Hallie watched the newscasts on the television hanging from the ceiling in her room. Fox broke the story, but by then the other news operations had gotten hold of it as well, so wherever she surfed—CNN, MSNBC, local news bulletins—she heard variations of the same theme:

". . . interrupt regular programming to bring you this special report. It appears that the nation may be under threat of an epidemic caused by a dangerous new bacteria. Early indications are that the new pathogen may have been brought here by military personnel returning from Iraq or Afghanistan. It's not clear whether this resulted from germ warfare by Taliban and Al Qaeda forces. But the infection is said to be highly contagious and drug-resistant. A government source, speaking on condition of anonymity, said that the president told his closest advisers this could be the worst threat to the nation since Pearl Harbor.

"The White House has announced that President O'Neil will hold a special press conference at three P.M. today. We will provide live coverage.

"We now return you to regular programming."

It's a whole new game now. She was not old enough to have witnessed the riots that tore Washington, D.C., apart after the assassination of Dr. Martin Luther King, but she had seen film and photographs and read accounts. It could be like that, she thought. No, worse. And not just in D.C. ACE would respect no borders, spare neither the innocent nor the young, would take no prisoners. Every city would erupt sooner or later. She had seen the images that came out of Haiti after the horrible quake of 2010. Chaos. Horror. It could get that bad here.

Europe's great cities during the plague years came to her mind, oxcarts filled to overflowing with rotting corpses, neighbors murdering neighbors, royalty fleeing, homes being set on fire with whole families locked in. She had a flash of what the future here could hold: the capital's sidewalks littered with decaying bodies, entire blocks in flames, hospitals under attack by mobs desperate for medicine. Services breaking down as policemen and firefighters and utility workers fled the city to be with their families. Mass suicides as groups chose a death fast and painless rather than days of lingering agony.

"Stop it." She pulled herself back to the present. The ward already felt different. There were more people bustling back and forth, more televisions playing with the volume too high, telephones ringing at the nurses' stations, patients calling out from their rooms.

She switched off the television and wandered out into the hall. *How odd it feels to know you're going to die,* she thought, but corrected herself. *No, that's not right. We all know we're going to die. What's differ-*

ent is that now I know when, and how. That feels different. But don't forget, there's a ten percent chance. Right. Her mind was spinning like a spooked horse in a corral, kicking and striking and looking for some way out of a place that had no exit.

Walk, she thought. *Put one foot in front of the other. Be here and now. Whatever time you have left, make the most of every moment. I should call Mom. No, I can't. Not right now. I need a little time. But, God, what about Mom? She'll be hearing all these news bulletins and wondering what the hell is going on. I have to tell her to get away. But where to go? She's probably as good on the farm as anywhere. But I have to call her. Just not yet.*

Hallie walked down the hall, turned left, moving without thinking, kept going to the end of the corridor, turned left again. She stopped in front of Lenora Stilwell's room. The door was closed. There was a sign on the door, red with yellow lettering: AUTHORIZED PERSONNEL ONLY.

I'm authorized if anyone is.

She pushed through the door, walked to the foot of Stilwell's bed, stared.

"Oh my God!"

She fled into the hall, where she stood screaming at the top of her lungs for doctors, nurses, anybody, to get down there *now.*

FIFTY-ONE

THE DOCTOR WAS PANTING FROM HIS SPRINT-WADDLE DOWN the hall in a Chemturion. He stood beside the bed, peering at Stilwell. His heavy breathing had fogged up the faceplate, so he kept tilting his head this way and that, trying to get a decent view. Several nurses in their inflated suits hung back, trying to see around him.

Lenora Stilwell smiled, waved. Weak, but a wave. "Hey there. Think I could get some orange juice?" Her voice was still raspy, but stronger.

Hallie stood and gaped. Stilwell's color had returned. The lesion on her forehead had shrunk. "Unbelievable. The colistin is working."

The doctor looked up from Stilwell's chart. "She hasn't received colistin since she got here. Wouldn't take it. Directed it to be used elsewhere."

More people, staff in biosuits and patients in johnnies, were crowding around outside the door now, peering in, trying to get a glimpse. Word had spread quickly through the ward that *something* was happening. Now pretty much everybody who could walk was coming toward Stilwell's room.

"Look at you!" Hallie laughed, sobbed, laughed. She turned to the doctor. "If it wasn't colistin, what happened?"

"Damned if I know." He put the clipboard on its hook. "It's . . . it's . . . hell, I don't know *what* it is."

Hallie was thinking the simplest thought: *A miracle, that's what.*

Stilwell let out a laugh of pure joy. "You don't get it, do you?"

"Get what?"

"It's *you.*" Stilwell pointed a bandaged hand.

"What?"

"It's you. Something about *you,* Hallie. You gave it to me, and now I'm getting better."

"The CPR." Hallie remembered the feel of Stilwell's mouth, the taste of blood, saliva and breaths mixing in their throats. Stilwell's chest rising. Over and over.

"Had to be. No other way to explain it."

"What CPR?" The doctor was looking at them.

"I arrested last night. No pulse, no respiration. Hallie was here. Did CPR. Something must have passed from her to me."

"How . . . ?" Hallie was still trying to understand. She looked down at her bandaged hand and remembered what had happened in the moonmilk chamber.

Was it possible? Could the substance somehow have synthesized, maybe even transfected, in her own immune system? Morphed biochemically?

"I don't understand."

"I don't either. But I tell you one thing, gal. You better come over here and let me give you a hug."

And that's what Hallie did.

Then she turned to the doctor, who was still staring, open-mouthed.

"My name is Dr. Hallie Leland. I'm a microbiologist with BARDA at the CDC. Biomedical Advanced Research and Development Authority. I need for you to call Dr. Donald Barnard, the director there." She repeated Barnard's cell number from memory. "Use any secure line you need to. Use WRAMC's national security hotline if you need to. But get hold of Dr. Barnard *now*. Understand?"

The authority in Hallie's voice took command of the still-stunned doctor. "Yes, sure, I can do that. But . . . what should I tell him?"

"Tell him he needs my blood. A lot of it."

FIFTY-TWO

"NOW I KNOW HOW IT FEELS TO BE A VAMPIRE'S GIRLFRIEND." Hallie was sitting up in bed, pale but showing no sign of ACE infection.

"It's a good thing the human body can replace a pint a day." Barnard had visited often. They had taken four pints of blood, one a day, with a day or two of rest in between each drawing, since the discovery of Lenora Stilwell's recovery.

"How're you feeling?"

"Light-headed once in a while. Sleeping more than usual. Otherwise, piece of cake. Are they getting it done?"

"Every government lab with the capability, and those of every major pharmaceutical company, are producing. Close to a hundred thousand doses already deployed. And since it's government property, which means everybody's property, every company has access to the drug's genome."

"So nobody gets filthy rich from this."

"Right. How's your mom? You finally talk to her?"

"She's relieved. So are Mary and my brothers. They all knew something weird was up, not having heard from me. They just didn't know what."

"Are they coming to see you?"

"They were. I told them to stay put until I get out of here."

"Did you think more about what we discussed?"

"About the lab? Yes. I would like to come back, and I appreciate the offer, Don. Have you found out anything more about all that happened down in Mexico?"

"We identified the two operatives that took you captive initially."

"You did? Who were they?"

"Their names were Brant Lee Kathan and James David Stikes. Kathan was former Army Special Forces. Dishonorably discharged for torturing prisoners in Iraq. Stikes had been a SEAL. Honorably discharged. Both worked for the security firm Global Force Multiplier."

"GFM? My God. The same contractor that provides security for VIPs in Iraq and Afghanistan."

"None other."

"We suspect that they were to kill everyone on the team, including Al Cahner, and retrieve the moonmilk. They knew nothing of its real value."

"So Cahner would have been double-crossed. And GFM was behind all of this?"

"No." Barnard frowned, sighed. "We're not sure yet who was the prime mover. But we do know someone else was involved."

"Well?"

"Nathan Rathor."

She gaped. "Rathor? The HHS secretary?"

"None other."

"Why would Rathor be part of something like this? And what did he do?"

"I'll take the second question first. We believe he was connected with David Lathrop's death."

She could only shake her head. "How about the why?"

"Before he was named HHS secretary, Rathor was the president and CEO of BioChem."

"Right up there with Johnson & Johnson and Merck."

"Yes. Biggest of the Big Pharmas. We're fairly certain that he was part of a larger effort to get the moonmilk directly to BioChem. With your whole team dead and missing, we could only have assumed that the mission failed. BioChem, meanwhile, would have been creating new antibiotics, effective against ACE and maybe other MDRBs as well. Their profits would have been obscene. Rathor's stock would have increased a hundredfold in value, if not more."

"Is he going to jail?"

"Sadly, probably not. The evidence is strong but circumstantial. More importantly, a criminal trial of a member of the president's own cabinet—and in particular one he personally recruited—would be disastrous for him."

"So what will happen to Rathor?"

"I understand that he was instructed to present a letter of resignation to the president. He did that late yesterday, in fact. His departure will be attributed to health reasons or the need for more personal time or some such. You know how it works here, Hallie."

"Indeed I do. How's it playing?"

"The media are chewing on it now, but it'll be forgotten by next week. They will know the reason given for his departure is bullshit. But they'll probably figure the real reason was his failure to react quickly to the ACE problem. And many insiders will figure he just pissed off the wrong people, something Rathor was very good at."

"And Al Cahner?"

"Tougher case, that. He had some very sophisticated software that we were able to track back to people in Ukraine, but not beyond. Turns out he had a secret Caymans bank account, but it had been drained and closed while he was in the cave. It appears that whoever paid him didn't expect him to be around long after he came out."

"What are we saying about the antibiotic? How we discovered it, I mean."

"We're simply saying that BARDA's brilliant scientists came up with the drug after working themselves nearly to death."

"How is Lenora?"

"She'll be heading back to her family in a couple of weeks, if not sooner."

"Brave lady, that one. Did anyone discover the infection's source? How the Z man got it, I mean?"

"You won't believe this. It was a tampon." Barnard looked like he still could hardly accept it himself.

"What?"

"They use them for bullet wounds. No one knows exactly when they started doing that, but it's common practice now."

"So somebody stuck a tampon in a soldier's wound and he got the infection from that?"

"Appears to be the case."

"How would a tampon become contaminated with ACE?"

"A very good question. That tampon was sold by a company called FemTech. Manufactured in China, shipped to the U.S. for distribution to all the big-box discounters. Some found their way into the military supply chain as well."

"So this whole thing started with an accidentally contaminated batch of tampons?"

"That's one possibility, certainly."

"There are others?"

"Someone could have contaminated the tampons intentionally."

"Why would anyone do that?"

"Suppose you could initiate an epidemic against which only one antibiotic on earth would be effective?"

"You mean that old drug, colistin?"

"Yes."

"Nobody had made it for decades, though."

"Because there was no market. Suppose you could create a market."

"You're suggesting that somebody intentionally infected people with ACE?"

"Here's what we know. Tampons are not required to be sterile, because the area of the body where they are used is not sterile. At no point in their production are they tested for sterility. So introducing bacteria into them would not be all that difficult."

"But how would the bacteria live? They need something to feed on."

"Tampons are mostly cellulose. Perfect bacteria food. Here's something else. In the year before the first case was diagnosed, one company, MDC Pharmaceuticals, produced a large amount of colistin."

"Possibly anticipating a sudden need?"

"Possibly."

"Anything else?"

"Nothing probative. But who do you suppose owns FemTech?"

"No idea."

"BioChem. And who do you suppose owns MDC?"

"BioChem?"

"None other."

"My God. Will the government prosecute?" She was becoming tired, her eyes drooping, easing toward sleep.

"Who can say? It's a long and very complicated way from an incident like this to the courtroom. All kinds of things can happen. I think of the ocean. You can see the surface and everything that's on it. But beneath the surface, there are countless invisible currents and forces at work."

Neither spoke for a few moments. Hallie's chin dropped, came back up. Barnard patted her shoulder. "Well, look. You need to rest, and I need to get back to BARDA."

"Before you go . . ."

"Yes?"

"I do want to rejoin BARDA, but not as a staff researcher."

"No? What, then?"

"Field investigator."

He hesitated only for a second. "Done. A good fit for you. We'll take care of all the official stuff once you're up and around."

He turned to go, but her voice stopped him again, the words soft, some slurred. "Jus' one more thing, Don?"

"Of course. What is it?"

"Need to get in touch with Bowman. Cellphone number? Email?"

He slapped his forehead. "My God. I almost forgot. I am getting old, Hallie. His services were needed elsewhere. He left town last night."

"Uh-uh. The man was shot, Don. Twice."

"Apparently he has amazing powers of recovery. With some help from his shadowy friends at DARPA, probably."

She had forgotten. It came back: him in her room, the fake sling, tossing the coin, catching it. "Where is he?"

"I can't say, Hallie. I mean, I don't know. Truly."

She frowned at Barnard. "Is his name really Wil Bowman?"

"That much I can vouch for. It is."

"I'll find him, Don. You know I will."

"Hallie, I suspect that when this new business is finished, he may find you first."

She smiled, lifted a hand, let it drop. Her head sank into the pillow. In that dim and soft-edged place between sleep and waking, she drifted out of the hospital and back to the blue house awash in the scent of oranges, opened the door, and saw Bowman, white Florida light flowing around him, around them, carrying her into sleep, a fine thing to dream on.

AUTHOR'S NOTE

This is a work of fiction, pure if not simple, so any resemblance between the novel's characters and real persons is coincidental.

On the other hand, any resemblance between everything else that happens in the book and true life is real.

During the height of the Iraq War, so many wounded soldiers contracted *Acinetobacter* infections that Army doctors started calling it "Iraqibacter." Military officials at first said that ACE in Iraqi soil was responsible, but that turned out to be untrue. In fact, soldiers were being attacked by a new ACE in the military's own hospitals. No one knows, or will admit to knowing, how it came to be there.

Soldiers do routinely use tampons as emergency wound compresses.

According to the National Institutes of Health, two million people acquire bacterial infections in U.S. hospitals every year. Some ninety thousand die as a result, a number that has *sextupled* since 1992. (And those are only the deaths attributed to such infections; the true total is almost certainly much higher, for the very reasons Mr. Adelheid discussed with Al Cahner in this book.) Each year, more and more such infections occur.

Seventy percent of these infections are resistant to at least one of the drugs most commonly used to treat them. Others are rapidly developing multiple resistances. "Various strains of bacteria that cause serious diseases, like meningitis and pneumonia, could mutate to the point that all of our available therapies are ineffective," said John Powers, an antimicrobial expert at the Food and Drug Administration, in 2006. And some bacteria are already resistant to *all* drugs.

Toward the end of the nineteenth century, biologists discovered that bacteria are nature's counterterrorists: in the proper conditions, some bacteria become able to kill their fellow bacteria. Understanding this, scientists identified, isolated, and distilled these bacterial ninjas into what we today know as antibiotic drugs. Their development was one of the greatest boons science ever delivered to humankind. That was the good news.

The bad was that most antibiotics used today are derived from one soil-based order of microorganisms known as Actinomycetales (Ac-tin-o-my-CEET-al-ees). Relying on this one order produced a generation of miracle drugs, but ultimately that has worked against us. Antibiotics benefit from inbreeding no more than humans do.

Indiscriminate use of antibiotics in everything from soap to sheep to farm-raised salmon has made it easy for bacteria to acquire resistance. And there is something else: perhaps more than any other organism, bacteria have a unique ability to exchange DNA not only with their own species but with others as well.

MDRAB, multiple-drug-resistant *Acinetobacter baumannii* (Ah-si-NEET-o-bac-ter bough-MAN-ee-eye), is a highly drug-resistant bacterium with yet another personality quirk that makes it inordinately dangerous. ACE may be the "great communicator" of all bacteria, able to pass on immunological mutations with speed that, in evolutionary terms, is lightning fast. When Don Barnard tells Hallie Leland that geneticists discovered, in ACE, the greatest number of genetic mutations ever found in a single organism, he is speaking the truth. They actually did, in 2005.

Antigenic shift, which produces the killer species of ACE, is a recognized evolutionary phenomenon.

Moonmilk is a real extremophile that lives in wild caves. A number of microbiologists believe that subterranean extremophiles are our best hope for developing new strains of antibiotics for use against microbes that, like ACE, are resistant to all existing drugs. Some—notably Dr. Hazel Barton, of Northern Kentucky University—have already synthesized new antibiotics from deep-cave extremophiles.

BARDA does exist and manages Project BioShield, which supports "advanced development of medical countermeasures for chemical, biological, radiological, and nuclear agents."

Several supercaves are found in southern Mexico: Huautla and Cheve are two of the most famous. Cueva de Luz is another character in the book, a combination of Cheve, Huautla, and several other such giants. These caves contain all the bizarre horrors described in the book, though no one cave—as far as we know—contains *all* of them.

Many—perhaps most—native peoples with sophisticated cultures dating back to prehistory truly believe that caves are sentient living beings.

Soldiers in Iraq and Afghanistan are using BADS, the boomerang anti-sniper detection system developed by DARPA. "Gecko Gear" was created by DARPA, which refers to it as Z-Man Tools and continues working in a "thrust area" called BIM, for biologically inspired materials. The DARPA devices are a bit different from those depicted in the book, but both operate on the same principle. While still experimental, the tools are thought to be deployed with certain special operations units today.

Soft robots that use "jamming skin enabled locomotion" to shape-shift and conform perfectly to, say, human hands and feet were developed by a private company called iRobot.

ACKNOWLEDGMENTS

Ethan Ellenberg, my intrepid literary agent, first saw potential in *The Deep Zone* and worked with me to make it better. My stellar nonfiction editor, Jonathan Jao of Random House, introduced me and the novel to Ballantine's editorial director of fiction, Mark Tavani. Mark helped transform the novel into the one I had dreamed of publishing for forty years. I am also deeply indebted to publisher Libby McGuire, editor in chief Jennifer Hershey, and deputy publisher Kim Hovey for their vigorous and unwavering support for the novel.

Kelli Fillingim masterfully guided *The Deep Zone* through the countless refits and refinements that transform a book from raw manuscript to published hardcover. Bonnie Thompson once again proved why she is the copy editor I would not write a book without. There are other worlds across the seas, and for introducing me to them I owe huge thanks to Denise Cronin, Rachel Kind, and everyone in subsidiary rights. And without the invaluable help of everyone in sales and promotion, the novel would have been like a tree falling in the forest. It might have made the most beautiful sound imaginable, but no one would have heard it.

Elizabeth Tabor, Wallis Wheeler, Steven Butler, Sheila Bannister,

Tasha Wallis, Lisa Loomis, Damon Tabor, and Jack Tabor all read early drafts of the novel and offered invaluable feedback. My good friend Jim Parker, an expert cave diver and perhaps the smartest and bravest man I've ever known, helped me avoid wrong turns in the diving passages.

My mother, Hallie Siple Tabor, contributed half of the heroine's name. Deputy Chief Joyce Leland of Washington, D.C.'s Metropolitan Police Department, the best supervisor any street cop could pray for, contributed the other half.

ABOUT THE AUTHOR

JAMES M. TABOR is the internationally award-winning author of *Blind Descent* and *Forever on the Mountain*. He was the executive producer for the History Channel special *Journey to the Center of the World,* after having worked as a Washington, D.C., police officer, a dockmaster, a nightclub manager, a national magazine editor and television personality, a corporate vice president, and a horse wrangler. He is a mountaineer, caver, and master diver. He lives in Vermont, where he is at work on his next novel. Visit him at jamesmtabor.com.

ABOUT THE TYPE

This book was set in Bembo, a typeface based on an old-style Roman face that was used for Cardinal Bembo's tract *De Aetna* in 1495. Bembo was cut by Francisco Griffo in the early sixteenth century. The Lanston Monotype Company of Philadelphia brought the well-proportioned letterforms of Bembo to the United States in the 1930s.